James Phelan is the bestselling and award-winning author of twenty-nine novels and one work of non-fiction. From his teens he wanted to be a novelist but first tried his hand at a real job, studying and working in architecture before turning to English literature, spending five years at a newspaper and obtaining an MA and PhD in literature.

The ex-CIA character of Jed Walker was first introduced in *The Spy*, which was followed by *The Hunted*, *Kill Switch*, *Dark Heart* and *The Agency*.

James has also written five titles in the Lachlan Fox thriller series, and the Alone trilogy of young adult post-apocalyptic novels. A full-time novelist since the age of twenty-five, he spends his time writing thrilling stories and travelling the world to talk about them.

To find out more about James and his books, visit
www.jamesphelan.com

Follow and interact with James
www.facebook.com/realjamesphelan
www.twitter.com/realjamesphelan
www.instagram.com/realjamesphelan
www.whosay.com/jamesphelan

ALSO BY JAMES PHELAN

The Jed Walker books
The Hunted
Kill Switch
Dark Heart

The Lachlan Fox books
Fox Hunt
Patriot Act
Blood Oil
Liquid Gold
Red Ice

The Alone series
Chasers
Survivor
Quarantine

JAMES PHELAN

THE SPY

CONSTABLE • LONDON

CONSTABLE

First published in Australia and New Zealand in 2013 by Hachette Australia,
an imprint of Hachette Australia Pty Limited.

First published in Great Britain in 2018 by Constable

13 5 7 9 10 8 6 4 2

A CIP catalogue record for this book
is available from the British Library.

ISBN: 978-1-47212-715-0

Typeset in Simoncini Garamond by Bookhouse, Sydney
Printed and bound in Great Britain by CPI Group (UK), Croydon CRO 4YY

Papers used by Constable are from well-managed forests
and other responsible sources.

Constable
An imprint of
Little, Brown Book Group
Carmelite House
50 Victoria Embankment
London EC4Y 0DZ

An Hachette UK Company
www.hachette.co.uk

www.littlebrown.co.uk

This one's for my agent, Pippa.

The Facts

In military time, to say 'zero-one-thirty' is to say 1:30 in the morning (written 0130). When someone says 'zero-dark-thirty', they mean a non-specific hour when it is very late or very early in the morning, and still dark.

At zero-dark-thirty on the morning of 2 May 2011 a CIA covert operation named Neptune's Spear was conducted in the city of Abbottabad, Pakistan.

The operators were members of DEVGRU, better known as SEAL Team Six, inserted aboard two highly modified Black Hawk helicopters of the 160th SOAR. Their mission was to capture or kill Osama bin Laden.

Within minutes of its start, the SEAL team leader radioed, 'For God and country: Geronimo, Geronimo, Geronimo,' and then, after being prompted for confirmation, replied: 'Geronimo EKIA.' (Enemy Killed In Action.)

The most expensive manhunt in history had come to an end. The terrorist Osama bin Laden – codenamed 'Geronimo' for the mission – was shot dead.

At the target compound, the SEALs retrieved a wealth of intelligence to use to counter future terror threats.

On bin Laden, sewn into his clothing, was 500 euros in cash.

And two cell-phone numbers . . .

PROLOGUE
BEYOND ZERO-DARK-THIRTY

Tuesday, 27 August 2013, 0630 hours
Yemen

Jed Walker. On a deep op, tracking a man whose phone number was sewn into the clothing of the dead terrorist Osama bin Laden. This guy was a courier, who with the right amount of pressure and persuasion could provide enough intel to get the next big break in the war on terror. Right now, on this hot morning in Yemen, after a couple of years chasing around the globe and two months scratching around the sand waiting for the right opportunity, Walker was mere minutes away from his goal.

The courier was due to arrive. They'd eyeball him, get more leverage, be one step closer.

Walker was the right man for the job. He was a patient man. Dependable to the last. A damned fine listener.

But he had limits.

Walker's limit proved to be Bob Hanley – the all-talking, no-pausing co-worker seated next to him – and he couldn't help but wonder what he had done wrong to have *this* guy assigned to him on *this* op.

'So I said, "You want to go get surgery for implants, fine, but I ain't paying" – and that was that. I got a Dear John email in 'Stan. She used my alimony for the implants. Shacked up with a guy from her book group a month after. You believe it? Fifty shades of *shit* is what it is.'

The fact was, Bob wouldn't shut up, and Walker couldn't just knock the guy out.

Well . . .

Before them stood what passed for a Yemeni roadhouse and shantytown. Six gravel roads collided here; the next nearest stop was a hundred clicks away. Locals did a boom trade in fuel, food, and khat, a chewable barbiturate leaf. Surrounding Walker's observation position was a junkyard of vehicles that hadn't survived the trip through the desert. Inside his battered, sand-coloured Land Cruiser was all the equipment he needed, and, among it, the most talkative CIA operative he had had the misfortune of sharing an op with.

'Yep,' Walker said. He scanned the horizon with binoculars. Waited.

'Yep? What do you mean, *yep*?'

Walker looked at the guy and considered simply not responding. But he didn't want to be trapped with a moody talkative guy any more than with a jovial talkative one, so he said, 'I believe it.'

Bob nodded slowly, letting out a low, slow whistle. 'Pfft, women. I can't even see my baby girl now. How'd her lawyer work that out? She's a teenager now. I can see her once a month, when I'm back in Philly, which is near enough to never.'

He showed Walker a laminated photo from his shirt pocket: a good, wholesome-looking girl like those Walker had grown up with in Texas.

'That's a tough break, Bob.' Walker passed back the photo, resumed his surveillance.

'I know, right?' Bob popped another can of ice-cold Coke from the cooler sitting between them. 'Damn it, I miss her.'

'The wife?'

'Hell no; the kid.'

Bob pocketed the picture and said, 'So, you married?'

'Was that a proposal?'

Bob snorted a laugh.

Walker shrugged. He squinted out at the bright landscape as the sun spilled across the sands, and put on his sunglasses. *This could be on Mars. And I could be sitting next to a Martian.*

Bob watched him for five seconds before continuing. 'Yeah, you're married.'

'It's complicated,' Walker said.

'Always the way, right?' Bob spat out his open window. 'It's always suckers like us doing the jobs we do . . . damn, they should worship us, be thankful for what we do out here. Instead they're happier with the local manager of Walmart moving on to his third wife. The whole world's gone to shit.'

Walker nodded; there wasn't much else to do. This was one reason he preferred to work alone. There were others – trust and dependability were at the forefront – but he had learned not to dwell on them.

'Pfft, women,' Bob repeated. 'A man's not meant to live with a woman full-time, that's what my pa always said.'

'Smart guy.' Walker watched through the glasses at a tiny dust cloud building on the road at the eastern horizon.

'Yeah, smart; the only guy in my family for four generations smart enough to never serve.' There was silence in the car for another five seconds, then Bob started to drum his fingers on the dashboard. 'Damn, I hate waiting. You hate waiting? I hate it. Always have.'

Walker didn't mind waiting. He had waited two years to get this close to his target; two years to get the chance to turn him over to their side. Walker knew how to wait. Waiting kept him focused, kept him sharp. And he knew that the possibility of death was around the corner for those who didn't know how to wait, for those who became impatient. For those like Bob.

'You don't talk much, do you?'

Walker shook his head, watching out the window, waiting. The dust cloud on the road slowly built from a dot to a smudge.

Bob fell silent, and Walker could sense that he was formulating his next talking points. Walker had worked with men like this before: men who liked to prove something, usually through talk rather than action, and when action was called for they couldn't wait for it to be over so they could talk about it.

While this mission was meant to be a soft op, one of surveillance, to observe and report, the man sitting next to him was tasked with *his* protection. On paper it likely seemed a smart move to those back stateside, to protect Walker, their intelligence-gathering specialist. But Walker in person was twice what he was on paper, and that was saying something. The truth was, if something went down, if things fell apart, Bob would just be in Walker's way, a liability.

And Walker had already left that kind of world behind.

He saw through the glasses that the dust cloud had disappeared. Not a vehicle, then, for there were no other places to go out here. Some kind of twister tearing up the sands.

'What did you do before this?' Walker asked.

Bob looked at him, danger in his eyes and excitement in his tone when he said, 'Guess.'

Walker shrugged.

'Come on . . .'

'Delta?' Walker asked, though he knew better: those guys had patience in spades. So, for Bob it was a compliment. Walker knew that it was always better to give props to guys like this, even if they were not due.

Bob shook his head. He replied, 'SEAL.'

Walker nodded. That made sense. The war in Afghanistan had built a new breed of SEAL: no longer was this kind of soldier training all his life for an occasional mission that may never happen; he had become accustomed to instant gratification, to completing three or four missions in a night, to chalking up a few more bad guys by sunrise.

A dangerous breed. One that made mistakes.

'Team Six,' Bob added.

Right, Walker thought, looking at Bob. *One of those* . . . Either Bob *was* in Six, DEVGRU, as it was properly known, or – more likely – he wasn't but was claiming it. Either way he had all the bravado markings of a soldier who had the skills to kill but not the right aptitude to survive post-Navy life in the high-paying world of private security contractors, so instead went to the CIA's Special Activities Division because they were desperate for door-kickers. The bulk of DEVGRU had rotated home not long back. Walker knew a few of them, had worked with them. The men on these elite special-operations teams went to war in shifts. For more than a decade they had been deploying to Iraq or Afghanistan for three-to-four-month tours, where they maintained a very high operating tempo. Nearly every night they would go hunting. When deployed, they were sequestered from conventional troops, living either at their own forward-operating bases or on a sealed-off portion of a larger base. Walker knew that it was a deeply satisfying business, and the good men in those units tended to stay. Most found it difficult to adjust to anything else; the skills required were not readily applicable to other kinds of work. For men who had been part of such operations – adrenaline-pumping missions in which they risked their lives and watched good friends die – and who enjoyed the silent admiration of everyone else in uniform, and believed their work was vital to their nation's security, little else compared.

Walker looked more closely at Bob. Like most special-forces operatives he was built for speed and endurance, and he liked to move quickly; sitting still wasn't easy for him. *The guy's bored to death out here . . .*

'How about you?' Bob said. 'Always a suit?'

Walker looked down at the grimy pants and combat boots he'd bought in country – sure, they hadn't been broken in yet, but what the hell made him a suit? If this were a movie, Walker thought, this would be the time to flashback to him wearing a suit to work, for a law firm in the Twin Towers, where on 9/11 he had watched his friends and co-workers jump out of the building, him alive today only because he had been in the forecourt when the first plane struck. Then there would be another flash to a scene a couple of years later, when he was working at a national-security think tank in London and saw a double-decker bus explode like a firecracker one day as he left work. The director would then cut to now, a close-up of his eyes: the eyes that had seen too much, the eyes that soon developed a determined edge, which had in turn compelled him to join the fight.

But this was no movie.

And Walker was no suit.

He'd been killing for the US Government his entire adult life.

'I mean,' Bob said, 'you're with the State Department, right?'

Walker scanned the glasses out his open passenger-side window. 'That's what they tell me.'

In itself, that wasn't a lie, but details weren't something he could afford to share; guys like Bob weren't cleared to know half the truth.

'Ha. I know, right? The two of us, working for The Man.' Bob was silent then for almost two minutes before he checked his watch, shuffled around in his seat to get more comfortable and said, 'Damn, where's our UAV coverage? Should have heard by now.'

Walker shrugged. He knew that there was no use looking up in the sky for the drone; it would be up there, somewhere, high above and out of sight, its powerful cameras doing their thing. Sure, if you looked long and hard enough you might catch a glint off the camera lens, but that was only if you knew where to look.

'Did you ever serve?' Bob asked.

'Yep.'

'Where?'

'Everywhere.'

'I mean, who with?'

'Twenty-fourth Tac.'

Bob was still, and quiet; the quietest Walker had seen him. Respect. Bob said, 'Your guys did some good work.'

'They still do.'

'Yeah, I'm sure. That's cool man, real cool.'

Walker stared ahead in silence.

'This one time, I had one of your boys back me in a bar fight in Kuwait. All started when some jarhead broke his fist on the back of my head, you believe that?'

Walker looked at him and said, 'Yep. It's a hell of a head.'

They laughed.

Walker went back to glassing the area. His reconnaissance the past couple of days had told him that there were two locals in the roadhouse, but they were the indoors type. A little wisp of smoke rose from the chimney as they made their tea.

'Your guy stepped in and stopped me from getting sucker punched,' Bob said. 'Kicked the hornets' nest, we did; it became a case of six SOCOM vets versus a platoon of Marines. The six of us owned that bar for the rest of our stay.'

Walker smiled. 'Ah, you're all right, Bob, you know that?'

Bob looked a little sucker punched. 'Thanks.'

Their encrypted DoD satellite phone bleeped.

'It's Qatar,' Walker said to Bob, reading the number on the display screen. He activated the speaker phone and answered with their call sign. 'Whisky Mike Bravo.'

'Copy that. Heads up, Whisky Mike,' the voice said. 'HVT rolling in from the east, make it twenty clicks out.'

'HVT inbound from east, two-zero clicks, copy.'

'Roger that. Make it as a three-vehicle convoy. Tango is in an SUV, make is a new Range Rover, possibly armoured, a couple of pick-ups with heavy machine guns riding fore and aft. Looks like they're heading for a meet with your target.'

'ID on the tango?'

'Negative over the net, Whisky Mike. But this is a category-five, NSA intercept confirm, and that's the extent of our intel at this stage.'

Which means nothing they are going to share with us, at least not over the phone. Walker looked to Bob, who tossed his empty Coke can into the back seat and readied his H&K carbine.

'Repeat last, Qatar,' Walker said. He scanned east and could make out the faintest plume of dust.

'Cat-five HVT, five minutes out, east of you, make it three mechs rolling in fast,' the voice repeated. Walker knew that the voice belonged to an Air Force captain with CENTCOM's intelligence section, JICCENT, calling in from Al Udeid Air Base in Qatar. The NSA intercept ID was likely a cell number or voice match on the High Value Target, relayed to and from the National Security Agency in Fort Meade, Maryland. Their information would be accurate – following the fiasco of going to war for mythical Weapons of Mass Destruction in Iraq, US intelligence agencies insisted on being methodical, absolute, and operating at all times with a paranoid sense of certainty at all costs.

'Copy that: cat-five inbound to our target,' Walker said. Category-five High Value Targets were the likes of terror-cell leaders and Al Qaeda lieutenants. There were none reported to be in this area of Yemen, a hundred clicks from the nearest town, the Gulf of Aden a crust of blue on the southern horizon. This changed everything. 'Comms between Tango and our courier?'

'Negative.'

No signals intercepts between these two meeting parties, which fitted the modus operandi of Al Qaeda's top brass: keep dark.

'How did this cat-five get made then?' Bob whispered. 'He called for a pizza?'

'Shh,' Walker mouthed to him, then spoke into the phone. 'Qatar, you're sure they're stopping in on our friends for a little face time?'

'Whisky Mike, from what I see, there's nothing else out there but rocks and sand,' the captain replied.

We're out here, Walker thought, then said, 'What are our new engagement protocols?'

'Stay on mission. Observe and report.'

Walker paused, then said, 'And the HVT?'

'He has to slide. Sorry, Whisky Mike, but this comes from the Admiral. Eyes in the sky will track him when he leaves. Rest assured the tango will be handled with extreme prejudice when the time is right.'

Bob shook his head. Walker admired his spirit. He wanted in, to take on the incoming convoy with small arms, despite the directive to do nothing coming directly from CENTCOM's Deputy Commander.

'We've got a Predator tracking, overhead your position in two minutes,' the captain said, as if this would appease them. 'Stay on station, Whisky Mike, and stay on mission, copy.'

'Copy that, Whisky Mike out,' Walker said, ending the call. His eyes scanned the road where it disappeared in the heat haze on the horizon.

•

Half a world away, in an office on Pennsylvania Avenue in Washington DC, a stone's throw from the White House, a man received a phone call about the category-five HVT sighting in Yemen.

The news was pleasing, because things were moving exactly as he'd planned.

He was in the business of intelligence, and his job was to be better at it than anyone else. Part of that meant making sure that he had all the cards. To him, this was a business. And business was big.

He knew that within seconds a certain order at the CIA would be made: that the meeting between the HVT and the courier could not take place. Right now, in Langley, a Deputy Director would be giving an instruction, and in turn several orders would follow, culminating in a kill order given to the UAV pilots at Creech Air Force Base, Nevada, who had control of a drone flying in Yemeni airspace.

Dan Bellamy ended the call and smiled. His business was making a killing.

•

'This is bullshit,' Bob said, grinding his teeth. 'Cat-five protocols are as clear as – we can't let this guy through the net, we've got to cook him!'

Walker knew the protocols, but Bob and a Predator drone were no match for all the hardware rolling towards the target complex.

'The Predator will be armed,' Walker said. 'This cat-five will be stacked up as another Targeted Killing in the middle of the desert later today, another scumbag scattered to the winds. However they do it, Bob, we've got our own job to do.'

'Yeah, but this is crap – you know those Nevada jockeys miss more than they hit.'

Walker knew that this was an exaggeration – he had seen Hellfire missiles fired from Predators meet most of their targets nose-on. And advances in Hellfire technology meant that the kill boxes were ever expanding. But that didn't *guarantee* that the target they fired on would die. Only a guy on the ground could guarantee that. Hence the decision to send in a SEAL team rather than a swarm of drones to kill bin Laden. For some missions a bullet to the head was the best outcome.

'I'm tellin' you, we should at least roll down to the road,' Bob said. 'Pass through, at the intersection, eyeball this new son of a bitch and—'

'And what? His guys will light us up with a fifty-cal as soon as they sight us. The best case? We get down there and spook them away and we miss everyone – including our courier.'

Walker and Bob went silent, both lost in their thoughts. Walker watched the horizon. He knew that although the Predator might get some imagery, the fact was that whoever was going to meet with his target would do their business and leave, and there was nothing he and Bob could do about it.

'Goddamned unknowns,' Bob said, rapping his fingers against the stock of his H&K 416, the danger-end pointed out the window. 'This is horseshit. Cat-five horseshit. We're here to put eyeballs on your courier's meeting. Now this. We've been here two days, shittin' in the sand and waiting; now this gift falls in our lap and we can't do nothin' with it?'

'I've been tracking this courier's movements for the best part of a year,' Walker said. 'Cool your jets, yeah?'

Bob met Walker's gaze, and nodded. *At least he respects the chain of command on the ground.*

'I'll watch for the UAV,' Bob said, scanning the blue sky out his open window with an identical set of Steiner anti-glare binoculars.

'UCAV,' Walker corrected as he watched a growing dust plume from the west, inserting the C for Combat, since he was sure it would be armed with four Hellfire missiles. Then again, this was a target-rich environment – the Predator might have discharged its missiles in the night, for this was never meant to be a kill mission, and might remain so.

Bob grunted.

Walker waited silently, watching. The dust cloud closing in from the west: their courier. The tiny cloud growing to the east: the HVT.

Two worlds colliding.

In less than three minutes their world would change.

•

The UCAV was not a Predator drone as the Air Force captain at JSOC had advised, but he was not to know that: his console had it tracked as such. That particular aircraft had been tasked off mission when another had arrived on station to take its place.

The aircraft making its way to the Yemeni target was a Northrop Grumman X-47B: a stealth UCAV, the most advanced remote-piloted air weapon the world had ever known.

Launched an hour earlier from the USS *Harry S. Truman* in the Gulf of Aden, the UCAV streaked through the sky at phenomenal speed.

There was no doubt about it: the X-47B was a mean killing machine.

•

Walker looked into the large side mirror on their jeep and used his water bottle to wash grit from his face. His clear blue eyes were sunken, skin dark from the sun, cheeks sallow for the too-little food he ate in country compared with the calories that his fear and anxiety demanded. His straggly two-month beard and unwashed hair made him look more like a castaway than an attempt at blending in as a local. Two months combing the sands of one of the world's richest terrorist hunting grounds would do that to the best of men. It was addictive work, once you lost yourself to it. It required focus; no time for dwelling on life back home, on what this job cost.

'Movement,' Walker said. 'Our courier's arriving.'

'Right on time.'

Walker took out the Canon EOS with telephoto lens and photographed his target getting out the back seat of a clapped-out Peugeot and moving quickly towards the building. A slight man, the courier: five foot nine, no more than 170 pounds, Saudi descent, raised in Algeria, schooled in Paris. He scanned his surroundings, not picking out Walker's jeep parked 300 metres out on an elevated position among a large graveyard of burned-out and battered vehicles. The target waved his driver to park around the back. The camera's shutter whirred away.

'Dust to the east is growing,' Bob said. 'A minute out.'

Walker looked at the eastern horizon, the single gravel road leading in from that direction: the plume was now huge. Several vehicles, heading in hot. Through the viewfinder's magnification he made them.

'That's our HVT,' Walker said. 'Range Rover's riding real low – it's armoured for sure.'

'Damn,' Bob said, watching. 'What I wouldn't give for a few AT4s.'

He pronounced it 'eighty-fours', the US military's man-portable rocket launcher of choice. Walker had seen them peel apart Iraqi Republican Guard armoured vehicles and punch holes through solid concrete walls of insurgent hide-outs. Nice toys.

The convoy pulled up to the squat mud hut next to the gas station, the only real permanent structures out here. Walker's camera snapped away as the courier greeted the category-five HVT. They looked a little wary of each other, unfamiliar, keeping a distance.

'This is BS, man, BS!' Bob said.

Walker remained silent, taking photos of the seven armed insurgents standing sentry by their vehicles.

Three things happened at once: Walker heard shrieking whooshes overhead; he saw the flashes as the missiles hit; and he felt the concussive force of the impacts.

Then, half a second later, the sound wave hit them.

KLAPBOOM!

KLAPBOOM!

The convoy was transformed into a bright, burning forest of wreckage. Only the carcass of the armoured Land Cruiser resembled a vehicle. No-one in a twenty-metre radius was moving.

'What the—' Bob's sentence was cut short as another missile streaked in, this one hitting the front door of their target building.

•

'Target down, sir.'

'Did we get them all?' CIA Deputy Director Jack Heller asked as he stood in the Langley op centre watching live satellite imagery and overhead drone images of the site in Yemen. Vivid colour and violent heat plumes in high-res. Beautiful chaos.

This was Heller's show. As Director of the Special Activities Division, he knew exactly who the category-five HVT was at the strike zone in Yemen. No-one else in the room did. Probably never would.

'Two five-hundred-pound JDAMs right on target, sir, and a Hellfire right through the front door. Our kill box is a good fifty-metre radius – there's nothing left alive down there.'

'The structure's still standing.'

'Incendiary Hellfire's still doing its thing; no-one's getting out of that.'

Heller said, 'Keep an eye on scene. Make sure.'

'We'll stay over target as long as we can, sir. The drone is loaded with another three Thermobaric Hellfire missiles – nothing's going to get out of there.'

'How long?'

'Sixteen hours' flight time remaining.'

'If you see movement,' Heller said, 'rain hell on them.'

'Roger that.'

'Good.' Heller turned to the room. 'Good job, people. Couple less dirtbags in the world—'

'Sir!'

Heller turned.

'Two figures in a vehicle just entered the kill box.'

'ID?'

The image from the drone above zoomed in but revealed little through the dust-covered windscreen.

'Negative. What do we do, sir?'

Heller smiled when he said, 'Toast 'em.'

•

Walker slammed on the brakes and their old Land Cruiser came to a halt ten metres out from the inferno ahead.

He knew that the craters in the road were not the work of Hellfire missiles. There was a large and very real combat aircraft somewhere overhead.

'I've got intel and the courier, you handle personnel,' Walker said as they exited the vehicle and moved quickly.

'Yes, sir.'

They each had wet scarves tied around their faces to protect them from the worst of the thick smoke. Walker was armed with his Beretta 9-millimetre in one hand and a dry-chemical extinguisher in the other, an empty backpack over his shoulder.

Bob was first through the gaping hole of what was left of the front wall, a double-tap ringing out from his H&K as he dispatched a wounded Al Qaeda insurgent.

Walker scanned the interior – the ceiling and roof blown out, the sky above sucking out the acrid fumes. Single room, door out back. No movement. He did an intel sweep, unzipping his backpack and bagging anything that looked worthy. A laptop computer was toasting but he blasted it with the white powder and took it. Singed papers. He couldn't identify anything else of value.

He moved on to the bodies, armed with his camera.

The category-five HVT, identifiable only by what was left of a scrap of his clothing, was beyond dead. The arms and legs were attached to what was left of his body, but his head and most of his torso were gone.

'Clear!' Bob called after checking out the back door.

The courier was immobile, face down, his back on fire.

Walker doused him with the dry chemical, then kicked him over.

The courier's face was locked in a grimace, a bubbling mess of charred flesh with a red gash for a mouth and bright white teeth where a side of his cheek had melted away. He was alive.

In his hand was a cell phone, its screen lit up.

Walker blasted him again with the extinguisher, putting out the little spot fires, then bent down to him, pistol pointed into his chest.

The man's eyes settled on Walker's and they softened, pleading.

'Walker.'

Walker looked up. Bob stood there, H&K aimed at him.

'Sorry, pal. Nothing personal. Heller's orders.'

'Bob . . .'

Walker looked at his colleague, the guy he'd underestimated. *He's doing this for Heller?* Behind Bob, outside the gaping hole, was the bright blue sky.

And the flash of a missile plume.

Too late.

The Hellfire struck the middle of the gravel road out the front and detonated on impact.

Their Land Cruiser bore most of the blast. What was left was engulfed in angry flames.

When the dust cleared, Walker worked his way free of rubble that was formerly part of the building and road. A fire raged outside. The Land Cruiser was a skeleton of its former self.

'Ah, shit,' Bob said as he tried to stand. He held a hand to his leg, watching blood seeping. 'I'm hit.' He collapsed to the floor, his back against the wall, his weapon still gripped firmly in his hands.

'We can head out the back for another vehicle—'

'No,' Bob interrupted. 'The drone . . . it'll hit us. Ah, shit . . . Heller. This was Heller, wasn't it? He sent me to kill you, and the drone's the back-up plan. Or I'm the back-up. Damn it . . .'

'They sent you because a bullet to the head's better than a Hellfire.'

Bob grimaced. 'You know those Nevada desk jockeys.'

Walker looked up at the sky. His stomach tensed as he saw a reflected glint of sunlight against glass as the aircraft banked around for another pass. He knew that even the latest-generation Predator could stay up there for a long time, and that the Hellfire missile had a range of 8000 metres. Waiting around wasn't an option.

'Have you got a strobe?' he asked Bob as he moved towards him, still scanning the sky.

Bob pulled an infrared strobe from his tactical vest. Walker activated it and tossed it onto the road outside. Back at Creech Air Force Base, the pilots should recognise that friendlies were on scene.

Should.

Walker tied off a tourniquet on Bob's leg.

'You got lucky,' Walker said. 'The shrapnel missed the artery.'

'Why're you helping me?'

Walker looked at him, said, 'Why wouldn't I? You're a soldier following orders.'

'Great,' Bob said with a pained smile, 'I finally qualify for a Purple Heart and I'm out of that game.'

'Hang tight,' Walker said. He moved to the back door and took in the scene; among the debris was the rusted-out old Peugeot 403 that the courier had arrived in.

He moved back to the dying man and bent to search for the keys, moving bits of debris out of the way.

'I'm . . . friendly,' the courier hissed out his wrecked mouth. 'Friendly.'

Walker looked down at the burned man's eyes. He was their target; their guy to track, to see whom he met with and then pressure and turn into an agent for the good guys.

'Why'd our own drone fire on us?' Bob said. He hadn't heard the courier speak.

Walker bent close to the courier.

'I'm . . . Louis . . . Assif.' The courier lifted a blackened hand to Walker. 'I'm working . . . this.'

'Who do you work for?' Walker asked, taking the man's hand.

The man struggled to get each sound out. 'DG . . . S . . . E.'

French intel; the French equivalent of the CIA and NSA rolled into one. *Was this guy already a double agent?*

'What were you working on here?' Walker said.

'Here to . . . meet him . . .' Blood dribbled from where his cheek had been. 'Working . . . for four years to get to this . . . meeting.'

Assif was fading fast. His eyes rolled back and his lids closed.

Walker touched the man on the shoulder, as gently as he could. 'What are you working on here?'

The man's eyes stayed shut. Life was leaving him. He said something, a single word but Walker couldn't make it out for the gurgling. Walker put his ear closer to Assif's mouth, and this time he managed a whole, stilted sentence. 'We must . . . deal with the devil . . . if we are to c-c-catch their . . . master.'

'Master?'

'Spies . . .' Assif gasped. 'Not . . . drones. Not intercepts. You want to . . . hear a conversation, you must be in the room, sipping . . . tea with . . . them . . . looking into their eyes. That was . . . my . . . job.'

Bright-red foam erupted from the courier's mouth and ran down his neck. His lungs were shredded. He was drowning in his own blood.

'We're bugging out,' Walker said. 'I'm getting the both of you to Aden, to a doctor.'

Assif looked at him blankly.

'Bob, give me a hand to shift this guy out,' Walker said. Then, with no answer, he turned to his comrade.

Bob sat silent, still.

Dead still.

Walker moved fast, checked the tourniquet on Bob's leg – it was tight. He felt for a pulse – nothing. Then he noticed the blood, a lot of blood, a sticky pool of it, from a wound on Bob's back, near his kidneys. He had bled out, quickly, quietly, against the wall, the blood running away out of sight.

Walker closed his colleague's eyes and took his H&K.

'Come on,' Walker said to the courier. 'It's me and you.'

'No, please . . . kill me.'

'I can move you. There's the car out the back—'

'No. No . . . time. Go. Your friend said . . . Why would they fire at you? Who would . . . want you dead?'

Assif's other hand released its grip – the cell phone clattered to the floor.

'You must . . . follow the . . . money,' Assif said. 'Follow the money – New York.' He convulsed twice, then closed his eyes. They remained closed.

As the sound of another missile tore through the sky, Walker saw that the blood-smeared cell-phone screen was filled with a text message: ZODIAC 0930 09.06.14.

1
Nine months later

Washington DC

Dan Bellamy looked at the highlighted screen of his unlisted cell phone and considered bumping the call. He'd had confirmation of the job just fifteen minutes ago, and now his field operative was calling him again. He had been expecting a call, but not this call. It was too soon. A complication, at their end. Calling him from the field.

He leaned back in his chair and rested his feet upon his desk. Looking out his window, he could see straight to the Capitol Building. It was after midnight. He had come by the office to handle some paperwork; at least that's what he told his wife. In reality he was here to make sure the operation was successful. Bellamy had a lot riding on it. Too much. Across the room – a modest wood-panelled space that was swept for surveillance bugs every week – his daughter slept on the couch. Still in her soccer uniform; she had won tonight. A good omen. His baby girl. Winning.

Bellamy answered the phone. 'This call came sooner than expected. You can't be outside Rome yet.'

'I'm still here. There's been a complication.'

'What is it?' He thought the worst: carloads of Italian cops have his operative's team surrounded. If that were the case, it would be gut-wrenching stuff until his lawyers did what they did and he did what he did to bury it all.

'There's someone on scene,' the voice said.

Bellamy relaxed a little. 'Some*one*?'

'A man.'

Bellamy paused, said, 'A man. On scene?'

'Yes.'

'Define "on scene".'

'Inside the target's apartment.'

Bellamy winced. 'I don't want to know such details.'

'It's a complication.'

'And you're still there?'

'Correct.'

Bellamy thought it through, then said, 'Forget it. Get out of there.'

'No. Not like this. I don't like it.'

Bellamy processed the implications: the op had started barely half an hour ago, they had been in and out within fifteen minutes, and yet his team was still there, watching the scene of their crime. *Why?*

'Who is it?'

'I don't know,' the voice replied. 'A guy. Could be a cop, but I doubt it.'

'But you're spooked by him. Enough to break protocols and contact me.'

'I thought I'd check in first.'

'First?'

'Before I proceed.'

Ah, right . . . it's about money. Trust, too, but money. To those guys in the field, this was another job.

Bellamy didn't have time for complications. He checked his watch. Eighty-one hours until deadline.

•

Rome

Inside the apartment in Rome it looked like a bomb had gone off.

Jed Walker entered warily, unarmed, using the heel of his boot to push the door closed behind him, leaving it unlocked as he had found it. The place was empty, but the trail was warm.

He scanned the rooms in ten seconds and learned all he needed to.

It was late nineteenth century, well made and maintained. A corner site on the second floor, with two windows looking south, three to the east. Opposite, two doors ran off to a kitchen and a bedroom with en suite. Everything was tastefully appointed, the furnishings sparse and modern: hardwood parquetry floors, herringbone pattern; an expensive TV and stereo the centrepiece of the living area; a set of custom-made golf clubs by the door. All of it fitted the profile of a successful banking executive – the cover job of the CIA operative who had lived there.

It had all been tossed. Recently.

Walker looked around each corner of the apartment and concluded that whoever had tossed the place was looking for something specific. They'd done a messy job of it, like cops do in the movies when they search a perp's apartment: lamps and vases broken, the sofas slashed and overturned, the carpets lifted, the bed flipped on its side, the kitchen cabinets emptied. The refrigerator had been pulled out and its panels separated; the oven and washing machine and dishwasher too. Piles of screws were everywhere: they had used cordless drivers to pull things apart quietly rather than pinch bars to wreck it loudly. The desk was upside down. A mess of cables remained, but at least two hard drives and a laptop were gone. Whatever was in the desk's drawers was also missing. No useful physical evidence remained.

This had been a search for something small, or a clean-up of anything incriminating that might lead back to the guy's employers.

Could have been by the CIA or another crew. Either way, no friends of mine.

Walker knew that this had been conducted by pros.

And he knew that the occupant had been killed here, within the past hour.

•

'It's your op,' Bellamy said quietly to his man on the phone while his daughter slept across the room. 'It must be clean, that was my main requirement. Clean and final . . . but that's not why you called me now.'

There was a pause, and then the man said, 'I thought maybe you sent another crew.'

'Now, why would I bother doing that?'

'I don't know.'

Bellamy was silent.

'Okay. Well, this guy,' his contact said, 'he's not local. He looks ex-military. Big guy. Late thirties. Caucasian. Can handle himself.'

The wheels in Bellamy's mind turned on that one. He trusted his operator on this mission, and trusted that like could spot like. *So, who is this ex-military guy in the apartment? A competitor? The target's protection, arriving too late? Could be anyone. Could mean anything. Could mean that they were too late . . . either way, this is getting messy.*

Bellamy said, 'Can you pick him up? Take him in? Question him?'

'When he gets out,' the voice said. 'Though it will attract attention.'

'What if he makes a call from inside the apartment?'

'We're scanning for that.'

'What do you want to do?'

'Go back inside. Deal with him in the apartment.'

'Do it,' Bellamy said. 'Question him first, see who he is and what he knows, then clean it up. Go in there and clean it up and be sure of it. Don't leave a trace. Burn it all.'

'Copy that.'

The voice was waiting.

Bellamy said, 'Something else?'

'My fee? This matter of another target . . .'

'Consider it doubled.'

Bellamy ended the call. He stared at his cluttered desk. This op was not meant to be messy. *Getting rid of a guy in the middle of Rome? Getting rid of two? All in a day.*

He looked across at his sleeping child. Some books and a field of McDonald's debris were spread on the table in front of her. *It's all getting harder, busier, less certain. It'll pay off, soon . . .*

He looked through his open doorway, to the large open-plan office empty of staff for the day; an office and business he had created from nothing more than a limited skill set and a lot of networking and risk-taking. Now INTFOR was on the verge of becoming the largest and most powerful private intelligence outfit on the planet. He swivelled around in his chair and focused on his collection of framed photographs: him with presidents and prime ministers and VIPs from around the world. Powerful men and a couple of powerful women. All of them more reliant on him with each passing day. He looked out the window to his left.

The sun was gone, now the streetlamps and uprights bathed the monumental town.

The end of another day.

A new dawn was just around the corner. Three more dawns before everything changed.

2

The blood the killers had left behind told Walker most of what he needed to know.

The mattress in the bedroom held a bloodstain – large, the size of a frying pan, and still red. After about two hours' exposure to oxygen, blood that has thinned and splattered and atomised onto absorbent material like a mattress oxidizes and turns brown.

They never got that right in the movies.

So, Felix was killed where he lay. Which meant that his killers entered quietly enough not to wake him. Which meant that this was an assassination: either to get what Walker had come here for, or to tidy up a loose end. Maybe both.

Two kill shots, through the chest, the heart probably. Not the head – less messy that way. Plus, like Walker they knew to protect the head; like Walker they knew what type of information was in it.

So, this was not a straightforward case of professional killers. This was the work of men in the know of current CIA tradecraft.

Maybe they had asked Felix a question or two before they fired, but probably not – this was a quick job, and what they needed most was not known to their target. Yet it was *on* his person.

They, like Walker, had come for what was sewn into the base of Felix's skull: a tiny chip containing information. Felix was a head-case courier, used by the CIA to transport intelligence from one wireless hot spot to another. Someone knew what was on that chip – if not the killers then whoever had hired them.

On the floor, blood had pooled where they had tossed the body from the bed. Once blood leaves the body, it begins to clot quickly, within five to ten minutes. After that the blood begins to separate as the clot retracts into a dark knot and squeezes out a halo of yellow serum. This process takes another hour or more, when the blood then dries to a rusty brown stain.

The blood here had clotted but not separated – this hit took place more than ten minutes but less than an hour earlier.

The bed sheets were missing, so the killers had wrapped the body in them and then placed it in a wheeled duffel bag. Judging by the track marks of blood on the floor, it was a 120-litre bag, which meant they had folded and stuffed the body in tightly. They weren't squeamish, these men, and they were strong. There were at least two, probably three, so someone stood sentry in the apartment while two dealt with the body. Or perhaps he had tossed the place while the others packed the body. The packers must have noticed the tracks the wheels had started to make, from where they had run through the blood pool, and wiped the castors clean with the quilt. The tracks then disappeared.

They had been careful and relatively quiet but they hadn't taken the time to clean up. So, it was a quick job. A three-man crew, on the clock.

Walker inspected the mattress. Two gunshot holes punctured the centre of the bloody mess. The underside was shredded. The floor below looked like it had been sandblasted, the surface pockmarked with dime-sized punctures, grouped more tightly in the centre, spreading out to a dozen chips in a diameter roughly the size of a dinner plate. Soft fragmentary rounds had been used, semiwadcutters with heavy grain, the slugs further slowed by a suppressor, fired up close, the soft lead tearing apart as it hit bone and bedsprings. So, the bigger and slower .45 calibre rather than a 9-millimetre.

Serious men doing a serious job of it.

Professionals.

•

Outside the apartment the three professionals in the back of the van readied and checked their weapons. Each had a Beretta .45 calibre, the PX4 Storm, locally sourced and made, custom silenced, untraceable, ten-round capacity apiece.

Their leader was Brendan Crowley, a contractor who did most of his work for the CIA, from extraordinary rendition around the Mediterranean to making people disappear completely. He spoke half a dozen languages and could pass as a local in Italy, France, Croatia, Greece and Spain.

As an intelligence operator he was a specialist in wet work; the messy end of the intelligence world. He and his team were known as 'outcome specialists'. Those back in DC didn't want to know specifics about the jobs these men took care of – just outcomes. Positive outcomes were their preference.

Crowley had planned that his team would stay on the scene for twenty minutes after their exfil from the apartment, mainly to be sure that their near-silent work had gone unnoticed, and partly to complete their cover. The van was marked as city-gas department, which in this middle-class but crumbling neighbourhood would not draw second glances. Outside the van they had erected a taped-off cordon around the street's main supply and left the hatch open. It had now been twenty-five minutes since they had left the apartment, and they had sat in the air-conditioned van, silent, watching, waiting. In the back were two large duffel bags of rubbish to drop, weighted down, in the Adriatic later that day. One bag contained the body of CIA courier Felix Lassiter, the other a collection of his papers and computer equipment. The spoils of a job done.

The disposal, however, would have to wait.

Crowley and his team had another job to do.

Time to go back in.

•

Walker knew better than to search the apartment hoping for a clue missed by those who had worked here this morning; this was the well-executed job of a well-trained team. Maybe not the best operators, but they weren't far from it. They were expensive, and not many entities had access to such men.

This fitted what he knew about the man who owned this apartment. Not so much a target as a person of interest and an unwitting courier – a perfect cut-out agent. For the CIA, and for someone else. It was the *someone else* that was of interest to Walker.

And clearly Felix Lassiter had garnered the interest of other parties.

Time to leave.

3

'What are you doing?' a voice said in accented English.

Walker stood still, in the middle of Felix's apartment. He had been making for the door, to leave, when the door had opened before him. A figure had stepped inside.

A woman.

She stared at him, standing there, for a few seconds. Then her eyes flitted around to take in the state of the room. Shock registered on her face.

'Visiting,' Walker replied calmly. 'Leaving.'

The woman took another step inside, and looked behind the door to check the blind spot. In a sweeping glance she had taken in the scene, and he could tell her version of what she saw: she had caught him red-handed in a robbery, maybe more. She appeared calm.

In under a minute she'd gone from shock to calm and that told Walker something.

'Where is Felix? Talk, or I call the police,' she said, placing one hand inside her shouldered handbag.

Walker remained silent.

Her eyes were locked onto his, reading him, his thoughts and motives and desires. Her hand remained in her bag.

She asked, 'Who are you?'

Walker did not see her as a threat. Her presence here, at this time, was intriguing. She was beautiful, in a classic, Italian way. Forty-ish, possibly late thirties, with a youthful fullness in her face. Dark hair and darker eyes. Tall and shapely. Toned arms. Bright red lips. Everything about her appearance was strong, exaggerated. Her simple summer dress did nothing to suppress the imagination. Desirable and disconcerting. Dangerous. He did not want to do her harm, yet she was in his way, asking questions. In English – she'd pegged him as American straightaway. Walker needed to get out of here, but he had to leave cleanly, calmly, which meant engaging with this woman long enough to make it quietly out the door.

'My name's Walker. Jed Walker.'

'You are American.'

'Yes.' *But you knew that as soon as you saw me . . .*

'And, Jed Walker, what are you doing here?'

'Visiting Felix.'

'Why?'

'He's a friend.'

'You made this mess?'

'No.'

She was silent for a moment, then asked, 'Where is Felix?'

'Gone.'

'Where?'

'I'm not sure.'

Her eyes were locked on his, measuring, then she asked, 'How did you get in here?'

'The same way you did.' Walker gestured slightly to the doorway behind her, but she did not flinch or look back. Instead she continued to watch him with those big eyes, her long black eyelashes unblinking.

'Do you have a name?' he asked.

'Clara Placido.' Her voice drew him in. Her next words were spoken calmly, carefully. 'What is your business here?'

'Like I said, visiting,' Walker replied, moving to the window and checking down onto the street. It was a bright day, with a few cars passing by and pedestrians aplenty. Masses of vehicles and scooters were parked, jammed in so there was not a free space. Illegally parked across the street was a city-works van that he had seen when he entered the lobby, the driver still at the wheel. The position of the rear slide-door had changed. Not shut completely, but almost, as if it had opened and closed but not fully engaged the mechanism. There were no workers in sight. He'd seen three men seated in the back of the van before. *They could be the kill team, could be with Clara, could be anyone.*

Walker faced Clara and said, 'I was visiting a friend. I was too late . . .'

'Too late?' Her expression changed.

Walker gestured to his left, her right, to the open bedroom door. Clara kept him in her line of vision as she headed for the room. Definitely time to leave.

4

Walker moved quickly to the open apartment door. There was nothing more to be done here. He needed to leave, now, before Clara reappeared. Before her reaction. Before—

Too late.

Clara let out a muffled scream from the bedroom.

Walker stopped before the doorway.

Footfalls reverberated in the stairwell. It was an old building, with a rickety steel-gated elevator next to a marble-tiled staircase. People were moving up the stairs. Men. Heavy. Fast.

He counted at least three sets of footsteps.

They weren't cops. Cops would be wary, they would move quietly, they would have cordoned off the street if they knew an armed killer was in here.

This was three men, possibly four, returning to the scene of their crime.

The professionals.

Which meant they had seen him enter the building. From the van.

In five seconds they would be at the apartment door.

Walker closed the door and locked it. The door was as thick and old as the flooring, but the lock and chain were rubbish. He scanned the room for a weapon, and selected the seven iron. TaylorMade, with a slim grip. Felix was left-handed.

Can't have everything . . .

'What are you doing?' Clara said, emerging from the room.

'Hide in the wardrobe,' Walker said quietly, raising a hand to her as a stop sign. 'If I don't come in for you in five minutes, stay in there, quiet, and don't come out for an hour.'

Clara paused for less than a second, taking in his demeanour, his stance with the club, the locked door. She went back into the bedroom, and Walker heard the wardrobe shut.

He turned his attention to the locked door. He stood to the left of it, so that when it crashed open they wouldn't see him until after the club was arcing through the air at face level. He mentally rehearsed his next physical movements. What troubled him was the unknown number of adversaries: three or four? There was nothing to be done about that but adapt on the fly.

In the corridor outside, complete silence.

Go time.

•

Most people would be surprised at the number of FBI agents stationed abroad, working in countries far outside the borders of the United States. The general public may have heard of legal attachés attached to embassies, but not the agents who work on cases that cross international lines.

As a decorated fifteen-year Bureau veteran, Special Agent Fiona Somerville was used to being woken in the middle of the night. She was less used to being woken in the daytime, having been doing a week's worth of night surveillance operations with local authorities.

This was the first time she had been woken by Brian Sedekis, the CIA Station Chief at the Athens embassy. She buzzed him up, opened the door to her studio apartment and went to the bathroom to splash cold water on her face.

Somerville was in country on an open-ended assignment, investigating money-laundering services that had come to light after the country's economy collapsed. She and her colleagues had discovered that several Greek banks had more foreign money passing through with links to organised crime, terrorist outfits and foreign intelligence services than they handled in local currency. She had spent the better part of two years chasing trails all around the Adriatic and beyond. It was a plum job, and not just because of the exotic location with its great food, amazing weather and cheap cost of living. Organised crime and big money deals were still the benchmark in the Bureau for how reputations were made, and finding international terrorist links to that kind of action was the icing on that cake. The fact was, nothing made promotion mythology better than bringing down an international criminal kingpin, and Somerville felt she was closing on several with this op by using good old investigate work: following the money.

Of French–Quebec heritage, Somerville's father had been in the

Bureau, while her mother was the atypical nuclear-family wife raising four kids and working part-time at the elementary school library at some of the places they were stationed: Houston, Atlanta, Washington, Seattle. Her father had been a good worker but never driven like she was: he wanted little to get in the way of family life and a steady, long career. That career had been cut short by four full-metal-jacket rounds from a Mac 10 during a siege in Utah. Somerville didn't have time for anything but putting bad guys away.

'You were asleep?' Sedekis said as he walked in, his characteristic shuffling of feet a legacy of a wrecked back from an IED in Iraq a decade ago.

'Workin' the night shift,' Somerville said. She saw that he carried two takeaway coffees in paper cups: this was a serious house call.

'Right,' he said, looking around the apartment.

Somerville's washing was hung on an indoor line across one length of the living room. Last night's clothes were in a heap on the floor. Empty food containers littered the coffee table. The dining table was covered in case notes. Her bed was unmade. She took the coffee from Sedekis and sat on an armchair on the opposite side of the room to her washing, making him turn towards her to maintain eye contact.

'Sorry to bother you,' Sedekis said. 'But I thought you'd want to know what a little birdie has seen today.'

'Oh?' Somerville said, sipping the coffee and feeling a little fresher, a little more awake.

'I couldn't talk about it on the phone, and I was in the neighbourhood . . .'

'Okay, out with it.'

His face broke into a grin that couldn't be shaken.

'You know you're a terrible poker player,' Somerville said.

'I know, you cream me every month,' Sedekis replied.

'So . . . is it good news?'

'We found a ghost.'

'Who?'

Sedekis's smile grew just a little wider. 'Jed Walker.'

5

Walker had exceptional hearing for soft sounds, which was surprising considering the amount of time he had spent at the range and in kill houses and on the front line, where most soldiers were boomed and blasted and from age thirty their hearing began to wane. Indeed, many front-line operators took a little side payout for hearing impairment when they left their corps.

Not Walker. Not for the little stuff.

At school it had enabled him to prank better, cheat easier and hear the opposition's play in whispered football calls. Now it told him to be alarmed.

He heard English being whispered on the other side of the apartment door. At least three voices. American accents.

That's interesting . . .

They counted down from three, at which point Walker settled his pose: a pace back from the door's swing, feet shoulder-width apart, body twisted like he was about to tee off.

On two, Walker held the club double-handed and arced it back behind his right shoulder to get into a full baseball swing.

Wrong club for the sport, but it'll do.

On one, he started his swing. He was going for a homer. Out of the park. Beyond the car park. There was no way the first man through the door would get up again, not in a hurry, maybe never.

The door burst open, the lock and chain proving as useless as they had looked. The first man rushed into the room blind. He had a pistol, a Beretta .45 with fat suppressor, held out in front in a double-handed grip, pointed forwards and down.

The murder weapon.

The seven iron caught him on the bridge of the nose and the left cheekbone. The kinetic energy of the swing forced his head back even as his feet carried him forwards. Within the same second his feet had left the floor and he was airborne, landing flat on his back as the pistol clattered past Walker and through the open bedroom doorway.

Walker was moving too, a constant, fluid motion. He continued through his swing and carried the momentum a couple of paces to his right, pivoting around on his front foot so that by the time the second assailant was through the door he was greeted with a right elbow to the temple. This guy was armed with a taser, and it dropped like a stone from his hand. He wobbled a little unsteadily on his feet, a stunned jig, in which time Walker brought the club down through the air in a vertical swipe. The man had moved enough that it missed his head, though the downwards force was enough to shatter his collarbone and snap the club in half. He went down, hard, and on the way his face met Walker's rapidly rising knee. Lights out.

Two seconds, two down.

The third assassin paused in the doorway. He was smart enough to be wary, but not smart enough to turn and run. He was the biggest of the trio, the kind of mass that came with injections and bulk protein and big weights. Bigger than Walker and maybe ten years younger. He looked at his two comrades – the first out cold, and the second writhing in pain and engaging in a subconscious flight response, doing slow circles to nowhere on the polished floor, his brain sending his legs primitive signals to flee but his body unable to properly comply. The big guy saw this carnage and Walker saw the wheels in that big fat head turning.

Thinking hard, but not enough.

Walker crouched down and picked up the other half of the club, an improvised weapon now in each hand. His eyes never left the third man.

For his part, the big guy took a step inside the room and pulled a blade from a sheath on his belt. A tactical, black-anodised KA-BAR, standard US Marine issue back in the day. A combat knife, one cutting side only: seven inches of American-made razor-sharp steel designed for killing. It looked tiny in the big man's oversized fist.

'You don't have to do this,' Walker said.

The guy took a couple of steps inside.

Walker took two steps back, his eyes glued to his opponent, his body taking in every slight move they both made and his subconscious registering that there were no others following this guy. This was it. Three bad guys, not four. He gripped both halves of the broken golf club.

Walker said, 'What's your name?'

The big guy spat at him. Shifted right. Walker mirrored him.

'Make this easy,' Walker said. 'Talk. Tell me where you're taking Felix's body. Or the chip in his head. Where's that going?'

'Fuck you.'

'Tell me,' Walker said. 'And I'll let you turn around and go home to Momma. Go back to picking corn and taters. With what brains you got left in that planet-sized head of yours.'

The guy glanced at his comrade doing the circles on the floor.

Walker said, 'Last chance to talk, hombre. Where's your drop point?'

Bloodlust shone in the eyes staring back at him. He'd settled in for a fight.

Damn. Walker had worked with plenty of these guys, those who had become accustomed to killing, were conditioned to it, thrived on it. They didn't value their lives like they should, not when the lust overcame them. At The Point, the finishing school for CIA field operatives in North Carolina, Walker had trained enough paramilitary guys like this. He'd broken them, busted them out at the first round. There was no place on A Teams for men like that. This guy was a dropout.

Certainly not CIA.

So, this was the B Team. They were good, but not the best. But good enough to put up a decent fight. Most likely ex-Marine, given the bulk and the haircut and the choice of knife. But this wasn't war, nor was it training at Camp Pendleton, where the big guy had been introduced to the knife and how to fight to the death. This was closer to the no-rules-out-the-back-of-the-gym-after-school-time stuff, to sort out some testosterone. Walker had lost a few of those back in high school. Never any since. Never when a knife was involved.

'Why don't you tell me who you're working for . . .' Walker said. 'Tell me, tiny, or I'll have to turn your head into a putting green.'

He was hit with stony silence in return. Walker had found that the biggest guys were often the least talkative. Marines especially, and this guy was a jarhead from a mile away.

He came at Walker, the knife in his right hand in a forward grip, breaking the golden rule of knife fighting taught in the Corps – namely, never charge with a forehanded knife grip, especially when you're up against someone you know is capable and expecting it. This told Walker that his opponent had been out of the service a while, and had forgotten that when you pull a knife it's do or *die*.

Walker retreated out of the weapon's strike zone, a simple shift of weight to his back foot. Before the guy could comprehend and compensate for a follow-up attack, it was too late.

Walker's offensive move was as swift as it was absolute. With nothing more than a shift back to his front foot and raising the club's handle in his closed fist, the fight was over: the ragged end of the broken golf club's titanium shaft buried into the B Teamer's left eye socket, stopping only when it met resistance at the back of his skull.

The jarhead fell like a dumped puppet. Game over.

Three guys. Three moves. Each exact and necessary in its own way. Forty seconds, all told.

Walker moved to the guy with the wrecked shoulder and flattened nose, who was now conscious and still on the floor. With each slow concentric motion he'd inched towards the apartment door. Walker checked through the guy's pockets – nothing.

Walker picked up the knife and knelt down near the guy, driving the thick blade hard into the timber floor near his face as he spoke. 'I don't suppose you want to tell me who sent you?'

The guy started to shake. With his head tilted to the side, he looked up at Walker.

Nothing. Nothing, but shock and a little fear.

'Have it your way,' Walker said, applying squeezing pressure to the guy's shattered collarbone. He could feel the compound fracture under the skin, grinding little splinters that would take a surgeon hours to clean out. 'What did you want with Felix Lassiter?'

The guy gritted his teeth.

Walker knelt close to him and pressed against the fracture again. The guy writhed and lunged at Walker with his good hand, which Walker pinned to the ground.

'See your buddy there?' Walker motioned to the amateur golfer lying in a pool of his own blood. 'I'm gonna knock you cold and the authorities are going to find you here with him. That's gonna take some explaining.'

'Fuck off,' the guy said.

'Ah,' Walker replied. 'You're from Connecticut. What's a well-bred boy like you doing hanging out with tater-heads like these? Hmm? Why'd you kill Lassiter?'

Silence.

'Where are you taking the head chip?'

Walker squeezed. The guy cried out in pain.

'Talk.' Walker pressed his foot on the guy's shoulder—

'Get away from him,' a voice said.

Walker looked up.

Clara stood in the bedroom doorway, the .45 in her hands, pointed straight at him.

6

The Beretta PX4 Storm was a match-grade semi-automatic pistol made of polymers and steel inserts. Fully loaded and fitted with a suppressor, it weighed close to one and a half kilograms. It wasn't the sort of pistol many people – apart from those who trained with it twenty-four–seven – could hold out, aimed, for an extended period.

But Clara's hands were steady. Her stance was true. Her aim was dead on Walker's chest. It looked as if she could stay like that for a while.

'What are you doing?' Walker asked, standing slowly and taking a long step towards her. 'Clara – give me the gun.'

'You – you are a . . .' she said, lost for a moment as she took in the scene of decimation before her, 'murderer.'

Walker looked down, then pointed at the dead big guy.

'He was going to kill me,' Walker said slowly, clearly, 'and after me he would have killed you.'

'I can take care of myself,' Clara replied coldly as she looked from the carnage on the floor – one dead, one unconscious, one writhing in pain – to Walker.

Walker moved close to her, said, 'These guys killed Felix. They're a clean-up crew. They killed Felix, and they came back in here to make sure the place stayed clean.'

She looked away from Walker for just a second and in that time he snatched the Beretta from her hands. He checked the safety and unscrewed the suppressor.

'And you . . .' Clara said, lost in the scene. 'You did this to them.'

'They started it. I finished it.' He stowed the suppressor in the pocket of his jeans and tucked the pistol into the back of his waistband, pulling his shirt down to conceal the weapon.

'But, why – why like this?'

'I had no choice.'

Police sirens chimed outside, their distinctive Italian duotone sounding that they were nearing, fast.

'You called the cops?' Walker said.

Clara looked defiant.

Walker said, 'You're coming with me.'

•

'This guy was the best,' Bellamy said to Senator Jack Anderson from Oklahoma. 'Did you think he'd just lie down and die, with no repercussions?'

'I thought he died when he looked around a corner of his bedroom doorway and our SEALs put a round through his brain,' Senator Anderson replied.

'And then another couple in his chest,' the senator's national-security aide added. 'And you're telling us what, Dan? That bin Laden's ghost is coming back to haunt us? It sounds to me like you're trying to get your little company more funding.'

Bellamy nodded. Anderson was Majority Leader, as well as chair of the Senate Intelligence Committee – the guys who held the purse strings to the intelligence budget; a good friend to have. Fifteen years ago Bellamy had started out in Washington as the senator's aide; now it was unclear who was aiding whom.

'What I'm telling you,' Bellamy said, looking directly at the senator, to show that no-one else in the room mattered, 'is that he's reaching out from the grave.'

'With what?'

'We're working on that.'

'How serious a threat?' the senator asked.

'Very. We've checked this a million times. So has the Agency. Something big is coming.'

'Define "big",' the aide said.

'Catastrophic. Nine-eleven big. Maybe bigger.'

The senator leaned back in his chair. 'I need more than that.'

Bellamy paused, then said, 'I can give you the codename they're using, that's all. Anything else is conjecture.'

'A codename? For what?'

'Their attacks.'

'Attacks – plural?'

Bellamy nodded. 'It's a staged attack. In steps.'

'Steps?'

'Several acts of terrorism. A chain reaction.'

'How many attacks?'

'We think a trigger event – significant in its own right – will set in motion twelve high-value terror strikes around the world.'

'Jesus . . .'

The aide asked, 'What's the trigger event?'

Bellamy said, 'I'm working on that.'

'Dan . . .' Anderson said, 'you gotta give us something.'

'I can't show you the raw intelligence just yet, just like the Agency won't show theirs,' Bellamy said. 'But I'll be ready to brief you fully. Soon.'

The aide asked, 'When?'

'Couple days.'

'New York,' the senator said. 'It's gotta be by New York.'

'That's what I'm working towards,' Bellamy replied.

'A win will really help your IPO,' the aide said, a smug look on his face.

'Win or lose, terrorism is what makes my business,' Bellamy replied.

Anderson looked with a middle-distance stare across his office, at nothing in particular, but it was clear his mind was racing. He asked his aide to leave the room, then, after the door clicked closed, said to Bellamy, 'Remember what you told me the first time we talked business? After the Iraqi handover? When you first came into this office and told me about your program?'

'Yes. I told you that we don't negotiate with terrorists,' Bellamy replied. 'We put them out of business.'

'How's that going?'

'Business is good. It could be a lot better.'

'What do you need?'

Bellamy smiled. 'Leverage.'

The senator nodded. 'Okay. I'll work on that. Tell me, what are they calling it? This plot?'

Bellamy replied, 'Zodiac.'

7

'Where are you taking me?' Clara said as he guided her onto the street.

'I'm making sure you get out of here safely.'

'I can—'

'Take care of yourself, I know.' Walker's left hand was clamped on her arm, his right hanging free in case he had to draw the Beretta. 'Do you have a car?'

'Yes,' Clara replied, her voice shaky.

The sirens were closing. Seconds away. Italian cops. Armed. Unpredictable.

Across the road the van roared off. A modern Ford with a diesel engine, relatively empty of weight. Walker clocked the driver.

Four guys, not three.

Damn.

'Your car?' Walker said, squeezing Clara's arm.

'There,' she said, pointing to a white VW Polo GTI hatchback.

'Get in,' Walker said.

She unlocked the car and looked at him blankly, unsure what he expected her to do next. He took the keys from her and pushed her into the driver's seat and then across to the passenger seat. He climbed in behind the wheel and stopped, confused.

'How do you start this thing?'

Clara pressed a button on the dash that was labelled START.

Two police cars skidded around the corner ahead.

Walker put the car in gear and took off with an unintentional wheel-spin. In the VW's rear-view mirror he saw the two small blue Fiat hatchbacks with flashing lights undertake sharp U-turns in the crowded street and start in pursuit.

Shit.

'Where are you taking me?' Clara demanded.

'I was planning to get out of town and then be on my way.' He downshifted through a corner, then hit the gas, the turbo engine revving quickly through the gears.

'*Was?*'

'Now I want to see where that van goes.'

Clara looked over her shoulder to the carabinieri cars behind them. 'They will not let you get away.' She watched Walker. 'But you know that . . .'

Walker focused on what was ahead: the Ford van with city-gas logos ran through the red light at an intersection. Walker changed up gears as the VW's engine whined and redlined.

A delivery truck flashed by in front of their eyes, millimetres from impact.

'You are going to get us killed!' Clara yelled, her hands bracing the dash. 'Slow down!'

'Tell that to the rest of Rome,' Walker said, applying the handbrake at the bottom of the hill and sliding through the bend in the road, veering right onto the insanely busy Via Sicilia. Walker weaved their vehicle in and out of the oncoming lane, mirroring the van's moves ahead.

'This van,' Clara said. 'You sure this is one of the men who killed Felix?'

'Yes,' Walker said. 'And I'm sure he saw us leave the apartment.'

'Then let the police catch him.'

The two Fiats made the turn behind him; one took the corner too quickly and spun out in a 180-degree turn as a bus clipped its bumper.

'They're chasing *us*, not him,' Walker said, taking a quick look behind to see the police in pursuit. 'And besides everything else, the guy in that van saw me, and he saw you.'

Clara hesitated, then said, 'So what? You have something to hide from the police? Perhaps that murder back there?'

Walker didn't reply, just hit the brakes as the traffic came to a standstill.

The van was five vehicles ahead. The cop car lingered somewhere in the chaos behind, the incessant siren sounding.

'We're getting out,' Walker said, dragging Clara out his door and then down the road towards the van. The driver climbed out and looked back.

He saw Walker, and ran.

Walker started in pursuit.

The van driver kept running, flat out. He turned around for a brief moment—

KLAPBOOM!

The force of the blast from the exploding van blew Walker off his feet. He smashed back-first against a parked car, leaving a Walker-sized dint in the door. His grip on Clara held but the .45 clattered under the vehicle behind him.

Debris rained down by the time the fireball reached its zenith. The car ahead of the blast was on fire; the one behind had its bonnet blown off and its driver sat, hands gripped with white knuckles on the steering wheel, stunned. Walker didn't stop.

He dragged Clara behind him as he ran in pursuit of the van driver.

Behind them the police car had come to a stop at the end of the traffic, and the two officers were out and running towards the scene. The other police car was further down the road, and took a side street.

Walker and Clara ran against a crowd of onlookers. The van driver was getting further away – he was small and fast. He took a left and disappeared around a corner.

'Ah!' Clara said, stumbling.

'Quick!' Walker said, steadying her as a whistle blew behind them – one of the carabinieri was closing in.

They made the corner onto Via Veneto.

Walker stopped. He had been on this street before. He had seen the building before him, at number 119a: large, imposing Palladian design, four storeys, shuttered windows, tall iron fence, reinforced concrete bollards designed to stop tanks, a squat guard box by the driveway and a blue police car parked sentry out the front.

The driver of the van showed his passport at the main gate and was ushered through, into the US embassy.

8

Walker watched as the van driver joined the small line of US citizens entering the building on the gated compound. In seconds the Italian policeman pursuing them would round the corner. Walker had a US passport on him, but going into the embassy was not an option.

'Where to now?' Clara asked. 'Or is this over?'

Walker thought for a few seconds and then made his decision. 'It's over, for you,' he said, letting go of Clara's arm. He crossed the footpath to the pole-mounted CCTV camera that faced the embassy. He looked up at it, made sure that it tracked him, and then returned to the footpath and sat down at an outdoor table of the nearest cafe.

'That's it?'

'That's it.'

Clara looked around, astounded that he'd just sit and wait.

'Sorry.'

'Sorry?' Clara said. 'That's it, and you're *sorry*?'

'If it's vengeance you want for the death of Felix, leave that up to me.'

Walker ordered a macchiato. Long. And a Scotch. Double.

Clara watched him silently as she rubbed her arm from where he had clutched it. She then sat at the table, opposite Walker, looking determined.

'You'd better go,' Walker said.

'I want answers.'

'Walk south two blocks, then head back to your car. Go home. When the cops come knocking, tell them I kidnapped you.'

'And what? You just sit here and drink coffee?'

'And Scotch.'

The drinks came. He drained the Scotch.

'What are you waiting here for?' Clara asked.

Walker remained silent.

'What was your interest in Felix? And that man . . .' She looked across to the US embassy. 'He just gets away? If he and the others back there were Felix's killers – you do nothing about that?'

Walker checked his watch. Waiting here like this he knew: his life would soon change.

'I really think you should go,' Walker said. He sipped the coffee. Sighed, settled himself, knowing what was to come. 'You don't want to get involved in what happens next.'

•

'Ma'am,' the tech officer in the CIA Rome station said, 'we have a Trapwire hit on a high-level Agency target.'

'Where?'

'Outside the building.'

'Outside which building?'

'This building. Like, *right outside*. Across the road, the cafe.'

She looked at the image on the iPad. 'Who is he?'

'Sealed file.'

She saw the notation, said, 'By the Director NCS?'

'Yes.'

'Get someone out there—'

'Whoa . . .' he said, seeing the image on his screen go blank.

'Tech problem?'

'No,' he said, tapping through screens. 'I'm still in the system – but so's someone else: the image was just wiped, from Langley. Everything outside has gone dark.'

'Get them on the phone.'

Her desk phone rang. Line one, from Langley.

'Beverly Johnson,' she said. She listened, then hung up and turned to her tech aide and spoke as she moved to the door. 'They've just ordered full rendition protocols against that guy, using an outside crew.'

'Where are you going, ma'am?'

'I want to see this.'

•

Clara sat opposite Walker, silent, watching him.

Walker sat, also silent, not watching, but *waiting*.

The waiter brought water. Walker ordered another Scotch; better to take the edge off what was coming.

'You are some kind of cop,' she said quietly.

'No.'

'Interpol or Europol or something.'

'No.'

Clara watched him.

Walker said, 'You need to go.'

'No.'

'Forget you saw me.'

'How?'

'Forget about Felix.'

'I can't.'

'Fine.' Walker stood, put fifty euros on the table, drained his next Scotch.

Clara stood, said, 'Where are you—'

Tyres screeched as a van pulled up to the kerb in front of them. Different to the assailants' van, this was a big, blacked-out Mercedes people mover. The side door slid open and four men in black ski masks emerged.

Walker dropped the first one with an uppercut, then kicked the next in the groin – then his world became one of rolling, unbearable pain as he was tasered. Twelve thousand volts running at .2 amps coursed through his body at 19 pulses per second, creating neuromuscular incapacitation by interrupting the ability of the brain to control the muscles in the body. Not a good feeling.

The hooded men loaded a semi-conscious Walker and a capitulating Clara into the van and were gone before the Italian cops arrived on the scene.

Seventy-nine hours to deadline.

9

London

Bill McCorkell was a veteran national-security expert with more than three decades' experience, including stints serving as the National Security Advisor to no less than three American presidents. He now headed the United Nations Special Investigations Unit. Supporting the UN Security Council, McCorkell and his team worked from an office space off Cabot Square in Canary Wharf, in a glass-and-concrete building otherwise full of bankers and financial planners.

'Knock-knock.'

'Yep?' McCorkell looked up.

'We just intercepted a phone message to your person of interest in DC,' Andrew Hutchinson said, entering McCorkell's office. On secondment from the FBI, Hutchinson served as McCorkell's counter-intelligence specialist. In his early forties and with a swag of successes in his back pocket, McCorkell had nothing but respect that the Bureau guy chose to fight the good fight alongside him.

'Which person of interest in DC would that be?' McCorkell said.

'Your INTFOR guy,' Hutchinson replied, taking a seat opposite. The office chair creaked under his weight.

'Dan Bellamy?'

'Yep.'

'Well, you've got my attention. What was it?'

'Police are reporting a van explosion on a street in Rome,' Hutchinson said. 'Right near the US embassy. It happened as part of a vehicle pursuit, where a hatchback with a male and female occupant seemed to be pursuing the van, and the cops in turn were pursuing them. CCTV of the scene shows that the van driver made his way on foot into the embassy, where once inside he called INTFOR's DC number. Their operations department. Left a message for Bellamy to get him out of there.'

McCorkell thought for a moment, then said, 'Sounds like an op went to shit.'

'Yep.'

'Does this van driver have a name?'

'Better. He has a file.'

Hutchinson handed it over. McCorkell flicked through the printout, then said, 'I'm seeing a tired old military jacket. Army, 101st, non-com, never made sergeant for a whole bunch of reasons. This all?'

'He's been a cleanskin since.'

'Too clean?' asked McCorkell.

'Yep.'

'So, he's a spook.'

'But not for any US agency. His last known employment was NSA two years ago. Security stuff. Discharged for disciplinary reasons.'

'He's gone private since?'

'Yep.'

'He's working for Bellamy?'

'All signs point to yes,' said Hutchinson. 'That kind of jacket is his recruitment's MO of paramilitary types.'

'Those we reject . . .'

Hutchinson nodded.

McCorkell said, 'Tell me more about his phone call.'

'He used an embassy line to call INTFOR's Berlin office. The call went from Berlin via an encrypted network to DC.'

'The Germans don't have a transcript?'

'Nope,' replied Hutchinson. 'INTFOR seems to have a more updated version of NSA encryption gear than the US Government has.'

'No big surprise there,' McCorkell said, turning slightly to look out his window. 'Bellamy's a big guy – he's a big player, in every sense. And getting bigger by the day.'

'What do we do?'

McCorkell faced his number two, said, 'Is this guy, the van driver, still at the embassy?'

'I'm waiting to hear back. Someone got to the legal attaché before I did.'

'Bellamy.'

'Fair assumption. I think we'll have silence there for a bit. The whole embassy in Rome is in lockdown due to the bomb going off in the street outside.'

'How about the Station Chief?'

'Uncontactable at the moment. I'm working on it.'

'Rome – that's Bev Johnson?'

'Yep.'

'She's good people. Keep trying,' McCorkell said. 'What was the car chase about?'

'There was a hit, in an apartment: Italian guy named Felix Lassiter, who ran cut-outs for a whole bunch of money men. Maybe even CIA. Italian CSI are arriving on the scene now. They'll work up DNA samples from the scene, but they'll take a while.'

'Nothing's fast down there.'

'Yep. I can have someone from Quantico reach out, to expedite things.'

'Do it.'

'Right.' Hutchinson made a note. 'They also found one of our van driver's buddies in the apartment: similar cleanskin ID to our van guy, but for an old Marines jacket.'

'Can we question him?'

'That'll be hard. He's KIA at the scene with half a golf club stuck in his eye socket.'

McCorkell swivelled back towards Hutchinson. 'A golf club?'

'Seven iron.'

'*In his head?*'

'Yep. Must have taken a decent swing. He mustn't have heard the fore call.'

'Who did that?'

'Probably our pair from the VW.'

'Who are they?' McCorkell looked closely at the grainy printout from an intercepted traffic camera. 'A man and a woman?'

'Yep. She's a dead end so far. And, in a sense, he is as well.'

•

Walker came to.

He was flexicuffed to a metal chair that was bolted to the floor in the middle of a bland room that contained nothing but a door, another chair, a table, and a long, horizontal mirror on the facing wall.

A CIA safe house.

Walker had been in plenty of such places, refuges for agents and field officers. He'd been in rooms like this, reserved for different types of houseguests, though he'd never been strapped to the interrogation chair. He breathed deeply.

Walker was exactly where he wanted to be.

A guy came in. Walker knew they had watched him wake, through the two-way mirror. The guy was average in every proportion. He kept his ski mask on: *smart move*. He moved with a slight limp – the guy who'd copped it in the nuts in the take-down on the street.

He held a bottle of water to Walker's lips, and Walker drank half of it.

The guy left, closing the door behind him.

Walker flexed his forearms against the plastic cable-ties behind the back of the chair. There was a little wriggle room – they hadn't done them as tightly as he would have instructed.

This will be interesting.

Seventy-eight hours to deadline.

10

Walker did not have to wait for long.

The door opened and four men entered. All wore ski masks, with just their eyes visible. The water boy with the limp now carried two eight-litre bottles of water. Another, out of shape, left-handed, carried towels. Another had a taser holstered on his belt, a hand resting on it for a quick draw. He was a big guy, capable, fit. The fourth bore nothing but a slight swagger. Lean and confident. Every movement predetermined and exact. He was their leader. He would be Walker's interrogator.

'Sorry about your nuts,' Walker said to Water Boy, who stood to Walker's right, arms crossed. He did not reply.

'Did I train any of you?' Walker asked. He looked from mask to mask. Nothing telling. He felt he had always been a fair instructor. Tough, but to the point. Methodical.

The leader gave a hand gesture.

The guy with the taser and the guy with the towels undid the padlocks that housed the front legs of Walker's chair to steel eyelets bolted to the floor. The back legs, still anchored by hardened-steel locks, acted like pivots, and the two guys tilted Walker's chair back forty degrees and held it steady.

Walker had been water-boarded more than once before. First at SERE Survival School, with the Air Force. Then at Fort Bragg, training with Delta to earn his place in the 24th. That's where it started, this interrogation technique; until recently, water-boarding was something that Americans only did to other Americans. It was inflicted, and endured, by those members of the Special Forces who underwent the advanced form of training known as SERE: Survival, Evasion, Resistance, Escape. In these harsh exercises trainees were introduced to the sorts of barbarism that they might expect to meet at the hands of a lawless opponent who disregarded the Geneva Conventions. It was something that American soldiers were trained to *resist*, not to inflict.

Later, after 9/11, when the world changed, Walker had shown recruits how to water-board at the CIA's training ground in North Carolina. The nation's defensive technique to show strength under duress had become an offensive means of obtaining information.

He'd spent six months training guys just like these. Maybe even one or two of these guys. In a way, Walker hoped that he had trained them, because at least then he knew that they'd be beyond proficient.

Walker settled his breathing. He knew he could last about two minutes by holding his breath. Decent interrogators, however, would be wise to his breathing rhythm and not allow him such a length of time to hold out.

If Walker were running this, he would not start this way. He would try talking to their guest first, then see where that went. Nice cop having a chat, bad cop to verify the story, then the confession afterwards to an even nicer cop. Two days of sleep deprivation, repeat process and compare results.

The chair improvising as board was a mistake too. A dangerous set-up.

Maybe these guys are on the clock.

Or worse.

Maybe they knew who he was. Or rather, who he used to be . . .

•

McCorkell looked at the photo of Walker and Clara.

'What do you mean he's a dead end?'

'Let me give you a bit of background,' Hutchinson said, flipping through his notepad. 'With that pic we got a match on facial rec to one Josiah "Jed" Walker. Former Air Force, officer in the twenty-fourth Tactical. Joined up after college, Georgetown, where he was first approached to join the Agency—'

'Wait – Walker, from Georgetown . . .'

'Yep, one and the same,' Hutchinson said. 'His old man was David. You knew him?'

'Knew him and then some. Go on.'

'Jed Walker turned the Agency down, the first time round. As an Air Force officer he did a tour in Iraq and three in 'Stan. Been decorated with everything from the Air Force Cross down, including three Purple Hearts.'

'A regular Billy Waugh.'

'You bet. Mustered out as soon as he became a Lieutenant Colonel, which he made pretty much as fast as you can get, and a short time later went to the CIA as part of the Special Activities Division.'

'Maybe he liked the field work,' McCorkell said. 'That last promotion would have seen him driving a desk.'

'Sounds like that's where the brass wanted him: they saw how good Walker was, how smart he was, and wanted him around the office to help steer the ship. Anyway' – Hutchinson checked his notes – 'at the Agency he stayed on a year at The Point, training their field operatives and whatever the fuck else they do there, then three years out in the big wide world running agents.'

'Where?'

'Everywhere there's trouble. It seems he specialised in a lost art.'

'And what would that be?'

'Running APs,' Hutchinson said.

McCorkell looked at the image again. There were two different kinds of agents that an intel officer ran: 'agents of influence' and 'agents provocateur'. The agent of influence tries to change opinion in the country where he operates; an agent provocateur, or AP, is sent to stir up trouble and create chaos.

'Walker literally wrote the book on twenty-first-century APs,' Hutchinson went on. 'The last record we have is that he bugged out days after the Arab Spring wound up. The final citation is a Distinguished Intelligence Medal to add to his collection.'

'So, he was a busy boy, and what, burned out? Took a job for some decent money? God knows he would have been fielding offers to make more in a few years than during a lifetime at the Agency.'

'Doesn't look like it. He came in from the cold within a year and did some odd jobs for various agencies and departments, stuff no-one else would touch.'

'The guy's an addict.'

'Looks that way. It's a hard life to leave behind, for those good at it.'

'Then why not sell out and do it for hire permanently?'

'Beats me.'

'Maybe he has. Maybe he joined INTFOR.'

'And maybe he hasn't.'

'He's too patriotic?'

'You knew his old man, you tell me.'

'Hmm. Maybe he's gone nuts. Too long at the coal face. Last location before Rome?'

'That's where it gets interesting. Very interesting.' Hutchinson leaned forwards in his chair and passed over the file he'd put together. 'Says there that around nine months ago Walker was listed as KIA. His family had a funeral for him, a coffin in the ground at Arlington next to his dad, but there were no remains to bury.'

Hutchinson passed over a separate file on the Yemen mission.

'So maybe MIA listed as KIA . . . who ran him then?' asked McCorkell, then opened the folder and saw the front sheet. 'Department of State? A guy like Walker?'

'That's what it says.'

McCorkell ran his eyes over the scant few pages on Yemen.

'My question,' Hutchinson said, 'is *why*. Why's he now come out of hiding?'

McCorkell was silent as he read about Yemen, then closed the folder and said, 'Hutch, you need to go talk to State. I want to know everything about this last op of his. It seems they're more than a little wrong when they say Jed Walker is dead.'

11

'Sure you guys don't want to ask me anything first?' Walker said.

Silence from the four men. The top of a large water bottle was removed. A towel was readied.

Walker said, 'Did you get an ID on those guys back at the apartment?'

The men remained silent. Each had a task.

The towel was placed over Walker's face and held in place from behind. One, two, three layers. He didn't flinch. The chair was tilted back further. He waited for what was next. Settled his heart rate down around seventy. Breathed a little deeper.

Walker busied his mind. He thought about the men at the apartment. The B Team.

Private contractors. Big money was moving through Felix. But who's paying them to take him out? If it's the government, neither the Pentagon nor the Agency have to worry about Congressional Oversight. Those guys were private, all right; ex-military working for the money, not a cause. What was their purpose? To stop Felix Lassiter? To make sure that whatever was in his head was buried forever?

The chair was tilted down to the point where the top of the backrest was leaning against the tiled floor. Walker's head was now lower than his heart: water-boarding 101. The trouble with a chair like this, though, was that it was reliant on the two guys either side being strong enough and quick enough to get him upright between sessions. A slipped hand on the wet metal frame, a second too long for Walker – it could be CPR time. Many Afghan insurgents had died in interrogations like this, via hastily improvised interrogation rooms in the field. *Sloppy work, this, for an A Team. Standards are slipping.*

The CIA officers started to pour the water over the layered towel covering Walker's face.

And here we go . . .

Walker held his breath and stayed calm.

Two minutes.

Walker knew that water-boarding had proved a useful enhanced interrogation technique in the war on terror. He could not deny that the gag reflex and drowning sensation it created were extremely effective; through the helpless terror it instilled came results that saved lives. He also knew there was a risk of death from actually drowning or suffering a heart attack or damage to the lungs from inhalation of water; and that long-term effects could include panic attacks, depression and post-traumatic stress disorder.

Walker didn't have time for any of that. And he didn't have time for this. The longer he stayed here, the colder the trail would become.

He too was on the clock. He'd come to this house for a purpose, and this wasn't it.

Walker exhaled. Then inhaled – and immediately started to convulse.

The towel was lifted and he coughed out water then breathed in a few settling lungfuls of air.

Seventy-seven hours to deadline.

12

'And then a CIA team picked him up?' The man spoke English with a thick Italian accent, along with a slight whistle through a gap between his front teeth.

'Yes, a rendition team. You have to clean this for me, quickly,' Dan Bellamy replied. 'I've just messaged you the address.'

'You should have had me handle this in the first place.'

The man's codename was Il Bisturi. The Scalpel. He specialised in getting rid of problems. He usually did mafia work around Naples, but he was not exclusive, not when the money was right. Bellamy had used him twice in the past year. He was effective, and expensive.

Bellamy said, 'It started as a simple courier intercept.'

'It does not sound simple,' Il Bisturi said. 'And now I am asked to fix others' mistakes. It would have been easier if you had contacted me at the start.'

Bellamy exhaled deeply, said, 'You don't usually concern yourself with such minor work.'

'So, what, you keep me on file as a clean-up guy?'

'Every tool has its function. I respect your skill set, and I am willing to pay a premium for the urgency required.'

'Okay. Fine.'

'When can you be there?'

'I am two hours away.'

'No. That's too long. I need this sorted right now. This man cannot be allowed to talk. You must have another option for me.'

Bellamy waited impatiently for the few seconds Il Bisturi kept him hanging in silence. Finally, 'I can have a team there in twenty minutes, nothing sooner – or there will be another mess to clean up. Okay?'

'All right. And I want Walker alive.'

●

54

Walker was tilted backwards, his head close to the floor again. The wet towel folded over his face.

These guys are playing bad cop. Good cop will come. He'll have questions. Maybe it's the taser guy. Or the leader. Get through it. You have time. Relax—

This time Walker's breathing cycle was interrupted, by hard fingers pressed hard against his solar plexus as the water was poured.

Finding out if I'm timing my breathing to the deluge . . . good boys.

'If you try that again, we will be forced to hurt you,' a voice said. 'And you know we have all kinds of enhancements.'

Walker breathed. Choked.

The chair came up. The towel came off.

Walker sucked at the air-conditioned air. Coughed out water vapour. Blinked at the bright room. Settled his elevated heart rate.

The two chair holders at the sides moved to the door, as did the water boy.

The leader told them to leave.

Walker watched as the leader waited for the others to depart, and then he turned to Walker. They locked eyes. Silence.

Two men, one seated, one standing, neither saying a word.

After a full minute the leader turned to the mirror and made a cutting motion across his throat.

He's killing the recording. Finally we're getting somewhere . . .

The leader turned to Walker and removed his ski mask. A balding guy with a buzz-cut, fine features and friendly eyes.

Walker knew the man. 'Hey, Pip.'

'Jesus-fuck, Walker!'

Walker had known Philip 'Pip' Durant, CIA counter-intelligence officer, for near on ten years. He liked the guy, had got drunk with him more than once, may even have sung karaoke with him at a KTV club in Beijing.

'I mean – what the fuck – you're *alive?*' Durant sat on the plastic chair in front of Walker. Behind him was the two-way mirror set into the wall. Behind it was all sorts of recording equipment, along with the landlord, the officer assigned to watch over the safe house and take in any guests. 'You know we had a funeral for you?'

Walker kept pressure on the cable-ties at his wrists. He had seen a six-foot-nine Marine break through three of them once, but he had been on crystal meth. *It would be easier to use something to pry open the toothed locking mechanism and pull it free, maybe using a rivet or seam in the steel chair . . .*

Durant asked, 'Where have you been, man?'

'Around,' Walker said.

'Around?'

Walker nodded. Silence fell between them. Durant's mood seemed to settle with every passing second. It was clear that this was not the reunion and catch-up Durant had in mind since pulling Walker off a footpath in Rome an hour ago.

'Walker, what are you doing here?'

'Same as you.'

Durant smiled. 'No, I don't think so. See, I'm working here. *You* – I don't know what you're doing, but it ain't work. At least, if it is, it ain't for us. Which makes me wonder . . .'

'Why not start with the talk?' Walker said. 'I like this. Why the watering?'

'To soften you up,' Durant said, with a small smile. 'You know the playbook. Hell, you helped write it, yeah? The infamous Jed Walker, as I live and breathe. You know . . .' Durant stood, and paced as though considering what to say or admit next, then sat down where he had been before. 'There were rumours about you, you know?'

Walker held his silence. He started to wedge the right-hand flexi-cuff in the tiny gap where the seat met the backrest.

'People were saying things.' Durant waited, clearly wanting to pique Walker's interest and draw him into conversation, but Walker wouldn't bite. 'You went KIA on a State Department op, along with an Agency grunt. Neither family got remains, not even ashes. Shit like that's hard to take, especially about a legend on a seemingly bullshit little op. That kind of thing makes people *wonder*. They *talk*. Whispers at first. Then they grew louder. Then – then I heard from Eve.'

Walker jolted his arms against the back of the chair, as though in a twitch of rage. He felt the right-hand cable-tie slip from the gap.

He wedged it back. *Couple more times, it might weaken enough to snap through . . .*

'See . . .' Durant said, pleased to be getting through. 'Eve came to me, a couple of months after I broke the news to her. She asked me to look into it: your death; the rumours and questions about you she'd heard via a couple of the other wives. From your father. He kept in touch with her, right up to the end. So, I helped her out. It was the least I could do, right?'

Walker shifted again. Pulled as hard and sharp with his arms as he could, felt the cable-tie looped through the bottom shaft of steel break free. His arms were still flexicuffed behind his back, but he could now lift them over the seatback. His ankles were still cable-tied around the front chair legs, but with the front legs unlocked from the ground he could tilt back the chair and be free of it.

'I mean,' Durant said, leaning forwards, 'we were friends from way back, *right*? We'd all gone out a lot, *right*? We – you and me – we were friends, man. And I mean, *damn*, Eve was always way too hot for you.'

Walker's muscles in his arms and chest tensed. His face remained passive, his eyes dead. He knew that in one swift motion he could take the weight of himself forwards and connect the ridge of his brow against Durant's nose: 230 pounds snapping down in a sharp whack that would drop the intel officer to the floor, collecting a knee or two to the face on the way down and then a sharply cracked boot to the side of the head to render him unconscious. It steeled Walker, knowing he had options like that. It eliminated panic.

There were always options.

13

'Where are we at?' McCorkell said as he entered the boardroom, which had been transformed into a situation room. Six staffers were manning computers or phones, or putting intel up on whiteboards dedicated to pertinent information on their three interconnecting targets: Lassiter, Walker and Bellamy.

'I just heard back from Bev Johnson in Rome,' Hutchinson said. 'They've picked Walker up, taken him to an Agency safe house on the outskirts of the city, with four Special Activities Division officers watching over him. Debriefing has already started.'

McCorkell said, 'Okay, where'd you get with State?'

'Nothing doing, they're saying they never heard of Walker, so I'm about to head to Heathrow for the next flight to DC.'

'Right. Where are we at with the van driver – the guy who went into the embassy and called Bellamy?' McCorkell studied the printout pic taped to the whiteboard that they'd pulled from the embassy CCTV.

'Gone. Disappeared. Bev's got a couple of people on it. And it seems the body of the dead guy from the apartment—'

'The golfer?'

'Yep, he's gone too.'

'How's a dead guy go some place?'

'Missing from the coroner's office. Guy was on a slab one minute, vanished the next.'

McCorkell sighed and looked around at the staffers in the room. 'Jesus, INTFOR's cleaning up their mess faster than we can chase leads. Do we have anyone in Rome that we can pull into the fold?'

'Nope, not like we need,' Hutchinson replied. 'The Feds are all tied up with a few big local cases. I thought you had a local source on Lassiter.'

'Gone quiet.'

'Damn.'

'Call in some favours, and I'll do the same. We need all the help there that we can get. We've lost Lassiter but this could be our in on Bellamy – if we can play catch-up fast enough. And I want to know more about this Jed Walker.'

•

'I mean, I looked into your death, as much as I could,' Durant said. 'I called buddies at State. Worked nights in the basement at Langley. Chased whispers around Fort Meade. Rumours in the Pentagon. Lies in Crystal City. I got the full goddamned runaround. In the end I was called into the Deputy Director's office and told to drop it. That was that. A month later I got the station gig in Berlin.'

'A reward for keeping your nose out of it.'

'Maybe,' Durant said, his smile receding. 'I think I earned it, though.'

'Don't be coy. They paid you off. You're a part of it now.'

'Am I? And what would *it* be, exactly?' Durant stared at him. 'What do you know, Walker? Hmm? Where you been? Who you working for?'

Walker stared at him silently.

'Sure, if you'd stayed around, Berlin would have been yours,' Durant said. 'Hell, a post like that should have been yours from the get-go. But that wasn't for you. You liked the chaos, not the plush stuff. And you bugged out a while back, right? That was your *choice*. Never good with commitment, were you, Walker? That's what Eve always told me.'

Walker was still. He put together a mental list of the actions he would take. He imagined Durant's warm blood between his fingers as he used the unconscious agent's teeth to open the cable-ties at his wrists. He saw himself hurl the chair through the mirror, slide the heavy bolt lock closed on the door, which he knew would be steel plate and set into a steel frame, terror-resistant up to small-arms fire. From there, to freedom, via the incapacitation of three guys – four, with the landlord, behind the mirror – in a couple of minutes. He would get what he came for, and bug out.

'Where you been, Walker?' Durant repeated. 'Hmm?'

Walker remained silent.

'What's this about? Why'd you go under? Why'd you walk away from everything you had?'

Walker pushed ever so slightly through the balls of his feet against the floor, readying, feeling the weight coming off the front chair legs.

'Eve said you might have lost it,' Durant said. 'That you were in this shit too deep, too long. You couldn't leave it – so she left you. You made that choice, right? This life over her?'

Walker smiled, waited. Answered a question with a question. 'If you were in Berlin driving a desk, how'd you end up in Rome so fast? On a rendition grab team? A little beneath a Station Chief, hey, Pip?'

Durant smiled in return and leaned on the desk. His hands were on his knees, his weight well forwards and out of balance for a counter-attack.

'You're getting sloppy, Walker,' Durant said. 'We got a facial-rec shot from a port in Spain four days ago. Then yesterday here in Rome as you passed an ATM's camera.'

Walker was a little surprised by that one. *Money machines linked into the surveillance net now?*

'Oh yeah, Trapwire's over here now too, didn't you know?' Durant said, all smiles again. Then he mouthed, silently: '*Talk, I can help. What's going on?*'

Walker shook his head, said, 'Where's my friend? The woman I came in with?'

'Friend?' Durant said, leaning a little closer still. '*I'm the only friend you've got left. Talk.*'

Walker began to imagine the pathway of each muscle from his feet up his legs and through his core and back and chest and neck as he would launch his attack.

'Okay, Walker, okay. Let me tell you what I know,' Durant said out loud. 'Stop me if I get anything wrong. Two years ago you bugged out of the Agency. No-one knows why, although Eve believed at the time that you did it for her. I know it coincided with the Syria op, which you saved but it burned you. You shouldn't have done that. But you wore it. You took the blame, and by doing that you saved the op. Agents' lives too. Patriotic. Stupid, dumb, but patriotic. So, you go home, play house, happy days for what – three, maybe four months? That's the last time I saw you – remember? You, me and Eve. Four days up at your folks' cabin in the White Mountains. You remember that? Yeah.

Shit, I remember it well. We had a moment there, me and Eve. Did she ever tell you that? Did you notice it? Yeah, Walker doesn't miss the little things . . . So that's it. A couple of weeks later you're back at work, this time for State. Right? You're doing fuck-knows-what for them, probably training fat wannabes in how to protect diplomats or investigating visa fraud or some shit. But then you're out in the field and you get a taste of an old op – and you can't *help it*, can you? You step outside your role, your mandate. You go into Yemen working on an op that should have been the Agency's all the way.'

Durant stopped, watching Walker. No reaction. 'So, you know what I figure? You did Yemen through State because you knew that the Agency wasn't going to go in there to shut them down like that. They have too much interest otherwise. You're chasing a money man through the mid-east who they don't want fucked with, but you work them into a corner because you sell it somehow to State. It's planned, all of it: you bugging out as the Agency hero who took one for the team, having your time out to appease Eve, go to the bullshit State job – all of it to get free rein to go mess around in the sandpit. Problem is, not only did you not *belong* there, you don't have a damned *clue* about the damage you were doing. Plans were in motion for a decade, and you go in there and fuck it up. You think you know more than the rest of us? Know better?'

Walker was silent but there was a slight smile in his eyes, which he allowed Durant to see.

'Why Yemen? Why go against the family?' Durant gave Walker the room to provide an answer but none came. 'You could have been part of something special, a big part, if you'd just stayed in your own lane. Instead, you think that protecting your country involves putting bad guys out of business. You know so, *so* much better than that, Walker. Shit, man . . . this business we're in? It's a goddamned gold mine, and it's only getting better as the world turns to shit. Syria, Yemen, all that wasn't your business to try and fix.'

'It's not a business, Pip.' Walker finally spoke.

'Really? You *really* believe that? Think about it. The Agency's outdated – hell, it was outdated the day it was founded. Didn't your father ever tell you that? Look around you, man. The world's not about governments and borders anymore. It's *all* business, and America's the best at it – at least, we were, and maybe still are, so long as people like you and me realise all it can be, and we do what we can to make it so.'

Walker looked at his old friend and wondered when he'd lost it.

'This isn't about what you can do for your country,' Durant said. 'It's about what you can do for *yourself*. We're all the authors of our own story, Walker. You need to see that. You need to see that the evolution of America is based on enterprise and expertise, and yours doesn't belong in the shadows anymore, nor in the ground. See what I'm saying?'

'I think so,' Walker said, his voice quiet, his head down slightly so that Durant had to lean in closer to hear. 'You want to privatise what's left of the intel community, and you want to be there from the ground up so that you can profit from it.'

'So that we can *all* profit from it,' Durant said. 'The country, every citizen, the entire world – we'll all be better off. It's evolution. You gotta move with it, or it moves on without you.'

'And you're offering me what?'

'A gift,' Durant said. 'A second chance.'

14

Special Agent Fiona Somerville arrived at the American embassy in Rome and was kept waiting. Fifteen minutes. Three times she checked and was told to wait some more. Finally the assistant head of mission for security, a young guy named Ben, came to assist her.

'I'm here to see the Station Chief,' Somerville said once they were in Ben's office.

'She's out. We've had some excitement here.'

'I saw, out in the street. A car bomb?'

'Van. It could just be a gas tank accident, but it looks more than that. What can I help you with?'

'You're not cleared for this.'

'I assure you, ma'am, I am.'

Somerville shook her head, made for the door.

'No, wait, I'm DSS,' Ben said. He handed over his business card.

Somerville summed him up: Ben Hobbs, RSO, US Diplomatic Security Service, a few years in, with a juicy posting; so, the kid was a rock star.

'Hobbs,' Somerville said, her tone somewhere between chastising and condescending, 'as of right now there's a category-one counter-intel operative in your backyard.'

'Jed Walker?'

Somerville nodded.

Ben Hobbs motioned to a seat, which Somerville took. Ben poured two coffees from a Thermos jug. Somerville took the cup: fine china, a short pour, the coffee rich and dark, the aroma only an Italian espresso could create.

'He was flagged as being in country, probably the same info you got in, where was it, Athens?'

'You've looked me up,' Somerville said.

'Hence you had to wait a bit. Quite the record,' Hobbs said. He sat on the edge of his desk. His posture made Fiona think that he was leering, playing her, trying to make up for something he felt he lacked. She got that a lot from male agents, mostly her juniors but often her superiors as well. Amazing, how women in law enforcement were still being underestimated.

'Hobbs, maybe you got to where you are by playing the bimbo,' Somerville said, draining her coffee and setting the cup down not on the saucer but on the timber side table-top right next to it. 'But I certainly didn't.'

Somerville took a typed letter from her briefcase and handed it to Hobbs.

'That's from my director,' she said clearly, firmly. 'As in, *Director of the FBI*. I have jurisdiction on this op, no matter who gets in my way. Walker's been in the wilderness a year, and he's mine – and mine alone – to bring in and debrief.'

Hobbs read the letter and was quiet for a moment. Then he folded it and returned it, before walking back around his desk, where he took a seat.

'You're too late,' he said, in a less cocksure voice. 'Walker's in the process of being rendered.'

'To where?'

Hobbs was silent.

Somerville stood and stared down at him. 'Where is he?' she demanded.

'Right now, he's at an Agency safe house,' Hobbs said. 'South of the city. It's an initial debrief, then they'll move him on. The Station Chief's headed there now. I'll call her.'

•

'What makes you think I want to come back in?' Walker said.

'Because you showed up on the grid, and that was no mistake,' Durant replied. 'Let me help you, Walker. Let me make sure you're protected. They listen to me. You do this, you follow me, and you won't have to be put into the ground – for real this time.'

Walker tensed his arms again, his chest, visualised the moves ahead.

'Tell me who you're working for,' Durant said.

Walker said, 'Why don't you tell me who it is that *you're* working for?'

Durant smiled. 'Last chance, Walker. Orders to pick you up came from up high.'

'Probably from the same person who ordered me dead in Yemen.'

'You were sticking your nose where it didn't belong. But this is a second chance. I'll vouch for you. You come back in. You work for me. And in ten years you'll see a world you could never have believed.'

'Okay.'

'Okay?'

'Okay, sure, count me in. Why don't you start by telling me who it is I'm helping out? Tell me that, I'll tell you all I know.'

Durant's expression changed. This was now the guy that Walker had seen beat an insurgent to death in Iraq. This was the operative who'd had more than his share of reprimands. This guy was a dinosaur, a relic of a short and dirty period of the Agency's recent past, when the pointy-end military and intel community had expanded too fast against a threat it never fully understood. Durant had always been as much a friend as an enemy.

'I'm not fucking around, Walker,' Durant said through his teeth. 'You need to tell me everything. Then we deal. Be thankful they sent me. I'm your only friend here, remember that.'

'And how about my other friend, the woman you picked me up with?'

'She's in the room next door,' Durant said. He could sense Walker changing then, a slight shift in demeanour, and pulled his face up close to Walker's, breathing stale coffee and cigarettes. 'Man, is she *sweet*. I'll get to her in good time. See how much duress she needs to make her talk. Show her what she's missing out on. Damn, Walker, you sure get women who are too hot for—'

Durant didn't finish his speech.

Walker went through his motions, rising fast and furious, his arms sliding over the back of the chair. At his full height he came back down, head-butting Durant on the way, the force of the downwards blow shearing the nose cartilage from Durant's face and sending him slipping forwards, into Walker's space.

As Walker rose, he slid the chair legs through the cable-ties that bound his ankles, freeing his feet, and in the same movement his rising left knee met the falling chin of Durant.

There was a satisfying snap of whiplash, and Durant was out cold.

Walker moved to the door and slid the steel bolt across. There was frantic banging on the outside as the officers in wait heard the bolt slide. In moments they would be in the viewing room. Then they would take another moment to react, perhaps up to a minute as they opted to either smash the mirror and rush through the shards of glass into the room, or wait Walker out from the dead-end interrogation room.

'I always knew what you were, Pip,' Walker said, then crouched down and used Durant's teeth as a chisel against the plastic flexicuff. 'Nothing personal, douchebag.'

ZIP.

The first wrist was free, allowing Walker to use Durant's metal pen to snap the other wrist free. For his part Durant remained still, his mouth agape. Walker pulled the officer's CIA ID pass and lanyard from around his neck and pocketed it.

Walker stood and looked at the mirror, the metal chair in his hands. He figured he had taken a full minute: enough time for the agents to be waiting on the other side of the two-way mirror, with their side-arms drawn. Not tasers, but the 9-millimetre pistols and sub-machine guns from the safe house's arsenal.

But they didn't yet have their weapons drawn.

And they weren't behind the mirror.

Walker knew this because that's when he heard the gunfire, coming from downstairs.

A lot of gunfire.

15

Walker threw the chair through the mirror. The glass shattered to show a black void beyond. The flying chair took out a digital camera that had been on a tripod. Inside the darkened room a young guy was cowering on the floor, bits of broken glass twinkling over him.

The landlord.

Walker counted at least eight separate firearms crackling off downstairs and figured there could be as many as double that; 5.56 mm assault rifles. The Agency 9 mms popped back in reply. This was fast turning into an OK-Corral type shootout. He didn't have much time.

Walker knocked out the shards of glass at waist level and climbed through. Jagged edges caught and ripped at his T-shirt on the way, and the floor on the other side crunched underfoot.

'Are you armed?' Walker asked the landlord once his feet were firmly planted on the other side.

The guy looked up, shook his head. Negative.

Walker dragged him to his feet, said, 'What's your name?'

'Bantram,' he replied. 'John Bantram.'

Bantram looked about twenty-five, fresh out of college maybe, a recent Farm grad, sent here to babysit a house that was probably lucky to host a guest per month. There were worse places to be posted. He probably had a local girlfriend, or two. Spent his time most days sitting in here with nothing to do but jerk off to internet porn. Rome wasn't exactly the mid-east but it was a better gig than driving a desk at Langley. *Poor kid never expected this.*

Walker asked, 'Bantram, where's the feed from the house cameras?'

Bantram pointed to a computer screen, said, 'Toggle the arrow keys to change views.'

Walker could see live footage from six vantages. The front and back doors had been breached. The hallway downstairs was full of gun smoke and plaster dust. At the top of the stairs the Agency men had set up their defence. It wasn't pretty, and it sure as hell wouldn't last.

A flash-bang grenade concussed through the house. Although non-lethal, this explosive device was effective in disorienting an enemy's senses, which told Walker that the attacking force was serious about one thing. These guys were well equipped, and they had a purpose – to get him, alive. Hence not shooting up through the floor, or burning them out, or tossing fragmentary or incendiary grenades up the stairs. They would soon storm the staircase and pick off the CIA officers on their way to the safe room, where they would probably blow the locked doors out with shaped C4 breaching charges.

That knowledge was an advantage for Walker; as long as they wanted him alive, he was virtually bulletproof. As an added bonus it made the attackers wary in their assault, buying him time.

Walker turned to the kid. 'Firearm?'

Bantram pointed, still unable to speak.

In a steel drawer under the computer was a factory-new Beretta 9-millimetre with two magazines of ACP rounds. Walker could hear the firefight raging through the house as he loaded and checked the weapon.

'All right, Bantram, I need to get the woman out of here,' Walker said.

Bantram was still, looking up at Walker, wide-eyed. Walker noticed movement on the CCTV screen: it showed two guys scaling the drainpipe at the rear of the building, clearly planning to enter the hallway at a window and assault the defending force from behind.

Walker shook the safe-house landlord. 'Where is she?'

'She?'

Walker pinned him up against the wall, feet clear of the ground.

'The woman! You've got a civilian in here! Bantram, where is she?'

'The room – next to yours.'

'Entry points?'

'Only the hallway.'

'Is the room locked?'

'Only from the outside – it's a storeroom.'

Walker set the guy down and took the lanyard from around his neck. It held an ID card and a USB stick.

Bingo.

'You can't take that,' Bantram said, reaching for the USB but not protesting convincingly when Walker brushed his hand away.

'How far off is back-up?' Walker said, hanging the lanyard around his neck and tucking it under his T-shirt.

Bantram stared at him. 'There is none. All the lines are down.'

'Won't that trigger some response?'

'Not until the next shift change. We've gone completely dark here.'

Walker paused. Assault rifles crackled. 'Cell-phone signal?'

'Whoever's doing this has blocked it.'

Walker recognised the MO as top-tier tradecraft in paramilitary assault. *The A-teamers, cleaning up where the B-team failed.*

'You're him, aren't you?' Bantram said. 'You're Jed Walker.'

'Get out of here, kid,' Walker said, taking position by the door.

'You can't leave me here!'

'You signed up for this,' Walker said, then slid back the heavy steel locks on the door. 'She didn't.'

16

The carnage was not immediately apparent. Standing in the doorway of the surveillance room, Walker was at a dogleg in the hallway. To his right was the locked door of his interrogation room. Beyond that was the storeroom door with its slide-across, hardened-steel lock on a plate steel door and metal frame. It was armoured against small arms, like the other doors on this level, only in this case the lock was on the outside. One room for keeping guests in; another for keeping others out.

Walker moved quickly past the doors to the hallway's first corner. The Agency guys were in cover positions at the end of the hall. One was giving another first aid, blood pumping fast from a gunshot wound to the upper thigh. He would bleed out in a minute, maybe two.

Time was ticking for them all.

Another flash-bang clattered up the stairs.

Walker turned and moved away, his back to it, hands over ears, eyes shut against the flash and mouth open against the concussive force that would reverberate through his skull.

BANG!

Walker kept moving, away from the doors and the stairs, ears ringing, the gunshots muffled as the Agency guys repelled an attack from the landing, firing blindly but trained well enough to empty their mags quickly, down towards the threat, to give hell to anyone wanting to rush them after that disorienting blast. A fine tactic, so long as their ammo held out.

Walker slid open the window at the end of the hall: a simple sash mechanism, timber frame, a nineteenth-century renovation to the older building. The 3-millimetre glass was original, the tiny bubbles of the early industrialised process distorting the view outside. Aside from the secure rooms inside and the neat technogear installed, the outward appearance of this building was as regular as any other house on the block.

Leaning out the open window and looking up, Walker eyed the small digital video camera aimed at the rear alley below.

The two guys he had viewed on the monitor were climbing the drainpipe, itself a modern improvement, thick plastic piping as wide as a grapefruit and pinned to the brick wall with half-inch threaded steel bolts. The first guy was almost within touching distance.

A turkey shoot.

Walker brought up the Beretta. Sighted.

POP. POP.

Two bodies fell to the cobbled ground. One squirmed for a moment, but the extent of his headshot told Walker it was just residual muscle reflexes.

Walker moved back towards the storeroom and slid the bolt at the door.

Clara was seated on a small cot bed in the bright room, no more than a ten-by-ten-foot box used to store 'guests'.

'Let's go,' he said.

She rushed him and held on for a second, then he showed her out to the hallway.

'The window,' Walker said, guiding her before him. On the way down the hall she picked up her handbag from a plastic tub of their personal effects.

A glance back told Walker that their time here was almost up: each Agency guy was injured in some way, with only two of them still managing to return fire. They had put up a defence against an overwhelming force for near on three minutes, and considering their 9-millimetre firepower they had done a pretty good job of it. If the attacking force had entered from above, through the window or ceiling, it would have been all over in less than half the time. This told Walker that it was a rush job, put together with minimal planning. Pros, no doubt, but on the clock.

Whoever wants me wanted to make sure I didn't have time to talk to anyone but them . . .

Walker steadied Clara as she reached out for the pipe and held on, her knuckles white with the fear and exertion, her bare legs tight against the pipe to add friction. Her slip-on shoes clattered to the ground, but she didn't falter in her descent.

Inside, someone downstairs fired from an assault rifle on full auto. A suppressing fire, full clip of 30 rounds, prepping to rush the stairs.

As soon as Clara was a body length down, Walker moved out.

Clara descended the last few metres quickly, too quickly, landing with a thud on a still-warm body.

Walker jumped clear from three metres above the ground as Clara picked herself up.

'Run,' he said, taking her by the hand and not looking back. 'Run!'

17

Somerville arrived at the safe house well after the local police. Hobbs had driven her, and to his credit he drove as madly as the locals. She had heard over the phone that Walker was not among the dead. The street was cordoned off with tape and carabinieri cars. No media were here yet, though a throng of residents had amassed. While her Italian was passable, Somerville caught enough to understand that rumours were flying about this being a mafia deal gone wrong.

'This is a shit storm,' a tall, red-haired woman in a wrinkled suit said to herself while exiting the house.

'Bev Johnson, this is the FBI agent,' Hobbs said, catching her on the footpath.

'Special Agent Somerville. We spoke on the phone,' Somerville said by way of introduction. 'Walker's gone?'

The three of them stood on the road. A fire crew exited, foam extinguishers depleted and the clear masks of their breathing apparatus, along with their uniforms, covered in foam and ash. Somerville knew that this likely meant that the landlord had followed protocol and set off the incendiaries in the control room, burning all the intel and sensitive equipment – and that meant that he might be alive for questioning.

'He's disappeared, and three of my field officers are dead.'

'I'm sorry,' Somerville said.

'You need to tell me about your boy Walker,' Johnson said, her accent southern, perhaps that of a genteel lady in another circumstance. 'Back at the embassy.'

'No, I really don't,' Somerville said. 'And he's not my boy. He was yours, once, and he's gone to the mattresses for good on a year – that's about as caught up from me as you're going to get.'

Johnson stared at her and, sensing something at least as hard as she, let it slide.

'Fine, he's your problem now,' she said, looking around as though salvation were a world away. 'I've got seven bodies: three of mine, four of theirs. Go get the son of a bitch, and his damned friends who busted him out in this shootout. Hang 'em all from up high, you hear? And they've got a good twenty-minute head start, so don't dawdle now.'

'I need to talk to any survivors,' Somerville said.

Johnson paused, considered Somerville's tone and poise, then pointed to a nearby ambulance.

Somerville walked over, Hobbs close behind her.

Inside the ambulance two men were being treated. One had a smashed face, gauze held to it by a paramedic; the other was a slight, young guy on oxygen.

'Leave us,' Somerville said in Italian to the paramedic. When he did, she took his place and closed the doors behind her, shutting out Hobbs and any witnesses.

•

Walker and Clara were fifteen kilometres away, in a pensione three floors above a street full of shops, cafes and bars. The little old lady who let the apartment to them insisted on bringing in a plate of cheeses and meats and bread and a bottle of Chianti. Walker waited until she left, then he locked the tiny wooden door and buckled over, clutching his side and gritting his teeth.

'What is it?' Clara asked.

'Busted ribs, I think,' Walker said. 'I had to hold my breath walking up those stairs just now.'

Clara helped him into a wicker chair at the small dining table by the open balcony door. Starting with the back, she carefully lifted his black T-shirt over his head, then off his arms.

Walker leaned back, and winced.

'Hurt?' Clara asked, prodding.

'Not bad,' he replied. He breathed deeply, in and out a couple of times, and self-diagnosed that his ribs weren't broken.

'Good news: your ribs seem fine,' she said. 'But you are cut badly.'

Walker looked down – he had a three-inch laceration, deep in the middle, where he must have caught himself on some mirrored glass getting into the control room. His adrenaline and focus at the time had kept it quiet. Now it screamed pain.

'You need a doctor,' Clara said.

'No,' Walker replied, looking at the blood oozing, running down his side and catching in his black jeans. 'I need a needle and thread. Some gauze. Maybe a drink.'

Clara looked in his eyes, saw his determination, and searched the apartment. She came back from a dresser with a needle and blue cotton thread. Walker went to the basin and wet a handtowel with cold water, pressing it against the cut.

'I'll do that,' Clara said. 'You sit.'

'I've got it.'

'Just do as I say.'

She took his hand and he followed. She led him first to the bathroom, where she stripped off his boots and trousers, then wiped him down, continually dousing the cloth in cold water to rinse it of blood. She then passed the cleaned cloth to him and he held it to the cut while she spread out a folded towel on the bed.

'Lie down,' she said.

Clara left the room as Walker carefully lowered himself onto the bed. He heard the gas stove spark alight. In a minute she came in holding the blackened end of the sterilised needle, thirty centimetres of single-thread cotton through the eye.

'This will hurt,' she said as she knelt next to him.

'I'm a big boy,' Walker said, watching her tanned hands as her delicate fingers pinched the cut closed with one hand and began to sew it shut with the other.

'Ouch,' Walker said.

He closed his eyes and focused his breathing, letting his mind wander away from the pain. Durant had made it clear: Walker was now on their radar. Whoever Durant was working for was the same person who had burned him in Yemen. The person who had placed the kill order on him and thought it a success for the past year now realised that they had a thorn in their side – a thorn who was looking into their dirty business. The head-case courier. The surviving assassin who fled to the embassy. It was someone still connected to or inside the CIA, of that Walker had no doubt.

'You've done this before?' he asked Clara, returning to the present.

'I have sewn before,' she replied, her fingers moving carefully, precisely.

Walker felt around his neck for the USB stick he had taken from the safe-house landlord.

'Done,' Clara said, placing a clean, dry face cloth over the wound and moving Walker's free hand to keep it in place. She closed her hand over his and applied gentle pressure for a moment. 'Not exactly Prada quality, but the bleeding will stop.'

'Thank you,' Walker replied. 'Now, I need to find a computer.'

Seventy-six hours to deadline.

18

'We've got new activity in Rome,' McCorkell said.

'It's Walker,' said Hutchinson, looking at the report coming in on a screen that was linked to Intellipedia, the information-sharing service run by the US intelligence and military communities. On the surface Intellipedia was a place for posting all kinds of mundane intel so that connections could be made and time saved, thus economising the intel community, an entity that had grown so bloated since 9/11 that it needed anything that might help. 'He was just busted out of the CIA safe house.'

McCorkell read over the details posted on the site.

'Question is,' he said to those in the room, 'do we think he's working for INTFOR? Is Walker Bellamy's man, like the guy who went to the embassy?'

'It's possible. They went in hard to get him from the safe house. Could have been an extraction.'

'Could have been a silencing op,' an analyst said.

'Then why not just blow the joint?' another countered. 'Says in the initial report that there was a sustained firefight.'

'They wanted him alive,' Hutchinson said. 'Whatever the case, we need to consider that Walker had been working with them all morning, not against them.'

'And the dead guy at the apartment? And the car chase through Rome? No. I don't buy it,' said McCorkell.

'We can't rule it out,' replied Hutchinson.

'Agreed. Keep it in the mix,' McCorkell said, checking his watch and turning from the report to Hutchinson. 'You'd better get your flight; we've got this. When you get to Washington, get everything you can on Walker and get it back to me.'

'Sure thing,' Hutchinson said, still lingering.

'What is it?' asked McCorkell.

'We're not the only ones interested in him.'

'That figures. Who else, pre the safe house?'

'Fiona Somerville.' Hutchinson pointed to an analyst, who brought up Somerville's personnel file on the screen. 'She's FBI, a counterterrorism specialist out of the Med, Athens posting.'

'She's working in criminal finance?' McCorkell asked. He looked at the photo of a no-nonsense woman in her forties with a short bob of blonde hair and intense eyes.

'That and some.'

'Do you know her?'

'Only by rep, and it's good. She's a pit bull, supernova bright.'

'Where is she now?' asked McCorkell.

'Rome,' an analyst said. 'Closing, no doubt.'

'What does she want with Walker?'

Hutchinson smiled. 'I haven't exactly asked her, but given her muster's technically counter-terrorism and counter-intel, I'd say she's looking at Walker as a double, at best.'

'At worst?'

'Take your pick,' Hutchinson said. 'Either a guy who wants revenge on those who listed him KIA . . .'

An analyst added, 'A terrorist.'

Another chimed in, 'Or he's a paramilitary officer who's always been bent.'

McCorkell nodded slowly. 'Whatever the case, she sees Walker as a threat to national security.'

'Yep.'

'What's his grab status with the Bureau? Do they want him dead or alive?'

'Alive, so far,' Hutchinson said. 'That could change real quick with a request from the Agency over the next twenty-four hours, if it's confirmed that he killed any of their agents at the safe house.'

'I hear you. Get on that flight to Washington, break down some walls at State and get everything you can on Walker.'

'You really think this guy's an in to Bellamy?'

'Right now he's the most interesting lead we've got.'

'I'm on it,' Hutchinson said and left the room.

McCorkell sipped his Irish Breakfast tea. A thought that had bugged him for hours started to play louder. *If a guy like Walker's been out in the wilderness all this time, how am I going to get to him before the rest of the world does?*

•

Walker sat at the computer terminal and inserted the USB stick. The encryption key it contained, along with knowledge of where to look on the internet, enabled remote access from any computer to Intellipedia.

He started with the head-case courier, Felix Lassiter. Basically the role of couriers such as Lassiter was to sit in a bar or cafe or other seemingly innocuous location for a pre-designated period, during which information would be wirelessly transferred to the chip embedded in his head. It was lucrative, and straightforward, the ultimate job for a cut-out agent: simply turn up for a while and then leave. It was the twenty-first century's version of physically passing over microfilm or printouts.

The identities of head-case couriers were protected in the Intellipedia system as deeply as any other agent run by one of the US's sixteen intelligence agencies. Walker had the benefit of knowing Lassiter's case number, something that had taken him two months to obtain and had led him from Istanbul to Riyadh and then, a few days ago, to Athens.

Walker knew from the prefix that it was the same booking officer that had been used then; he figured that Lassiter had taken over the runs that the courier from Yemen, Louis Assif, used to make. So, killing Assif in Yemen had not cut that money and communications line. It had been taken over. By someone inside the Agency. The same someone who'd issued the drone strike and listed Walker KIA because he'd got too close.

Walker checked over his shoulder and saw Clara standing outside, holding two espressos. With the sunlight behind her he could see the shape of her body through her thin summer dress, and in a glance he traced her legs from her ankles up to the top of her thighs.

He refocused on the screen in front of him, typing an access code into the protected-field-officer area. The case files loaded within seconds. As with all head-case couriers, Lassiter's file went only one rung deep, showing the last locations of his service.

The pick-up was at a cafe in Greece, yesterday.

The delivery was two nights from now, in a public space in Hong Kong, the exact location TBA an hour out, to be instructed at a hotel where Lassiter was booked.

Walker looked up the officer running the courier: CIA Deputy Director Jack Heller.

Now, why would a guy like you be using an Agency head case . . .

Walker logged out of the ops centre, then went to the Intellipedia message boards. They were hundreds-deep in topic, and he searched through for the one he had not looked at in six months, hoping that his contact would be as diligent as ever.

He left an anonymous post: *OMEGA DOWN*.

Two words that would mean nothing to anyone other than the intended recipient.

Now, Walker had to wait.

Seventy-five hours to deadline.

19

Dan Bellamy was in an off-site PR meeting when the next call came. This time it came not from the field but from his DC office. He listened and was updated on everything the CIA knew about Rome.

Another cluster fuck. He couldn't afford any more mistakes. He had no doubt that The Scalpel would succeed, but he didn't have time to wait for another chance.

Bellamy replied with just a few words. 'Get Durant back stateside before we proceed with Zodiac.'

Seventy-five hours to deadline.

•

Walker sat on the edge of the bed while Clara showered. He hadn't expected her to come back to the apartment. They had lingered on the street outside; he apologised for getting her involved, and she said she needed the bathroom. When they had made their way back into the apartment, she had said she felt like she had death on her skin from all that she had seen, and she needed to wash it off, to think, to take it all in. Walker had been so caught up in the business of day-to-day survival that he hadn't reflected on how she was coping. Now that he thought about it, he was a little surprised that she hadn't fallen apart.

Yet.

He knew from a lifetime of experience that it would catch up with her. Best case: she would crash and want to sleep. Worst case: she would be traumatised, shut down, become a liability.

Walker knew that whoever was hunting him was USA all the way. His pursuers wouldn't call the local cops, nor Europol or Interpol. Cops of any sort have questions, and his answers could not be heard outside the intelligence community. That was good and bad, but it was what it was.

Right now, he needed to use this window to get Clara out of here.

The water was turned off. Clara came out wearing a towel.

'We need to talk,' she said.

'Okay.'

'Well, *you* need to talk.'

'Okay.' Walker could sense that the cleansing shower had steeled her resolve and cleared her thoughts. He regretted letting her back up here.

'I mean it,' Clara said, 'or I call the police.'

'Fair enough.'

Clara sat on the edge of the bed next to Walker and waited.

'So . . .' Walker said.

'Felix.'

'Right. Well, like I said, I was visiting him—'

'How do you know him?'

'We worked together.'

'What kind of work?'

'International relations.'

'Felix does not work in international relations. *Did* not. He was in finance.'

'I know. I dealt with him on a business deal once, about a year ago. He told me to look him up if I was ever in the neighbourhood.'

'And there you were, in the neighbourhood at the time of his murder.'

'It wasn't exactly the house call I wanted to make.'

Clara paused, then said, 'Why did you not call the police?'

'The phone line was down.'

'Why did you not use your cell phone?'

'I didn't have one on me.'

'You could have gone for help.'

'I only got there about two minutes before you.'

Clara nodded. 'Okay.'

'Okay?'

'Okay. I believe you. About Felix.'

'Thanks.'

'Now tell me: who were those men who took us from the street before, took us to that house?'

'Americans.'

'I know that much. Were they in "international relations" as well?'

Walker smiled at the way she said that. 'No, no they weren't.'

'You are American. They were American. A coincidence?'

Walker stood and walked to the bedroom's balcony window. He spoke over his shoulder. 'You should probably go.'

'No. I want to know.'

'It's better you don't.'

Silence.

Here it comes . . .

'Who were they? You must tell me this. You must. Who takes people from the street and locks them in a house like that? I want to know what is happening.'

Walker said, 'Those guys worked for the CIA.'

Clara laughed.

He turned back to her. 'I'm serious.'

'Okay,' she said. 'And why did they do that? Take you, take me, from a street in Rome?'

'Because they want something I have.'

'You stole something?'

'No.'

'That,' she said, pointing at the USB around his neck. 'They wanted that.'

'No,' Walker said. 'Not this. This is what I went to the house for.'

'Went? They abducted *you*.'

'I needed this,' Walker said, tapping the USB. 'So I let them take me.'

Clara's expression changed, and she said, 'When you looked up at that camera, outside the embassy, you wanted them to pick you up, to take you there?'

Walker nodded. 'I needed to go to that safe house.'

'You call that a *safe* house?'

Walker smiled. 'They are usually a lot safer.'

'Then what is it you have that they want?'

'Information.'

'Information?'

Walker nodded.

'About international relations?'

'Maybe. I'm not sure. I'm still figuring it out.'

'They want to kidnap you – and me – for some information that you do not even have yet?'

'They don't know what I know and what I don't, so that makes me dangerous to them.'

Clara seemed to be taking it all in. Adding it all up. Weighing it. Testing it. She looked him directly in the eye for a long moment, then asked, 'Are you a spy?'

'No. I'm just a guy.'

'A guy who works in international relations.'

'More or less.'

Clara nodded, stood. 'Okay. I should go.'

•

Andrew Hutchinson sat in business class on the BA flight to Washington DC, working through his notes. He highlighted an interesting little fact: Jed Walker had been in Iraq the same time as Dan Bellamy. But then so were a couple hundred-thousand other Americans. Hutchinson's gut told him that Walker wasn't the type to sell out . . .

He switched to the personal information. The data on Walker's family, namely his father, was substantial. Walker senior had been a foreign-policy specialist and senior advisor to several administrations, right up to his death. The guy was a legend, surpassed in his field perhaps only by Kissinger, a man he'd had a lifetime of run-ins with.

Hutchinson moved on to Walker's wife, Eve. The little he'd found on her raised more questions than answers. He made a note: *talk to the wife*.

•

Walker moved to the tiny kitchen to give Clara privacy while she dressed. She left the door open, dropped the towel and slipped into her dress, nothing underneath. *Damn*. Walker went to the apartment door and opened it. No sign of the little old lady. He checked the cut on his side while he waited for Clara. The bleeding had mostly stopped, but the walk before had opened the wound and a slight ooze of bright-red liquid trickled.

'Why don't we get you a dressing for that?' Clara said, her handbag over her shoulder.

'I'll be okay.'

'And something to eat.'

'I thought you were leaving.'

'I will. After. I . . . I cannot think. I have nowhere to be. I was headed to the countryside with Felix today . . . now this.' Clara looked at Walker, her gaze steady. 'What will you do now?'

'Not much. Rest, then leave.'

'You need taking care of.'

'I'm fine on my own.'

'You're still bleeding.'

'A scratch. I can manage.'

'Yes. But everybody needs looking after sometimes.'

Walker laughed.

'What is it?'

'Nothing,' Walker said, then pulled down his T-shirt. 'Okay, let's eat.'

Seventy-four hours to deadline.

20

Walker scanned faces as they walked. The Beretta was tucked into the waistband of his jeans at the small of his back beneath his T-shirt.

After finding a pharmacy and some adhesive bandage and painkillers, Clara made Walker stop to buy a new shirt. He chose a black one: cotton, long sleeves, slim fit but enough room across the shoulders to allow a full range of motion. He rolled up the sleeves and binned his torn T-shirt on the way down the ancient cobbled street. A police car flashed by, its siren wailing.

'You are not afraid of being arrested?' Clara asked.

'I've done nothing wrong,' Walker replied.

They walked in silence. Summer in Rome. Even on this tiny out-of-the-way street it was impossible to escape the tourists. Walker scrutinised faces as they moved, wary, assessing the physical capability of each person they passed. It was tiring work, and he had been doing it for years. Always ready. Fight or flight.

'Here,' Clara said. 'This looks good.'

They entered a restaurant with pale yellow flaking plaster, buckets of flowers rowed against the front window and wooden tables that had seen a century's worth of patrons dining upon them, red-shirted waiting staff floating about the twenty or so diners.

Walker sat with his back to the wall, the front door to his right, the kitchen to his left, the bar ahead. Clara sat opposite, the waiter pushing in her chair.

She ordered Campari and soda, he a double of Scotch, neat.

She smiled, settling herself in her chair while Walker took note of each of their fellow diners.

'Excuse me,' he said as he stood and left the table. Beyond the kitchen was an outdoor paved area, the single toilet a brick lean-to that was occupied. Walker didn't need the bathroom. He checked the back alley through a rickety wooden door set into the brick fence. A dark, cobbled space, too narrow for cars. To his right the next street was ten metres away. To his left was sixty metres of uneven ground, winding around out of sight as it followed the curve of the road. Behind him a toilet flushed.

A man came out: late sixties, thin white hair, could handle himself once, maybe former Navy, face cragged with sun damage, now a happy tourist.

Walker went into the tiny bathroom and washed his hands. The mirror was rusted around the edges, the surface dulled and pocked with age. He didn't need to see his reflection to know that he looked tired. He did not need to pause and question why he was staying with this woman longer than he needed to. They both knew what was happening. An early night. An early morning, leave before she wakes. Check the message board. Head to Hong Kong.

Walker returned to find bread and oil and their drinks on the table.

Clara had applied more lipstick, a deep red painted on the full contours of her pout. Extra eye shadow too, blue–green highlights above those dark eyes. Framed by thick eyelashes. Detailed by perfectly shaped eyebrows. Poised. Expectant. Seductive.

Walker sipped Scotch. It tasted like home. He relaxed.

'You are interesting, Jed Walker . . .' Clara said.

'I bet you say that to all the guys you stitch back together.'

She smiled as she watched him. 'I have never met an interesting American before.'

Walker smiled through his Scotch glass. 'An endangered species, but we do exist.'

'So I see.' Clara turned to the waiter and ordered for them.

'What am I getting?' Walker asked.

'A surprise,' Clara replied.

•

'Agent Somerville,' Captain Spiteri said. Middle-aged with tanned skin and a big smile, he exuded success and confidence.

'Captain,' Somerville said, shaking his hand. They stood outside Rome's police headquarters in the warm afternoon sun, the traffic sounds humming a background soundtrack.

'You've come to see your Trapwire system in action,' Spiteri said.

He led them inside, through a warren of corridors to a large open-plan room full of LCD screens. The room was vast, and loud. No fewer than fifty police were at workstations, watching and collating data as it was being mined. Every camera in the city that was accessible via the internet was linked to this room.

'It's impressive,' Somerville said.

Spiteri nodded. 'You have the picture file?'

'Yes, here.' She passed over her cell phone, and the captain passed it to a subordinate who uploaded the image of Walker onto a computer.

'The facial recognition will run until you tell me otherwise,' Captain Spiteri explained. 'But I'm sure we'll find your man before then.'

'You're very helpful.'

'It is the least I can do,' he replied. 'Are you able to enlighten me as to why you want this man?'

Somerville looked at the photo of Walker and replied, 'He's a person of interest.'

'Ah, one of those.'

'I'm sorry I can't tell you more, at least not yet.'

'It is fine; it was the expected answer,' Spiteri said, with an eyebrow raised. 'One would presume it has something to do with this afternoon's attack on your CIA safe house?'

'He may be involved.'

'Ah, well I think that unlikely,' Spiteri replied.

'How so?'

'You see, the four dead men in the downstairs of that house are all known to us,' the captain explained. '*Well known*. Heavy hitters, Camorra types, now plying their trade here in the capital. They were scum, born and bred. But they were good at what they did. Very good.'

'Do you know who they would have been working for?'

'Well, I am just a local police captain. You'd have to talk to the judicial department, for they are the only ones liaising with your CIA on this . . .'

'But you knew the men.'

'Like I said, that is all I know. They work for hire, no known long-term affiliation with any one person or group. That is what has made them difficult to pin down, and dangerous, for a long time.'

'Okay. Thank you.'

'And now you tell me one thing. One friendly cop to another.'

'I'll try.'

'This man you are looking for,' the captain said. 'Is he friend or foe?'

Somerville didn't hesitate. 'Foe.'

Seventy-four hours to deadline.

21

Entrees of grilled, stuffed calamari had cleared and the mains were almost finished. Veal for Walker, with a sauce of Prosecco, cream and mushroom; a side of assorted steamed vegetables. Clara had a bitter-leaf salad topped with grilled branzino.

'See, if I'd known what you were ordering for us,' Walker said, 'I'd have insisted you get yourself something decent.'

'Decent?'

'More substantial.'

'Ah, Americans, telling the world what to do, and along the way making sure you glutton yourselves.' Clara smiled. 'Perhaps you would like a large soda to go with your meal? Or a bucket of fries?'

'Touché.'

'Perhaps Italian women have different eating habits to their American counterparts?' Clara leaned forwards, added, 'Or perhaps it is just that you have not dated in a long while and have forgotten your manners?'

Walker smiled, checked the surroundings as he sipped water.

Clara's voice changed tone when she said, 'They're out there, aren't they?'

'Somewhere.'

'You're worried.'

'I'm wary.'

'They are looking for you. Do they want you dead, like our friend Felix?'

Walker leaned back. 'No, I don't think they want me dead.'

'You don't think?'

'They would have killed me if they wanted to. They've had chances.'

'Right. They just want information, as did the CIA men.'

'Exactly.'

'But they're out there, looking for you, and here you are, on a date.'

'This is a date?'

'I mean—'

'I know what you mean, and I know what I'm doing,' Walker said. 'Being normal. Blending in. Hanging around. The borders will be covered. Airports are impossible. They'll presume I'm running, as fast and as far as I can. Meanwhile, I'm waiting right here, within the same city as that safe house, the embassy, Felix's apartment.'

'So . . . staying put is sometimes a smart move?'

'And running away is often overrated.'

'Why were you in Rome?'

Walker looked around. He saw tourists, a few locals, the waiting staff. Smiles everywhere. A microcosm of happiness. Good food, wine and company. It was another world, one he had never had enough time to appreciate: always one foot out of it, always ready to flee.

Clara watched him closely. 'Felix?' she said.

'Yes.'

'But you were not there because he is – *was* – your friend.'

'No.'

Clara paused, then said, 'And are you lying about anything else?'

'No.'

Clara nodded.

Walker waited. He was probably being more honest now about his working life than he had ever been about it with Eve. Here, with this unknown woman, when all certainty of his next move was lost. It was an unaccustomed, uncomfortable realisation, one he didn't want to dwell on.

'Tell me one thing, and please be honest,' Clara said. 'Were you there to kill Felix?'

'No.' *Incapacitate him and cut the tiny chip from the back of his head, yes. Kill him, no.*

Clara seemed to accept the truth in his answer. Then she asked, 'What is next?'

'Next?'

'When will you know what your next step is?'

'Hopefully by the time I wake,' Walker said.

Clara watched him closely. 'You will leave soon?' she asked quietly but clearly.

'Yes.'

'You must?'

'Yes.'

'And what do I do?'

'I think you should stay with friends. Out of town. Go to the countryside, like you said. Don't go home for a few days. Just to be safe.'

'What will change in a few days?'

'Everything.'

Seventy-three hours to deadline.

22

Bellamy sat in his home office. His family was asleep. He had never been a big sleeper, and usually managed on four to five hours per night. Since his first serious job in Baghdad's Green Zone in the days after Saddam's fall, to heading his own company eight years later, he had held the firm belief that anything more than a few hours' shut-eye per day was a waste of time.

Tonight he was not alone in his evening work. Opposite him sat an old family friend turned current business associate. Between them, a bottle of Old Forester Bourbon, two glasses, and a growing problem.

'What could Walker know?' asked Senator Anderson.

'We can't afford to wait around to find out,' Bellamy responded. 'We have planned for too long for this to go off track now. One slip-up this close and the whole chain could break. We've got to put a stop to this guy.'

'True. What can I do?'

'Nothing. We're doing it all, everything that can be done.'

'One man can't stop this.'

'Of course he can. A man can do pretty much anything, if he's driven enough.'

'Maybe you're right.'

'Maybe? You've been on the Hill too long. One man can do plenty in the big wide world. And you've read his file.'

'The wrong man in the wrong place at the wrong time.'

'That's about the sum of it,' Bellamy said.

'His old man could have stopped us. God knows he tried.'

'We don't have to worry about that SOB anymore. And soon, this Walker either.'

'We're not in the business of killing Americans, Dan, you know that.'

'It's the price you pay.'

'Excuse me?'

'Think of it as a tax.'

'For what?'

'For daring to live in the shadows.'

'I'm not living in the goddamned shadows, Dan, you are.'

'Okay,' Bellamy said. 'But you're a part of this. And you know as well as I do that secrets have a way of coming out.'

Anderson stopped himself from saying something and took another sip of his drink. 'We're so damned close to being on the other side of it all . . .'

'We're going to be heroes, that much hasn't changed,' said Bellamy, trying to reassure them both. 'Rich heroes.'

'You're already rich.'

'As are you. But we're the haves; soon we'll be the have-mores.'

Anderson chuckled. 'Now you're talkin' my language.'

Bellamy raised his glass and leaned forwards, and the senator clinked the crystal.

'To the future of American intelligence,' Bellamy said.

'To *our* future.'

•

Walker woke early. He moved silently from the bed, careful not to wake Clara. Her dark hair was spread out like a halo on the white sheets, the shape of her sleeping form precise, as though she had appeared from a Jack Vettriano painting. Peace personified and at the same time something worth going to war over.

Dangerous.

Walker showered and dressed. Drank a glass of water as he looked out the window at the city not yet awake. Watched as Clara turned over on the bed, as beautiful asleep as awake.

He left the apartment and walked down the street in the direction of the internet cafe. In the dark alleyway Walker entered via the rear door, itself sturdy but the lock defeated by a debit card in two seconds. His observations yesterday told him that the security system was simple, something available from RadioShack back home. The alarm was disengaged by a simple crossed wire. The digital cameras in the customer area – two, in opposite corners – were easily switched off in the office.

Walker switched on the internet router and then a PC, listening as it booted up; sounds he hadn't heard in years – old tech, grinding away along silicon pathways outdated the moment it was designed, probably bought second-hand from an office and installed here for grimy tourists to destroy. Still, it did the job he needed it to do.

Accessing Intellipedia was completed in a matter of minutes: the USB inserted, the webpage accessed, the chat room opened.

He found his simple two-word line: *OMEGA DOWN*.

It was a code for help, to his old mentor, the man who had not only recruited Walker to the Agency but been like another father to him well before his own had died.

An answer was waiting: *ALPHA CLEAR 4239-185*.

Walker shut down the clunky machine and left the room, locking the rear door behind him. He made his way back to the apartment in a roundabout way, constantly checking to make sure he was not being tailed.

The streets were starting to brighten as people began their day.

Time to leave Rome.

Fifty-eight hours to deadline.

23

'Walker is back on the grid,' Zoe Ledoyen said. Formerly an agent with France's Direction Centrale du Renseignement Intérieur, she had been recruited by McCorkell two years ago after he'd seen how good an investigator she was, and now in the absence of Hutchinson she was quarterbacking the situation-room efforts to find Walker. It was the first time she'd had to wake McCorkell at home.

'Where is he?' McCorkell asked into the phone, rubbing sleep from his eyes and switching on his bedside lamp.

'He is still in Rome. We have confirmed facial-recognition images from a traffic camera and a street security camera, two blocks apart.'

'How'd we get it?' He checked the time: 4:40 am in London meant it was 5:40 am in Rome.

'Trapwire,' Zoe replied. 'Via the Guardia di Finanza. I got it through a Europol contact assigned there.'

'How old are the images?' McCorkell sat on the edge of his bed, scrunching his arthritic toes against the carpet. *You're getting old, Bill . . .*

'About twenty minutes,' Zoe replied. 'But we're not the only ones who know.'

'Figures. Who else, besides the Italians?'

'The FBI agent who requested the Trapwire search.'

'Somerville?'

'Yes . . . wait . . . I have just received email confirmation that it has been accessed by another party: the CIA.'

'Does it say where their search request came from?'

'One moment.'

McCorkell walked to the kitchenette and put coffee on, the phone between his shoulder and his ear.

'Langley. Office of the Director of the Special Activities Division.'

'Okay, thanks,' McCorkell said, pulling on his trousers. 'Get everyone up, keep Hutchinson in the loop, and book me on the next flight to Rome.'

Fifty-seven hours to deadline.

•

Walker had made as many mistakes in life as anybody else. He figured that an hour back at the apartment would not be one of them. At the time there seemed no harm – in fact, the opposite – in waking Clara on his return and spending the time as they had when they had returned from the restaurant: in a sweaty tangle that ended in her moans and his shudders and a sleepy aftermath.

They showered together, and then Walker dressed. By 7 am he was waiting by the kitchen's open balcony window watching the street below come to life, filling with people buying coffee and breakfast and getting to work and beating the rush. He glanced at Clara in the bathroom, naked in front of the mirror, her small bag containing make-up next to her as she lined her eyes.

Walker tensed as he heard a noise in the tiny hall outside.

Getting louder.

Footsteps.

•

Il Bisturi received his nickname during a training operation with the French Foreign Legion in Madagascar where he killed a man with a surgical scalpel in a bar fight. The scalpel had been pulled on *him*, and he was of the opinion that if you pull a blade then you are prepared to kill or be killed. The man had been their battalion's chief medical officer, and Il Bisturi had been on the run ever since.

The thing he had hated most during his six years of service with the Legion was the lack of sleep. He was a man who liked sleep. So, when he had been woken earlier with an alert, he was curt but courteous. Being an hour's drive from the scene of Walker's last sighting, he placed a call to those who had survived the previous day's mishap at the CIA safe house.

For those men, it was a chance to make amends. He made it clear to them that failure a second time would not be tolerated, and that if they were not killed in the advent of mission failure, then they would be, by him, in their sleep, in the near future.

24

Walker quietly closed the bedroom door without alerting Clara, and moved to the door of the apartment and listened.

A pair of feet shuffled outside, the floorboards creaking. Not heavy. Not trying to be especially quiet. A slightly uneven gait.

Walker exhaled.

The landlady.

Walker opened the door.

She stood there, slightly stooped with age, a tray of breakfast in her hands.

'Buon giorno,' she said, her little round face full of smile and age lines.

'Good morning,' Walker replied, letting her in. She set down the wooden tray on the table and spread her hands out over her offerings: a French press of coffee, buttered toast with scrambled eggs, a bowl of sliced fruit, a jug of milk. Perhaps her version of an American breakfast.

'You stay another day?'

'No, thank you,' Walker said, handing her a hundred euros. 'We will leave in a couple of hours.'

'No, no, too much,' the lady protested at the money but Walker refused its return, and she made a sign of prayer for him and exited.

Walker took the tray into the bedroom. Clara sat on the bed, the white sheet covering her left leg and contrasting against her tanned skin. He poured coffees and sat next to her.

'You will leave today,' Clara said, curling her legs up and turning to face him, taking her coffee and resting the cup on her raised knees.

'Yep.'

'Where to?'

'I'm not sure,' Walker said. That wasn't the truth, but he felt it would be better for her in the event she were questioned that she would not have to lie for him.

'You are not sure, or you will not tell me?'

'A bit of both.' *4239-185. Latitude and longitude*, Walker thought. *And the coast was clear.*

'Why not stay another day?' she said quietly, smiling. 'With me. Here. In bed.'

'I wish I could,' Walker said. 'But I can't. I have to keep moving.'

She was silent, then nodded. 'Okay. I will walk you out.'

•

'I'm getting nowhere with State,' Hutchinson said to McCorkell over the phone from across the Atlantic. 'I even used your name to get through a few doors. It's like Walker never even worked here.'

'Meanwhile, it looks like we've lost him in Rome,' McCorkell said. 'The guy has vanished. A ghost. FBI and CIA have got a whole bunch of resources at play, alerts at all exit points. He's either gone to ground, or slipped out undetected.'

'For Walker, Italy's an easy place to do either.'

'Which makes me think: I'd like to know if he's operated there before, if there's some old contacts he might be working with.'

'I might get further with Langley. I'll let you know how I go,' Hutchinson said. 'First, I'm stopping in at Crystal City.'

'What's there?'

'A State overflow office,' Hutchinson said. 'The human-resources department managed to get the name of the person who signed for his life-insurance cheque for his wife.'

'I'm guessing that was his boss,' McCorkell said.

'I'm going to find out.'

'They might want their money back.'

'Tell 'em Walker's alive?' Hutchinson asked.

'With the amount of heat on him now, they're bound to know already.'

'I don't know . . .' Hutchinson said. 'Things were ice cold at State.'

'Ever the optimist.'

'Realist.'

'Good luck with that.'

'Thanks.'

'And, Hutch?'

'Yeah?'

'The wife, too. Speak to Walker's wife. He may have been in contact.'

'On it, boss.'

•

Walker and Clara passed the corner of Via Toscana and Via Sicilia near the internet cafe, and turned towards the busy Corso D'Italia. Local traffic on the road, and tourists on the sidewalk.

Clara stopped and smiled at him.

Walker sighed.

'We can go together, to my friends,' Clara said, her arms linked around his waist, her head rested on his chest. 'They have a little farmhouse near Palermo; we can catch a train or bus there. Drink wine. Relax in the sun. Sleep. Or not sleep . . .'

'In another life, absolutely,' Walker said, resting his chin on her head. 'Another time.'

Walker felt Clara's body tense.

'Let's find a cab,' Walker said.

Clara walked from him, and he watched her settle at the kerb, looking right and left for a passing taxi. Walker knew that there were certain truths in the world, and one of them was that with a body like Clara's, cab drivers would fight for the fare. *In another life . . .*

Walker looked back towards the internet cafe. He spotted someone, but his eyes didn't linger. A split second, that's all it took, all he needed to know that the moment had changed.

Walker made a guy who didn't belong, the type of guy who had no place in an internet cafe full of backpackers and tourists. He was not from the security company, responding to Walker's soft break-in. And he was not alone – his accomplice was across the street, waiting.

25

Italy had the most police per capita than anywhere in Europe, and at least two of them were tailing Walker. Plain-clothes cops.

Walker did a casual sweep of the area and could not see any others.

These two could be checking the break-in at the internet cafe; they might even have a lead that it was—

Walker knew what they were there for when one of the cops scanned the faces in the street and locked on Walker: *recognition.*

Damn.

Two career cops, used to dealing with criminals of all kinds. Not used to former special-forces operatives who had no time to be detained and no desire to answer questions. Walker almost felt sorry for them; then he remembered Clara. They had seen her with him just now. *Maybe they were specifically looking for her, too.* It was an unfortunate complication, and he knew in that moment that returning to the apartment this morning went counter to everything he had learned in year after year of training and practice. Instead, it was a decision based solely on a primeval part of his brain that yearned for company and comfort; that same tiny speck of grey matter that said going to the farmhouse in Palermo to drink and fuck was a great idea; the same bit of him that wanted to take Clara in his arms and let no harm come to her.

'In here,' Walker said, taking Clara firmly by the elbow and guiding her into a bridal shop. He led her quickly towards the back, her feet sliding on the floor as he pulled her along. He glanced behind.

The two cops were in pursuit, entering the store at a wary half-run, talking into police radios.

•

'Local police are pursuing Walker on foot,' Ben Hobbs said, driving an Alfa Romeo from the US embassy's pool down the oncoming traffic lane to overtake a jam, a Bluetooth earpiece relaying information from the police net.

'I told them not to approach!' Somerville cried.

Car horns blazed as Hobbs bleeped the Alfa's hidden siren and blasted through an intersection.

'They must have been made,' Hobbs replied.

'Tell them to back off.'

He touched his ear, said, 'We've lost contact with them.'

'How far away?'

'Just up the road here.'

'Hurry!' she said. 'We can't let Walker slip through again.'

26

The shop attendant shouted something but Walker could not make out the rapid-fire Italian. The tone he recognised, though, as he led Clara into the rear of the store and through the first door: a storeroom set up with a maze of stuffed clothes racks.

'What is going on?' Clara called, struggling to keep up with Walker's pace.

Walker pulled Clara behind the doorway and pressed her against the wall.

He turned, waited a beat, then held his arm out straight to the room—

Clothes-lining the first cop through the doorway, Walker's forearm chopped hard against the guy's windpipe. The wide-eyed cop's hands clutched at his throat, as though trying to pull it open to let air pass through.

The second cop was a step behind and hesitated, seeing his partner down and now out as Walker kneed him hard in the ribs and then brought the Beretta down on the back of his head.

The cop raised his hands at the sight of the pistol, but his forward momentum and surprise worked against him, and Walker rushed the two steps to close the gap.

The policeman's reaction was instinctive and showed some decent training and street smarts as he tried to disarm Walker, grabbing his wrist and twisting it into a compliance hold, the weapon pointed away.

Walker had no intention of shooting the guy, not here, not like this, not when he had other options. He pulled his arms in, drawing the cop close, then quickly twisted his arms across to spin the guy around him into a choker hold, holding, squeezing, tightening his biceps and forearm around the cop's neck until he felt the guy go limp. He slid to the floor with a dull thud.

'Come on,' Walker said to Clara as he grabbed her wrist and pulled her behind him through the doorway.

'They were police!' Clara said, pointing back at the guy's open jacket to his badge and holstered pistol.

They exited the rear door, out into the service alley he'd been in earlier this morning. Walker headed right, to the busy street forty metres ahead, still holding Clara by the arm, when she suddenly stopped.

•

Andrew Hutchinson was in the plain office of a State Department official named Stephanie Nell.

'So, you're telling me that Walker's alive?' Nell said, after hearing Hutchinson out.

'Yep.'

Nell didn't seem shocked by the news. 'What's he been doing?'

'We don't know.'

'Where's he been?'

'Don't know that either.'

Nell scratched at a notepad and said, 'And you want what with him, exactly?'

Hutchinson said, 'He's touched on an ongoing investigation that we are running.'

'We – you and McCorkell's little UN intel outfit?'

Hutchinson nodded.

'What's that about?'

Hutchinson said, 'Can't say.'

'Walker's involved how?'

'It's too early to tell.'

'And why are you here,' Nell said, leaning forwards on her desk, 'aside from telling me that our guy didn't really die in the desert?'

'I need a better sense of Walker.'

'A better sense?'

'Motivations. Alliances. Suspicions. The kind of thing that doesn't make it into human-resources reports.'

Nell leaned back, considering Hutchinson. 'My advice would be to let him be,' she said. 'Whatever he's doing, it's not as bad as you think it might be. Whoever he's up against, that's where you should be looking. That's it.'

'That's it?'

Nell nodded. 'That's all.'

Hutchinson pushed his luck, said, 'What work did he do for you?'

'I can't say.'

'Has he been in contact with anyone here since Yemen?'

'You mean, since he and an Agency paramilitary officer were killed by a CIA drone strike?'

'Yes.'

'No.'

'You're sure?'

'Yes.'

'What can you tell me about Yemen?'

'It's a shit hole.'

'The mission.'

'Nothing.'

'You know I'm here representing Bill McCorkell.'

'I know. And if he wants to go begging the President to change a whole bunch of secrecy laws, then good luck to him.'

Hutchinson smiled, looked around the office. 'What sort of work does this office do?'

Nell returned his smile. 'We could go round and round in circles all day, but I really do have important work to do.'

Hutchinson stood, paced around the room. There was nothing telling. An American flag, several legal books, a computer, a plastic plant. It looked like the room had been set up just before he arrived.

'You know,' Hutchinson said, 'I've heard rumours of a secret State Department group. The Magellan something-or-other. A group of special investigators, travelling the world, setting things right, stuff no-one else could do.'

Nell matched his stare, allowing silence to fill the room for a few long moments. 'Sounds like fiction.'

'Yeah, you're probably right.' Hutchinson fell silent.

A minute passed, and then Nell leaned forwards on her desk and said, 'All right, Agent Hutchinson, I'll give you something. But this doesn't come back to me.'

27

'Please, stop, tell me what is going on!' Clara was panicked, and Walker didn't have time for her to fall to pieces.

Walker looked both ways in the busy street and led her onwards, merging them with the mass of pedestrians as he replied. 'They're after me. I pushed my luck being here. I was careless.'

'Who are you running from – the police? The CIA?'

'Them, and the guys who killed Felix.'

'But back there – they *were police*!'

'And if they found us, then the others won't be far behind.'

'Us?' Clara said, and Walker could see her face cloud over with mistrust and worry.

'I'm sorry you got involved in this,' Walker said. 'You need to get out of town, stay with a friend, lie low for a couple of weeks.'

'Why? Please, tell me, what is going on here?'

'Clara, I can't tell you.'

'You *are* a criminal, aren't you?'

'No. It's . . . this is something I've been trying to piece together for almost a year, and I need to keep going just a bit longer.'

'Why?'

'Because something terrible will happen if I fail.'

'When?'

'Soon.'

'But what *is* it?' She stopped walking in the crowd and looked at him, her big dark eyes wet, the tears holding but not for long. 'I want to know. I need to know.'

'I'm trying to set something right,' he said. 'There are people involved who will think nothing of hurting me or you to stop me from doing this.'

'The men who killed Felix.'

Walker nodded. 'He was killed for a reason, and he was killed on an order.'

'And you want to find out who was behind it.'

'Yes.'

'Why you? Let the police handle it.'

'They can't. They won't.'

'Let it go while you have a chance.'

'I can't do that.'

'I do not understand!'

'Look, Clara, just get out of town, okay? Some place quiet and safe – your friends' place in the countryside sounds good. Go there and see them. Take a holiday.'

'A holiday?'

'Out of town. Stay there for a week. Maybe longer. As long as you can. Forget you ever met me.'

'What about you?'

'I'll be fine,' Walker said. He took her hand and they moved to where the street met a bustling four-lane road. As they emerged onto the corner footpath, Clara started to say something but Walker had tuned out as a new threat appeared.

A black BMW sedan pulled up hard in front of them.

28

'We've lost all contact with the cops on scene,' Hobbs said, hammering the embassy's Alfa Romeo, blue magnetic light on the dash, a Chevy SUV with DSS agents riding close behind them.

Somerville hit the dashboard with her fist. 'Shit! Where is it?'

'We're two blocks out,' Hobbs said, leaning on the car's horn and blasting a way through the traffic to enter the oncoming lane. 'Thirty seconds!'

•

Walker did not stop moving.

From the passenger seat of the BMW a large guy got out – Walker dropped him with a heel-kick to the kneecap, followed by an elbow striking down squarely on the guy's forehead where his brow met his nose. The guy stayed motionless on his knees, as though frozen in time and stuck in a shocked state of semi-consciousness, his nose running with blood.

Walker kept moving. He knew these guys were not cops, even before the driver pulled a silenced pistol from inside his jacket.

'Down!' Walker called, spinning around and grabbing Clara's arms and pulling her out of the line of fire.

PFFT. PFFT.

Two silenced gunshots hit the brick wall behind them, the passers-by oblivious to the gunfire and the dust kicked up by the slugs.

Walker lifted the large guy to his feet to face him. He was sucking for air through the running blood flow.

The driver aimed.

Walker had the big guy between him and the shooter, held his Beretta in hard against the guy's chest and fired two rounds that were muffled by the close contact, the 9-millimetre slugs drilling through him and into the driver. The dead man's chest cavity acted as a suppressor, so the sound was little different to a car's backfire, and did not draw attention. Carrying through with the same movement, Walker put the big guy back into the passenger seat, closed the door, hid the Beretta under the back of his waistband and then spun around to Clara.

'Move,' he said, and grabbed her hand. They walked quickly and deliberately down the street, joining the morning commuters. 'Keep moving, that's it, keep going . . .'

Ahead of them a taxi pulled up to the kerb and a couple got out. Walker had Clara in the back seat before she could protest. He told the driver to take her to the Stadio Olimpico, then paid fifty euros and shut the door. The cab took off into the morning traffic. In thirty minutes she would be at her destination across the Tiber, a safe distance from here. With any luck, by then he would be heading for a border.

The last image he had of Clara was her looking back at him, her face over the back seat and framed through the rear window, her lips mouthing something he could not hear.

29

Il Bisturi watched the shooting of two of his Camorra employees and was impressed.

Walker was a resourceful man. Quick to react. *A challenge.*

He'd seen the gunfight from across the road. Saw Walker put the woman into the cab. Saw him a moment later get into a cab of his own, headed the opposite way. And now, he watched as a black Alfa Romeo pursued the cab at a safe, precise distance, driven by a young black guy; a woman next to him. Another car was behind them, this one a big SUV with blacked-out windows. *Americans.*

Il Bisturi kicked his Ducati into gear and followed the convoy.

•

Walker sat in the back of the cab, headed to the Termini railway station.

His hands shook from the adrenaline of recent action. He breathed deep, settling breaths. The wound in his side stung. He concentrated on that to calm his thoughts and plan his next moves.

•

'Easy. Don't spook him,' Somerville said.

Hobbs nodded, and concentrated on driving coolly and calmly, the blue light of the Alfa stashed away.

Ahead, Walker was in the back seat of a cab. A little old VW beetle was between the cab and their car.

Somerville checked her side mirror to confirm that the SUV was still close behind.

'What's our move?' Hobbs said.

'Follow him, see where he goes,' Somerville said. 'Take him down when we have him cornered.'

•

'The Americans are following,' Il Bisturi said via the Bluetooth connection to his cell phone, riding behind the SUV chase car.

Bellamy said, 'Who?'

'Walker.'

'No, who are the Americans?'

'I don't know.'

'Describe them.'

'Black man driving, woman passenger. SUV chase car following.'

'Send me a photo from your phone for ID.'

'Okay.'

Bellamy was silent, then said, 'Watch and report to me. Let them take him in if you have to.'

'Why?'

'I want to get an ID on them before you move. Stick close to the embassy; they'll be taking Walker there. I'll work at having him released. Don't let him out of your sight until then.'

•

Walker pushed through the throng of tourists passing through Termini station and headed for the storage lockers.

He opened the locker. His backpack was as he had left it yesterday before heading to Felix's apartment. He checked its contents: a clean passport, more than a thousand in used euros, a couple of new throw-away cell phones and a change of clothes.

He put on his cap and sunglasses, took the backpack from the locker, slung it over his shoulders and pulled the straps tight. In the confines of the locker he emptied the Beretta, wiped it down and then left it behind the locked door.

Walker turned and headed for the ticket booths, ditching the old passport he had forged himself and clocking the train times as he moved. Fifteen minutes until the next Eurostar left for the two-hour journey to Naples. *Perfect.*

But Walker never got to buy a ticket.

He didn't even make it halfway to the booth.

A voice – American, female, assertive – rang out, shouting, 'Down! Down! Down!'

30

Bill McCorkell touched down at Rome International Airport and skipped the immigration lines, flashing his UN diplomatic passport and heading for the taxi rank. He called Hutchinson as he moved.

'Are your ears ringing?' Hutchinson said.

'Nope. How are you getting on?'

'State's all done. I'm about to walk into Langley now.'

'Get anything from their Crystal City office?'

'A little bit of the Yemen op.'

McCorkell stopped at the cab rank. 'And?'

'A cell-phone number.'

'Whose?'

'That's just the thing: no-one knows, not for sure, except maybe Walker.'

'Anything else?'

'You sitting down?'

'No.'

'Well, don't go falling down and breaking one of your frail old-guy hips,' Hutchinson said. 'The number? It was one of the cell numbers found on bin Laden.'

McCorkell let out a sigh, part whistle, part wonder. 'Walker was working on that? For State?'

'Yep. His CO there told me that Walker had tracked it to an SMS message placed to a courier, the guy in Yemen; the one he was watching when he was supposedly cooked by a drone strike.'

'The op he was running when he was listed KIA?'

'Yep. And there's more. I ran that by a guy I know in the Joint Chief's office, and he's just got back to me. It's not just Walker.'

'What's not just Walker?'

'There's been a few unusual deaths relating to that cell-phone number Walker was chasing – some of the guys who inspected bin Laden's body after the DEVGRU team brought him back to base, and a couple of analysts who were working on it at CIA.'

'Who's investigating this?' asked McCorkell, moving towards the front of the taxi queue.

'Everybody did, at first, because it involved Navy deaths. DIA, NCIS, FBI; you name it. Open cases, all of them because they got nowhere. The thing is, none of those investigations linked the deaths to the cell number – and they're all unrelated but for that fact.'

'Who do you think is doing it?'

'My first bet would be revenge hits, for bin Laden,' Hutchinson said. 'That list is a mile long.'

'Maybe . . . but I don't think so. That's a smaller list than you'd think.'

'Maybe, maybe not,' replied Hutchinson. 'What we do know is that Al Qaeda wants revenge. Seems like they're now taking it.'

'Seems that way, yet this is the first I've heard of AQ reprisal killings attached to OBL,' McCorkell said. 'But it doesn't match their MO – I mean, they'd be gloating all over the net with their successes, right?'

'Maybe things have changed a bit since they lost their figurehead,' Hutchinson countered. 'Maybe their new playbook is to do their thing but not announce it until the whole objective is in hand.'

'That's a damn big maybe.'

'Yeah, well, look at what we've got: Walker was the first casualty, about a year ago. Since then the two Navy corpsmen on board the *Carl Vinson* who inspected bin Laden's body and found the phone numbers stitched into his clothing have died, one on an op in 'Stan, the other while on leave. As have a couple of CIA analysts who went through the intel at the compound. And when I say they died, I mean graveyard dead, no mistaking it like with Walker.'

'They found a lot of intel in that compound,' McCorkell said. 'I'm surprised we haven't seen AQ engage some of the plans we found in the house. They weren't planning on stopping after nine-eleven; they had plenty more big moves up their sleeve.'

'Maybe Walker knows about this.' Hutchinson was silent for a few seconds. 'Maybe he's the one *doing* this.'

'I've seen nothing to point to that. And it creates a big *why*.'

'Nothing pointing to it other than being listed KIA and living in the shadows for a year?' said Hutchinson.

'Your other idea is more likely: that we're looking at AQ revenge on those who came into contact with the intel retrieved from the bin Laden compound, perhaps specifically those cell-phone numbers. They may all be related, as you say, but maybe Walker's not related to that. Keep your eye on our prize.'

'It's *all* related.'

'Maybe. I'm still not convinced.'

'Work with me here for a minute,' said Hutchinson. 'Assume I'm right. How did the killer or killers track them down? The corpsmen, the analysts?'

'Pentagon for Navy, and Agency for their people,' replied McCorkell. 'Human Resources records or some such. Citations records maybe.'

'Whatever, it's an inside source, right? It's got to be – that cell number is the only thing connecting the deaths.'

'Could they have hacked the info?'

'Via the Pentagon?' said Hutchinson. 'Doubt it. Far easier to turn someone. Maybe it was innocuous.'

'It's traitorous,' replied McCorkell.

'Maybe not, if sold the right way. Think about it. Some HR lackey with access to addresses of Navy personnel, next of kin and all that . . .'

'The corpsmen attached to the DEVGRU personnel are protected files,' argued McCorkell.

'Then that's just made our job to find the leak a hell of a lot easier.'

They both paused.

'There was no other way,' McCorkell said. 'Someone on the inside gave up details of our men.'

'I know,' replied Hutchinson. 'Jesus.'

'This isn't a reprisal,' said McCorkell. 'It's a clean-up op.'

'Then maybe we should be asking ourselves: what else did they find in that compound that needs to be silenced? I mean, is this just about that cell number?' Hutchinson paused, then added, 'I'm arriving at Langley now. I'll call you straight after with an update.'

'Okay. Don't let them dick you around. They know about Walker, even if they don't want to know about him.'

'Someone dick *me* around? Pfft.'

McCorkell ended the call as he climbed into the back seat of the taxi and said to the driver, 'US embassy.'

•

Walker was in the back of an Alfa Romeo Giulia sedan, his wrists handcuffed in front of him with old-school steel police cuffs. The driver was American, though Walker wasn't sure about the provenance of the two guys in the Chevrolet Tahoe chase car behind. Maybe they were local cops, under secondment, Feds of some sort, similar to those he had met near the internet cafe – but quicker, more agile.

The woman seated next to him had introduced herself as Special Agent Fiona Somerville, FBI. She had Walker's backpack on her lap and had gone through its contents, none of it a worry but for the US passport made out to a fake name.

Walker guessed they were headed for the one place he didn't want to go: the US embassy.

31

'The last place we have you is Yemen, a year ago,' Somerville said.

Walker did not respond.

'It's easier to talk to me,' Somerville said, 'than those you'll meet at the embassy.'

Walker watched the world outside, Rome's morning traffic in full nightmarish flight.

'I need to know where you've been since Yemen,' Somerville pushed. 'What you've been doing. Why you're here in Rome. How it is that we have your DNA found yesterday at a homicide scene. What happened at the safe house. All of it.'

Walker remained silent.

Somerville continued, 'I'm the closest thing you have to a friend left in this world.'

Walker smiled.

'Your old pal Pip Durant spent the night in hospital having a plate put into his face,' Somerville said. 'He'll be black and blue for a month and will be forever setting off metal detectors. Why'd you do that?'

Walker was pleased to hear that Durant got out of the safe house alive, and better yet that he was in serious discomfort. He looked forward to meeting him again some day. He wouldn't be as gentle next time.

'Who busted you from the safe house yesterday?' Somerville asked.

Walker also wanted to know the identities of the guys who crashed the party but he remained silent.

'Walker, I'm trying to do this differently, don't you see?' Somerville said.

As long as he was silent, he had time. But he also needed to convince her to take him some place other than the embassy.

'I saw the footage from the safe house,' Somerville said. 'What the Agency guys did to you in the debrief room. I saw that you were stoic, that you said nothing. Look, I don't do that CIA shit. But your time in my custody may be limited. Understand?'

Walker watched the cars career in and out of non-existent lanes, somehow managing to avoid impact.

'If you give me something to work with, maybe I can help you,' she said. 'Tell me who you're working for, working with. Where you've been all this time. Why you came in from the cold. Tell me what you're doing.'

Walker waited for her to talk herself out. To reveal something, anything that he didn't yet know. Being picked up was a complication he didn't have time for, and going to the embassy was not something he could allow to happen. 4239-185: that's where he had to be. *Gotta get out of here . . .* When the time was right, he'd make a move. He imagined incapacitating the driver and taking Somerville by surprise, using her as a shield against the guys in the chase car.

'Talk to me, Walker. Why don't you start with Yemen.'

In this traffic they were twenty minutes' drive from the embassy.

'Why you?' Walker asked her.

'Why me what?'

'Why are you here, taking me in?' he said. 'Because you're in counter-intel?'

'Maybe. Why, would a counter-intelligence specialist be interested in you?'

'I need to know.'

'Why?'

'I need to know what you know.'

'Funny, I was thinking the same thing.'

'You want me to talk, tell me: what's your interest in me?'

Somerville paused for a beat, said, 'My interest was not in you, but then we had a partial hit on you in Greece. Do you remember being in Greece?'

'Yes.'

'Right. At the time we thought the partial was bullshit – it was a seventy per cent probable match; you were obscured, in profile, in a grainy CCTV pic. Hell, you were dead then. We thought it was a ghost. A false match. Couldn't be you, right? Because you're dead.'

'That's what they tell me.'

'What were you doing in Greece?'

'Looking for a friend.'

'Who?'

'No-one special.'

'Felix?'

Walker did not respond.

'What was your interest in Felix Lassiter?' she persisted.

'What's yours?' he countered.

'Did you kill him in his apartment yesterday?'

'No.'

'Did you kill him?'

'No. Now give me something.'

'Okay,' Somerville said. 'I wasn't tracking him. My surveillance focused on some people he was seen near on a couple occasions. People he was working for.'

'Felix worked for the CIA. He was a courier.'

'That was one employer.'

Walker smiled.

'Tell me what you know about him,' Somerville said.

'You're taking me to the embassy,' Walker said, looking out the window.

'Yes.'

'I wouldn't do that if I were you. Not if you want me to remain alive.'

32

At the US embassy Bill McCorkell was shown to the corner office of the CIA Station Chief, Beverly Johnson.

'Hey, Bev,' McCorkell said, standing in the doorway.

'Bill, come on in,' she said.

'You look as I expected.'

'That good, huh?'

McCorkell nodded.

'Jed Walker. Jesus. This has been such a cluster fuck. Walker's about fifteen minutes out, got a Fed bringing him in. Take a seat.'

McCorkell sat opposite. 'I need to talk to Walker when he comes in.'

'Well, Bill, I would say that you'd have to talk to Special Agent Somerville, as she was lead agent on this because of some dinky piece of FBI paper she's got.'

'*Was* lead agent?'

'She's bringing him in, but she's out of the loop once she gets here.'

'I don't follow.'

'I've got the stronger hand,' Johnson said, flipping her laptop screen around so that he could see. There was a letter, on the letterhead of the Director of National Intelligence, assigning Bev Johnson as the lead on the Walker case. 'Since he was one of us, and he's had a hand in the death of three of our SAD front-line operators at the house, the DNI has been good enough to ensure things stay in-house.'

'There's a little conflict there, don't you think, Bev?'

'Conflict?'

'Looking into one of your own. Especially if he *has* had a hand in the deaths of your three operatives at the safe house.'

'He had a hand in it, all right – Pip Durant confirmed it after he woke up from surgery.'

'So . . .' McCorkell said. 'Do I get any face time with Walker?'

'What for? No, you know what, I don't want to know, not yet.

Just hang around, let me see what we're going to do with him, then I'll talk to you.'

'Hang around?'

'Yeah,' Johnson said, smiling. 'You're in Rome, Bill. Go look at the goddamned Colosseum or something.'

•

Somerville and Walker were locked in a gaze. She was a few years older than he, and wore a dark suit that was clearly European rather than American in make and design. She was short, five-two or five-three, but he knew that she was capable, from the way she had taken him at the station: pressed her knee hard into his back and her snub-nosed .40 cal side-arm into the base of his skull. Quantico built some very fine agents. This was one of them.

Agent Somerville was not to be underestimated during his escape plans.

'I can protect you,' she said, 'but only if you tell me everything. Give them all up. This is the only chance you'll get. If this goes beyond me . . . well, after that safe-house shit, you'll be handed over to someone far less accommodating. They'll consider you a traitor, maybe even an enemy combatant, and you know what they'll do to you. Guantanamo, at best. They'll get you to talk. A federal or military tribunal will determine you're a traitor and murderer of US intel personnel. Then, a lethal injection. So, talk to me. Take the chance.'

Walker shook his head.

'I can help you.'

'I'd like to believe that,' he said. 'But you have no idea what these guys are capable of.'

33

A hundred metres behind Walker's car, Il Bisturi answered a call on his cell phone.

'This photo you sent me . . . the woman with him in the car is a problem,' Bellamy said. 'Walker too. This has changed things. I need you to deal with this. Quickly.'

'Define "deal with".'

'Kill them both. Before they get to the safety of the embassy.'

'Understood.'

Il Bisturi ended the call and accelerated the Ducati, the third gear taking a second to spool up revs from the 1500cc engine but then it bit, hard, and spat him down the road, splitting the lanes between the cars as he eased off a little and reached into the pack strapped onto the gas tank in front of him.

•

Walker weighed his options. He could talk to Somerville, tell her just enough to persuade her to take him somewhere other than the embassy. But what would he give up? He had so little that would make sense to anyone, let alone convince them to put their neck on the block and career on the line. An FBI investigator would want something more solid than a stack of hunches and suspicions.

Something concrete.

To Walker, the culmination of a year in the shadows, working on his own – taking a few odd jobs for associates, old and new, to fund his investigations with untraceable cash – summed up to little more than a bunch of people getting killed. He couldn't just announce that he had inadvertently unravelled an operation that would bring down the CIA . . . not if he wanted to be believed.

'Felix Lassiter's man in Athens; I can give you that,' Walker said. 'The last guy to use his Agency courier service, just a couple of days back.'

Somerville shook her head. 'That's nothing new to me.'

'He's an off-books Agency asset.'

'I know.'

'So far off the books, he's got two sets.'

'And? That all?'

'It's a good lead. Solid. The guy's a money man that the Agency uses as a source while also being one of the largest financiers of a whole bunch of trouble makers. You could look into him and put away several cells of arms traders and war mongers in the mid-east and Africa.'

'Walker, you don't understand,' Somerville said. 'He's old history. And we have him. What was left of him. Did you kill him as well?'

Walker didn't display surprise. *He's dead too?* If there was a pattern emerging from the past few days, it was one of a clean-up. The people involved were being silenced, permanently.

Which told him: *the deadline was more than real.*

This news confirmed his strongest piece of intel so far: a date and time. But he didn't have a location. For that, he needed to keep moving.

'I need to know your involvement in this,' Somerville said. 'Everything you know, everything you've done from Yemen onwards. Give up who you're working for and with, and maybe we can make a deal.'

'First up, there's no grand conspiracy on my part,' Walker said, looking out the side window. 'I'm working solo.'

Somerville nodded, but Walker could see that she wasn't buying.

'I was the start of something that's now coming to a head. Something that's happening very soon.'

'How do you know?'

'The body count is tallying up fast, and in public view. That's worrying, I would think, to someone in your profession.'

'I investigate crimes. Do you want to confess any?'

'Yeah, well, I'm investigating a crime too.'

'So, what, you're some kind of cop now?'

Walker remained silent.

Somerville said, 'What crime are you investigating?'

'Murder.'

'Who was murdered?'

'Me. Bob Hanley. A DGSE agent named Louis Assif.'

'Your op in Yemen.'

Walker nodded. He could see that it got to Somerville a little.

'You need to tell me what happened there,' she said.

'I can't.'

'Because you're a part of some Agency conspiracy to undermine our government's interests in the war against terrorism?'

'What? No.' Walker paused for the slightest moment, filing that away. *Maybe she knows . . .*

'The time to confess is now, make no mistake,' Somerville said, starting to grow impatient. 'It'll only get harder when we get to the embassy, because there's all manner of agencies and departments who will be lining up to have a crack at you.'

'Talking would go against some Agency papers I signed when I joined up.'

'You'll be protected.'

'You keep saying that.'

'I mean it.'

'What, I'll be another Bradley Manning or Edward Snowden? That's hardly a comforting offer.'

'I protect people who deserve it, so you'll have to prove to me that *you* do – because right now I've a mind to turn you over to the masses and give someone else the headache.'

'You really think you can protect me?'

'It depends what you've got that's worth protecting.'

'Why don't we pull over somewhere up here and talk?'

'Give me a reason to.'

'Or at least just drive around awhile.'

'So you can work out a way to escape?'

Walker was silent.

'That's not it, is it?' She looked at him hard for a few long seconds. 'Why don't you want to go to the embassy?'

'I learned long ago that a dead man doesn't have many rights,' Walker replied. 'Give me that: give me an hour some place, and I'll tell you what I know.'

Somerville looked down at the bag on her lap, and Walker could see that she was considering his offer.

'Fifty-six hours,' said Walker.

'What?'

Walker spoke clearly and firmly. 'We've got fifty-six hours to stop an attack.'

'What attack?'

'A terrorist attack.'

'By you?'

'No.'

'Who?'

'Don't take me to the embassy,' Walker said. 'And I'll answer your questions as best as I can. That's all I can offer.'

Somerville nodded. 'Okay.'

THUD.

Walker glanced out his side window. A Ducati rider in black leathers had just bumped against their car. There was plenty of room; it didn't need to happen. He saw in the reflection of a shop window as they passed that their vehicle had a new addition – a dark object, about the size of a small shoebox, was attached to his door. It stayed there due to magnets, Walker knew. He had seen similar charges used in Iran. He had trained agents how to make them, and how to use them.

'Stop the car! Get out!' Walker shouted. 'Bomb!'

34

Andrew Hutchinson had been to Langley plenty of times, and it never failed to impress him with just how normal the spook-land seemed, just across the Potomac River from DC. When he'd first come here as a fresh-faced Bureau agent, he'd expected to see all sorts of secretive behaviour on display. He soon learned that the operations staff were segregated from those accessed by visitors. But that had changed some time ago, and now it was all very . . . governmental. Just a big ol' office building, not unlike the Hoover building in that regard, where people turned up, did their job on paper and computers, and then went home to their families.

As a visitor he filled out the required paperwork and his vehicle was thoroughly examined. He was fingerprinted, his retina was scanned and his photograph was taken, all of them cross-checked to his previous visits. He stated an oral oath and agreed to wear a high-visibility ID badge at all times. Only then was he permitted inside the building.

The staff was young – more than half of the current Agency personnel had started after a hiring freeze that was unfrozen after 9/11. Waiting for his contact in the lobby made Hutchinson feel like a dinosaur.

'Andrew Hutchinson?' said the guy who approached him.

'Yes.'

'Joe Baer.' They shook hands. Baer had the look of a middle-aged guy who'd recently had lap-band to lose a lot of weight due to doctor's orders, and hadn't changed the style of his mop of grey hair since the early eighties. 'Come with me.'

Hutchinson followed.

Baer said, 'You've been here before?'

'Bunch of times,' Hutchinson said. 'I worked counter-intel with the Bureau for a long while.'

'Ah, one of them,' Baer said, his tone good-humoured. 'Don't get me wrong, counter-espionage is an incredibly serious threat to national security,' he continued as he led Hutchinson up a set of stairs. 'I just always thought we'd be better at the role.'

'Yeah, you're probably right.' Hutchinson had heard that argument many times before, and the intel community would forever be in-fighting to see who got what share of the budgetary pie. The role of CIA field operatives was to acquire intelligence, or as they described their job, 'manipulating people for information'. Deception was the key, everything was off the record, and agents worked undercover using encrypted phones and false identities. The Cover Operations division provided cover for operatives by creating and supporting the illusion of false identities. Hutchinson's role in the FBI had been to bust such operatives, albeit foreign nationals working in the US. Jed Walker was among the few Hutchinson had encountered who were possibly domestic-turned-foreign. A traitor. The worst of the worst.

'Here's me,' Baer said, showing Hutchinson into a tiny office with no windows. 'Take a seat.'

Hutchinson removed a pile of papers from the spare chair and put them on the floor, for the desk was full. 'I see you haven't heard of the notion of a paperless office.'

'Old habits,' Baer replied, leaning back in his chair and cracking his neck with a quick side-to-side movement, some kind of habitual settling action. 'So, what's what?'

'I need to know about a former intel officer,' Hutchinson said. 'Everything you've got.'

'Officer got a name?'

'Jed Walker.'

'Wow,' Baer replied, genuinely surprised. 'Up until twelve hours ago, that's a name I hadn't heard for near on a year. Now I'm hearing it all over the place. How long have you got?'

•

In the Alfa Romeo time stood still for a moment as Walker shouted again, 'Out!'

Somerville's eyes went wide at the same time as Hobbs stomped the brakes, the ABS ratcheting away. Walker pushed Somerville out her door as the car was slowing to a stop. They hit the road and rolled with the momentum until Walker had enough purchase to stop them both.

KLAPBOOM!

Walker heard bells ringing after the blast. He felt a wave of heat wash over him, and he closed his eyes against debris and was suddenly back at high school. The ringing in his ears reminded him of the pealing of the bell, of autumn leaves crunching underfoot, of ending lunch breaks and trudging back to class; of long, hot summers filled with laughs and shenanigans only a kid could get away with; of wet nights training with the football team – a carefree time, some of the sweetest memories of his life, the go-to moments he escaped to when in times of extreme duress, like his SERE training back at Fairchild AFB, Washington. The gruelling weeks at Bragg. The time in the field. His time as a dead man, on the outer, looking for a way back in, for reasons why . . .

BRRRR!

Walker snapped out of his daze.

Daylight. Rome. The car bomb.

He was on his back on the road.

Somerville had rolled clear.

He looked across, at the direction of oncoming traffic—

BRRRR!

The incessant, deafening noise of a truck's compression brakes locked on full. A semi, closing, jackknifing its trailer as the driver reacted to avoid running over the two figures on the road and smashing into the flaming wreckage of the Alfa twenty metres beyond.

Too little, too late.

Twenty tonnes of steel and glass and rubber and cargo were headed Walker's way and little short of a main battle tank could halt it in time.

Walker spread out flat against the road, his arm brushing against Somerville's.

She was next to him, semi-conscious, her forehead grazed but her eyes blinking, watching him. Her mouth formed around words but no sound emanated, or maybe it did and Walker couldn't hear it over the brakes and the eighteen wheels locked in a slide against the bitumen.

Walker's grip clamped around Somerville's forearm and he pulled her to him and flat to the ground.

The truck passed over them, Walker and Somerville pressed together in the void between the cab and the trailer, wheels either side. The sixteen-litre diesel engine roared overhead, its exhaust gas being compressed and used to brake the wheels.

Walker was momentarily deaf but that did not stop him moving. As soon as it coasted over them, he looked up. In the wake of the truck, traffic was inbound – slowing but still incoming, oblivious to the true scene of destruction ahead that had been shielded from view by the massive vehicle.

He kept Somerville close to him, wrapped his arms around her and rolled them to the kerb.

Walker sat up, clutching at his side, where he was sure the stitches had pulled apart, ignoring his grazed hands and knees and elbows from the roll across the bitumen.

Somerville's eyes were unsteady as he propped her up against a parked car.

The SUV chase car had pulled up ahead of the inferno, and both agents were out with hand-held extinguishers, dousing the flaming chassis with foam.

Walker could see a vague human form blended into the driver's seat. Hobbs hadn't made it out.

'Walker . . .' Somerville said.

'I have to go,' he replied, picking up his backpack from the street and shouldering it. He bent down to look at her. 'You'll be fine.'

He could see through the car's windows that one of the officers was headed over, taking a route around the fire.

Walker fished in Somerville's pockets and pulled out the handcuff keys, and freed himself. She grabbed hold of his hand, her grip surprisingly strong, but it faded quickly. A crowd was gathering. Walker melted into it, moved towards the back and then ran from the scene.

•

'So, now you know as much as I do about Walker,' Baer said. 'Anything above that, you'll need to speak to the Deputy Director of NCS.'

'Jack Heller,' Hutchinson said, making a note of it.

'Yep.'

'And you were Walker's direct superior up until the moment he left?'

'Yes. I head up the Political Action Group within the Special

Activities Division, and Walker worked for me for most of his time here. Before that, he was a Targeting Officer supporting the SAD recruiting APs. But he was too good for them, so I poached him.'

'Why'd he leave?'

'Personal reasons is what he said. The wife, I think. He'd just come off an op that didn't work out, but it had nothing to do with his competence – and even if it did, the guy's Teflon. He could have been sitting in this chair by now, what with his record, and his pedigree.'

'He doesn't seem to me the office type.'

'You're right there.'

'What do you think happened at the safe house in Rome?'

'Internal cameras were down, and there were no witnesses of interaction between Walker and the assaulting party,' Baer said. 'Preliminary ballistics point to two of the assailants being taken down by Walker with the landlord's Beretta. So I'd say there's another group hunting him.'

'Walker did attack Durant.'

'SOB probably had it coming,' Baer said. 'But he's not my territory, never has been and never will be, so don't ask me about him.'

'Not a fan of Durant?'

Baer was silent.

Hutchinson nodded as he looked over his notes. 'There's nothing that ever pointed to Walker as being suspect?'

Baer shook his head. 'I'd trust him with my life. If you think he's up to something, it ain't sinister; he's no threat to the US. You know his old man's a legend around here?'

'Yeah.'

'I think that was another reason he left. His father's shadow cast a long way. When Walker left, his father was stormin' around here, wanting an explanation. His old man was pissed – saw our Walker as the future of this place. His mother's pretty much lost it, but then, she lost it a while before that.'

'What do you mean?'

'Dementia. At least a decade. It was a real sticking point about her care, and Walker senior never could walk away from his work. The old fool had a heart attack during a sixteen-hour shift in the White

House. Dropped dead in the stairwell heading up from the Sit Room. Not the way for a guy like that to go.'

Hutchinson noted that down, then asked, 'What happened in Yemen with the blue-on-blue hit?'

'Like I told you, Walker ran into the kill box with our Agency guy. Best I can tell, it was to retrieve intel. It became a blue-on-blue incident, with the operators hitting the target again, unaware that we had a couple of our own in there. Maybe State knows more than me, but I doubt it.'

'No, they don't. They pointed me here.'

'Yeah, well, Walker's been a ghost for a while now.' Baer leaned back. 'He served in the Air Force before us. Try them.'

'Yeah, I checked, but I couldn't get much of a file.'

'It's there, if you know where to look.'

'Where?'

'Pope would be my bet.'

Hutchinson knew that Pope meant Fort Bragg. And that meant Special Forces, home to Delta. But Baer said Pope: the Air Force contingent. That meant Air Force Special Ops. *Which meant . . .*

'The twenty-fourth?'

Baer smiled. 'Look,' he said, 'until yesterday we had him listed as KIA – and that was while he was on State's dime. And from what I'm hearing from you, if he's not dead yet, he soon will be – and that's a damn shame.'

'There's *nothing* he worked on that made you suspicious?'

Baer smiled again. 'We're done here. Whatever Walker's got himself into, it's no business of ours.'

'You're sure?'

Baer didn't answer.

There was a rap of knuckles on the door. Hutchinson turned to see a tall man, wearing an expensive suit and polished shoes.

'Speak of the devil,' Baer said.

'Are you the guy asking about Walker?' the guy in the doorway said.

Hutchinson nodded.

'Come with me.'

35

The tall man in the expensive suit was Jack Heller, Director of Clandestine Services, reporting to the Deputy Director of National Intelligence, and his boss answered directly to the President.

Hutchinson sat opposite him in a plush top-floor office. There was a quote from General William T. Sherman on the wall: '*War is cruelty. There is no use trying to reform it. The crueler it is, the sooner it will be over.*'

'You know my role?'

'Yeah,' Hutchinson said. 'You're kind of like Deputy God for all human intel. The spymaster.'

Heller chuckled.

Hutchinson was at the top of the tree in the CIA. He knew that as DCS Heller oversaw a smaller offshoot of the Special Activities Division, responsible for covert operations known as 'special activities', and Walker's former employer.

'When Walker handed in his resignation, he cited family reasons,' Heller said, 'so I offered him a role I thought he couldn't turn down: heading up the Domestic Protection Division.'

'It was a slap in the face when he knocked you back?'

'No – the DNI wanted me to offer Walker the job. I knew he'd never go for it. Walker's not a desk man. And certainly not one to be caged here at home. He's an animal – a wild animal. Hell, he can barely be tamed, let alone caged.'

'So, he left the Agency and went to State. Then you guys led the drone strike that listed him as KIA.'

'He should never have been there. I didn't feel bad about that for a second, except that he got one of our front-line guys killed. But who knows – maybe he's still alive too. Hell, we get people all over the place saying that bin Laden's still out there. And don't get me started on Elvis or Kennedy.'

Hutchinson didn't buy the easier banter but went along nonetheless to get what information he could.

'You were surprised by Walker's reappearance?'

'Yes,' Heller said. 'Completely.'

'What do you think Walker's been doing all this time?'

'No idea. He was a Specialised Skills Officer, and as such he knew that if he was compromised during a mission, our government would deny all knowledge. He's used to going solo. He could be up to all kinds of mischief.'

Hutchinson nodded. 'So, no-one ever went to Yemen to check the bodies?'

'No.'

'Why?'

Heller didn't reply. Instead, he said, 'We do not negotiate with terrorists, we put them out of business. That's what was done that day. Walker fucked up and got himself killed. Or not, evidently.'

Hutchinson tried a different tack, asked, 'Who did you get in that house in Yemen?'

'I can't say.' Heller leaned back. 'I looked into you.'

'Oh?'

'You were involved in a high-profile case involving an Agency double in New York City a few years back – the Patriot Act thing.'

Hutchinson knew that was classified but accessible to someone of Heller's clearance.

'Then you went off the radar, but you're still in the FBI. So, either you've turned family man and are driving a desk, or you've been tasked some place else.'

'I'm at the UN.'

'Those guys? Damn. I could use a guy like you. That said, the best people are all leaving these days. Going private, mostly. You thought about that?'

'The private sector?'

Heller nodded.

'Maybe. Not really,' Hutchinson said, flicking back through the pages of notes he'd made while talking to Baer. 'What about Pip Durant?'

Heller shifted in his seat, said, 'What about him?'

'He trained with Walker, then they worked together in Afghanistan and Iraq for a few years. They were tight. Durant was the one who broke the news to Walker's wife, Eve. If anyone had heard anything about Walker being alive, it'd be him. And he's the one who went to debrief Walker at the safe house in Rome.'

'So?'

'So,' Hutchinson said, 'he's just returned home for a couple of weeks' R-and-R following injuries sustained during the hit on the house.'

Heller eyed Hutchinson slowly. 'No,' he eventually said.

'No what?'

'No, you can't contact him.'

'A few questions about what was said in the safe house—'

'Leave Durant be. And that's not a request.'

Hutchinson thought Heller looked uneasy but hid it well behind aggression.

'What if they're still tight, him and Walker?' Hutchinson said. 'What if they're working together on something here, something well off reservation?'

'That's not happening. This isn't Hollywood.'

Hutchinson nodded.

'Something else?' Heller said.

'I've been hearing some rumours,' replied Hutchinson.

Heller laughed without humour. 'Rumours? In Washington? No way . . .'

'I'm serious. Some serious rumours. Dangerous.'

'Rumours *are* dangerous.'

'Especially this one,' Hutchinson said, eyeballing Heller long enough to ensure he had the man's complete attention. 'It's about the compound at Abbottabad, and the cell-phone numbers found on bin Laden.'

Heller was silent.

•

Walker hitched a truck ride to Frosinone, then within ten minutes was sitting in a van to Naples. The trip took around three hours, which was not much longer than he had planned by train. He walked small alleys and streets through the city, stopping to buy coffee and bottled water, which he drank on his way down to the edge of the Port of Naples. Out on the water, cargo ships, fishing boats and pleasure craft competed for space, colourful and chaotic, an explosion of noise and movement. Walker headed around the port, to the south-east, between the water and the rail tracks, looking for the guy he doubted had changed location since he had last seen him six months ago, out of desperation for funds and for new ID papers.

A criminal, and a useful one at that.

Leo Andretti liked to be considered a businessman. Well, he *was* all about commerce, and Walker had heard rumours about Andretti owning a legitimate cargo freighter that did a Sicily run.

Walker spotted Andretti by the water's edge. He watched the Neapolitan carefully and he walked slowly, deliberately bringing himself into Andretti's line of sight.

Andretti did a barely disguised double-take before letting out a low whistle. 'Walker,' he said, not pleasantly. 'A walking ghost.'

Walker gave him a smile, outstretched his hand. It was left hanging.

Andretti said, 'You have nerve showing up here like this.'

'How's that?' Walker said.

'You ran out on me.'

'No, I did what I promised,' Walker replied.

Andretti looked around, sucked his teeth. 'You still owe me.'

'How's that?' Walker said again.

'Tunisia.'

'I repaid that debt.'

'No. That was a blood debt.'

'So, I have to bleed for you?'

'Yes, that would do it.'

Walker gritted his teeth. 'Andretti, I need to get to Croatia. Get me there, and it'll be two I owe you. I'm good for it.'

'So, what? I look like a travel service?'

'I know you have a boat going across the Adriatic out of Bari every night.'

'Lots of boats do that trip.'

'Not like yours. I'll pay you, once I'm on the other side.'

'I don't need your money.'

'Just my blood?'

'A deal's a deal.'

'Evidently,' Walker said, looking around, the surrounding landscape mostly concrete and blinding in the day's full sun. 'I need to be on a boat tonight.'

'That's not going to happen.'

Walker breathed deeply. 'Andretti, you're a smart businessman. Make me a deal.'

'So you can run off on it again?'

'No. Give me something, whatever job you need done: I'll do it, but I get on the boat tonight.'

'Fine. Do a Tunisia run.'

'When?'

'Tomorrow.'

'No can do.'

'Then we have no deal.'

Walker moved a few paces away, looking around at the boats. This place was teeming with smugglers, going back and forth all over the Med. Andretti's Croatia run was a squid boat; Walker had done it a few times, though the real cargo being run between Croatia was vast quantities of stolen goods courtesy of local mafia. All manner of stuff came back on the return voyage: drugs, prostitutes, illegal immigrants. Whatever needed to be transported, Andretti had a boat and cover to do it.

'You must be desperate,' Andretti said, lighting up a cigarette.

'I am.'

'Trouble with the law?'

'Something like that.'

'You always were mysterious . . .'

'No more than you.'

'Tell you what,' Andretti said, blowing smoke at Walker. 'I've got an old debt that needs collecting. You do that for me, you get your boat ride tonight.'

'Where?'

'In town.'

'How old's the debt?'

'Just a couple of days.'

'It's not like you to let money slide. Why haven't you got someone else doing it?'

'I would have, but the local boys I use have been busy.'

'My lucky day.'

'If you say so.'

'How long will it take?'

'A guy like you: an hour.'

'If I do this, you get me onto your fastest boat out of Bari.'

'Deal.'

Fifty-three hours to deadline.

•

'CIA was a whole load of BS,' Hutchinson said into his cell phone.

'You expected something different from those guys?' McCorkell replied.

'I guess not. Jack Heller's a jerk.'

'So I've heard.'

'Gave me the runaround, told me zip about Walker, said to leave Durant be.'

'Durant?'

'Walker's CIA buddy, and a surviving witness to what was said at the safe house. Other than that, he was talking about going private.'

'Heller?'

'Yep.'

'No great loss to national security. Hell, you should have told him to go work for Bellamy.'

'Yeah. They'd fit well together,' Hutchinson replied, and then spent the next five minutes while he was driving out of Virginia updating his boss on all he'd learned about Walker from the Agency.

'So, you're no clearer about Walker's motives?' McCorkell asked.

'Nope. My read was that Baer was full of praise for the guy, while Heller was full of envy. Neither seemed aware that he was alive until the last twenty-four hours. And Heller seems content to let the FBI handle bringing him home.'

'Yeah, well, it's not going to be that easy,' McCorkell said, then explained the bomb blast that disabled Somerville's car and killed a DSS agent.

'So, Walker's gone, again?'

'Yep,' asked McCorkell. 'I'm gonna go now and see Somerville, see if she wants to do a Marvel team-up. What's next for you?'

'Walker's wife,' replied Hutchinson. 'Maybe she knows she hasn't been a widow this whole time.'

•

Walker looked at the strip of shops in front of him. The street was like so many in this part of town, adjoining stone buildings with tiled roofs that could have belonged anywhere around the Med. He was in a northern district called Secondigliano, an old farming town that was swallowed by the city and evolved into one of Europe's largest open-air drug markets and a working-class stronghold for their mafia, the Camorra.

This street was full of tiny no-name bars that catered only to those who knew the owners, where cards were played and money was made and lost by everyone from simple fishermen to those who plied their trade in Naples' seedier side of life. Between some of the bars were workshops, the fronts of which sold handbags and sunglasses; for those brave enough to go inside, the better counterfeit stuff was for sale; and for those willing to pay a premium, the really good stuff would be delivered on the back of a motorbike.

Scooters and motorbikes were lined along the footpath, the road just wide enough to navigate through. The place was packed with young guys, gangly and with greasy hair and dirty looks, in T-shirts, jeans and leather jackets. For those working this street and so many others like it, crime was a generational thing, in their blood, all they knew. Most of the kids would be armed, Walker knew. None of the bikes and scooters had legible licence plates. Italy 2.0.

Walker moved as he always did in such places: like a guy who belonged, and was not to be messed with, at least not by the lower-tier kids. He passed over a patch of dried blood on the road, a day old. Maybe the result of a collision, but more likely a stabbing or shooting over some bullshit turf quarrel. The police wouldn't bother to identify the assailants, but the Camorra would. Street justice would be done. Perhaps it already had been. In Naples murder was a language that all understood, while silence under questioning was a birthright; police and the judicial system had little sway here.

Walker found number 42 and entered, no hesitation. The inside of the shop smelled of old cigarettes, bad cologne, stale coffee and cheap red wine. The space was filled by four small tables, and along the side walls sat bench seats that had probably been church pews once. The front of the store was glazed but most of the clear glass had been painted over with white paint. At the back was a closed door.

Four guys sat around one of the tables, playing cards. Walker pulled a chair up to the table and spun it around, straddling it, his forearms resting on the table.

All four guys stopped playing and looked at him like he had just dumped a turd right in the middle of their card game.

They were maybe five years older than Walker. Guys who had risen from doing street work to running their own small gangs. Mid-level management in the extortion, protection, narcotics and counterfeit-goods trade.

'Hey, what's up?' Walker said. They seemed surprised that he was American. 'I'm looking for someone.'

'You have the wrong place,' the guy to his left said. 'Leave.'

Walker stared him down.

'Who would you be looking for?' the guy to his right said. Walker pegged him as his man, and he was surely the leader here, what with the pile of cash in front of him; these other guys would be letting him win. He was around forty, balding, yet his arms and the back of his hands were as hairy as any primate Walker had ever seen.

'You, evidently,' Walker said. 'Dom Fontana.'

The guy opposite Walker pulled a pistol and clunked it down on the table. An old .22 that looked like it had never been cleaned. Walker could probably have leaned across and reached it before the other guy knew what was happening, but he felt safer without it.

Dom Fontana said, 'What the fuck you want, Americaaan?'

'I'm here on behalf of Signor Andretti,' Walker said. 'Collecting.'

There was dead silence around the table. Blank stares.

Walker said, 'Look, Dom . . . Can I call you Dom? We're all grown-ups here. We've all been around. We all know how this works. Let's just be quick about it, yeah?'

Fontana smiled, stood, left the table and retrieved a black rucksack from behind a makeshift bar.

'This is what Andretti wants,' he said, dumping the bag in the middle of the table and sitting back down. 'But I must tell you, unless he comes here to this table and negotiates a better deal for the future, *my* future, he's never going to get it.'

Blank stares continued around the table.

Walker knew that these four hadn't been in a serious fight for probably ten years. They had others to do it for them, and even before that they were always part of a brotherhood, and that offered a degree of protection against the kind of street fights that are anything more than a little warning shot from a rival group. A bit of a slap around here and there, maybe occasionally shooting a blindfolded and tied-down guy in the back of the head to show their boys that they still had it, but that was the extent of the last decade of hands-on involvement for the guys around this table. It had been a long time, if ever, since any of these muppets had partaken of a do-or-die tussle. Too bad.

The gun was unfortunate, though. The .22 round, while tiny in stopping power, did have good penetration, even when fired from a pistol. So, using the body of one of the guys either side of him as a shield was not a great option.

'I'm not leaving without that bag,' Walker said, his voice even and calm. 'And I'm on the clock.'

'Then we have a problem,' Fontana replied.

'I've got about ninety-nine problems,' Walker said, 'but you ain't one of them.'

The guy to Walker's left drew a thin stabbing blade. While he was quicker than Walker expected, he was an amateur through and through. In one motion Walker stood, reached left and wrapped his arm around the neck of the knife man, leaning back and twisting, feeling and hearing the vertebrae snap loose and the weight of the head heft forwards.

The body was still falling when Walker moved to the next guy.

Fontana was up from the table and took a step back, while the gunman reached forwards and brought up the pistol in a two-handed aim.

Walker kicked the table up at him and charged; the guy's arms and hands and pistol were forced straight up towards the ceiling and a round pinged off with the pathetic PANG! of the tiny calibre. Walker grabbed the guy's right wrist, the index finger still in the trigger guard, and pulled it down as the guy to his left charged. Another shot rang out, this time into the rushing guy, boring a hole clean through his shoulder and sending him howling around the room.

Walker buried an elbow into the gunman's face and sidestepped, twisting his body and getting a good, solid stance. Still holding onto the pistol hand, Walker picked him up and flipped him flat onto the ground, where his head cracked onto the hard tiled surface. Walker picked up the pistol and field stripped it to pieces with little more than a clap of his hands.

'This,' Walker said to Fontana, picking up the rucksack, 'is what I'm taking. You want to try to stop me, there will be no more gambling days in your future.'

Fontana nodded.

Walker slung the rucksack over his shoulder and left the shop, wary as he walked up the street and rounded the corner, where he paid a kid on an old Honda 250cc to give him a lift to the docks.

Walker checked his watch as they wound through the traffic.

Fifty-two hours to deadline.

•

'Tell me what's happening in two days,' Senator Anderson said.

Bellamy leaned back in his office, his hand tight on the phone.

'You've never wanted to know before,' Bellamy replied. 'All these years, you've never wanted details of an operation.'

'Well, I've got – *we've* got – too much riding on this one.'

'I need you to trust me.'

Anderson paused, his breathing steady but deliberate on the other end of the line.

'I'm not going to tell you,' Bellamy said carefully. 'For all kinds of reasons.'

'In person then.'

'No. You do what you do, I do what I do, and never the twain shall meet.'

'But the President will never—'

Bellamy interrupted, said, 'I know, so forget the President for now. The Vice President will get the NSC to budge, if you're patient.'

'There's no more time for patience,' Anderson replied.

'When I see the VP in New York, he'll learn a new urgency.'

'Urgency or not, one man is not going to change the administration's view on letting INTFOR off the leash. The Snowden fiasco, Walker's father – they've been too spooked to outsource more of the intel world, even to us.'

'Off the leash?' Bellamy said. 'I prefer to think that we are achieving our aims and being rewarded accordingly. And besides, I think you'll be surprised by what one man can do . . .'

36

'You'll be fine,' the embassy doctor said. 'Take it easy for the rest of the day. Or at least try to avoid jumping from a moving vehicle and close proximity to bomb blasts.'

'Thanks, Doc,' Fiona Somerville replied, a small piece of gauze plastered to the graze on her forehead and the heel of her right hand. 'I'll do my best.'

'Knock, knock,' Bill McCorkell said, standing in the open doorway after the doctor departed.

'Yeah?' Somerville said, sitting up from the bed and slipping her feet into her shoes.

'Bill McCorkell,' he said. 'Do you mind if I come in?'

'McCorkell?' Somerville did a double-take. 'You were NSA to the President,' she said, not hiding her surprise to see him standing before her.

'Three presidents, though one of them rarely heeded my advice.'

Somerville stood and shook his hand a little gingerly because of her wound. 'That's pretty much my dream job,' she said.

'It made me grey. Then balding. Then a heart thing.'

'So, be careful what you wish for?'

'Nah. I like me a grey, balding woman with a weak heart.'

Somerville smiled. 'You're here for . . .'

'Walker.'

'Oh?'

'How about I buy you a cup of coffee,' McCorkell said, 'and we compare notes?'

•

Walker found Andretti in what passed as his office: the back of a Fiat van. From the outside the faded blue paint gave the impression of just another delivery vehicle used around the docks for small jobs. Inside, the rear was carpeted and housed a reclining chair, a small table and plenty of paperwork.

'Quite the paper trail for a crook,' Walker said, dumping the rucksack on the floor. He leaned half in and half out of the van, not wanting to get comfy, not wanting to linger. 'I'm ready for my ride to Bari, and then the boat.'

'A *crook*, you say . . .' Andretti said, checking the contents of the bag and seeming pleased. 'I'll let you get away with that one. Besides, I hate computers, and with the amount of gear I handle across this little sea, if I don't have things written down I wouldn't know if I were being ripped off by my contacts or not.'

'Well, I gotta say, your friend Dom isn't pleased about your current arrangement with him; he told me that much.'

Andretti shrugged dismissively. 'Okay, Croatia it is. But, there's one more thing.'

'What's that?'

Andretti gestured to his cell phone, which showed a photograph of the knife guy whose neck Walker had snapped. 'Did you have to kill him?'

'He pulled a knife, so it was him or me.'

Andretti looked at the image like he was weighing up that thought. 'I knew his family,' he said, then sighed. 'They will ask for a price. I will pay it. It is how things work around here. And you know what that means for you?'

'I won't be getting my Christmas bonus this year?'

'It means you will owe me. Again.'

'And let me guess,' Walker said, 'you don't take cash?'

Andretti smiled. 'I like you, Jed Walker, you are a good man; a man who understands the way things must be.'

'See you around, Andretti.'

'Ciao. Until next time.'

Walker was sure that there would be no next time.

•

'I've been conducting a long-term investigation into a private intel outfit,' McCorkell said, stirring his double espresso at the cafe across the road from the embassy.

'Oh?' Somerville said, looking around the outdoor cafe and then back to McCorkell. 'For the UN?'

'Yep.'

'Ah, the burgeoning intelligence industrial complex. Which outfit? Academi?'

'Nope.'

'Total Intel?'

'Closer.'

'Booz Allen?'

'Hell, no.'

'Stratfor?'

'No.'

'I give up.'

'INTFOR.'

'Ah, the new kid on the block.'

McCorkell nodded, watching on as Somerville sipped her macchiato. He said, 'What do you know about Dan Bellamy?'

●

Jack Heller said, 'But there's nothing to deliver.'

'I know,' replied Dan Bellamy.

'The courier's information was lost when they blew up the van.'

'Yes.'

'And his contact was killed in Athens, after the courier was spooked that he was being watched.'

'Yes.'

'So, it's lost.'

'Lost.'

'And better lost than in the wrong hands, so I don't see a problem.'

Bellamy said, 'That's right. But this is no longer about a delivery, or having the information out there.'

'What *is* it about?'

'Someone getting too close,' Bellamy said.

'Jed Walker?'

'Yes. And those surveilling in Greece – the FBI, we think.'

'Well, I had a guy here today, asking after Walker.'

'Who?'

'Some FBI nobody. I'll handle it. Leave it to me.'

'Like you had Walker handled in Yemen?'

Heller was silent. He thought about responding, thought about the fact that it was *his* name that would add credence to Bellamy's aims for INTFOR to take over the bulk of the hands-on intel role currently being played by the CIA. But he let it be. That was a fight for another day. Being a business partner was never going to be all his way. At least, not at first.

'There's still a link left in the chain,' Bellamy said. 'Lassiter's next stop: the money man in Hong Kong. Well, money woman. She's still expecting a courier to show up.'

Heller sighed impatiently. 'We never should have put the money down like that.'

'But we did. We had to buy back our client list.'

'And so, what? She doesn't get the info delivered tomorrow. The chain's broken, link left or not. We've got bigger issues right now.'

Bellamy said, 'My worry is, when we're this close, if this woman doesn't get what she needs? She starts looking. Talking. Digging. And who knows what she might find.'

'I'd be more worried about Walker finding her.'

Bellamy was silent. Heller could almost hear the gears turning in his mind, playing catch-up.

Heller said, 'Walker *will* go there. I know the guy.'

'We need to break this final link,' Bellamy said, 'and get Walker in the process.'

'This one's a public figure, in Hong Kong.'

'I'm sure your office is adept at that sort of thing. If you can kill political leaders, you can kill a high-profile business woman, in Hong Kong or wherever.' Bellamy paused, then said, 'And, Jack, remember, we're just two days from the rest of our lives. We're on the home stretch.'

'Fine. I'll sort it out. You do what you gotta do.'

'And Walker?'

'Leave him to me.'

37

Dubrovnik

'You lousy old drunk.'

The guy turned and made eye contact with Walker. After a few seconds of silence he broke into a smile, stood and hugged him like a son.

'Jesus, have you spent your whole pension on food over here?' Walker said. 'You've put on, what, four hundred pounds? You look like Templeton the rat, after the fair and Christmas lunch.'

'And I've enjoyed every bite. Croatia's my smorgasbord.'

Walker laughed. He'd known Bloom in his prime, when Walker was just a boy and Bloom had worked for his father. He'd always been all-American football solid, but his appearance now was one of a hopeless gourmand.

'You look tired,' Marty Bloom said. He pulled out a chair for his old friend and protégé. 'Long flight?'

'Long life,' Walker replied. They sat in a little bar in Dubrovnik, surrounded by tenth-generation local drinkers.

'When I saw your message on the Intellipedia boards, I freaked,' Bloom said. '*Omega Down*? You know that's only a life-and-death message for help.'

'I think you'll find reports of my death were grossly overstated.'

'Well,' Bloom said, leaning back, resting his hands on his huge girth. 'Yet here you are.'

'Here I am: 4239-185. Latitude and longitude for this fair city, the location of my saviour.'

Bloom's demeanour changed, from smiling to serious. 'What's up?'

'I need help getting into Hong Kong.'

'Ah, it figures. You're still on your one-man mission. What do you need?'

'A Gulfstream G5 would do, landing at a private airport with no customs.'

Bloom smiled. 'Nice. And in the real world?'

'I need papers. Cash. Travel docs. Made out in the name of a CIA courier.' Walker handed over a piece of paper with 'Felix Lassiter' written on it. 'I can't get by on my own handiwork. And I'll need another set to get into the US – bulletproof ID. I can't be held up and made.'

'The full works, hey?'

Walker nodded.

Bloom nodded. 'When do you need all this?'

'Yesterday.'

Bloom hesitated a moment, then said, 'Damn, okay, give me a minute.' He finished his beer and left the bar.

Walker watched through the tiny windows as Bloom walked up the street, perhaps to find privacy to place a call, or to speak quietly to someone in the flesh. Probably the latter, for this town, and most of new Europe, was the kind of place where you could get things. Dubrovnik was like any big international city in that regard, only on an intimate scale. It had centuries of smugglers and entrepreneurial types passing through. *No wonder Bloom loves the place.*

The barman brought water, and Walker ordered a beer. His car and boat rides to get here had been uneventful, an otherwise nice way to lose an afternoon. A good way to decompress from the last day of mayhem. He resolved he would never show his face in Naples again. Within the week he would be back in the States; all going well, that's where he would stay. He had been a ghost for too long.

Walker was going home.

Forty-three hours to deadline.

•

Bloom returned by the time Walker finished his first beer.

'I've got a guy working on your docs through the night,' Bloom said. 'It'll be ready by morning. They'll tape the parcel under this table by opening time. The cash you can take from me; add it to the tab.'

'Thanks, Marty. You know I'm good for it.'

'Hey, I'm kidding, I hardly earned it. And someone else is doing the all-night work.'

'False modesty to the last.'

Bloom looked sideways at Walker. 'Don't think I don't know how badly you want to watch while these docs are made, to try and speed things along, to pick up the papers the second they're ready and then run.'

'Pretty much.'

'But this is as quick as things will move, if you want them as good as they need to be,' Bloom said. 'In the meantime, you can stay on my couch. We'll book you on a flight to Hong Kong, and I'll get you to the airport first thing.'

'Sounds like a plan.' Walker leaned back. 'So . . . seems we have a few hours to catch up.'

'Seems we do.'

Bloom ordered a bottle of Scotch. 'Johnnie Black do?'

'Good enough for Churchill and Hitchens.'

'I got a taste for it dining with the Ba'ath party and Hamas in the eighties.'

'Now you're just showing off, and showing your age.'

'Me?'

'Yeah, how was it on that trip with Rumsfeld and kickin' it with Saddam in the palaces? What was that, must have been around eighty-three, right? When Rummy was Reagan's man?'

'Okay, you're right, I'm an old man.'

'Old as dirt.'

'Old as Dubrovnik maybe.'

'To Dubrovnik.' They clinked glasses and drank.

Walker said, 'What *is* it about you and this place?'

'What's not to love?'

Bloom gestured around, and Walker couldn't argue. The beautiful stone buildings in the medieval walled town were so spectacular that UNESCO had long ago declared its heritage status.

'Too bad you're too old to chase the local women.'

'There's a pill for that, so the old codgers in my fishing club tell me.'

'Seriously, though, why did you retire here? Why not the Keys? You always used to talk about the Keys. Catching big fish. Hell, looking at you now, you could enter their Hemingway lookalike comps.'

Bloom chuckled. 'I fell in love with this city when I passed through while working on Yugoslavia falling apart. Then when the JNA were shelling the crap out of this town, I fell in love with it some more, and I came back before the Bosnian War properly set in.'

'I forgot that this was once an Agency hot spot, that you operated so much around here.'

'Long time ago.'

'Before my time.'

'Hell, you were probably still at high school.'

'Probably preschool.'

Bloom smiled, his gaze far off into his glass as he spoke. 'There's something I'll never forget about those early trips. During the evacuation one of the UN people I helped get onto a boat said to me, as a way of trying to explain the war, "Those who can make you believe absurdities can make you commit atrocities."'

'You quoting Voltaire at me?'

'Yeah, though I didn't know Voltaire from my elbow back then, college boy,' Bloom said, again looking into his glass as though the memories were somewhere in the bottom of it. 'It struck a chord with me, is all. It became something I kept telling those who would listen about the Taliban. But there's too many deaf ears these days.'

'Yeah, well, I listened to you,' Walker said. 'And I read a lot on those cold nights in Afghanistan; took a stack of my old man's books with me on my first tour. Voltaire also said, "The art of government is to make two-thirds of a nation pay all it possibly can pay for the benefit of the other third."'

'Which we know is now bullshit, because today it's about ninety-nine per cent to one.'

They laughed and clinked glasses.

'And I got one more,' Walker said. '"No problem can withstand the assault of sustained thinking."'

'Yeah,' Bloom said. 'And how about, "Objectivity is the search for truth even if it leads you to unwelcome conclusions."'

'Who said that?'

'Your father.'

'Ah.' Walker was silent as he gazed down into his Scotch.

'Good old David.'

'Yeah.'

'Look, Jed, take it from an old – old*er* – man, you're reading too much into this Yemen op,' Bloom said. 'Do you know how many agents I know who were burned for no good reason other than that their sacrifice was deemed the lesser of two outcomes?'

'A few.'

'Few? A shit load. Count the stars on the wall at Langley. Go speak to other old hacks like me – I mean, the Cold War? We were cycling through guys like the army goes through boots. Agents especially. Lose a few, gain a few, keep your eye on the prize.'

'Winning the war.'

'Fuck that. So long as we beat the other guy, that's what it has always been about. And we only beat them in the end because our bureaucracy was smaller.'

'So *that's* where I always got it wrong . . .' Walker said with a smile and topped up their whisky.

'You ran *into* that damned house in Yemen against orders,' Bloom said. 'If not for that, hell, you'd still be shovelling their shit for them.'

'You know that's crap. Sure, you're right about going into the house, but . . .'

'But?'

'They cooked us. KIA. Do I look KIA to you?'

'I've met a lot of dead men.'

'I'm serious about this,' said Walker. 'It's bigger than someone on high at Langley pulling the plug on an op and cooking a couple of field guys for the sake of bagging a big fish.'

'And what?' Bloom countered. 'You've obsessed for the past year, all so you can clear your name?'

'No. It's not that. I want justice. There's a lot I have to set right.'

'Then you're in the wrong industry, bub. Just bug out while you can – this is your chance, don't you see? You're a dead man, about to get a couple of new passports and a nice little pay day courtesy of your Uncle Marty. Take it and disappear. Start again. You won't get another chance. If you keep kicking this hornets' nest, you're gone. For real this time.'

'So, you agree there's something there.'

'We all know there's something there, but what? And what are you going to do about it? Hang them all up by their bootstraps and shake 'em until they confess? Water-board the executive arm of the Agency until they all come clean and sing a tune you want to hear? Then what? It'll never see a court, whatever *it* is, because it's under ten layers of national security BS and then some.'

'I'm getting close, Marty. I feel it. I made the courier, Lassiter, and his next contact. They were there too; they killed them both.'

'Who is they?'

'The same crowd who wanted Yemen to disappear.'

'Why?'

'Because of Zodiac.'

Bloom shook his head.

'It's a real thing, Marty.'

'It's a goddamned ghost, more transparent than you. Zodiac's probably some bullshit op, delivering food stamps to some shitty place in exchange for God-only-knows-what.'

'No. It's not. I tracked it and confirmed it in Yemen. It's as real as me sitting here. And it's still in play.'

'Says who?'

'Says the actions of many. Because someone is still chasing me all over the world. Because I've seen people getting killed and bombs going off – that was yesterday, Marty. Because I was grabbed and taken to an Agency safe house, and someone in the CIA knew it and sent in another team, killing three of our own paramilitary guys.'

Bloom sat back and looked at Walker, processing this latest bit of information. 'I didn't know . . .'

'Right?' prompted Walker. 'See what I'm getting at?'

Bloom drank. 'Shit,' he said, stunned. 'What are you going to do?'

'What I've been doing: chasing leads.'

'What aren't you telling me?'

Walker swirled the Scotch around in the glass.

'Jed . . . talk to me.'

Walker looked up to him. 'Yemen,' he said. 'My CIA guy, Bob Hanley.'

'Listed as KIA with you.'

Walker nodded.

Bloom said, 'What – you're gonna tell me that he's alive too?'

'No. Bob's as dead as they get. But it's what he did before he died . . . he drew down on me.' Walker leaned forwards, said quietly, 'It was an assassination. A clean-up. He was meant to walk out of there alone. The whole thing was meant to be a hit and clean-up and only he would have been witness to how things really went down.'

38

Pip Durant took two pain-killers and phoned Bellamy from his hire car. The call came in over the car's radio speakers, the voice loud and clear.

Bellamy said, 'You okay?'

Durant turned the volume down, said, 'Yes.'

'You okay?'

'Yes.'

'You sound like shit. All nasally.'

'Busted nose, cheekbone and eye socket will do that.'

'You should be resting, recuperating. I want you to be there with me in New York.'

'I've got a little work to do first,' Durant replied. 'And I'll be there. I'm always there when you need me. Heller too. I'm that guy, aren't I? Dependable.'

'Yeah, you're that guy.' Bellamy paused, then said, 'I heard about the trouble at the safe house.'

'Yeah . . .' Durant replied, wary.

'You shouldn't have been there,' Bellamy said.

'I heard of the Walker sighting and hauled ass – I wasn't gonna miss out on that.'

'You could have been killed by the guys we sent in.'

'I know. In a weird way I should be thankful that Walker took me down, because it meant that I was left alone by your team.'

'Like I said, I didn't know you were going to be there.'

'Field operations move quickly. That's why you need guys like me and Heller driving things like this. You worry about your upcoming IPO and pressing political flesh and all that.'

'Yeah, well, now there's a lot of interest in you,' Bellamy said. 'An FBI guy went to Heller asking questions about Walker, and your name came up.'

'So?'

'Just disappear for a bit. You've done enough. Hang in the hotel in Manhattan and enjoy the show.'

'Fuck you disappear,' replied Durant. 'I'm part of this, a big part.'

Another pause from Bellamy. Then he said, 'All right. We need to find Walker before anyone else does. You can help with that.'

'I'm working on it. I owe him a smashed face.'

'Where would he go?'

'He's wounded. He's got only the clothes on his back. He's on the run.'

'So, where would he go for help?'

'That's the thing,' Durant said. 'The guy's been a ghost. He could be anywhere.'

'Then think harder. He's up against it. Maybe he knows we piggybacked trading info on the Agency's courier network.'

'So he'll be headed to Hong Kong.'

'Better he's held up there than New York,' said Bellamy.

'My point is, he has to travel internationally.'

'There's a lot of heat on him; we're not the only ones looking for him. He'll need iron-clad travel docs.'

'A guy like Walker could get documents anywhere.'

'But he won't, not when there's this kind of heat on him, because he's a pro. He doesn't trust just anyone.'

'*Was* a pro,' corrected Durant.

'By the by. He won't take unnecessary risks. You worked with him all that time. Where would he turn for help?'

Durant paused, then said, 'There's a guy you could check in on. A guy he used to look up to, like a father. Marty Bloom. Retired spook from way back, lives in Europe some place. Trained Walker in the early days. Recruited him in Kabul back in the Afghan war, when Walker was still a DoD boy. The way I heard it, he secretly made sure Walker got his promotion to Lieutenant Colonel because he knew that'd bring a desk job that Walker couldn't abide. Next thing you know, Walker leaves the military for the Agency.'

'Okay, I'll talk to Heller about this Bloom guy, get him tracked down. Where are you?'

'Texas,' Durant said, merging onto the I-81.

'What's in Texas?'

'Leverage.'

•

The Croatian night was a veil of bright stars in the dark blanket above the Adriatic. Walker leaned against the outside wall of the bar and waited while Bloom stubbed out his cigarette.

'Those things . . .' Walker said.

'Will kill me? Please.' They headed back into the bar and sat at their table. The plates from their meal of cured meats, cheeses, and preserved and pickled vegetables had been cleared. It took a while for Bloom to say, 'Hong Kong?'

'Yep.' Walker looked around, then said, 'Lassiter was due to be there tomorrow, and I'll be there instead.'

'It's the wild west over there. Whole different set of rules. You get caught, they take you to mainland China and you're fucked.'

'Yep.'

'I mean dead for real this time; it's not a place you'd want to get caught.'

'Nope.'

Bloom was silent, then said, 'You know what you need?'

Walker looked at him with a raised eyebrow.

'You need a place, Walker, your own place. Somewhere, something that means enough to you to make you want to walk away from all this. When I got shot here in ninety-one during the siege, I should have died, but I didn't because of the help of the good civilian folk who stayed behind. They stayed here with no water, no power, for *months*. They stayed, even while the place was occupied, because it was their home and they were prepared to *die* here. They saved me. And at the time I swore that if I lived through it, and all the other shit that followed, I'd come back one day and join them.'

'That's a sweet story.'

'Damned straight. And you know what I meant by it?'

'You're more sentimental than you look?'

Bloom raised an eyebrow in return.

'Fine, I get it,' Walker said. 'You're saying that I need my Dubrovnik.'

'Damned straight. We all do. Everyone needs a place to settle down. Somewhere to live. Somewhere to die. Somewhere to settle and stop looking over your shoulder every other second. It's as simple as that. I'm a fat old man with plastic knees and yet these have been the best years of my life. I'm not saying you have to run head first into it. Just take your leave while it's given to you. Open your eyes, man. Look at your so-called death as a gift. Walk away while you can. Be thankful for what you have. Find your Dubrovnik.'

Walker couldn't, not yet, and Bloom knew that.

'Jed, before all this, there was a long time, while I was working,' Bloom said, 'where I couldn't live in the world of sobriety. Shitty time. Cold War ending, my friends getting shafted all over the place, plenty of excuses to drink with plenty of people who no longer had a place to fit in. You get to the point where you've done so much for your country and you think, *What's the point of staying sober?*'

'I can't remember you as a drunk. I was joking before, when I walked in here and called you that.'

'I know, I know.' Bloom smiled. 'I gave it up after the siege. I've eased back into it since my demons have departed.'

Walker could see the change in the man in the four years since they'd last met in person: in his face, his eyes, the smile lines, his stance, his body language and his demeanour. 'This place really changed you, hey?'

'Yep,' Bloom said. 'And Yemen was your siege. Let it be. Just leave all this be.'

'Nope.' Walker shook his head. 'My siege is yet to come, Marty. Yet to come. They started this war. I'm going to finish it.'

Forty-one hours to deadline.

39

Somerville broke her conversation with McCorkell and looked down to her phone sitting on the embassy desk between them: Captain Spiteri. She answered it and the voice came through on the hands-free speaker.

'The Trapwire system picked up images of Walker in Bari, on the eastern coast, a few hours' drive from here,' Spiteri said. 'I am messaging you the shots now.'

Somerville looked at the grainy images. One was taken through a convenience-store glass door, another from a petrol station as he had passed by, another from a security camera at a dock.

'There,' Somerville said. 'The one on the docks. What's he doing with that guy?'

'Talking,' Spiteri said.

'He's doing more than talking,' Somerville said. The photos showed Walker passing over the bag; the other guy checking its contents.

Spiteri continued, 'Walker handed him a rucksack, which we later intercepted and searched.'

The corresponding enhanced footage showed wads of euros and wrapped parcels that appeared to be drugs.

'When was that? Who's he with?' Somerville said.

'Six hours ago. We haven't confirmed ID on his contact yet. We arrested another guy with the bag during a vehicle stop.'

'Run him. Find that guy. It can't be hard: a haul that big, he's got to be a player. Have your local carabinieri get hold of him as soon as he's made. I want to know what Walker said, and where he's now at.'

'We are working on that,' Captain Spiteri said.

'Call me when you know more.'

Somerville ended the call and turned to McCorkell. 'You still think Jed Walker's a poster-boy for good intentions?'

•

'Let me help you out a little,' Bloom said.

'You've done enough,' Walker replied. There was a third of the bottle of Scotch left, and the bar was almost empty but for a few patrons seeing the night through, though their vision and memories would be suitably impaired. Walker suspected that this bar was the kind of place that didn't have a regulation closing time.

'No, no, I'm serious,' Bloom said. 'One professional helping another. Tell me.'

'Tell you . . .'

'Yemen. The mission. What was it about?'

'Marty . . .'

'What, after all you ask of me, you can't tell me this?'

'It's . . .'

'Against the law?'

Walker shrugged. 'No, not that. I just didn't want to disturb your new-found peace.'

'Let me worry about that. Talk.'

'Okay, Yemen . . . I was in and out of country for a few months, chasing a guy. A courier.'

'How'd you get assigned?' Bloom asked. 'I know you were out of the Agency then.'

'That's right. Remember the story about that office in State, about how they ran DSS-type officers to handle sensitive investigations into diplomats, politicians, royalty and the like in foreign countries?'

'Yep.'

'That's how.'

'No.'

'Yep.'

'No . . .' Bloom looked into his empty glass, to the bottle, then set the glass down and drank from his water glass instead. 'That outfit at State was just a bullshit rumour.'

'Nope. As real as you and me sitting here.'

'Who runs it? Where's it headquartered?'

'What, you looking for a job?'

'No, forget it. Go on.'

'I was in Yemen, had been ghosting a member of the House of Saud. He kept meeting with a guy. A courier. Louis Assif.'

'One of about ten thousand princes, meeting with a courier. And?'

'Yeah, well, Assif was already a suspected courier within Al Qaeda, dealing with Saudi money moving around in return for AQ not fucking around in their sandbox. And I'm talking *big* money. Intel initially pegged him as one of bin Laden's personal guys. Turns out that wasn't right, but he had links to one of the guys they got at bin Laden's compound, probably his number-one runner.'

'But?'

'But at the Agency I could never get close – Heller always shut me out whenever the guy's name came up,' Walker said. 'And it turns out that Assif had already been made and turned. He was an agent, for the French.'

'DGSE?'

Walker nodded.

'That could be why Heller shut you out.'

'Could be, but I doubt it.'

'So then you went to State and looked into it anyway.'

'Yep. And before I could get shit out of Assif, my Agency minder turned on me and then, quick as you could blink, we were hit by the drone strike. All told, a couple of years' work up in smoke, and whoever Al Qaeda's using now is an unknown.'

'Because the HVT rolled in and the Hellfires rained down.'

'That's about the sum of it. If you believe that.'

'Did you follow any DGSE leads?'

'Assif's French handler was a dead end. And when I say dead end, I mean it: he's dead. Car accident, they said. He was among the first to die in this clean-up, nine months ago now.'

Bloom nodded, staring down into his drink. Walker could see his legendary old mentor's mind working overtime, connecting dots. 'Who was the HVT who rolled in?'

'They had him made as AQ's premier bomb-maker. Now he's supposedly compost for the desert.'

'He's probably got a date palm growing out of what was left of his butt.' Bloom looked up at Walker. 'And only you got out of there alive.'

'Yep, saved by a bit of mud-brick wall and a whole lot of luck. I stayed hidden in what was left of the place for the next two nights, then I hot-wired a car and bugged the hell out. And you know the rest.'

'Why didn't you tell me about this sooner?'

'This isn't your fight. You're out, remember? Retired.'

'Yet I feel I'm more than just your travel agent, you know.'

Walker laughed. 'Yes, Marty, you are. You're a friend. You're a champ. But your days of fighting are over. You said so yourself. Hell, look at you, man. Your fight's against angina and diabetes, not this.'

'I've still got a little fight left in me.'

'Save it,' Walker said, and gestured towards a couple of women seated at the bar, 'for the ladies.'

Bloom laughed, then turned serious once more. 'Hong Kong,' he said. 'Lassiter's contact. How are you going to proceed?'

'I'm going to question her, direct.'

'Her?'

'Yes.'

'You know his contact?'

'I know of her.'

'Is she protected?'

'Very well.'

'Okay. I think I have a better idea.'

Forty hours to deadline.

40

Bloom's better idea involved a scalpel, a tiny plastic pill that contained a wireless storage chip, and surgical stitching gear. They sat in Bloom's apartment, not a few minutes from the bar. The old man had a grin on him that Walker didn't like.

Walker said, 'You wanna stitch that into the back of my head?'

'You'll be the new head case.'

'I can't just keep it in my pocket?'

'They're not designed for that. Besides, what if you get caught? This way, it's hidden.'

'They booked Lassiter but they get me . . . But I'm supposed to be delivering info, not receiving, right?'

'You deliver some crap and download whatever she's got.'

'Download?'

'Yep.'

'These things do that?'

'It seems you have much to learn, my young Padawan.' Bloom looked at the tiny head-case chip in the clear plastic container. 'It's not standard, but I had my guy back in the States make them two-way for a little project I did when I first moved here.'

'Of course you did.'

'It's simple, and ingenious: you'll be going to Lassiter's agreed location at a designated time, and his contact will connect to your chip to download what you've got – and this little baby will automatically take all the data off whatever device she's using.'

'She could be using a smart phone, tablet, computer . . . that's a lot of data.'

'This will hold one-twenty-eight gig, and it can wirelessly transfer real-time data via the chip to a smart phone or tablet if need be.'

'And how am I posing as the head case?'

'The same way they all do,' Bloom replied. 'Five minutes before you arrive, she'll get the automated message, the picture of you sent to her phone.'

'That's risky – that can be hacked; it's how I made Felix Lassiter in Athens in the first place.'

'Yeah, but you were already on site and waiting for a head case to show up. This time, who's going to be waiting for you?'

'Okay. And how will you get me listed as the head case?'

'I didn't get a gold watch from Langley for being a boy scout,' Bloom said. 'The Station Chief in Hong Kong is one of the best gigs on the planet, and the SOB sitting at the desk owes me more than you do. You're already using the courier's name – we'll just get you logged into their system as the guy.'

'If he knows who I am, he'll never give me cover – it'll be his career over.'

'He's never going to know who the new head case is.'

Walker was intrigued.

'I'll tell him to give me a one-time access key to the secure network in the Hong Kong station. One use, to do something for an old buddy. He'll give me that.'

'If he manages to trace what you've done—'

'He won't, he's not that kind of guy. He'll look the other way on this.'

'But if someone sees, some IT desk jockey notices that my ID has been uploaded into the system.'

'It's not part of the Intellipedia network, it's internal, a LAN, so it'll be buried in the local server in Kowloon.'

Walker nodded, the plan now making sense. 'Head cases are like any other cut-out agents – no-one runs them but the officers who recruited them in the first place . . .'

'So, you're going to be a ghost in the system. Life imitating art, or something.'

Walker looked at the scalpel. 'I don't know, Marty.'

'You want to forget about it? Fine.'

'How about we wait until we're sober before you cut my head open?'

'We can, but it'll hurt less now.'

Walker grimaced, paced the tiny kitchen and then sat down. 'Fine. But if you butcher me, I'll give you a vasectomy with that thing.'

'Ooh, kinky.'

41

'You know I fully support INTFOR, John,' the Vice President said to
Senator Anderson. 'But the Cabinet just won't pass it. It's the wrong
administration for it. Especially in the wake of Snowden and all the
press that got. You should bug out and lay low some place, like the
Blackwater guy is doing.'

'Academi,' Anderson said.

'Whatever they call themselves now. There's too much heat on this
sort of private enterprise right now for it to be all you want it to be.
A couple of smaller programs, sure. But not what you and Bellamy
presented last year. Wait a while, you'll see.'

Senator Anderson stood and walked over to the window, looking
down at the grounds of the United States Naval Observatory, the official
office and residence of the Vice President.

Anderson said, 'I came here today hoping there would be some
movement before the IPO.'

'They feel we're winning this war on terror, winding things up,' the
Vice President said. 'They don't see the urgency to hand more to the
private sector this fast. Under the last President, sure, INTFOR would
have been a gift. But now, with bin Laden gone and us bugging out
of Iraq and Afghanistan, there's just not the urgency on the foreign
front. Maybe you should have made things more domestic, taken on
the DHS instead of the CIA – since the Boston bombing, that's where
the public support for more action against terrorism is. So either wait
it out, or change your focus.'

'What we're about is smaller, leaner government,' Anderson said,
facing his old friend. 'And I can make it work. You know that. I've got
cross-party support on this from the leadership down.'

'I know. You've worked hard at this, but, like I said, this is the wrong
administration to be selling to. Wait a few more years, then it might
have a better shot.' The Vice President paused as his Secret Service
detail chief appeared in his doorway and made a signal at his watch

and departed from sight. 'Right. I've got to go see a guy about a thing. I'm going to see you and Bellamy on Monday at the exchange, right?'

'Wouldn't miss it.'

'It'll be big, even without what you're asking of me. A great day. The start of something – you boys just need to stay patient.'

Yes, it will be big, it will be the start of something. Like you wouldn't believe.

Thirty-four hours to deadline.

•

Walker woke to the sight of blood on his pillow. Not much, just a little reminder that he was now walking around with a tiny chip sewn into the back of his head.

The smells woke him. Ground coffee, and sizzling bacon. He trudged to the kitchen, where Bloom had set out plates and piled fried eggs onto dark toast, with sides of mushrooms and spinach.

'You're quite the homemaker,' Walker said, flicking open the *Herald Tribune* and sipping the coffee. Black, hot and strong.

'You've got about an hour before you leave for your flight,' Bloom said. 'You remember what I taught you?'

'Hell, all of it?'

'The important stuff.'

'Never put ice into Scotch.'

'Good.'

'Follow the money.'

'And find your man.'

'My man . . . what man? There's no man here, he's dead.'

'Bullshit. Your contact's dead. Who's he working for?'

'Originally? Osama bin Laden.'

'I don't want to know. But that SOB is dead too. So keep looking for the next guy.'

'The next guy . . .'

'There's always a next guy.'

'Always?'

'Always. People like to cover their ass.'

'Times have changed, Marty.'

'Not this much.'

'But this lead's gone.'

'Without a trace?'

'Yes,' Walker replied through a mouthful of toast.

Bloom smiled.

Walker finally did too, then said, 'Nothing disappears without a trace.'

'You missed something. Go back, figure it out. Make a list.'

'You and your lists.'

'Have they ever let you down?'

Walker paused, then took another bite. 'No.'

'Good. You know what to do. Now, enough shop talk. Give me a few minutes of bullshit. How's your sex life?'

Walker cracked up.

'I'm serious. I'm old, and the best I can do is look at all the beautiful women around here.'

'Oh Jesus . . .'

'I remember, back in the day, when I was younger than you are now, a posting in Micronesia, and there was a Polynesian honey. Bow Bow, that was her name.'

'I've heard this.'

'Damn, she was fine. Why I never stayed there . . .'

'You liked this game too much. Your whole life was ahead of you. You thought there would be a million more Bow Bows out there.'

'Mistakes, all of them. I'd be watching my grandkids by now if I'd stayed there.'

'Great-grandkids.'

'I'm serious, Jeddy boy. Don't get stuck in a quest and lose what's important.'

Walker was silenced. He knew there were only so many jokes he could make before he would have to have this conversation. 'You're talking about Eve.'

'She's a fine woman. She loves you more than anyone should.'

'She's moved on, long ago. I'm history.'

'She thinks you're dead, jackass.'

The truth hit Walker in the gut.

'You never reached out to her; just watched from afar as she moved on, from grief to whatever semblance of love again she could muster.'

'What could I have done?'

'You could have walked away from all this.'

'And walked back into her arms?'

'Maybe.'

'And Jack Heller and whoever else at the Agency wanted me dead would have killed her too. I couldn't go back.'

'Yeah, I know.' Bloom sipped his coffee. 'I trained you too damned well. You watched me too damned close. Don't make the same mistakes I did, that's all I'm saying.'

'I already have.'

'Listen. This op you're running solo, the forces you're up against? This ain't no training drill; hell, this ain't no op against a cell of bad guys. This is national security up the wazoo against you and God only knows who else. You're one man. And when they catch up with you – and they will – then it'll be too late. Too late for anything and everything.'

'So what – just walk away?'

'I did. Look at me now. Sitting here in the sun. Looking at the women.' He leaned towards Walker. 'Walker, you're the closest thing to a son I have. You've got options.'

Walker looked away, couldn't face the man who had been as much a father figure than the man who had raised him.

'I want to have more moments like this with you. I want to go fish the Caribbean like we always said we would. At least the Adriatic. Stay here. Drop this. There's no rush.'

Walker smiled. 'Fish from some drug-runner's boat, and we'd use the crew as bait, like we used to say.'

'We'd catch a monster. Maybe two.'

Walker looked his mentor in the eye. 'I have nothing but this right now,' he said. 'And if I don't do this, no-one will. I'm on the clock – there's a deadline. I'll get through it. We'll go fish the Caribbean, you'll see; hell, I hear there's even salmon fishing in the Yemen these days.'

Bloom wasn't having it, but he let it slide. Walker saw that the old man's eyes were wet. He passed over an envelope containing Walker's new ID and a wad of cash.

'Thanks. For trying to talk me out, yet again.' Walker stood. Bloom too. They embraced. Walker couldn't meet his gaze as he left, hoping to someday return and take that fishing trip.

'Oh,' Walker said, turning back, 'there's one last thing . . .'

42

Two hours later, Bill McCorkell sat at a table in a cafe in Dubrovnik and said, 'Hong Kong?'

Bloom nodded. 'But I never said that. You did.'

They had spoken for barely ten minutes, and promises were made, one old professional to another.

McCorkell stood, left a few euros on the table and patted Bloom on the shoulder.

'Enjoy your retirement.'

•

At the next table, Il Bisturi heard everything.

It made life easier. He had come here prepared to make Bloom talk, had looked forward to the challenge. Instead, all he needed to do was eavesdrop.

He waited for McCorkell to leave, then he walked to the bathroom, went out the back door and placed a call to Bellamy.

'Walker is on a plane, headed to Hong Kong,' Il Bisturi said.

'I know,' Bellamy replied.

Il Bisturi was silent a beat, then said, 'You didn't think to tell me?'

'I'm doing your job now, am I?'

The Italian was silent.

'I need you to get back to Rome.'

'What's in Rome?'

'The woman who was with Walker.'

'The American – the agent who was in the car?'

'No, not her. An Italian. Her name is Clara. I will send you the details. I need you to pick her up and bring her to New York.'

'What for?'

'Insurance.'

'But this target is going to Hong Kong—'

'And I have Hong Kong covered. But I may need you and Clara in New York.'

'I'm finishing this job, this guy.'

'You will. Get to Rome, get the woman, bring her to New York.'

43

Walker flew into Hong Kong as the sun was going down. The city was all golds and blues and studded with lights, twinkling, strobing, still, every beautiful detail of capitalism roaring along, illuminated.

Back in the day, when still on the government payroll, Walker had experienced the international transport perks otherwise out of his civilian league. Private entrances and exits, private customs contact, all of it expedited and proficient, thanks to diplomatic privileges. Today, however, Walker had to take the everyday, traceable route through the long line of international customs; fortunately the forged documents were faultless, complete with the used passports.

Customs cleared, Walker found a cab and made his way from Hong Kong International Airport to Kowloon, where he had a reservation at The Peninsula hotel. Outside, a roll-up of luxury cars delivered well-heeled guests to the 1928 hotel, amid white-gloved bellboys with pillbox hats buzzing like flies in the evening air. Walker passed the rows of the distinctive hotel-owned Rolls-Royce vehicles lined up in the driveway off Salisbury Road, the outside air heavy with tropical humidity that didn't discriminate. He checked in with only his backpack, and handed over the credit card issued in the same name as the Canadian passport Bloom had provided: Felix Lassiter.

The receptionist worked with practised felicity and handed over the room card. Walker's room was on the twenty-seventh floor and looked out over the twinkling nightscape of Victoria Harbour. The interior colour scheme – caramel, walnut and dark chocolate – was soothing, and the attention to detail, including vintage leather travel-trunk drawer handles, mahogany dining tables, Chinese ink paintings and Poltrona Frau dining chairs, were all things Walker would have enjoyed at another time. Contrasting it, or accentuating the hotel's place in the twenty-first century, was the room's technology, designed to provide touch-of-the-button access to almost anything the modern guest could desire: an in-room tablet, available in five languages and from which one could order room service, operate the TV, adjust the lighting and air conditioning and open and shut the curtains.

'Probably could have launched the Apollo program off this thing . . .' Walker said, taking a Heineken into the shower and washing the past twenty-four hours from his body, careful to avoid the wound at his side. He then dressed the wound with supplies provided by Bloom, shaved, and sat with a towel wrapped around his waist at the room's compact desk, inspecting a map of the area.

Still waiting on Bloom's confirmation, he was sure that the head-case meeting would go down in the chaos on Hong Kong Island rather than where he was now. From there, he would go home, for the first time in a year.

He dressed in his jeans and shirt and pocketed the passport and ID papers he would need for entry to the United States, along with the credit card and the US$5000 Bloom had provided, and the map. The final piece he took from his backpack was Pip Durant's CIA identification card.

Tonight, he was posing as a head-case courier and needed to blend in to the corporate banking world that would be on Hong Kong Island. While the former was merely a matter of being in the correct place at the pre-arranged time, the latter meant that he had to look the part.

Calling the concierge, Walker obtained the address of the closest Paul Smith store, where he availed himself of a black suit, black shirt and a black tie flocked with a charcoal pattern of ivy. The cut at his side still wept, and the stitches at the back of his head, hidden beneath his hair, itched.

On the way through the mall he bought a pre-paid cell phone and sent a text to Bloom: CONFIRM HK.

He swallowed two more pain-killers as he made his way harbourside, to the ferry, where he paid the HK$2 to get across to Hong Kong Island.

The cell phone chimed in his suit pocket: CONFIRM. HV RACE COURSE, Stable Bend Terrace. 2100–2130. FRIENDS EN ROUTE.

Walker looked around to make sure the coast was clear and then leaned with his back against the railing and dropped the phone overboard.

He had no friends here, and knew Bloom's addition to be a warning.

The 'friends' tracking him were a known entity, which meant either a CIA grab crew or the B Teamers.

As he passed under the frenetic light show colouring and strobing the Hong Kong skyline, his mind swirled and eddied around the possibilities: how to deal with these friends, and whether Bloom's assurances about the two-way chip in his head would be accurate. Anything and everything was possible.

Twenty-five hours to deadline.

44

Hutchinson picked up a Ford Taurus at the Houston FBI field office. On the passenger seat he had a street map open, Eve Walker's address circled on it. He figured the drive was about half an hour.

●

After exiting at the Star Ferry terminal on Hong Kong Island, Walker spent fifteen minutes strolling around Central looking at architecture and shop fronts in order to be certain that he was not being tailed. Convinced he was clean, he took a cab from Central to Happy Valley Racecourse.

Outside the taxi window the scenery changed from densely packed glass-and-steel skyscrapers to generic concrete apartment towers, set among a backdrop of black–green tree canopies dotted with the houses of the über wealthy stretching up to Victoria Peak. They passed bustling night markets and steaming street food, a technicolour of organised chaos that knew neither limit nor constraint. Walker had once heard a description that living in Hong Kong was like being inside a pinball machine: being propelled at high speeds through space, bouncing between bright lights and dark passageways, a never-ending sequence of shadows and shines, a place where it didn't cost much to play and when you started you soon realised that it was addictive, making you crave that high score, never really being able to tear yourself away, always remembering what it was like at those magical moments when everything seemed to come together and, for an instant, the world was just you and this city.

To Walker it seemed like New York City's Chinatown had been bitten by a radioactive spider and in turn exploded exponentially into a seething, bubbling mass that refused to acknowledge physical limitations to its size. As the taxi drove and wove, he took in the effects of eight million people inhabiting an area a quarter of the size of New York City.

This was the centre of the world. There was no night, no day, only the light of the sun and the light of neon. Whatever you wanted, Hong Kong would sell it to you. Anytime.

Walker was counting on that.

His taxi driver, a guy the other side of fifty who had seen Hong Kong through many phases, was talking rapid-fire, giving him tips on the races from a form guide that he studied all day, every day.

Walker nodded and listened and felt at the tiny bump at the back of his head, the urge to scratch it overwhelming. In an hour's time he would be headed back to the airport, the data transferred. Downloading and deciphering it was a different story, but he would be one step closer to the culmination of a year's work.

Walker knew it was time for him to step from the shadows and into the bright light.

Like a pinball machine, sometimes life needed a tilt, a shove, to produce the desired outcome.

Just a day from the deadline, he knew the time for a bump or shove was over. He had entered a period of consequences. The time to smash and crash was upon him.

Twenty-four hours to deadline.

45

Durant was on the road, having picked up his hire car at Houston Airport. He had the satnav system programmed with Eve Walker's address, and figured he was about twenty-five minutes out.

•

Walker queued to get into the Happy Valley Racecourse. He checked the time: 8:34 pm.

Plenty of time.

It was Wednesday night; busy, but the queue was orderly and he moved through along with groups of guys and girls who had come here after work and knock-off drinks or after dinner – either way, they had been drinking, and they were loud, happy, full of smiles and without a care in the world as they started the next part of their evening with a punt or two. Give it more booze and some losses and missed attention from someone they admired and they would leave the place with a whole different disposition.

He would be out of here by then.

In another life he would have put the $10 coin in the turnstile and joined the throngs enjoying the atmosphere of the public area: a broad spectrum of punters in attendance, numerous food and beer options, and the palpable buzz of lives being lived. Instead, he paid the $100 to enter the members' concourse.

The beer garden was wall to wall with more expats and tourists than locals and he blended in, casually looking around, glancing up to the terraces where he was due at 9 pm. High grandstands and buildings enveloped the lush green track, which saw the field of horses pass the main straight and finishing post twice in even the shortest of races, giving the crowd plenty of opportunity to view and cheer on their selected pony.

Behind Walker two guys wearing jeans and polo shirts spoke to each other, occasionally looking around, their sweeping gaze taking him in too.

Walker moved on towards the enormous mounting yard. The two guys remained where they were. All bets were placed with a central betting authority, with numerous booths placed around the public area, complete with clipboard-carrying attendants hovering to help tourists complete their betting slips. Walker followed his cab driver's advice and put HK$100 on horse seven in the next race, then did a circuit of the beer garden, which formed a clear path between the tents and stalls.

Always watching, always scanning faces and reading body language. To the average punter Walker was just another race-goer. To a fellow professional he might be considered a person of interest, someone worthy of a second glance and further thought.

The two guys may well be nothing more than two guys, he figured, for they were still there, standing and talking, looking around, not interested in punting, the races or the women.

DJs played tunes between the races, which were set twenty minutes apart.

He clocked the Stable Bend Terrace overlooking the entire track and headed for the third floor.

8:43 pm.

46

Walker had learned early on that when you needed to blend into a crowd, it was best to do so early. To settle in. Melt into the background. Make a few friends. The terrace was crowded, and he took a complimentary beer from a waiter and did a quick lap to choose his target. Walker knew that all he had to do was stand here, blend in, until 9:30. Sometime during those minutes, the person who had booked the head-case service would be in the vicinity and would access his chip.

Then he had to do little more than make it back to the airport without losing his head.

Piece of cake.

After listening to several back-and-forths among groups, Walker struck up conversation with a crowd of eight people standing on a terrace, eating and drinking and not paying any attention to the horses being loaded into the stalls for the next race.

Six men, two women. From late twenties to early fifties. All worked in finance.

'Felix Lassiter,' he said. 'Reuters.'

Like most intelligence operatives, Walker had often used the cover of being a reporter and was comfortable using it. A second skin.

'What area?' a tall guy asked.

'Finance,' Walker replied. *Why not have a little fun?* 'Financial crimes, specifically.'

'Working on anything big?' a smug guy with silver hair asked, leaning an elbow on a stand-up table and sipping champagne.

'You know, all in a day,' Walker said, draining his beer and catching the waiter as he passed. 'Bruno Iksil is ongoing.'

'Hmph, those JP Morgan guys . . . what'd they call that Iksil guy? The White Whale? Voldemort?' the tall guy said. 'You'll be digging through files and in and out of courtrooms over that story for years.'

Walker shrugged. 'I've got time.'

'What was wiped off the bank's value after that story broke?' the woman closest to him asked. 'Ten billion?'

'Closer to fifteen,' Walker replied.

'What's your secret?' Silver Hair asked. 'When investigating financial crimes?'

Walker recognised the guy from TV interviews – some kind of economic advisor to Germany's finance minister.

'I follow the money.'

'You make it sound simple,' the woman replied.

'I'm patient.'

'It took more than that,' she replied. 'If it was that simple, it would have come out sooner.'

'I'm persistent.'

'You're clever.'

'Tenacious,' Walker said, sipping his drink.

'He's modest,' the woman said.

Walker took her in in a glance. Sultry. Spanish maybe. Or Portuguese. Accented English from one of the top British finishing schools. From money. Around money. Obsessed with money.

'You are smart enough to figure out the clues and outsmart the villain,' Silver Hair said.

'Resourceful,' the woman added.

Walker said, 'Are you trying to make me blush?'

The gathering laughed.

Walker took the time to take in the wider mass. He clocked the man across the room: six foot four, 250 pounds. Ex-military. Bodyguard to someone here. No telltale earpiece with wire snaking under his shirt. Then again, such gadgets were small these days, especially for the well heeled. And this was such a soiree.

'Tell me,' Silver asked, 'where did you get your investigative experience?'

'I've worked in a lot of places,' Walker said, casually glancing around the room. 'It's added up to a variety of tough life experiences. From Baghdad to Kabul, Tripoli to Damascus.'

'Ah, so you've lived tough and documented it so we don't have to,' the tall guy said, 'and for that, I'm getting your next drink.'

They laughed.

'Is that true?' the woman asked. 'You've lived tough?'

'I'm good at adapting,' Walker said. He spotted two security operators by the main doors, and another pair by the kitchen throughway that was being used by the waiting staff. Plain clothes, trying to blend in, doing a bad job of it.

'I must say,' Silver said, 'I don't always believe what I read. Nor what I see.'

'That's a good philosophy,' Walker replied. He sipped his drink, his head turned away from the group, looking over his glass. He made another guy: similar look to the 250-pounder, only with less neck. Walker assessed the two of them as either German or Austrian. He had trained with guys like them; they were good, damned good, at the physical stuff. One guy like that watching him wasn't such a big deal. Two of them? This was becoming an issue.

And they *were* watching him.

This was good: good that he knew they were there, and that he knew their type. It was also bad: bad that they clearly wanted to be seen. Their training and the fact that they were in a visible space meant that they would not kill him unless their lives were threatened, and they wanted him to know that. Perhaps they were fitter and stronger than Walker, but he doubted it; the past nine months spent with the constant fear of violence had been as good a motivator as any to keep sharp and in shape.

'I have a question,' a woman's voice behind him said. 'Have you ever worked for the US Government?'

Walker turned around.

Special Agent Fiona Somerville stood before him.

47

'For a bit,' Walker replied pleasantly while his mind began to run through his options. 'I figured a little public service is good for the soul.'

'Treasury Department?' Somerville asked. She was wearing a similar suit to the one she had worn in Rome, this one dark grey with light-blue shirt. She held a glass of champagne, the graze on her forehead hidden under a side-parted fringe of blonde hair.

'State.'

'Ah, other people's economies,' Silver Hair said.

Walker shrugged but kept his eyes on Somerville. 'Not quite the same as you're used to, I'm sure.'

'How's that?' Smug asked down his nose.

Somerville gave him a look.

The guy remained silent.

'You were saying,' Somerville said to Walker, 'that you are determined.'

'When I need to be.' He could not immediately locate her back-up on the terrace. *Maybe they're inside. Maybe they're outside, scoping from afar.*

'And what's next for you?' Somerville asked. 'Looking into more financial crime? Or have your interests broadened?'

'I'll keep on doing what I do,' he replied. He had counted just three CCTV cameras in here, all trained at the entrances and exits. The bulk of the cameras would be outside and in the back-of-house areas. There was little need to watch people once they were in here – there was enough physical security personnel for that. He thought through his options.

'Well, Felix, lovely as it's been to meet you,' the tall guy said, 'don't go embroiling the rest of us in your next breaking-news scandal.'

There was an awkward beat among the group. Walker's welcome was over. Somerville's had never started.

'Don't ever leave a paper trail,' Walker said as a parting piece of advice, and left the group.

Somerville followed.

•

'Walker?' Bellamy asked over the phone on his G5 jet, headed north.

'Consider him out of the picture,' Heller replied, looking at a surveillance image of Walker from the racetrack.

'You've said that before.'

Heller paused, biting off a comeback, then said, 'This time it's gospel.'

Bellamy said, 'Okay. What else?'

'Tying off loose ends.'

'Walker's the only loose end I'm worried about. Everything else is in place.'

'You worry about our business. I'll handle the operational details.'

Heller ended the call.

48

Walker knew trouble when he saw it, and Somerville had it in spades. He also knew that, given some of the visible threats in the room, getting out of here was going to be a bitch.

'So . . .' Somerville said.

'So.'

'You got any hobbies aside from running from federal agents?'

'Hobbies?'

'Yeah.'

Staying alive, Walker thought. *Making lists. Counting down the clock. Take your pick.*

'Fly fishing.'

'Really?'

'No.' Walker leaned with his back against the bar. 'I used to like watching football on Sundays. Sitting with the family. Me wearing a jersey, Dad yelling at the Birds to do what they were trained to do. Ma making a roast and pretending she didn't know how the game was played.'

'You wanna tell me about your family? I think that'd be an interesting story.'

'No, I'm talking about football. What, you don't like football?'

'Sure. When America's team is playing.'

'Cowboys? Damn.'

'What's wrong with the Cowboys?'

'Everything. Dallas was my wife's team, and she tried for years to make me think otherwise, but they're just awful.'

'You want to talk to me about Eve?'

'No.'

They were silent for a beat and Walker felt her watching him. One of the big guys left with a group of race-goers, hanging outside the main doors. The bigger one remained thirty feet across the room, failing so admirably to blend in that he was making it clear he wanted to be seen watching. Waiting.

'You don't like being here,' Somerville said. 'Gatherings like this.'

'You're a psychologist now?' Walker asked, looking at her. He tried to look away from her eyes but couldn't.

'In another life,' Somerville said, then continued quickly, as though appraising, 'You're passionate, but not overly emotional. Often calm under fire, steadfast. Not one to break under pressure. Often intense about what you feel is right and wrong. A strong, silent type who detests gatherings such as this one. You feel a calling for something . . . you're searching for justice in an unjust world. You are destined to remain unsatisfied.'

Walker smiled.

The other watchful guy had re-entered the room, near the southern emergency exit. Walker had a built-in compass, even indoors, even with his eyes closed and turned around a million times. These two were pros, no doubt. Either they knew why he was here, or they represented someone who wanted to talk to him about Felix. Intriguing. And a little annoying, though Walker seldom allowed himself to feel annoyed: it got in the way, like being flustered or stressed or worried. Push on, put your head down and smash through whatever's in your way to get to your objective: he had been taught that long ago, and it had steered him well in life.

'How did I do?' Somerville asked.

Walker said, 'Uncannily inaccurate.'

Somerville smiled.

'Are you here to arrest me again?' Walker asked.

'I didn't arrest you last time.'

'Really?'

'Sorry if you had that idea.'

'You were just going to hand me over to the embassy.'

'I hadn't planned to hand you over, but they would have taken charge, I've since learned.'

'Because of the safe house.'

'Yes, because of the safe house. The Agency doesn't take kindly to losing three of its own.'

'They lost one a year ago in the desert. They didn't seem so hell bent to get whoever did that.'

'Why don't you tell me about that?'

Walker fell silent.

Somerville said, 'Why don't you tell me why you're here tonight, waiting?'

'What makes you think I'm waiting?'

'You'd have left by now, either when you saw me or those big guys.'

'They with you?'

'Nope.'

'Maybe I'm waiting for this.' Walker held up his wager. 'Next race, horse seven.'

'I didn't pick you as the gambling type.'

Walker looked around. 'I didn't kill those CIA boys at the safe house. I gave Durant's face a little improvement, but that's it.'

'I know.'

'You know?'

'I've seen the security footage. I talked to the landlord. And I've identified the guys who assaulted the place. It was a hit. They came for you.'

'So,' he said, 'if I *had* made it back to the embassy in Rome yesterday?'

'The Station Chief would have taken over.'

'Bev Johnson; she's good people,' Walker said, smiling as he finished his beer. 'She'd have followed protocol, which would have seen me bagged and put aboard a plane and I would have woken up in some hellhole where the rules on torture are a little lax.'

'At least it would have been a nice plane. A Gulfstream maybe, on the government dime. You wouldn't have had to worry about lining up at customs either.'

Walker knew, then, how Somerville had found him. It wasn't due to an intercept of the throwaway cell phone, nor her brilliant investigative skills and catching up to his year's worth of work in getting here.

'You spoke to Marty Bloom,' Walker said.

'Not me.'

'Who?'

'Another interested party. A friend.'

'I can't believe Bloom ratted me out . . .'

'My friend is persuasive.'

'My friend Bloom is a vault. Or so I thought.'

'He's a good guy; don't let this change your opinion of him. It's just that my friend managed to convince him that your life would be better preserved if you had some help.'

'Help?'

Somerville nodded.

'From who, you?'

'Maybe.'

'"Because you're a part of some Agency conspiracy to undermine our government's interests in the war against terrorism?"'

'What?'

'That's what you said to me, in the car, in Rome. Verbatim.'

Somerville smiled. 'Good memory.'

'It comes in handy. But I need to know: what conspiracy?'

'You tell me.'

Walker scanned the place. No sign of either security guy. He looked back to Somerville. 'Your two heavies have disappeared.'

Somerville's face changed and she said, 'I told you I came alone.'

Then, Somerville's phone bleeped.

49

'Yeah?' Heller answered his secure office phone. He listened to the field report from Hong Kong, then said, 'Good. Keep me posted. If you get to Walker first, make sure that when he's taken in, the Chinese put him away in some mainland jail for the rest of his miserable days.'

•

Somerville's body language changed as she stared at the screen of her phone. She then looked at Walker. 'Bloom never did tell my friend *why* you were in Hong Kong,' she said, holding up her phone. 'Is it because of her?'

Walker looked at the screen and saw a picture of a young local woman.

'I've never seen her before.' Walker scanned the terrace. The exits were still clear, but he knew there were at least two guys, likely more, nearby. The first two had been the visible threat, perhaps to corral him, make him flee the other way.

'You need to tell me what you're doing here, and what you did at The Peninsula hotel before coming to the racetrack.'

Walker looked at Somerville, knowing there was more to it. 'How about we get out of here first?'

Somerville scrolled through the message. 'Five minutes ago the body of this local woman was found by police in your hotel room, along with a trafficable quantity of drugs and several firearms. There's an APB out for you.'

'Why would the police search my room? They were tipped off?'

'Yes.'

'Convenient, don't you think?'

'Did you—'

'No. Good plan by someone, though; they want me tied up here in Hong Kong.'

'The local police have already gone to the Canadian embassy with a copy of your passport and discovered you to be a fraud,' Somerville said, reading, then looking him in the eye. 'It won't take them long to get a facial-recognition hit and make you for who you really are.'

'I'm just a dead American, remember?'

'You're not worried by all this?' she asked, watching him closely.

'Worrying doesn't fix anything,' Walker said. 'And if there's something to be immediately concerned about, it's the two big guys who were here until about a minute ago.'

'Do you have any idea what will happen to you when you're arrested by Hong Kong PD?'

'That's not going to happen.'

'Hong Kong's a small world.'

'How long do I have?'

'Minutes. Security cameras here would be networked into the police system.'

Walker checked his watch: 9:24 pm. Six minutes to go. 'I can't leave just yet.'

'Why?'

'Call it stubbornness.'

Somerville saw the determination.

Walker had already worked out the distances in the room. Head chips had a wi-fi range of twenty metres, meaning anyone in here could be relaying the data to any point on the terrace. He also knew that he could go up or down in the complex, as long as he stayed within a three-dimensional twenty-metre bubble.

'Let's go,' Walker said and headed for the stairs that would take them up towards the roof.

'Where?'

'Anywhere but here.'

'You don't have an escape plan?'

'I planned on spending the night on a flight out of here, sleeping like a baby.' Walker held the exit door open for Somerville.

'How's that working out for you?'

'Not great, I've got to say.' He checked his watch. Three minutes to go. He led the way up the stairs, and they exited at the next level: private boxes, with as many staff milling about as there were patrons.

Two uniformed security guards headed their way, walking along the wide hallway, their demeanour suggesting that no threat had yet gone out over their radio network. Walker checked his bearings and the time; another minute before he could flee this zone.

'We need to keep heading up,' said Walker.

'We need to get you down to the harbour,' Somerville countered, following Walker up another flight of stairs.

'What's at the harbour?'

'Not what, *who*,' Somerville said, dialling a number in her phone. 'That persuasive friend I was telling you about.'

'I'm not heading straight for the harbour,' Walker said, emerging onto the highest level: a service area of open steel mesh walkways behind the lights that illumined the track for those in the grandstand. He stopped, knowing he was now at the edge of the twenty-metre range. He checked his watch: 9:31 pm.

Job done.

'You have something to do?'

'Yeah: not get caught,' Walker said. They made their way past all sorts of warning signs telling them not to be up here. 'They'll be at the harbour.'

'Who?'

'Cops. Those guys who've been tailing me all night. Whoever put that dead girl in my bed. They'll be covering all the exits.'

'My friend will be able to get you out.'

'Is he a magician?'

'Of sorts.'

'Right, well, meantime in the real world . . .' Walker said, looking down from the roof of the racecourse. Wind shot up from where it hit the structure below. 'How are you with heights?'

'Fine.'

'Then follow my lead.'

'I'm not the fugitive here.'

'Then don't follow me.'

'I'm taking you with me.'

Walker looked at her, his expression saying, *How you gonna do that?*

'Okay,' Somerville said. 'I'll follow.'

Walker made his way along the steel lattice gangway, the radiant heat from the huge floodlights to his left as intense as the sound from the grandstand as the horses thundered towards the finish line.

There was an emergency exit ladder that went from the roof structure to the ground below, and Walker took it down, fast. It ended several metres short of the street level, where he had to break through a security tape and kick down the final section of ladder.

At street level Walker led the way through the throngs of people who left after each race. There were red cabs lined up, but he didn't want to be stuck in one. There were shady guys milling about, spruiking lifts in illegal taxis, but he didn't want that either. He needed to stay in control. Mobile. Fast.

He threaded between the long rows of scooters and motorbikes in the car park.

'So, how do you plan on leading the chase elsewhere?' Somerville asked, her gait cumbersome, somewhere between a power walk and a jog, as she kept up with Walker's fast stride.

'I don't,' Walker said. '*You* do.'

'I'm not letting you out of my sight.'

'I'm flattered. But you won't have to. Make a phone call.'

'A phone call?'

'To the embassy,' Walker said, stopping by an old scooter but then thinking better of it. He started up the search again. 'Place a call to their regular open line. Tell the RSO that you have me, that you're in Kowloon and headed for the airport with me in custody, that you'll need assistance on arrival.'

'You're assuming that those hunting you here are listening in?'

'I know they are. They're CIA.'

Somerville nodded, dialled the number and relayed the message, the perfect sell, every detail. Thirty seconds later she said, 'Done.'

Walker stopped at the perfect vehicle: a Husqvarna 400 Cross motorcycle, probably older than he was but in gleaming condition. He sat on it and kicked up the stand.

Somerville said, 'You're stealing a motorbike?'

Walker reached to her hair and took a hairpin, which he used to undo the steering lock, and then he kick-started the engine.

50

Somerville rode pillion position, her hands on Walker's rib cage, which made him wince, and he moved them down to his hips.

'You're injured?'

'A scratch,' he said.

'Central,' Somerville said into his ear. 'Head for the westernmost pier at Central.'

'To your friend?'

'Yes.'

Walker was silent as he considered his options, the bike slow going as the junction ahead clogged with all manner of traffic. *Going with Somerville could be the best way out of the county – but will she get me to the US?*

'Not yet,' he said, toeing up into third gear as he wound through Queens Road East. 'We wait for them all to converge on the airport. Thirty minutes. They'll then be tied up there for a couple of hours, looking for us.'

Somerville said, 'We can be on a flight out of Macao by then.'

'I don't have time for that. I have to get to America. Fast.'

'You're on a deadline?'

'Yes.'

'What is it?'

'I'll tell you when we're safely in the air and headed stateside. Can you organise that?'

'If you tell me everything, yes, I can. Where you've been since Yemen and what you've been doing. You tell me all that, then yes, we can take you home.'

Walker nodded almost imperceptibly, noticing the headlights behind him take the same turn he did for the third consecutive time.

Walker stuck to his speed and made the amber light. Just.

The car behind flashed through the solid red.

At the next traffic light he stopped.

The sedan – Walker could just make out the BMW badge – stayed back, as though not wanting to be seen at close distance under the street lamps and red-vapour glare of his tail-light.

The intersection was full of the ubiquitous Hong Kong red cabs, old Toyota workhorses. This was a business area, and outside of 7 am to 7 pm things changed to dining and drinking and tourism. It had just ticked after 9:50 pm. The other way was still green but there were no vehicles passing through.

Walker turned into the oncoming lane, through the intersection.

'What are you doing?' Somerville shouted against the wind as he moved up through the gears, her voice alarmed.

'I got sick of waiting,' Walker said, his eyes on the side mirror.

The chase car made the same manoeuvre, but the driver had hesitated, as though weighing up the move since it would be the clearest sign yet that they were tailing him. They sped to catch up. The BMW was nowhere near as nimble as the bike, but it was big and powerful. *Better keep them at arm's length.*

'So much for being patient,' she said.

Walker grinned. Eyes on the road ahead, stealing glances at the side mirror.

Behind them, the BMW announced itself by way of a blue flashing light mounted on the dash. The car closed in on the bike's rear tyre, the light strobing in the night. Somerville noticed it, looked behind her.

'Police,' she said. 'Seems your little stunt got noticed. What's next, genius?'

Walker kept at his speed, on the limit, and considered his options. It was highly unlikely that these guys were cops. *Maybe the Special Duties Unit, modelled on Britain's SAS before the handover and still staffed by a lot of expat types . . . that would explain the grizzled old meat-heads back at Happy Valley.* While they weren't in the habit of making traffic stops, they would be after a prized and dangerous catch such as Walker, the killer, his guilt by association to a false passport and a dead woman in his hotel bed.

They could be part of the same crew that hit the safe house. Or someone posing as cops. Or Agency goons, outsourced heavies.

Too many variables. Better to deal with it here and now.

Ahead was Staunton Street, lined with bars and restaurants, and plenty of people.

Walker pulled to the kerb.

They flashed headlights at him, a hand out the window, signalling him to drive around the corner into an alleyway. It wasn't a good option, but it also told Walker something useful: whatever they intended, they didn't want it to go down in public view.

Walker drove on towards the corner.

'Maybe I should let you off here,' Walker said, motioning to the packed line at the door to a speak-easy marked Feather Boa.

'It's not my scene,' Somerville replied. 'Besides, you might need me.'

He looked back at the federal agent: about five-three, maybe sixty kilograms, soft yet fit. Capable.

But he had to get out of here as quickly as possible. He had to get to a computer and log onto a secure network to download the data from his head chip.

And he had no intention of losing his head.

Walker pulled into the side street.

51

Walker and Somerville had climbed off the bike by the time the BMW pulled up behind them.

The driver said, 'Police. Hands in the air.'

'You're not cops,' Walker said as the two guys he had seen back at the racecourse got out of their car. They moved from the vehicle to stand a couple of metres away from Walker. Somerville stepped up to his side, and her bravado made him smile.

'Then why did you pull over?' the other one said.

His accent was Afrikaans, which to Walker confirmed them as outside muscle: private contractors; mercenaries; soldiers of fortune. Used by the Agency for the same reason anyone hired them: deniability. They may have been good once, but now that all the piss and vinegar of being a young man fighting for God or country had worn off they wanted a sweet life with a big pay cheque.

If they want to meet their maker so badly, Bloom used to say in weapons training at The Point, *we're here to help*.

'Why did I stop?' Walker said. 'Because I wanted to get rid of you guys here.'

The two men shared a smug look.

Good, feel confident.

'How did that work for you, Mr Walker?' Afrikaans said.

'I'll let you know in a couple of minutes,' Walker said.

The two men chuckled.

'Who's your lady friend?' Afrikaans asked.

Walker watched the guy, a level gaze, never faltering. He replied, 'She's the person who's going to clock your lights out in about a minute fifty.'

'A minute fifty?' Afrikaans said, his eyebrows raised to his cohort. 'Quite specific in his dreams, this one, hey?'

Walker said, 'One forty-five.'

'Okay,' Afrikaans said, 'enough shit, hey, mate. In the car.'

Walker said, 'Why would we do that?'

'Because I said so. Come on, then.'

Walker remained silent.

The other guy said, 'We want to talk.'

Walker said, 'So, talk.'

'Not here.'

Walker said, 'I'm not going anywhere.'

'Get in the car.'

Walker said, 'I don't think you guys understand what is going down here.'

The two guys chuckled, then opened their suit jackets to reveal holstered automatics: Glock 19s.

'We're not going to ask again,' Afrikaans said. 'We can give you all kinds of pain, mate.'

'You know,' Walker said, taking a couple of steps to close the gap, 'you really should be careful who you try to bully in dark alleyways.'

The repartee stopped as a large group of loud, drunken tourists made their way through the laneway, a couple of them hurling obscenities at the driver of the BMW for taking up so much of the road.

'We've seen your record, Walker,' the other guy said, this one with an Irish accent. 'You were a good operator in your day, but you've been out of it. We never have. And there's two of us, and we're both armed. So, don't be a dick, yeah? Get in the car, and make this easy. We want to know what you know, simple as that. Otherwise, well, look at her, she's real pretty. Shame to have to hurt her.'

Afrikaans added, 'It's not just you who's going to get hurt tonight, Walker, see?'

'Ah, now I see,' Walker said, looking back to Somerville, who had an unreadable expression plastered onto her face. He turned to face the two guys. 'The thing is, I'm on a bit of a deadline.'

'A deadline to die?'

'That's just the thing . . . I'm *already dead*.' Walker smiled the kind of knowing, dangerous smile that these two hardened men had likely seen before. 'So, you see, I've got *nothing* to lose.'

Behind that smile, if they were really paying attention, if they knew what they were doing, they would have noticed Walker's adrenal response: the monosyllabic speech, furrowed eyebrows, dropped chin, white cheeks, the bared teeth in the smile. These tiny motions, all within the same split second, indicated that an attack was imminent.

Most people will not back down from an attack once their adrenaline has surged. The two guys saw that in Walker's smile, but they were not quick enough. They were good, but not great. The B Team.

Three things happened within three seconds.

First: both guys reached for their Glock pistols. That was their biggest mistake – aside from taking on Walker up close and in a confined space. They were both right-handed, with the holsters on their right hips, which meant they had to bend their arm at the elbow to remove the pistols, moving their shoulder and arm back as they did, index finger pointed straight at the ground, other fingers and thumb curling around the grip, as had been drilled into them thousands of times at some military training ground. They also knew that for a close-contact firing position, the grip must be perfect or more time is wasted adjusting to aim, so their quick draws became a split second slower still.

While they were in motion, so was the second thing.

Walker.

He descended upon them. Fast.

Walker took the two short steps and punched forwards and up with two fists, one in each target's solar plexus; he positioned his fists like he was holding a mug handle in each hand, so that the force on connection did not reverberate back or transfer through his wrists and elbows. Two hundred and thirty pounds delivered in a lined-up kinetic chain through to two hard fists.

The guys never got to draw. Walker's blows damaged nerves, which would result in serious organ dysfunction, and caused diaphragms to spasm, knocking the wind out of them.

And then the third thing happened.

Somerville. Her attack came in the form of a kick to Afrikaans under the jaw. The uppercut from the toe of her boot targeted the guy's chin by coming straight up, minimising lateral movement. A spectacular sound emanated as the recipient's head snapped straight up, then his knees gave out, collapsing as if the puppeteer had cut the strings.

The Irishman in front of Walker was winded and staggered back a step, wide-eyed. In that passing second his survival instinct kicked in, and his brain told him to drop his right hand back down to the still-holstered Glock.

Walker caught the hand reaching for the gun, twisted it around the guy's back in a compliance hold and applied increasing pressure. First the wrist snapped, a double pop from the ulna and radius as they splintered apart.

Walker didn't stop there, because the guy wouldn't give in. Walker turned him around to face the car, and used his left hand against the guy's shoulder and continued the compliance hold to the point of shoulder dislocation, while hammering his head down onto the car boot.

The guy slid from the car to the ground and didn't move.

Somerville was silent, taking a step back, the moment of violence settling in.

Two minutes, start to finish.

'German engineering isn't what it used to be,' Walker said, admiring the dint in the BMW. 'Time to go.'

She turned to look back as Walker guided her by the arm and they joined the throng of Staunton Street, where Walker kick-started the motorbike and Somerville climbed on behind him. He headed for the westernmost point of the Central Piers, the night's summer breeze in his face as he descended from the Mid Levels.

52

Walker winced at the tearing pain in his side as he brought the bike to a stop. Bill McCorkell waited inside a helicopter, the Chinese version of the Augusta 109, its rotor spinning as they arrived. Somerville dismounted and then Walker followed and dropped the bike. He took the packet of pain-killers from his pocket and swallowed three. He walked under the rotor wash.

'Bill McCorkell,' McCorkell said, offering his hand.

Walker shook it. Firm grip.

'I hear,' McCorkell said, as they climbed aboard, 'that we have a deadline.'

•

McCorkell's contribution to the deadline factor was providing two flights. First in the chopper, which took them to Macao International Airport, where they ran to a private terminal and boarded a Gulfstream G650. The sky's speed queen, the G650 had a record speed of close to Mach 1, making it the world's fastest passenger aircraft. With a range of 7000 nautical miles on long-range cruise, it would get them non-stop to their next destination: Washington DC.

'What's our deadline in DC?' McCorkell asked.

Walker said, 'It's not in DC.'

'So what's in DC?'

'Answers.'

The G650 climbed fast.

Somerville looked at Walker, expectant: they'd come through, buying him time and a trip back to the United States. Time for the payback.

'I have to go to DC first,' Walker said, settling back in his chair. 'For two reasons. First, I need to use a secure terminal at Langley. Then, I have to visit Jack Heller.'

The pilot's voice came over the speakers, announcing their flight plan: they would be flying north-north-east, over mainland China, Korea, Russia, the Arctic Circle, and down through Canada to DC.

Nine hour flight time. Walker checked his watch. They'd arrive 5:30 pm NY time.

'What's Heller got to do with this?' McCorkell asked.

'I'm not sure,' Walker said. 'But he has everything to do with Yemen.'

Somerville said, 'This is about revenge?'

'No,' Walker said. 'It's about another target. An imminent attack.'

They both looked at him, expectant.

Walker said, 'In New York.'

•

Somerville said, 'And were you planning to stop this attack alone?'

'Who says I'm working alone?' Walker said.

'Marty Bloom,' McCorkell said. 'Great guy, one of the best. But this is the A League. And times change.'

'Yeah, so I hear,' Walker said, drinking from a bottle of water. He checked his watch.

'How do you plan to stop what's coming?'

'Call in a warning,' Walker said. 'Prevent it, or at least get the intended victims out of harm's way. Maybe all of the above.'

'Is that still your plan?' Somerville asked.

'Do you have a better one?'

'Ah, yeah,' Somerville said. 'How about telling the world's intel agencies about this impending apocalypse?'

'You don't think I tried that?' Walker said. 'The first few months, I sent anonymous messages to everyone I've ever been in contact with and trusted. CIA, FBI, Homeland Security, NSA, MI5 and 6, DGSE . . .'

'And?'

'And nothing.'

'They could be working it,' McCorkell said. 'I mean, you wouldn't know, right? You're out of the loop.'

'They could be. But I can't take that chance. I can't assume it's going to be beaten. They've got contact from me, giving them a date and time. *A date and time.* And that deadline is getting close with nothing being done for all I know.'

'You could have come forward,' Somerville said. 'Put your name to the warnings, to lend them credibility. Or go public, or at least go to the Agency or Bureau. Once they see that you're a legit operator—'

'Yeah, because it's worked out really well for me since the world's intel agencies have known that I'm alive,' Walker said, then sighed. 'Look, I've done what I can, working this on my own. I've backtracked through my last mission, in Yemen. I made other couriers in the network. I've been able to operate with extreme . . . let's say, *prejudice* to uncover this target. I'm getting close and I'm not giving up yet. There's still time.'

McCorkell said, 'What's the target?'

Walker said, 'All I have is a city. New York.'

'We're hours from deadline!' Somerville said. 'And all you have is the *city*?'

'There's still time,' Walker repeated. 'Have a little faith.'

'I have faith,' McCorkell said. 'And you should too.'

Walker looked at him.

McCorkell said, '*I* got your message.'

Twenty-three hours to deadline.

53

Andrew Hutchinson had Eve's work and home addresses written down on a small notepad. All the young agents used smartphones or tablets these days. Hutchinson wasn't old – just on forty – but he didn't have time for those things. The batteries could die, and they could be hacked, read from afar. Plus you could drop them or get food on them and that would mean an expensive repair or replacement. Impractical for the working man. A small paper notebook? Five for a dollar. Paper and pen were dependable. The time-proven perfect technology.

Hutchinson liked to cover bases and worry only about the things over which he had no control.

Take his current house call.

Across the road he watched Walker's former wife, Eve, leave work. She was five-seven or close to it, dark brunette, with the toned and tanned figure of someone who did a lot of running. She was a nurse, on night shift. Leaving a little late. Overtime. Understaffed. America today . . . She got in her car, a five-year-old Camry, and took off, soon heading through streets of tree-lined, picket-fenced homes that made up the American dream.

She drove like a maniac, and he broke at least three laws just staying in her wake. At first Hutchinson thought she was late for something, then decided it was simply her regular driving style.

He slowed a few houses down the street as Eve pulled up into her driveway and waved to the kids playing catch in their front yard next door. Hutchinson pulled up closer. Her wood-panelled home was painted white with light-blue shutters, the upstairs loft space with a slanted roof like an oversized bungalow design. The garden was well kept, the lawn mowed in the past couple of days. A long-haired Golden Retriever bounded out the front door when she opened it – a quick sniff and then it dashed off the porch, sniffed her car, did a quick loop around the front lawn, selected a spot in the garden and then lifted a leg and peed on a shrub.

Eve called him in, having to repeat herself a couple of times until he bounded up the stairs and into the house.

She closed the door, not looking out. Not wary. Not worried that someone might be watching.

A dead end, this one. Still, he had to do it. The Taurus was due back before his afternoon flight to DC. It would be back in plenty of time. He would file his report to McCorkell from the airport bar.

Hutchinson stepped from the car and headed for Eve's house.

•

'When you sent out those warnings, you included Bloom,' McCorkell said, 'and he passed the intel on to me. He didn't mention it had come from you, just a source that he trusted like no other. Yesterday, he contacted me again, confirming the source was you, because he was concerned for you.'

'I guess I should be thankful he has a big mouth,' Walker said. 'How do you know him?'

'He does consulting for me at the UN and for the International Court of Justice, tracking down those still wanted in the area from the siege and Balkans war. He's a good guy. Without him, this conversation might not be happening – not this way.'

'Bloom's word was enough to convince McCorkell that you were not a threat,' Somerville added. 'And he convinced me.'

'And don't hold it against Bloom,' McCorkell said to Walker. 'He was looking out for you.'

'I'm not angry at the guy,' Walker said, then chuckled. 'Should have known the old dog wouldn't walk away from work, not completely. So, how much did he tell you about this threat?'

'Only that you – we – are on the clock. He gave me a date and time,' McCorkell said. 'I've spent the past couple of days playing catch-up regarding you. I know that you got burned in Yemen.'

'And does that mean anything to you?'

McCorkell nodded. 'What do you know about a guy named Dan Bellamy?'

'Private spies,' replied Walker. 'His INTFOR supplies the intel community with private contractors. He wants it to become what companies like Blackwater were to the military when we went into Iraq and 'Stan.'

'Yep. That's what he's working towards,' McCorkell said.

Walker said, 'Smart opinion says that the intel community is a good decade away from outsourcing half its workload to private contractors.'

'That's the smart opinion,' replied McCorkell.

'You think that Bellamy is the one driving this deadline?' Walker said.

'Who do you think it is?'

'I'm not ready to say.'

'Why?' Somerville said.

'Because I need to be sure. It's where things have been pointing since Yemen. But I'm not ready to call it. Not quite. Not for sure.'

'You don't have much time.'

'I'll get it done.'

Somerville looked to McCorkell and then asked Walker, 'What did those guys back in Hong Kong want?'

'My head on a plate,' Walker said.

'Who were they?'

'Working for the same people as the guys at the safe house.'

'The guy on the bike that hit our car back in Rome?'

'Him, I don't know,' Walker said. 'That was a kill mission. Maybe because I was with you. Maybe those guys back there in Hong Kong's Mid Levels didn't want to talk either but wanted to get us in the car to finish us. It makes more sense doing it that way.'

'So, they're all working for the same guy?'

'A guy who has wanted me dead since the safe-house cock-up.'

'Bellamy,' said Somerville.

McCorkell nodded.

Walker shrugged. 'You say so.'

Somerville asked, 'Who was the girl in the safe house with you?'

'Nobody,' Walker replied.

'No, not nobody,' McCorkell said, leaning back and looking at the other two. 'Clara works for me.'

54

Walker thought back to when he first saw Clara, standing in the doorway to Felix Lassiter's apartment. Then he thought about how calm she had been when aiming that pistol at him.

'She'd been following you for three days,' McCorkell said. 'Picked you up when you got back from Greece, when you crossed Lassiter's path.'

'Who is she?' Walker asked.

'Clara works for AISI,' McCorkell said.

'Italy's domestic intelligence agency,' Somerville said.

'What was her mission?'

'With you?' McCorkell said. 'First she was to observe and report. Then, when she saw you go to Felix's apartment, I told her to make contact. It took me until yesterday to put your name to Bloom's warning, then I had a sit down with the guy.'

'Clara's good,' Walker said, leaning back and feeling the stitched-up cut in his side. 'Not the best seamstress in the world . . .'

'Let's get back to Yemen,' McCorkell said. 'The HVT that crashed the party. Did you ever find out who he was?'

'He was supposedly a bomb-maker,' Walker said.

'Supposedly?'

'I'll get to that. A goddamned good bomb-maker. Asad Kamiri.'

'That's a lot of heat to bring for a guy who makes things that go boom,' McCorkell said.

'I thought so too, until I uncovered more,' Walker said. 'This guy was legitimately on our most-wanted list. Bomb-maker to the stars. The guy rewrote the IED playbook. Not only could he fashion a bomb to look like pretty much anything, he refined the explosive mix. He's got shit that has about ten times the explosive charge of C4.'

'You're talking about ONC,' Somerville said.

'Yep,' Walker replied. 'He could turn something the size of a pack of cigarettes into a car bomb.'

'Okay, now I know who you're talking about,' McCorkell said. 'It was never reported as Yemen, but I remember the hit being announced through the community – it was a happy day around the office.'

'Yeah well . . .' Walker stared into his drink. 'I'm sure the Agency sold the Yemen angle quietly because they didn't want every other bomb-maker in the world sending their CV to Al Qaeda's top brass. Not that that'd slow things down much.'

'Okay, so it's making more sense now,' said McCorkell.

'Sense?' replied Walker.

'Why they'd strike the house even though you and another operative ran into it.'

'Does it?'

'We believe that Asad has had a hand in major strikes against the US, from the ninety-three World Trade Center bombing to the USS *Cole* attack to sending home God knows how many of our uniformed in body-bags from Iraq and Afghanistan.'

'As well as connections to London and Bali,' Walker said. 'The guy works to the highest bidder: Al Qaeda, their affiliates, whoever.'

'And they got him,' said Somerville.

Walker shrugged. 'Supposedly.'

'What? What do you know?'

'I saw him,' Walker said. 'The body. In the house, at Yemen.'

'After the strike?'

'After the first strike. He was cooked, but I saw him.'

'And?'

'It wasn't our bomb-maker.'

Somerville looked at him sharply. 'The body in Yemen – it was someone else?'

Walker nodded.

'How do you know?' McCorkell asked. 'His face was never on file.'

'This body had no face,' Walker said. 'He was a mess.'

'But?'

'Asad had lost a hand, early in his career. Occupational hazard for guys in his field. His was major, because he'd always played with the big toys. Lost everything below the left elbow, and he was known to have a prosthetic.'

The look on McCorkell's face showed that he now knew. 'This guy, in Yemen,' Walker said, 'had two hands.'

55

Hutchinson knocked on the wood panel next to the screen door. The dog barked as the sound of footfalls came to the door. Eve opened it. Up close Hutchinson saw the small freckles dotting her face; she was no more than five-four, with dark-brown hair tied back in a loose ponytail.

'FBI, ma'am.' Hutchinson showed his ID. 'Special Agent Andrew Hutchinson. I need a couple of minutes of your time, please.'

'What's this about?'

A car sped past.

Hutchinson looked around, then turned back to her. 'It's sensitive.'

The dog barked again.

Eve shushed him, then opened the screen door. 'This is about Jed, isn't it?' she said, standing on the threshold.

'Yes.'

'Ya'll alone?' she asked, looking about outside, seeing his unmarked car parked out in the quiet street that she knew well.

'Yes. This won't take a minute.'

Eve nodded, stepped aside and Hutchinson entered the house.

•

'Tell me about the connection with Bellamy,' Walker said.

'He ordered the strike on the house in Yemen.'

'How?' Walker asked. 'Is his little private company operating their own fleet of drones now?'

'No, not yet,' McCorkell said. 'But be careful what you wish for. And they're not so little anymore.'

'How did he order it?' Walker said. 'Everything I've learned says that the order came from the SAD Director, Jack Heller.'

'That's who you're pegging this on?'

'We'd had run-ins before,' Walker said. 'He had personally pulled me off this op when I was still at the Agency. And his guy that was with me in Yemen – he drew down on me, mentioned Heller by name as he checked out.'

'Well then, it's Heller, *via* Bellamy,' McCorkell replied. 'I heard it from a source that I do not doubt.'

'Who?'

'A senator on the intel committee.'

'And why would Bellamy do that?' Somerville said. 'Order the strike, I mean?'

'The official reason is because of Asad,' Walker said. 'The bomb-maker. It was a cover. The world stops looking for him because he's dead. Meanwhile, he's now working for Bellamy. And I'm out of the picture.'

'That's about the sum of it,' McCorkell said.

'Until ten minutes ago I thought Asad was now working for Heller . . .' Walker said. 'Now I know he's working for INTFOR.'

'Why would a private intelligence company and the CIA want a bomb-maker listed as dead? Because he's working *for* them as a spy?' Somerville asked. 'As an agent? I mean, he can't infiltrate AQ anymore if they think he's dead – he's of no use. Or have they got the real Asad in a room somewhere, like Gitmo, bleeding him of intel?'

'None of the above,' Walker said. 'They've got him working for them doing what he does best: making bombs.'

56

Hutchinson said hi to the dog in the hallway. The house was timber floored, wide old boards that looked like they'd been reclaimed from some place far older. The paint scheme was muted but for a wall in each room that was painted a vivid colour; violet in the hallway, emerald in the lounge room, burnt orange in the kitchen. A distraction maybe, some kind of therapy, something to shock the senses into remembering to keep it together. He wondered how Eve had taken the news of Walker's death when their friend Durant had broken it to her.

'Take a seat,' Eve said, motioning to a row of stools at a marble-topped kitchen bench. 'Coffee?'

'Thanks.' Hutchinson could see that the backyard was unkempt: shrivelled plants, the ankle-high grass burned in patches from the heat of the sun and not enough water, a dead tree fallen over. It was in stark contrast to the front. Hutchinson looked out the back and saw Eve's private turmoil let to go to pasture, as if she did everything she could but as much as it was and as hard as it had to be, she couldn't do it all.

He knew then that this was a dead end.

•

'So, they have Asad making bombs,' McCorkell said. 'And we have a deadline and a city: New York.'

'And think about the bomb,' Walker said. 'It'll be small, and powerful. That's Asad's specialty.'

'So,' McCorkell said, 'it could be anywhere.'

Somerville said, 'Could be more than one. Could be multiple targets.'

'It doesn't need to be,' Walker said. 'It's a public space. It's for show, more than anything. This attack is designed for a specific purpose: to show the world that the imminent, persistent threat of terrorism is still out there.'

'Damn,' Somerville said. 'That'd help Bellamy out some, right?'

'Him, the Agency, anyone in the intel community,' Walker said. 'And I think I've figured out the place.'

'You know the target?'

'The target, no, just the location – and with Bellamy involved, it makes a whole lot more sense now . . .'

'Sense? Where?'

'Think about the time,' Walker said, snapping out of his thoughts. 'What happens at nine-thirty in the morning in New York?'

'People are at work,' Somerville said. 'Kids are at school.'

'It's a specific time, though,' McCorkell said. 'What's it mean?'

'I followed the money,' Walker said. 'That's where I found the answer. I kept searching and looking, and with the New York location, and the time, it became clear.'

'I don't follow,' Somerville said.

'You will,' Walker replied. 'Think about 9/11. Remember what happened to the money markets?'

'They closed,' McCorkell said.

Somerville added, 'And went haywire.'

'It was havoc,' Walker said. 'Billions, trillions were wiped. People lost big . . . but not *everyone*.'

Somerville stared at Walker as she figured it out. 'Bellamy's outfit is going to make a huge profit out of a terrorist attack, in New York, one that's going to affect the markets.'

'I didn't know about Bellamy,' Walker said. 'You guys brought that to the table.'

'You're talking put options?' McCorkell asked, nodding.

'That's right,' Walker said, and he could see that McCorkell was starting to get it. 'Put and call options are contracts that allow their holders to sell or buy assets at specified prices by a certain date. They allow their holders to profit from *declines* in stock values, because they allow stocks to be bought at market price and sold for the higher option price.'

'Just like on 9/11 . . .' Somerville said.

'Yep. Two of the corporations most damaged by the attack were American Airlines, the operator of Flight 11 and Flight 77, and United Airlines, the operator of Flight 175 and Flight 93,' Walker said. 'The spikes in put options occurred on days that were uneventful for the airlines and their stock prices. On September 6 and 7, when there was no significant news or stock-price movement involving United, the Chicago exchange handled almost five thousand put options for United stock, compared with just a couple of hundred call options.'

'People were betting those stocks would fall,' said Somerville.

'And fall *big* they did,' Walker said. 'On September 10, an uneventful day for America, the volume was a few hundred calls and almost five thousand puts. Bloomberg News reported that put options on the airlines surged to the phenomenal high of hundreds of times their average. And add to that, over the three days *before* the attacks, there was more than twenty-five times the previous daily average trading in a Morgan Stanley "put" option that makes money when shares fall below forty-five dollars. When the market reopened after the attack, United Airlines stock was almost cut in half, and American Airlines wasn't far behind it. Those who had bet the shares would fall made fortunes.'

'There were similar calls on stocks for defence contractors like Raytheon,' McCorkell said. 'While most companies would see their stock valuations decline in the wake of the attack, those in the business of supplying the military would see dramatic increases, reflecting the new business they were poised to receive.'

Somerville said, 'If something big happens again, the New York Stock Exchange will immediately close.'

'For a day or two, maybe longer,' Walker said. 'After 9/11 it came out that huge put options had been placed on airlines, on banks and insurance companies that would be hurt by the attacks and crashed markets. In each case the anomalous purchases translated into large profits as soon as the stock market opened a week after the attack: put options were used on stocks that would be hurt by the attack, and call options were used on stocks that would benefit.'

'That's the target, isn't it?' McCorkell said.

Walker nodded.

'That's what happens at nine-thirty in the morning, in New York City,' McCorkell said. 'The New York Stock Exchange opens.'

57

'Has anyone been in contact with you about Jed?' Hutchinson asked.

Eve replied without turning to face him, filling the kettle. 'Contact?'

'Since – after you were given the news.'

'You mean has anyone been here asking about him since?'

'That's right. Has anyone called? Any contact at all?'

'No. Not for ten months. At least. Not since wrapping up his affairs, the life insurance and all that. Before that the State Department sent me a flag; I forwarded it to his mother. Before that a friend from the CIA – Pip Durant – visited, to tell me what happened. And that's it, the sum of all contact.'

'Nothing else?'

'No.' Eve stopped still, lost for a moment, then went on. 'It's great, isn't it? You die for your country and your wife gets a visit and a flag and then all's forgotten.'

Hutchinson could see that she had tried to move on. Pictures on the mantel showed her with another guy. Happy snaps. Different places. The Grand Canyon. The ferry going around the Statue of Liberty. Disneyland. Hutchinson felt bad bringing all this back to her.

The place was not a museum full of old memories – it was an art gallery with blank walls, ready to be filled with new ones.

Eve made the coffee. Ground the beans, put them in a French press. Hutchinson sat on the stool at the kitchen bench. Eve set the coffee plunger on the bench, alongside two mugs, a sugar bowl and a small carton of milk.

'Agent Hutchinson, what's this about?'

'It's due process, is all. I thought I'd . . .' Hutchinson trailed off as the dog sniffed him, tail wagging, a well-chewed toy in his mouth. 'It's really nothing that need bother you – I'm sorry to have disturbed your day.'

'No,' Eve said. 'I know that look. I saw it on Jed's face enough times. You're not lying to me but you're also *not* saying something, to protect me. But you know what? Leaving things unsaid doesn't do anyone any favours.'

Hutchinson was silent. He closed his notepad.

Eve said, 'Tell me, Agent Hutchinson. What's going on?'

•

'Before he was CIA, Jack Heller used to be in banking,' Walker said. 'Until 2002 he was chairman of an investment bank that was acquired by Banker's Trust.'

'One of twenty major US banks named by the Senate as being connected to money laundering,' Somerville said.

'That's right,' Walker said. 'And Heller's last position there was to oversee "private client relations", giving him direct contact with some of the wealthiest people in the world – and their money.'

'Yemen?' McCorkell said.

'Yes,' Walker said. 'I was tracking a courier for financing operations. Thanks to him being a double, through the DGSE I was able to get details of some of his transactions.'

'They pointed back to Heller?' McCorkell said.

Walker nodded. 'That's why he shut me down when I was at the Agency; he didn't want me looking into it. When I went to State, I picked up where I left off.'

'And then Heller ordered you dead,' Somerville said.

'That's what I thought, though via Bellamy, you say,' Walker said. 'And they weren't taking chances – my Agency guy riding shotgun turned on me, then the drone strike came in. They wanted me dead and they left nothing to chance.'

'Jesus,' Somerville said. 'If you have this, I can take Heller down. I can have a team of agents—'

'He's Director of the SAD,' McCorkell said. 'It'd have to be beyond watertight, and a guy like that is cautious.'

'The kill order on me would have been recorded, in Agency files,' Walker said. 'If I get that, it's enough to take him in and get a federal warrant to comb through all his affairs.'

'You'll never get that kill order,' McCorkell said. 'It'll be buried under so much national-security red tape that you and a room of lawyers would take a thousand years to get to it.'

'I'm not going to ask for it,' Walker said. 'I'm going to take it.'

McCorkell fell silent.

'That's what Felix was getting from Athens . . .' Somerville said, making the connection. 'We knew that he had a list of buyers, money men, laundering through Greek banks.'

'And those people in the know who made put options that certain stocks would crash tomorrow morning,' Walker said.

'I'd bet on it, but we'll never know the names,' McCorkell said.

'Though maybe I have them now,' Walker said. He touched the small bump at the back of his head. 'They've been using Agency couriers like Lassiter to communicate with each other. Probably for years.'

Somerville asked, 'How did Heller go from banking to leading the pointy-end division of the CIA?'

'He joined the CIA in 2005, as counsel to the Director,' McCorkell said. 'He was promoted to CIA Executive Director by President Bush in 2008, then sidestepped to the role he's now in.'

'The short answer,' Walker said, 'is that Heller's made a career out of taking down competitors.'

'That's something he and Bellamy have in common,' McCorkell said. 'Bellamy has been brutal in his intelligence operations against his competitors.'

'Bellamy has competitors?' Somerville asked.

'The legit agencies,' McCorkell said. 'CIA, NSA, MI5 and 6, Mossad, you name it. Bellamy's people at INTFOR infiltrated the internet chat rooms where hackers would boast about their achievements; from there they developed contacts and recruited agents. They employed former police detectives and intelligence operatives of many nationalities, including a former head of Scotland Yard's criminal intelligence bureau. These agents used their contacts with state agencies, bugged phones, burgled homes, set traps and employed every device familiar to readers of crime fiction – with apparent disdain for the law. As in the high times of maritime piracy, one man's pirate would be another man's privateer.'

'So, he's chasing the American dream, forging ahead as the titan of a new industry, getting filthy rich and powerful in the process.' Somerville shook her head. 'Sounds like a true patriot.'

'That and more,' McCorkell said. 'If Heller goes over to INTFOR, it lends a hell of a lot of credibility to their operations.'

'What can we do about it?' Somerville asked.

'A lot, I think,' replied McCorkell.

'I've got my own battles,' Walker said. 'I've got a deadline to beat, and I've got Heller to take down.'

'No,' McCorkell said. 'This is the main game. This is the World Series. This is do or die.'

'I was never much of a baseball fan,' Walker said.

'Really?'

'The Phillies depressed me too many years growing up. Nearly gave my old man a heart attack thirty years before he had one.'

McCorkell shifted position. 'I knew him, you know.'

'Most in Washington did,' Walker replied.

'He was a good man. Honest. Never turned his back on a fight.'

'I can't fight Bellamy for you. I've got my own battle waging right now.'

'I hear you. But you're soon going to realise that all roads lead to Bellamy.'

Walker looked out his window. 'What could I possibly offer you that you don't already have?'

'Two things,' McCorkell said.

Walker looked at him, waiting.

'Ability,' McCorkell said, 'and deniability.'

58

Hutchinson could see more detail with each passing moment. There wasn't even the barest trace of Walker in this house, but then, it had been a while, and Hutchinson understood that each person was unique in their grief. Twenty years at the Bureau and he had seen it all when it came to grieving spouses. He had to admit, he preferred these ones; those who picked up and moved on. However long that process took, it was better than spending the rest of your days sitting in a chair and looking at a photo and wondering *what if . . .*

'It's something that Jed was working on,' Hutchinson said. 'It's still unravelling.'

'The mission that got him killed?'

Hutchinson nodded.

'For the State Department?'

'That's right. Did he tell you much, about his work?'

'No. Only arcane things. Broad brush-strokes of places he went and things he saw.' Eve smiled. 'And minute details of the food he ate, interesting things he saw in cultures, stuff like that. He'd tell me about every little thing, but never any details about the work. Never any secrets. Nor the people he met. Not even a reason for being away so often, for so long.'

'What do you remember him saying about that last assignment?'

•

'In Yemen,' McCorkell said, 'you were tracking a lead from one of the cell-phone numbers that was found on bin Laden.'

Walker nodded. 'It led us to part of their funding network, before Heller dead-ended it citing ongoing operational reasons.'

'What do you remember about bin Laden getting hit?' McCorkell said.

'I remember a buddy in the 160th SOAR telling me that we got him. That the SEALs had killed him.'

'When did you find out?'

'An hour after the event.'

'It was under wraps until zero-six-thirty,' said McCorkell.

'Like I said, my friend flies with the 160th,' Walker said. 'He took the SEALs and the body out on a Chinook to Bagram. I was told that at zero-six-thirty it would go out on the Intellipedia net.'

'Did you worry about reactions?'

'Hell yeah,' Walker said. 'I was in the field. You know the drill – the world was gonna light up when the news broke. Back home, people would celebrate in the streets. And elsewhere, just like Newton's third law of motion, there'd be equal and opposite reactions. I laid low that day.'

'Then?' McCorkell said.

'Then, I got ready for a shit storm. Prepared for anything and everything. We've all got something in a glass case to break on a rainy day when the devil's breathing down our neck, and I got ready to break mine.'

'You know why I'm asking, right?'

Walker nodded. 'Because of Heller. And Bellamy. For them, and for INTFOR, that was a bad day.'

'A bad day?' Somerville said.

Walker said, 'Our SEALs killed their cash cow.'

'They need a new war,' Somerville said, the dots connecting. 'So, they're starting their own.'

McCorkell nodded.

Walker too. Then, he said, 'And they're calling it Zodiac.'

59

Eve exhaled. There was a broken woman behind that mask, Hutchinson saw. She could put up a good front, set things up in her life just so, but it would never completely leave her. Maybe she kept a box of Walker's stuff up in the attic, out of view from her new life, but there for when she needed it.

'Jed was gone for months, and I had no idea that he was in Yemen,' Eve said. She poured the coffees and added milk to hers and stirred it ten times, then tapped the spoon on the rim of the mug as if out of habit. 'We were already apart then, and that – it was the final straw. He emailed a few times; I deleted them without reading them. I was so angry that he'd gone away . . . But he – it's like he was addicted to the job, and they knew it.'

'They?'

'Whoever he was working for. The Agency, State, whoever. It's like they had an emergency Rolodex with one name in it: "You need a long-term mission done well? Call Walker, he'll do it."' Eve was quiet for a while, looking into her coffee. 'But that's all in the past. Is there anything else?'

'Have you ever had any contact?'

'Contact?'

'Has – I thought maybe he might have left something behind, a letter or email, that came later, after he—'

'No. He died. That's it. Are we done?'

'Yeah,' Hutchinson said, finishing his coffee. She didn't know anything that he couldn't get from the files. 'Thanks for your time.' As he stood, the dog came up to say goodbye and get a scratch behind the ear.

Eve opened the door and stood aside.

'Will they get them?' she asked.

Hutchinson turned around. 'Sorry?'

'Will they get the men who killed my husband?'

My husband. Hutchinson was looking at a woman who still cared.

'I'm working on it,' Hutchinson said. 'Everything I can do, I will do.'

•

'The mood at the CIA has shifted,' Walker said. 'It started a few years back. A big change was the path they'd gone down with interrogations and tortures. The new administration came in, and they meant it when they said we couldn't torture any more. A lot of guys were left disgruntled. A lot bugged out, in case they were the ones left holding the ball when the lawyers came knocking.'

'And add to that the scaling back of activities in Afghanistan and Iraq,' McCorkell said. 'It meant that for Agency personnel, times had definitely changed.'

'So, Bellamy has designed a series of attacks to – what, make his private-spy company viable?' Somerville said. 'That's what Zodiac is?'

'Viable, necessary – the big player on the block,' McCorkell said. 'He can scale up a hell of a lot faster than the Agency can in order to respond to the new crisis. He was a junior counsellor on the 9/11 commission. Worked for Senator Anderson. Got a sweet gig in the Green Zone for a couple of years, running the oil ministry, re-building and securing billion-dollar contracts for companies back stateside.'

'Have you ever met him?' asked Walker.

'Only in passing. He recently did a bit of work for the Agency.'

Walker raised his eyebrows in surprise.

'He was never payrolled,' nodded McCorkell. 'Just a few jobs here and there. Ran a few ops for them.'

'But not payrolled?'

'No. He gifted his services, or, rather, those of his company.'

'Showing them what INTFOR could do.'

McCorkell nodded. 'Yes. Think of it as proof-of-concept type stuff. Clamped down on some big-time computer hacker in Spain operating out of a decked-out van. And I gotta tell you, a *hell* of a lot of folks on the Hill like what he's selling. He's got the Vice President in his pocket. If Zodiac's big, it just might see INTFOR become the next multi-billion-dollar security company.'

'More than that,' Walker said. 'It'll be an intelligence apparatus with no government oversight.'

60

Hutchinson pulled the Ford Taurus from the kerb and did a U-turn. As he drew his seatbelt to stop the chime of the warning, he glanced over and saw that Eve had closed her front door.

A Dodge Charger passed him. Dark-grey metallic.

Hutchinson checked his rear-view mirror, his mind catching up with the Dodge's bright-red flaring brake lights. He took his foot off the gas, allowing the Taurus to coast. His mind replayed the pass. Male driver, thirties, plaster tape over his nose and dark eyes like he had suffered blunt-force trauma right between them. He had been looking at the street numbers on his right like he was visiting the place not for the first time but it had been a while.

The guy was familiar.

Hutchinson saw the driver pull over to the kerb and get out.

Hutchinson stopped the Taurus at the intersection. A car behind him tooted to pass through, but Hutchinson ignored it.

It took Hutchinson another few seconds to make the guy.

He turned right, floored the gas, did another U-turn, then turned left back down Eve's street.

Ahead, he saw Pip Durant on the front porch, knocking on the timber cladding by the door.

•

'INTFOR means smaller government,' McCorkell said, 'and for the majority of the House and Senate, that's all they care about.'

'And they're just going to hand over the keys to our spy kingdom?' Somerville said.

'Yes,' Walker said. 'They will. It's the dawn of the intelligence-industrial complex.'

'The way Bellamy's been spruiking it is: you've spent all this money finding bin Laden, and where did that get you?' McCorkell said. 'How long did it take? How many lives wasted?'

'Heller used to say a similar thing,' Walker said. 'He said, essentially, that we've had eight years to find bin Laden – and all we've got to show for it are a bunch of photos of naked Arab men peeing on themselves and wearing dog collars and black hoods.'

'Well, those days are over,' McCorkell replied. 'The government wants nothing to do with that kind of thing. Not in this day and age.'

'So, outsource it?' Somerville said. 'Keep it at arm's length?'

'Damn sight easier,' Walker replied. 'With OBL, there was no secret group up on the top floor looking for him. We were chasing ghosts around the world. We took our eye off the ball for too long, when at the end of the day it was our priority – it was our job to find him, and it took far too long.'

'Did Bellamy have a hand in it?' Somerville asked.

'Abbottabad? No, not directly,' McCorkell replied. 'But he helped put a rocket up the Agency by telling the President that INTFOR could find bin Laden within twelve months. He said to give him that chance, and they'd do what the CIA and the other intel agencies couldn't do. And, if proven effective through that op, INTFOR would rise to become everything that Bellamy wanted it to be.'

'And that pushed the Agency?'

McCorkell said, 'Damn straight. The President said no. He wanted to give the proper channels time, and had his new DCI say, *Go find bin Laden – and don't use torture. Torture is morally wrong. Torture is the coward's way. C'mon – we're smart, we're the USA, and you're telling me we can't find a six-and-a-half-foot Saudi who's got a twenty-five-million-dollar bounty on his head?*'

Walker said, 'Makes sense.'

'I know,' said McCorkell. 'So, they do their thing. The agents switch from torture to detective work – and guess what happens? They find bin Laden! Eight years of torture – no bin Laden. Two years of detective work – boom! Bin Laden! So, where does that now leave the big fat intel community?'

'They've spent umpteen billion dollars on the war on terrorism,' Walker said.

'Yep. Terrorism. People fell for it, and these rich men and their friends made billions of dollars from contracting deals and armaments and putting a Burger King on every US base in Iraq. Billions more were made creating a massive internal spying apparatus called "Homeland Security". Business was very, very good, and as long as the boogieman Osama was alive, the citizenry would not complain one bit. That's been part of Bellamy's case since. He wants the private spy of tomorrow to be what the private contractor is today.'

'And make a killing in the process,' Walker said.

McCorkell nodded. 'We're not talking small change here. This is tens of billions in government contracts every year.'

'Okay,' Somerville said. 'Well, now that bin Laden's gone, there's no poster-boy of evil to hunt, so the war on terror isn't what it used to be. So, what's Bellamy's leverage? A cheaper, more efficient intel community?'

'That's because we don't know it all,' replied McCorkell. 'What are they doing tomorrow morning, when the Stock Exchange opens?'

'They've set up an attack. A bombing.' Walker headed to the small galley area and took a bottle of water. He stayed standing, drinking, then said, 'We get to Heller, and we get to Bellamy. If we get them both, we can shut this down.'

61

Hutchinson killed the engine a house down from Eve's.

He watched as the front door opened. Eve looked Durant up and down questioningly. His boots and jeans and chequered shirt were like any other Texan's around here. His face, however, was all banged up. Durant replied with a shrug and few words. Eve hesitated a moment, and then embraced him. They went inside the house.

She looked outside as she closed the screen door, and saw Hutchinson getting out of his car. She called for Durant as Hutchinson walked up the driveway.

Durant came out to the porch. 'Can I help you?'

Eve made the introductions, explaining how Hutchinson had just been inside for coffee and a chat about Walker.

'Right,' Durant said, his gaze never leaving Hutchinson. 'Can I see ID?'

Hutchinson showed his FBI credentials.

'Why don't you come on in again?' Durant said with a smile, revealing he had lost a front tooth from his run-in with Walker at the safe house. 'Maybe I have some information that will be helpful to you.'

'Thanks,' Hutchinson said. It was not the greeting he'd expected. Hutchinson paused as he saw the look in Eve's eyes. She seemed uneasy with the little get-together. He asked her, 'Would you like us two to go talk some place else? We can go to my car?'

'No,' she said, 'it's fine, come on in.'

Hutchinson entered, walking past Eve, who held open the screen door. He walked a few paces up the wide, antique floorboards and paused.

Durant was to his right, outside the line of the hallway, in the space where a wall used to be but had been cut out in a renovation to make the living room open to the hallway.

Durant motioned onwards, towards the kitchen. Hutchinson headed for the kitchen again.

Durant attacked him from behind.

Hutchinson hit the floor hard, dazed but conscious, the blow to the side of his head having just missed his temple. He rolled to his left—

WHACK!

A boot heel stomped down where his head had just been.

Hutchinson turned—

Durant pulled a Smith & Wesson revolver. Hutchinson kicked out and tripped Durant. The .38 boomed.

Plaster rained down from where the round hit the ceiling.

Eve screamed.

Durant was on his back and reached for the spilled revolver.

Hutchinson grabbed Durant's ankle and pulled him towards him.

Durant sat up and made to swing, but Hutchinson was ready, sideswiping the blow and grabbing Durant's arm, twisting him around on the slippery polished floorboards, getting behind him in a sleeper hold.

The upper hand was short-lived – Durant dropped to the floor, Hutchinson's grip lessened, and Durant had the .38 in hand and whipped around—

CRACK. The steel butt caught Hutchinson across the chin and he fell to the floor.

Eve tried to run, but Durant caught her by her hair and slammed her against the wall.

'You're going to get what's coming to you, bitch,' Durant said, his left hand pulling down hard on her hair. His right hand was by his side, with the Smith & Wesson hanging.

Eve was stunned. Wide-eyed. Dying inside at the betrayal.

'First, you're going to see me kill this guy. Then, you're going to feel what it's like to—'

Hutchinson crash-tackled Durant to the ground, ploughing him into the wall. The Agency man turned with the hold and pulled Hutchinson into a headlock.

Eve screamed at them to stop.

'Get out!' Hutchinson yelled to Eve, his face and neck red with the effort of fighting against the hold. 'Get out now!'

Eve ran out the front door.

Hutchinson fought for purchase on the slippery floor and found it. He rose on a knee and snapped his head back, using the back of his skull to crack Durant in the face, but the CIA man took the blow to the forehead and kept his hold.

Hutchinson twisted but Durant held tighter, gripping his arm around Hutchinson's neck and pulling him deeper into the sleeper hold.

Hutchinson squirmed, bending his legs to steady his rubber-soled shoes on the floor and then pushed back, moving them both across the floorboards and crashing against the wall, Durant bearing the brunt of the impact.

The FBI agent repeated the move, and again, until he felt the grip slacken and he twisted from the hold – he felt bones in his right wrist snap as he broke free. He let himself fall to his right, his left hand reaching across his body for his service pistol, but Durant caught him by the ear and threw his head down to the floor.

CRACK.

Hutchinson saw stars in a black sky, though he was still conscious. His head rolled to the side and his focus found Durant, his face covered in blood from his re-shattered nose, getting to his feet, the Smith & Wesson in hand. He was turning as Hutchinson reached for his pistol.

'Hey,' Hutchinson said. He was lying on his right side, his left hand holding his service pistol sighted on Durant's chest.

Durant turned and showed more of his body, raising his revolver to aim—

Hutchinson fired twice. Both shots hit Durant in the chest, a little to the right side of the rib cage, blowing him away.

As Durant fell, he returned fire, two shots. One bullet flew wide, gouging through the floorboard to Hutchinson's right.

The other was on target, and grazed Hutchinson as he turned in reaction to the first shot, the slug burrowing a groove across his forehead. The last thing he saw through a curtain of dark blood was Durant, dragging himself to his knees and crawling out of the house.

Twenty-two hours to deadline.

62

Walker had been to Langley hundreds of times, but he had never felt like this. He was nervous as they entered the grounds.

Just inside the gate, which looked a lot like a customs stop, was a traffic light. When it turned red, people stopped their cars. If they didn't, the steel barrier that was poised to rise from the roadbed would stop their cars for them.

McCorkell parked the hire car and led the way from the car park, Somerville and Walker behind him. The three of them walked in silence.

There were two main office buildings, one occupied in 1961 and another in 1988 after the Agency outgrew the first. By the piercing floodlights Walker could make out the lesser buildings on the grounds: the steaming block that was a gas turbine back-up power plant; The Bubble, an auditorium; the tall water tower; and a modern house out of character with the rest of the architecture, which served as a day-care centre.

The CIA's white marble lobby set a tone of austerity. No-one got in without going through one of a battery of special gates, inserting an ID card and punching in a code. Even then the cards didn't always work, and sometimes an arm of the gate would stick. The visitor's ID card was unmistakable, with a large orange V and the words 'Visitor – Escort Required'. Everyone wore ID here, all the time. Not long ago Walker felt at home here, but tonight he was slapped with a big, conspicuous V. His biometrics would be stored, and when he made his move, and security files were checked, there would be a few surprises for the security guys.

He couldn't help but cast his eyes over the memorial wall as he passed. Each of the hundred-plus stars commemorated the life and service of a CIA officer who had died trying to protect the United States.

Walker was one of those stars. He wondered how many others were like him – presumed dead, but not.

Not many. Maybe none. It had been Agency lore that there was another, far larger, list of bright stars in the night sky that represented field officers listed as MIA.

Inside, Walker headed for tech services in the basement to search for his kill order, while McCorkell and Somerville went to confront Deputy Director Jack Heller.

'I need the bathroom,' Walker said to his escort, a young guy who looked like he belonged in high school.

The guy gestured to a door, and Walker went in – followed by the escort.

'Really, in here too?' he said.

The guy shrugged.

As he headed for a cubicle, Walker surreptitiously unhooked his ID pass and it fell to the floor. He turned to retrieve it.

The Agency escort bent to pick it up by the lanyard, and Walker kneed him under the chin as he rose. The guy went limp, falling unconscious to the floor. Walker dragged him into a cubicle, sat him on the toilet with his head slumped against the wall, and locked the door, then hoisted himself over it to the other side.

He slipped Pip Durant's ID pass over his neck and left the bathroom. On the way to tech services he passed four people working the night shift, none of whom he recognised.

•

Somerville stood next to McCorkell, waiting outside Heller's office.

'Don't mention anything about Bellamy until Walker gets up here,' McCorkell said quietly.

Somerville smiled. 'I can't wait to see the look on Heller's face when Walker appears.'

'I can't wait to see the look on Heller's face when you arrest him.'

The secretary came out. 'The SAD Director will see you now.'

•

Tech services was located in what used to be a storage area before most of the paper files were digitised. It could fit four football fields per level, and it was four levels deep.

The attendant was vaguely familiar to Walker, and it went both ways, with a mutual 'Hey there' greeting. Walker wore Durant's ID lanyard, the face and name turned around so that only the colour of the back, which signified his Above Top Secret clearance level, showed.

'I need a head-case scanner,' Walker said, rapping his fingers on the desk.

'Which station do you need it sent to?' the guy asked, reading off a computer screen as he continued with the task Walker had interrupted.

'No, I mean right here, right now,' Walker said, tapping a finger to the side of his head. 'It's in me.'

'Oh,' the tech officer said, looking at him queerly. 'That's odd.'

'I got in a tricky situation,' Walker said, playing with Durant's ID card. 'It's lucky I'm here at all.'

'Right. Well, have you got your Agency phone handy?' he said.

Walker paused briefly and said, 'No. I kinda need a new one of those too.'

'Right . . .' The tech tapped away at his keyboard and then produced an iPad with a requisition order. 'You field spooks – this ain't the army, you know. These ain't boots and blankets we're issuing. We have budgets to answer for.'

'Yeah, sorry about that.' Walker looked at the screen, uncertain.

'You need to put your thumbprint where it says.'

'Right.' Walker did so, and the image of his print stayed on the screen, lit up in bright blue. He saw the print flash three times then stay green, IDing him as field officer Pip Durant. *Nice work with the switch, Marty . . .*

'I'll have the phone pre-loaded with the one-time app.'

'The one-time . . .'

The tech looked at him. 'You haven't done this for a while, have you?'

'I've kinda been stuck in the field, living under a rock, if you know what I mean.'

'Well, hang on a sec,' the tech said, and he left his station and disappeared between stacks of metal shelves that used to hold file boxes and now held all manner of tech and IT gear. The office was open plan, and by the glow of the screens and dim lamps Walker could make out six other staffers working away in the cavernous space.

'Here, this one's old tech but compatible, and secure,' the tech said, handing over an iPhone 4. 'You want to use a computer room?'

'Room – yeah, for sure.'

'Number seven, down there.'

Walker took the phone and its charger and went to the computer room. He locked the soundproof door behind him and then opened the phone's head-case application. He watched the screen. It said it was scanning, and then a 'downloading data' message came up along with a progress bar that moved slowly across the screen.

While waiting, Walker used the browser to access the CIA's secure wi-fi network and looked up Dan Bellamy. In paper terms the file – full biographical information – was the equivalent of a couple of inches thick. The private bio ran at just a couple of pages. Walker downloaded Bellamy's home address and phone number, along with the family details of his wife and daughter, and a thumbnail sketch of the guy's life. Walker then entered Bellamy's financial and cell-phone details in the shared database that all intelligence and law-enforcement agencies could access. The system did a search of real-time location, bringing up details of when and where credit cards were used last, Trapwire image hits, phone calls made and vehicle location.

Bellamy's location popped up within a few seconds: he was currently checked into a hotel in lower Manhattan.

The phone beeped. 'DOWNLOAD COMPLETE.'

Walker checked his watch.

Fifteen hours to deadline.

63

Bill McCorkell told Jack Heller that he had debriefed Walker.

'And?' Heller said. 'I have no further interest in Walker; he's as dead to me today as he was last week. He's got nothing to do with this Agency.'

'They put a star for him in the lobby.'

'A gesture as erroneous as his decision to go to Yemen in the first place.'

McCorkell and Somerville shared a look.

'He has some interesting things to say,' Somerville said. 'About Yemen. About Asad. About his CIA guy turning on him . . .'

Heller's face gave a slight tick.

'You really should hear it from him,' Somerville said.

'I've heard that dead men tell tall tales,' Heller replied, smiling, leaning forwards. 'I'm sure he's got some outlandish story about how the drone strike in Yemen was a hit, to cover something up. Am I right?'

McCorkell looked to Somerville and smiled. 'Why don't you bring Walker in?'

•

'Thanks for this,' Walker said, waving the phone on his way out of tech services. 'I was never here. You didn't see me.'

'And you never got that from me, Walker,' the tech said.

Walker paused, took a moment, nodded in appreciation. 'You know me?'

'I ran that pass number. You're not Durant – I know *him*, unfortunately. So I brought up your file via facial rec.' The guy looked around, pointed to a security camera above, then whispered, 'I heard rumours, you know. You really are alive, hey?'

'That's what they tell me. You gonna rat me out?'

'Should I?'

'No.'

'Okay.'

'Okay?'

The tech nodded. 'Is this some *All the President's Men* kind of op?'

'I think you'll find that, once all this dust clears,' Walker said, 'you'll be on the right side of this one.'

Walker looked at the phone's screen.

'What is it?' the tech asked.

'Oh, so *now* you want to know?'

'Occupational hazard,' he said. 'I want to know everything.'

'The head-case info . . . it's a stock listing,' Walker said, scrolling through the pages of stocks. 'And a directive, for certain clients, to buy before nine-twenty-nine am tomorrow Eastern Standard Time.'

'What's so special about nine-thirty tomorrow?'

'That's my deadline.'

•

Somerville came back into the office empty-handed.

'He can't be far,' McCorkell said, turning to face Heller. 'Probably went to the bathroom.'

'He's here?' Heller said, and stood behind his desk. 'Walker's here? *In the building?*'

'Yes. In archives, getting the transcript of your order of the drone strike.'

'And that's just for starters,' Somerville added.

Heller looked hard at McCorkell, as if trying to read his thoughts. He spoke slowly. 'You brought Jed Walker *into* Langley?'

'Yes.' McCorkell returned the stare.

Heller picked up his phone and dialled security.

•

'Nine-twenty-nine is a weird time. Why not nine-thirty?' the tech said.

'Timing is everything, apparently,' Walker replied. 'Especially on the stock market. Can I print this?'

'I'll do it,' the tech agent said, taking the phone and hooking it up to the printer. 'Something's happening?'

Walker nodded, reading the two printed pages. 'At nine-twenty-nine, the bell is rung to start the day's trading at the NYSE. Have to get these in before then, so they say.'

'Well, you're in good company,' the tech said, his fingers flying over his keyboard as he Googled the New York Stock Exchange. 'INTFOR's going public tomorrow. You know who's going to ring the bell?'

Walker looked at him expectantly. Something inside him started to churn. 'Dan Bellamy?'

'Yep, and a special guest.' The tech turned the screen around for Walker to see. 'The Vice President of the United States.'

Walker looked at the screen in a daze.

'The Vice President!' the tech said. 'Man – you need help on this op? I've got clearance. My shift leader always promised I could go out in the field and—'

'No,' Walker said.

'*No?* No I can't tag along? Or no—'

A constant, no-nonsense alarm started to wail.

'What's the quickest way to the car park?' asked Walker.

The tech smiled. 'The quickest, or the sneakiest?'

64

Walker bought two pre-paid cell phones from RadioShack and used the first to call Marty Bloom.

'Thanks,' Walker said.

'It worked?' Bloom said.

'Like a treat. McCorkell brought me to the US, totally bought that I didn't know you fed him information.'

'What can I say?' Bloom said. 'I've still got it. And your ID switch at Langley?'

'It worked – just. I gave them the slip thirty minutes ago.'

'Nice. What now?' Bloom asked.

'Now I finish this.'

'What about Heller?'

'He can wait. Got a bigger fish to fry first.'

'Good luck, buddy. Keep your head down.'

'See you for a drink once this has all blown over.'

'Some place like Dubrovnik?'

'Yeah, some place like that.' Walker ended the call and tossed the phone, then took the car and headed north.

•

McCorkell and Somerville made their way through the car park at Langley. The security alarm had died down after four minutes of wailing and a biometric sweep had accounted for every person and corresponding security pass in the building. Walker had disappeared.

'Heller will wait,' McCorkell said. 'We'll pick him up tomorrow once this blows over. It's better we get to Bellamy.'

'Where did Walker go?' Somerville said.

'New York,' McCorkell replied.

'How?'

'Not flying. Train, or bus.' McCorkell stopped and looked around the car park full of Fords and GMCs and Toyotas. 'Didn't we park here?'

Somerville raised an eyebrow as McCorkell patted his pockets – the car keys were gone.

Walker.

'Son of a . . .'

65

Walker ditched the car three blocks from the train station and left the driver's window down and the keys in the ignition. As he sat in a window seat on the second carriage, he mapped out what he knew, a mental list.

Louis Assif. A double agent, working for Al Qaeda *and* the French. Dead not because he was a double, but because he was unravelling this. He had told Walker to follow the money. His cell phone had given Walker the date and time of the Zodiac attack.

The money had led to Felix Lassiter. To Hong Kong. To the put options being put on the New York Stock Exchange that morning. Walker thought back to the put options placed in the days before the 9/11 attacks. Some people made a lot of money from those attacks.

Dan Bellamy and INTFOR. His company was having its IPO today. He would be there, at the Stock Exchange, with the Vice President.

Ringing the bell.

Were they working together? The Vice President was Bellamy's biggest supporter in Washington, but what kind of attack would help them secure support for INTFOR? Or was it the aftermath that mattered rather than the means: the established, government-run and -funded agencies had failed, yet again, to stop a terrorist attack, this time focused on the very heart of America – its money and its executive government?

But wasn't this administration against the expansion of INTFOR?

The put options meant that someone was betting *against* the market.

Bellamy had the world's best bomb-maker on his payroll.

Walker rubbed his temples, popped another pain-killer. He checked the departure time for the next train to New York.

Twelve hours to deadline.

•

Hutchinson figured that Walker would arrive by train.

Airport security was too much trouble, and with the Vice President due in town in the morning, the security services at JFK, Newark and

LaGuardia would have been beefed up for the past forty-eight hours, the cost billed back to the Secret Service.

The roads – well, the roads getting in and out of Manhattan were chaos at the best of times.

So, Hutchinson figured the train. Quicker than the bus. Still, he had a couple of agents from the New York field office at the Port Authority Bus Terminal just in case, along with a detachment at Grand Central.

He bought a takeaway coffee and waited for the Amtrak Acela Express to roll in to New York City's Penn Station. He touched the thick wadding of plaster gauze over his forehead under a loose Yankees cap, the wound courtesy of Pip Durant's .38 slug. He had been patched up in the Texas Medical Center before speaking to Bill McCorkell and commandeering a Bureau helicopter to take him to the FBI's New York City field office. He was then driven into Manhattan, to Penn Station, where he stood now, waiting, sipping his coffee, watching for Walker.

•

Walker made Hutchinson first, but the latter was hardly trying to avoid being seen. He looked like hell. Worse than hell. The whole left side of his face was swollen, his bottom lip was threatening to explode with pressure and had angry black stitches in it, and the plaster above his left eye pushed his cap up and was weeping blood.

For his part the federal agent was waiting at the end of the platform and scanning the faces of every male over six feet two inches tall.

'Let me guess,' Walker said to the FBI agent. 'Andrew Hutchinson.'

Hutchinson left Walker's outstretched hand hanging.

He said, 'You ditched McCorkell back at Langley.'

'He can handle himself.'

'And the SAD Director?'

'Heller? What about him?'

'You didn't want to talk to him about Yemen? Get some kind of retribution?'

'No, not yet. I'm on a deadline. He'll get what's coming to him.'

'And what's that?'

'The full force of the law, I would hope. What is it that they do to traitors these days? Or what – you worried he's going to run away to Ecuador? He'll keep.'

Hutchinson smiled. 'But why ditch McCorkell?'

'He was surplus to my needs.'

'Which are?'

'Fairly minimal.'

'What do you hope to do?'

'Hope? No. Not hope. I'm going to kill the guy who killed me.'

'You're going to kill Dan Bellamy?' Hutchinson said, slightly out of breath as he kept up with Walker, headed south on Seventh Avenue.

'Yep.'

'How are you going to do that?'

'Whichever way first presents itself.'

'And you think that'll stop whatever's coming at nine-thirty?'

'It's his show, so I don't see why not.' Walker stopped at the red light at West Twenty-Ninth. 'Have you got a better idea?'

'Lock the city down. Get the NYPD to call in National Guardsmen to sweep the place for our bomb-maker.'

'Really?'

Hutchinson shrugged. 'It's a start,' he said. 'It's an option.'

'It'll drive them underground at best. You're not going to catch these guys like that. You have to end things, first chance you get. If we had got bin Laden when we knew where he was, 9/11 would never have happened.'

'So, what – just go bump off Bellamy?'

The walk signal changed, and Walker set off. 'Cut off the snake's head,' he said. 'Something like that, yeah.'

'Jesus, Walker, wait up.'

'Walk faster.'

'No, I mean in your mind, in your – I've gotta tell you something.'

Walker stopped on the footpath.

Hutchinson looked uneasy.

'Can we sit, get a coffee?' Hutchinson said.

'Out with it.'

Hutchinson nodded, then, a little uneasily, said, 'It's about Eve.'

66

Hutchinson and Walker were in an all-night diner on Twenty-Eighth.

'Eve is all right?' Walker said.

'Completely,' Hutchinson replied.

'What were you doing there?'

'That's the thing,' Hutchinson said, stirring sugar into his coffee. 'The past couple of days I've been asking around about you, to get a better picture of what your motivations could have been for faking your death.'

'You thought I *wanted* to be KIA?'

'I had to look into it.' Hutchinson leaned back in the booth as the waitress topped up their coffees. 'I looked into your old jobs, that sort of thing. I spoke to some people. I spoke to Eve.'

Walker gave Hutchinson a look he reserved for special occasions, the kind he was waiting to level on Bellamy.

'Hang on there, hermano,' Hutchinson said. 'I told her nothing about you being alive and all; it was purely for background.'

Walker gritted his teeth.

'The thing is,' Hutchinson said, 'I wasn't the only one to pay her a visit.'

'Who was it?'

'Durant.'

That surprised Walker, and it didn't, in equal measures. 'Eve – did he tell her about me?'

'I'm pretty sure he didn't,' Hutchinson said. 'I didn't give him the chance.'

Walker nodded. 'How'd it play out?'

'Let's just say he won't be paying house calls anymore. At least not in this world. Two rounds in the SOB, he got away, they found his car, crashed into a road pylon and burst into flames. Guy's barbecued to charcoal.'

Walker saw Hutchinson in a new light. 'And that's how you got your face and arm banged up?'

'Yep,' Hutchinson said, looking at the hard plaster cast.

'Eve?'

'FBI have her secured. She's fine. I spoke to her on her protective agent's phone before I flew here. I told her that Durant had gone rogue, that we have to watch over her a couple days.'

Walker nodded and sipped his coffee. 'Thank you. I owe you.'

Hutchinson smiled. 'Normally I'd say forget it . . . but not this time.'

Walker knew what was coming.

'Work with me here,' Hutchinson said. 'Tell me what you know. What you're going to do. It's better that the two of us go up against this, together.'

'You sound like McCorkell.'

'I'll take that as a compliment.'

'And what, you're some kind of boy scout for him, running around collecting patches?'

'No. I'm just like you – I like getting the bad guys.'

'How's that going for you?'

'We do all right.' Hutchinson looked around. 'You know, you and I have something in common. What we do – this – we can't walk away from it. We have to keep going till the job's done.'

'Who says?'

'Me. I know it. Knew it as soon as I started talking to people about you.'

Walker watched Hutchinson for a moment before he spoke. 'You don't know me.'

'You're chasing this on your own. You can't let go. You don't see the world as grey and flexible; it's black and white. You're a blunt instrument. You see the division of good guys and bad guys and *nothing* in between. And you can't rest until you've tallied it up when you die. I know that, because that's me.'

Walker paused. *Not so dumb, this Hutchinson.*

'You believe you can change things?' Hutchinson continued. 'You're smarter than that. It breaks you, no matter how good you are. You're content to go and fuck up the bad guys; life goes on, the sun rises, a new day is born. But what have you really achieved? They're still out there. Shit still goes down, every second of every day. So, you go back, start it all over again. And again. It's addictive.'

'That's a nice story. Excuse me, but I've gotta be some place.'

'Not without me you don't.'

'I don't play well with others – ask McCorkell.' Walker drained the last of his coffee and stood. 'You're good people, Hutch. Don't make me add you to the wrong pile.'

'Let me tag along. No harm in that.'

Walker checked his watch.

Less than five hours to deadline.

67

'I don't like it,' Hutchinson said.

'What's not to like?' Walker replied. They stood on the dark corner of Sixth and White Street, looking at the entrance to the Tribeca Grand Hotel, a six-storey brick structure that was probably once a warehouse when America still made stuff, and was now a place where you could sleep for five hundred dollars a night. 'I know he's staying there.'

'And he'll probably have security. Better we wait until the sun's up and he comes out; take him in the open.'

'I get you now,' Walker said, a sideways smirk. 'You're a one-armed, one-eyed lawman who likes fucking up bad guys. Nice. The thing is, in another hour from now this city starts to wake up good and proper. In another two, you're going to have thousands of people streaming along this footpath. Our window's *now*.'

Hutchinson grunted. 'Damn it. Come on.'

They walked into the hotel lobby. Behind the reception desk stood a young hip guy. He looked at the two dishevelled newcomers like they were something stuck to his shoe.

Hutchinson showed his FBI badge. 'We need the room number for Dan Bellamy.'

'Yeah,' the clerk replied, sliding his large black-rimmed glasses up his nose. 'My roomy sells those IDs on Houston Street for ten bucks apiece. You crackers can go back outside; we don't want what you're selling.'

'What about this?' Hutchinson said, removing his Glock and placing it on the counter.

'Yeah, my roomy sells them too,' the clerk said.

Walker smirked, looked to Hutchinson and then to the clerk and said, 'What, we don't look like Feds to you?'

'*He* does, a little, if it weren't for all that Frankenstein shit with his face and arm. You, not so much.'

Hutchinson re-holstered his weapon. 'It's Frankenstein's monster, shit for brains.'

'What *do* I look like?' asked Walker.

'A big, tired, angry motherfucker who's trying to get details on the rich guy staying in our penthouse so you can go hassle him. Not on my shift, Jack. Be gone with you, Frankenstein *and* his monster.'

Silence reigned for a moment as they all realised what had been said. *The penthouse.*

'That was like some kind of Jedi mind trick,' Hutchinson said to Walker.

'I know,' Walker said to Hutchinson. 'You wait here with our new friend. I'll go and visit the penthouse.'

'Not on your own.'

Walker was already headed for the lifts but turned and said, 'If I'm not back in fifteen minutes with an unconscious dirtbag over my shoulder, come looking for me. Besides, we don't want our little friend here warning our suspect, do we?'

'Listen to you, talking like a cop.' Hutchinson half smiled. 'I'll give you ten minutes. Don't do anything I wouldn't do.'

'Ha,' Walker said at the lift lobby and pressed the call button. 'We're the same, me and you.'

Walker got off at the top floor. The corridor was deserted. He looked up the hotel on the CIA-issued iPhone and saw via Google maps that the penthouse had a private rooftop garden, accessible via its own set of stairs. At the end of the hallway he opened a sash window and climbed out, reaching up to the eave and hauling himself up.

The roof terrace was flat and had a glass balustrade fence, which he quietly stepped over before creeping through the garden. The stairs leading down into the penthouse ended in a locked door.

He used Pip Durant's plastic ID card to jimmy the latch.

CLICK.

The door opened out, and he left it ajar, silently taking in the dark room; all its curtains were drawn. As his eyes adjusted to the darkness, he was able to make out a large sitting room with chairs and sofas. Walker could see enough to navigate the furniture, and he found the bedroom with its door closed.

Walker opened the door, the latch making a slight clicking sound as he turned the handle. He walked forwards, slowly, seeing a sleeping figure in the bed.

Bellamy.

Walker leaned in and clicked on the bedside lamp.

Four hours to deadline.

68

Bellamy woke with a start, his eyes fighting to focus as Walker shone the lamp light into his eyes.

'Game's up, buddy,' Walker said. He stood over him, lamp in hand, looking for the slightest excuse to brain him.

Bellamy looked from Walker to the door of his room, as if he were struggling to comprehend how his day was starting.

'You got close to your goal,' Walker said. 'That's gotta suck.'

'You really think you can stop me, Walker?' Bellamy said, sitting up and leaning back against the bed head. 'You? You're a *dead man*.'

'So they keep telling me.'

'Yet here you are.'

'I like to disappoint people.'

'So, what are you going to do?'

'I'll figure it out. But first we're going to chat. I know why you had me killed. Felix Lassiter, too. And Bob Hanley.'

'Oh?'

'To cover your tracks.'

Bellamy raised an eyebrow.

'You had the CIA hit the target and called it as taking out Asad. But it wasn't him, was it?'

'You tell me, it's your story.'

'It wasn't Asad. I know that, because I was there, and I saw him. So, it was a cover. But then, there was a double agent there who'd been working on this from another angle: Louis Assif. He was getting close. If he had really met with the bomb-maker, he'd have been a step closer to making you.'

'So *you* say.'

'But you'd made the double. You have links with all intel agencies; you called in a favour from DGSE for his ID, and you ordered Heller to kill him. You replaced Asad with a fill-in, obviously not telling the guy that it was a one-way job. You sold that intel – intel that you made up – to the CIA. Then you had the place cooked via Heller to make a whole heap of problems disappear – me included.'

'I can see that you've been thinking about this for a long time. Obsessing . . .'

'I haven't had much else to do, what with having my life taken from me,' Walker said. 'And I've been wondering: why would you – supposedly an intel expert – have a bomb-maker on your payroll? Why would a guy in your profession be working with a guy like that?'

Bellamy was silent.

'Then I saw the confirmation of the stock options from your money people in Hong Kong – and it made some more sense. You're buying up stocks before crashing the market at nine-thirty this morning.'

Bellamy watched Walker, still silent.

'But they're not regular purchases of stocks, are they?' Walker said. 'They're put options. Just like in the days leading up to 9/11. You're betting against those stocks rising – betting the other way, because you know better. You *know* that those stocks will crash and you're going to make a packet out of it.'

'Well,' Bellamy said lazily, 'if all this is true, that I *do* know that something will happen at nine-thirty this morning that will cause the market to crash and those stocks to fall, and if I *am* linked to those put options, then it would make sense to make a little money along the way, right?' He paused, then said, 'But why? Why do this? It all seems a lot of trouble to make a little money.'

'It's a lot of money. Could be a hundred million, depending how far the prices dive.'

'A hundred million? *Please.* That might buy a decent jet and the costs to run it for a couple of years. You're thinking too small, Walker, that's your trouble. You're failing to see the bigger picture.'

Walker thought about it. Thought about 9/11. Those in the know made money in put options, but that was just on the side. The real show was the act. Four passenger airliners changed the world and started a war. A war worth *trillions* of dollars.

What was the show here? A bomb blast? Where . . .

'You know what he said to me?' Walker said. 'The guy in Yemen, the words on his lips as he died?'

Bellamy shrugged. 'Do I care?'

'He said, "Follow the money." And that's when I first saw it. The word on his cell phone: Zodiac. Along with the date and time.'

Bellamy smiled. 'You know your biggest mistake?' he said. 'Being a loner. Not telling someone else all this. Not letting others in. Not having a team working against me instead of one lonely, bitter, *dead* man.'

'What makes you think I don't?' Walker said. 'Maybe there's a whole department at the FBI working around the clock on this. Maybe the Deputy Director in charge of the New York field office is waiting downstairs, right now.'

'That's bullshit,' Bellamy said.

'Sounds like you're a betting man.'

'No, not at all. I just deal with differing degrees of certainty. For instance I know that if you had gone bigger with this, then Bill McCorkell's meeting with Jack Heller would have gone very differently.'

Walker knew then without a doubt that Heller was working with Bellamy. He also knew something else: the tone and content of what Bellamy had just said showed that he was confident. Confident that Walker could do nothing to stop what was coming at 9:30. Confident that Walker hadn't shared all the relevant information with anyone. Confident that he was safe, alone in this penthouse, with Walker.

Which meant one of two things, and maybe both. Either that whatever was coming at 9:30 would not stop if Walker painted Bellamy's brains on the wall, or . . . that they were not alone. *There's someone else in the penthouse. Someone capable.*

Walker tensed, then started to move. 'Heller,' he said. 'It's all down to Heller. He made Felix as a double and knew that when I got to him I'd learn what you guys were up to; he sent the fake Asad to Yemen, set up the meet. Had one of his operators there to make sure I didn't walk out alive. All of it. He called the air strike. He ordered my death.'

Bellamy shrugged. 'He didn't order it; *I* did. He just gave me the facts and lined up our threats. I gave him the order. He relayed it.'

'What's in it for him?' Walker said, taking a step to the side so that the door to the bedroom was not in his blind spot. 'What is it? He's going to come work for you when he bugs out of government service? There's gotta be more than that.'

Walker heard movement from the dark living room, like a person struggling with something heavy.

Bellamy looked from the bedroom door to Walker and said, 'Why don't we go and see who that is?'

Walker motioned with the Glock for Bellamy to head out to the living room. He kept a few paces behind. The desk and reading lamps in the room came on.

'Walker, I think you know who this is,' Bellamy said coolly, calmly.

Walker could see why Bellamy acted as he did.

He had a hostage.

69

It didn't take Hutchinson long to realise that there was no way he could wait ten or fifteen minutes. Walker could get killed up there; Bellamy could get killed; there could be all kinds of innocent, public collateral damage if bullets started to fly through hotel walls.

'I'm going to check on my friend,' Hutchinson said to the night guy at the desk, writing down some numbers for him. 'If you want to call the cops, do it. But do me a favour – if I'm not downstairs in five minutes, call the FBI New York field office, give them my ID number, and tell them to send a tactical team.'

•

Walker took in the scene before him. It took just a second for him to see that he had made a mistake.

A big mistake.

A couple of big mistakes.

Clara was there.

That was his first mistake. He had got too close to her in Rome; they had been seen together, and now here she was, a hostage.

Leverage.

Clara was on the floor, seated against a long sofa, her butt on the carpet and her legs out in front of her. Duct tape was wound around her ankles, and probably around her wrists too, which were behind her back. Another couple of lengths of the black, near-on-indestructible tape were wrapped around her head and through her open mouth as a gag.

She was there, in the centre of the room, where she hadn't been just a couple of minutes ago. That meant that someone had just put her there. That meant that there was at least one other person in the room.

His second mistake was walking into a trap.

Fewer than four hours to deadline and everything had unravelled within the passing of a single second: that's all it took for Walker to know that two mistakes had been made. Had he had longer, he may have thought of others, such as leaving Hutchinson downstairs, and not dragging Bellamy out with a gun to his head, but he didn't have the luxury of time.

It was in the next second that he heard movement.

Behind him the skilled motions of a professional doing a good job, light on his feet, the carpet absorbing the footfalls.

WHACK.

Walker slumped to the ground. Lights out.

Il Bisturi stood over the unconscious form of Walker. 'There's a guy downstairs too.'

'Go get him,' Bellamy said. 'Quietly. Bring him up here and take care of it. No witnesses.'

'What about this one?' Il Bisturi said, his boot on the back of the unconscious Walker. 'Shall I finish him first?'

'No,' Bellamy said. 'Leave him to me. There's something I want him to see.'

•

Hutchinson walked to the lobby's lifts and pressed the call button, then saw that a lift was already on the way down. He knew that he was heading into a bad tactical situation: approaching a potentially hostile environment from the ground up, alone, without back-up. Just him and his cell phone, going into the unknown.

He shuffled from foot to foot, waiting for the lift, weighing his options.

He started to type a text message to Bill McCorkell.

•

Walker came to. He felt heavy, too heavy to get up, like he was in a lucid state of sleep and his body refused to completely wake. Darkness beckoned, but he forced himself to become alert.

A numb, throbbing pain in his right side. The cut, the stitches.

A ringing in his head.

He made a list of what he could feel and see.

He was face down on plush carpet.

It was dark but for the dull light of a lamp in the next room.

His head ached, his ears were ringing . . . He had been struck, from behind.

The hotel. Bellamy . . . New York.

His hands were behind his back and his wrists taped tightly together, one on top of the other, while his legs were straight out and his ankles stuck together.

Clara.

Walker rolled over. He saw that Clara was in the same position as before. Her eyes locked on his. They were desperate. They were the eyes of a professional, not a lover. The look said that this situation was going to hell, fast, and that any and all drastic action had to be taken. It also said that action or not, the odds were against them.

Walker looked up to Bellamy, who stood over him, smiling, now fully dressed in business suit and tie. *How long have I been out?*

'Let her go,' Walker said.

'That's not what's going to happen here,' Bellamy said. 'You know that.'

'She's got nothing to do with this.'

Bellamy was silent.

Walker rolled onto his back and looked up at him. 'What do you want?'

'I want things to go to plan,' Bellamy said. 'And now that you're here, like this, I'm sure that they will.'

'What do you want with me?' Walker asked. He could tell that Bellamy understood the unspoken qualification: what do you want with me *alive*?

'I want you to know what a failure you are,' Bellamy said. 'I want you to realise the new world that you're leaving behind.'

Bellamy crouched next to Walker. He slapped him a couple of times; short, sharp taps to the side of the head. 'I want you to go knowing that. And I want you to go knowing that you could do nothing to protect the women you care about.'

Walker wondered about Hutchinson. Bellamy had sent Durant to kill or capture Eve, and Hutchinson had foiled him. Maybe Bellamy didn't know that yet. No news from Durant did not necessarily signpost that the mission was a failure; it was just no news. Walker wondered how much time had passed while he was out.

As if in answer to his unspoken question, Il Bisturi came into the room, dragging behind him the bound and gagged form of Hutchinson, and then the night clerk. He propped them up next to Clara. The clerk was taking in the scene and starting to hyperventilate. Il Bisturi dropped him to the floor with the butt of the pistol cracking behind his ear.

'Ah, now it's getting interesting,' Bellamy said. Then to Hutchinson, he ordered, 'On the ground.'

Il Bisturi pressed the silenced pistol into Hutchinson's back. The FBI agent complied.

Bellamy taped Hutchinson's wrists and ankles as he had done to Walker, and then did the same to the unconscious hotel clerk.

'Why?' Walker said to Bellamy as he watched him wrap the tape.

'Because,' Bellamy said to him, 'I want you to witness your failure.'

'Failure?'

'Sometimes in life, we get what we want, and sometimes we get what we need. Il Bisturi here is going to give you what you deserve.'

Bellamy dragged Walker over to the sofa, where he sat him against the furniture, next to Clara, then turned on the television to Fox Business.

Bellamy opened a case. Walker ignored the television and took in the details of the case: black, about the size of a regular briefcase, made of some sort of hard plastic or Kevlar or carbon fibre – something near indestructible, even if dropped from an aircraft. Designed to store sensitive equipment, to protect what was locked soundly inside. The case was lined with pointed foam – like the inside of a pistol case – so the contents would be held tightly, immovably in place.

This case did not contain a weapon. At least, not an obvious one.

Bellamy reached into it and carefully removed what looked like an ordinary cell phone. He held it gingerly, as though it were precious.

'Did Asad make that for you?' Walker said, trying to buy conversation. *Asad could make a car bomb the size of a cigarette case . . . what's he going to do with that?* He watched as Bellamy carefully placed the phone in the inside breast pocket of his jacket.

'You really don't remember me, do you?' Bellamy said. He looked at Walker. A blank stare going both ways.

'It's Zodiac, isn't it?' Walker said. 'It's the first step in Zodiac – that tiny device will set in motion the first of twelve attacks that will ensure INTFOR becomes the big boy on the block.'

Bellamy smiled. 'As much as you think you know, you're wrong.'

'I know you're mad,' Walker said. 'Delusional.'

'Maybe, but you know what *I* know?' Bellamy said. 'I know it *all*. I know that you'll be dead soon. I know what's coming here, and I know what's coming there.' Bellamy pointed to the TV screen, which showed the trading floor of the New York Stock Exchange. 'And make no mistake, Walker. This time you'll be graveyard dead.'

Walker saw the time on the television.

Two hours to deadline.

70

McCorkell and Somerville touched down at the Downtown Manhattan Heliport. Their helicopter lifted off immediately and headed out to the west over the Hudson. Soon another helicopter would touch down: a VH-60N WhiteHawk operated by the HMX-1 Nighthawks squadron. Today that aircraft would be designated Marine Two, the call sign of any US Marine Corps aircraft carrying the Vice President of the United States.

'The place is locked down for the VP's arrival.' Somerville looked around. 'What's our move?'

There were a dozen uniformed NYPD officers either in or around their squad cars by the road entrance. Four blacked-out Chevy Suburbans were parked, their Secret Service agents milling about. A small gaggle of news crews were kept at bay, bustling around their tech vans.

'Hutchinson isn't answering his cell,' McCorkell said.

Somerville checked her watch. 'It's eight-thirty.'

'Let's make our way to the Stock Exchange,' he said, trying Hutchinson's cell phone again as he headed for the road.

•

Walker could see that the clock on the television news channel read 8:25.

Il Bisturi sat in a plush, orange, velvet, high-backed chair watching the four of them. Next to him, on a small side table, lay an unfolded set of cutting instruments, along with Hutchinson's Glock and the silenced pistol.

'We've met before, you and me,' Bellamy said.

Walker remained silent.

'At your father's funeral,' Bellamy said. 'I was there. I was the guy smiling.'

Walker remained still.

'Do what you like with those three,' Bellamy said, taking one last look at the captives. 'Make sure Walker watches the start of trading. Then kill him.'

•

'Hutchinson's still not answering,' McCorkell said.

'Maybe he and Walker are already inside the security bubble,' Somerville replied.

'Maybe. I told him to wait for us, though.'

'Walker doesn't strike me as the patient type,' Somerville said.

'Really? I thought the opposite.'

'Not my read.'

'To be fair,' McCorkell said as they walked up Broad Street towards the New York Stock Exchange, 'the first time you met him they did try to blow the both of you up, so he wasn't exactly in a situation to show patience.'

'True. Though ditching us at Langley was just rude.'

'Or genius, depending on how you look at it.'

'Have they found your car yet?'

McCorkell shook his head. 'Are your people ready?' he asked.

'I've got the local agents from CCRS Branch on standby around the corner at the Court Admin Building, along with a squad from HRT in case things get sticky.'

'Good.' McCorkell didn't know which he would rather see in action today: the Hostage Rescue Team, the FBI's heavy hitters with all the weaponry that the best of Special Forces could muster, or the CCRS with their computers and ledgers, specialists in dealing with financial crimes and public corruption.

'How do you think this'll play out?' she asked.

'Best case: we confront Bellamy with whatever evidence Walker retrieved from Langley, and he confesses.'

'Not gonna happen.'

'That was best case.'

'More like dream case.'

'Right.'

'So, in the real world?'

'Real-world best case?' McCorkell said. 'I think we're going to get nowhere today. But our presence will show Bellamy that we're onto him, and it might stall this so-called Zodiac terrorist attack.'

'So called?'

'Crashing a market? Look, I think us being here might break some of Bellamy's alliances, such as that with the VP. And, whatever the longer term consequences, it should prevent whatever chaos he's trying to stir up on the ringing of the bell.'

'You're not afraid of Asad and whatever part he may have played in this?'

'Of course I am,' McCorkell said. 'But I think that's a distraction, or unrelated. I mean, Bellamy's going to be there, standing next to the VP, and he's hardly going to blow himself up, is he?'

•

The hotel clerk passed out again when Il Bisturi made the cut. It was a small lateral incision in the wrist, about an inch long, but it would not seal, Walker knew, without medical attention.

Blood pooled to the carpet. It would be a slow bleed out to death.

'Two hours,' Il Bisturi said in his Italian accent. 'That is how long it will take him to die.'

Next to the clerk Hutchinson squirmed against his duct-tape binds, his mouth wide open against the tight tape wound through it, watching as Il Bisturi wiped the blood from the scalpel, its blade small and straight. He replaced it among his tools and selected another. This one had a curved cutting edge with flat back. A slicing instrument.

Hutchinson started to rock from side to side, sweat pouring down his face.

Next to Walker, Clara was still. Eerily calm.

Il Bisturi moved close to Hutchinson, crouching down, and sliced off his shirt with three precise swipes of the blade.

Walker had nothing to cut through the duct tape around his wrists, which had been taped together at an angle, one over the other, forming an X, with five layers of tape. There was plenty in the room that would get through it, including the scalpels, but to get to them or anything else he would have to get past a man who was an expert in wielding them.

Hutchinson was starting to panic as Il Bisturi felt down the side of his ribs, as though counting them off and finding the point of entry that he desired.

Walker leaned back as hard as he could into the sofa, putting more tension against the tape and preparing for his next movement.

Next to the television, across the room, were two pistols: Il Bisturi's silenced FN, and Hutchinson's Glock. Next to that Hutchinson's cell phone, disassembled.

Hutchinson screamed through his mouth tape.

Walker let the fear in. He knew the process, had been in countless sudden dangerous situations and lived through his body undergoing the changes. The release of adrenaline and noradrenaline as he moved to the state of readiness that helped him confront danger; the rise in his heart rate; the increase in respiration; the dilation of his pupils and – perhaps most importantly – the rapid contraction of muscles.

Walker felt each movement. He was now more agile, able to take in more information and use more energy. He was ready.

Hutchinson continued his muffled scream.

Walker couldn't see what was happening. Behind his back, his wrists taped tight together, he pushed his elbows down – a fast, sudden movement – with every ounce of strength he had, and then just as quickly he lifted his hands up, moving through an X motion.

The violent action against the duct tape ripped off hair and skin.

And snapped the tape.

Walker's wrists broke free of the binds.

Il Bisturi, still crouched in front of Hutchinson, turned to face him, the bloodied scalpel in his outstretched hand, as Walker lunged towards him.

Hutchinson lifted both his feet in a kick, knocking Il Bisturi's arm high.

Walker was on his knees and pulled Il Bisturi to him, a hand on the back of his knife-wielding wrist and another on the back of Il Bisturi's neck.

Il Bisturi twisted hard and fast to get away.

Walker held onto the small man's wrist, twisted it and pulled.

The scalpel dropped free.

Walker expected the guy to chase after his weapon, opening himself up for an attack.

He didn't.

Walker could tell that Il Bisturi knew how to fight, how to survive, how to kill.

The Italian elbowed Walker in the jaw and rolled away, Walker a second behind and pulling him back in. Il Bisturi kicked Walker's arm, pulled himself in and delivered two short jabs to the chest.

Walker bent into the fist blows and retaliated with a swipe, his backhand connecting with Il Bisturi's face.

The move only served to make Il Bisturi faster. He was already more agile, particularly with unbound feet, and he moved out of the strike range.

Walker reached for a table lamp, gripping the stem.

Il Bisturi made for the curved scalpel, holding its handle in a forehand grip. He was on his feet, moving sideways, crouched forward ready to pounce.

A blunt tool versus a fixed blade. Walker would choose the blunt tool any day.

Walker was on his knees, his bound ankles behind him. He transferred the lamp to his left hand, the power cord, which he yanked from the wall, in his right.

Il Bisturi lunged forwards – not for Walker, but for Clara.

Walker let his full weight fall forwards as he swung the lamp in a backhander that was flat and hard.

Il Bisturi ducked the blow, but the lamp caught him on the shoulder, twisting him.

Hutchinson kicked again and tripped him as Walker threw his full weight on top of him.

Il Bisturi wriggled on the ground to get up, but he couldn't move under Walker's weight.

Walker passed the power cord around Il Bisturi's neck and pulled, yanked, with every fibre of strength he had. There was an audible crunch as the quarter-inch plastic-coated copper wire tightened around the neck and compressed all the air, leaving only bone and muscle.

Il Bisturi went limp.

Walker dumped the body to the carpet. He picked up the scalpel, cut his feet free and then Clara's binds.

'Thank you,' she said.

Walker nodded, breathing hard from the efforts.

Together they freed Hutchinson and the unconscious clerk.

'You okay?' Walker asked Hutchinson.

'Yeah,' Hutchinson replied, holding his cut-up shirt as a bandage to his left side at the front of his chest between the fourth and fifth rib. 'Just a flesh wound. I think the little fucker was going to fillet me.'

Walker moved to the clerk. He took one of Il Bisturi's knives and cut a section from his uniform shirt to wrap tightly around the bleeding cut, as Clara cut her ankles free.

'Keep the pressure on this guy's wound, keep it elevated,' Walker said to Clara, and she moved to do as he instructed. 'I'm going to get to the Stock Exchange.'

'Not alone,' Hutchinson said.

'You're out of this round, buddy,' Walker said. He made for the minibar and drank a bottle of Coke in seconds. He tossed Hutchinson the penthouse's cordless phone. 'Call in an EMT.'

'I will come with you,' Clara said to Walker.

'No,' Walker replied, crouching down to her.

'I've got this guy,' Hutchinson said, taking over the first aid on the clerk. 'You two get out of here. Get Bellamy.'

Clara nodded. Walker helped her to her feet.

One hour to deadline.

71

Walker re-assembled Hutchinson's cell phone and it rang.

'Yes?'

'Walker?'

'Yep.'

'McCorkell. Where's Hutchinson?'

Walker gave him a quick rundown as he sat in the back of the cab, headed south on Broadway. McCorkell spoke off the phone for a bit and Walker could hear him relay the information to Somerville.

'Somerville and I are almost at the Stock Exchange,' McCorkell said. 'You'll need to get out at Beaver and walk up to Broad; NYPD has the whole place shut down. I'll be waiting for you.'

•

Dan Bellamy greeted the Vice President of the United States like the good friends they were.

'Thanks for doing this,' Bellamy said to him as they walked into the NYSE building on Broad Street.

The Vice President's press secretary asked them to turn at the top of the stairs for a photo op.

'My thanks to you, Dan,' the Vice President replied to Bellamy. 'I just wish that everyone saw your company as the future of defending this nation, as I do.'

'Give it time,' Bellamy replied, smiling as the cameras flashed. 'They will.'

•

There were thirty minutes to deadline when Walker found McCorkell at the NYPD roadblock at Beaver and New Streets.

'You look like death warmed up,' McCorkell said to him.

'That's how I feel.'

McCorkell nodded to the sergeant on the gate and Walker was

ushered through and handed a visitor pass for those cleared to access the streets around the Stock Exchange. Press, mainly, gaggled around their tech vans that bristled with satellite dishes.

'Clara?'

'She's gone with Somerville,' Walker said.

'She's set up with her colleagues around here some place,' McCorkell said. 'She's got several agents here, ready to move in and arrest Bellamy as soon as he shows his hand.'

'I think I know how that'll be,' Walker said. He described the cell phone and the case in which it had been so carefully stored.

'You think it's an IED?'

'Yes.'

McCorkell shook his head, said, 'Can't be. You can't bring cell phones inside the Secret Service's protective bubble.'

•

'Sir,' the Secret Service agent said to Bellamy, his metal-detector wand lighting up during the pat-down search. 'Do you have a cell phone on your person?'

'Oh, yes,' Bellamy said, removing the ordinary-looking smartphone from his inside jacket pocket. 'I'm expecting a call from my daughter.'

'Sorry, sir. Protocols,' the agent said. 'You'll have to surrender that.'

Bellamy looked to the Vice President.

'Let me take that, Dan,' the Vice President said.

'Sir, I must—' said Agent Bronson, the man in charge of the Vice President's Secret Service detail.

'It's fine,' the Vice President said. 'Dan is one of my closest friends, and when my goddaughter calls, we're going to answer.'

Agent Bronson looked uneasy, but after a moment's hesitation he capitulated.

'You put this on vibrate, right?' the Vice President said, patting his breast pocket and flashing his trademark smile of bright white teeth as he and Bellamy strode into the Exchange and entered the trading floor.

'Of course,' Bellamy said. 'Don't worry. When it rings, you'll feel it.'

•

At the end of Broad Street was another security cordon, with more NYPD officers – these ones in black combat gear and carrying M4 assault rifles – standing around another ring of temporary barricades. Secret Service agents in dark suits were stationed between them and the Stock Exchange building.

McCorkell showed his ID and the NYPD sergeant called over a Secret Service agent.

'Bill McCorkell.'

The agent looked from the ID and said, 'I know who you are, sir.'

'Good,' McCorkell said. 'I spoke on the phone to your agent in charge, Bronson, before. We're cleared to enter.'

'Yes, sir,' the Secret Service agent replied. 'Follow me. Leave all cell phones, wallets, everything loose on your person in a tray with these officers here; pick them up again on your way out.'

The bubble, Walker knew: the protective zone around the President and Vice President wherever they travelled. Nothing in or out that the Secret Service couldn't control.

Walker and McCorkell complied and were then patted down and scanned by metal-detecting wands.

'See,' McCorkell said. 'If he's using the phone as an explosive device, how's he getting it past here?'

'I don't know. But I'm sure he's found a way.'

72

Walker watched as the Vice President worked his way around the trading floor, shaking hands and smiling.

'I'm sorry, Mr McCorkell, my hands are tied,' the Secret Service agent said. 'I can't let you onto the trading floor; you know our pre-vetting procedure.'

'We just need a minute,' McCorkell said.

'Hey Bill, the Vice President's here to ring the bell for trading,' Agent Bronson said. Through his work in the Secret Service he had known Bill McCorkell throughout his entire career, as McCorkell had spent almost twenty years in the White House as an advisor to the President. 'He's got a twenty-two minute window afterwards for meet-and-greets: I can push you to the front of that line.'

From a pamphlet he had picked up by the entry, Walker knew that the NYSE opening bell was rung at 9:30 am EST to mark the start of the day's trading session, and at 4 pm the closing bell was rung and trading for the day ceased. There were bells located in each of the four main sections of the Stock Exchange, and they all rang at the same time once the electronic button was pressed.

That button, today, was being pressed by the Vice President. Ostensibly it was to mark the passage of a new bill being passed on financial-market reform, but there was no mistaking another reason: INTFOR was going public. Since 1995 the Stock Exchange had started to invite special guests to stand behind the NYSE podium and ring the bells, and these ceremonies had become highly publicised events involving celebrities or executives from corporations. Many considered the act of ringing the bells to be an honour, and due to the amount of coverage that the opening and closing bells received, many companies coordinated new product launches and other marketing-related events to start the same day the company's representatives rang the bell.

Today, on either end of the podium, below the Seal of the Vice President of the United States, was the company logo of INTFOR.

Bellamy stood before the podium, taking it in: this would be a photo op for him that would be broadcast and recorded and replayed time and time again.

'Hey, Bill,' the Vice President said, spotting McCorkell. He strode over, smiling, and shook McCorkell's hand. 'What the hell are you doing here?'

'Working, sir,' McCorkell said. He saw that Bellamy had his back to him, talking to the camera crew. 'Do you have a couple of minutes?'

'I will, right after this,' the Vice President replied.

'Sir, I have an emergency situation that you need to hear about,' McCorkell replied. 'Right now.'

The Vice President looked at McCorkell, and Walker could see that the old man's eyes took in the tone and the speaker, and knew what had to be done.

'I'll give you three minutes,' the Vice President said, checking his watch. 'Let them through.'

Agent Bronson nodded to the thickset agents to let McCorkell and Walker through, and then led them, along with the Vice President, into a side room.

Ten minutes to deadline.

73

'So, what is it?' the Vice President asked once the door was closed. 'Have you got a tip on a hot stock?'

'Hardly. Sir, this is Jed Walker,' McCorkell said. 'He's a deep-cover operative for the government.'

'Which agency?' the Vice President asked.

'Pretty much all of them, sir,' Walker replied.

The Vice President put his hands on his hips. 'So, what is this about?'

'Sir, we have reason to believe that an incident will occur as you ring the bell,' Walker said.

'Define "incident",' Agent Bronson said.

'Catastrophic,' Walker replied. 'At nine-thirty, as you ring the bell, an explosion will go off in the near vicinity.'

'We believe it's designed to close the market,' McCorkell added. 'Minimum of today, maybe a few days.'

Agent Bronson said, 'What's the intel?'

'Human intel, and intercepts of put-option transfers that back it up,' Walker replied. 'I've worked on this for near on a year. It's rock solid.'

'This is credible?' the Vice President said to McCorkell.

'I vouch for Walker,' McCorkell said. 'This is as solid as intel gets.'

Agent Bronson spoke a hushed code phrase into his sleeve mike.

'My team's just stepped up a threat level,' Bronson said to those in the room. 'But I've got to tell you, Mr McCorkell, with all due respect, we've had bomb units going through this place every day for the past two weeks.'

'He brought it in,' Walker said. 'Today.'

'Who's that, son?' the Vice President asked.

Before Walker could answer, Dan Bellamy entered the room.

Seven minutes to deadline.

•

Clara stood next to Somerville, watching as the FBI agent hovered between her troops – eight suited federal agents, seated at laptop computers. A radio uplink kept them connected to an armed team; HRT she'd heard them called.

The whole time that Clara stood there, watching, listening, she wondered, *Do I kill Somerville and run, or will I have to shoot them all?*

Clara took a couple of paces towards the agent seated at the tactical communications console, her eyes transfixed on his holstered Glock.

74

There was a moment when Bellamy saw Walker and Walker could see that all manner of violent options were being considered. It passed within a second.

'You were saying?' the Vice President said to Walker.

Walker stared at Bellamy.

Bellamy turned to the Vice President.

'They need us out there,' he said.

'Okay,' the Vice President replied. 'We'll continue this later, Bill.'

Walker reached out and took the Vice President by the arm – and in the same moment Agent Bronson had his Sig P226 pressed into Walker's side, hidden from all view, but Walker could feel it and got the message. He let the Vice President go.

'He's using you,' Walker said to the Vice President. 'Bellamy is staging an event here today that will be the catalyst for getting INTFOR the lion's share of the intel community's budget.'

The Vice President looked to Bellamy and then back at Walker.

'Son,' he said to Walker, 'you're exactly right. That's why we're here.'

'Not like this, sir. He has a bomb.'

The Vice President chuckled. 'Bill, is this some kind of joke?' He then focused on Walker, and the chuckle died. 'Son, you are gravely mistaken. Dan Bellamy is a true American hero. The work he's doing with INTFOR will save more American lives than anyone will ever know. And you know what? He's a friend of mine. And I've heard enough from you, Walker.' He turned to Agent Bronson. 'Get him out of here.'

'Get one of your guys here to look me up!' Walker said, the Sig again pushed into his side. 'You'll see. Jed Walker.'

'Okay, Walker, you're out of here,' Agent Bronson said.

'You're making a big mistake,' McCorkell said.

'Maybe he's in on it,' Walker said, staring at the VP.

The Vice President said, 'Bill, leave us be a moment.'

McCorkell left the room, his glance to Walker signalling it was up to him.

'Sir, I've spent my life defending this country,' Walker said. 'I've worked my whole adult life so that you can sleep soundly at night.'

The Vice President shook his head. 'And where did you go wrong, son?'

'When Bellamy ordered me to be killed when I was on assignment with the State Department tracking down terrorist financiers. And right now, if this goes ahead.'

'And what's going ahead, exactly, hmm?' The Vice President turned to Bellamy. 'My friend here is a patriot. He's taking INTFOR to the next level today. And it's my hope that it will become everything that I know it can be, because we will all be better for it, for generations to come.'

'It'll never be that big, and you know it,' Walker said, looking at Bellamy.

'He's disgruntled,' Bellamy said to the Vice President. 'He was looked over too many times. Rejected by our HR department. He was good, once, but he's cooked.'

Bellamy leaned in closer to Walker and said, 'It's because of what this country's intelligence agencies have done to good men like you that I' – he looked to the Vice President – '*we* need an entity like INTFOR.' He patted Walker on the arm. 'You go get the help you need, soldier. Find your peace.'

Bellamy stood back and motioned the Vice President towards the door, and they left the room.

Five minutes to deadline.

75

Walker thought through what he knew.

At 9:30 am the Vice President would ring the bell.

The put options: they were just the sideshow.

The phone bomb, made by Asad. Ten times the explosive force of regular C4. A hundred grams of the stuff would easily make a bang; kill a person, if it were on him.

Wherever, whatever, it was going to be a spectacle, an attack on the very symbol of the American economy, all in the presence of the second-in-command of the nation and a wannabe intelligence kingpin.

Why was Bellamy here? To make sure it occurred? To be there when the dust settled, to cement his place as the all-American hero with the answers that his country needed to go forward against the next eleven Zodiac attacks?

Agent Bronson said into his sleeve mike, 'We're going to need a pick-up as soon as we bug out. No, one unit will do it. What? No, not a trader, just a random crack-head in here talking about some grand conspiracy against the country. Yeah, another one. No, let's not make a scene. I've got it until you get here. Copy that. Later.'

He looked at Walker.

Walker looked at the sleeve mike, his mind racing. He knew that the public were not permitted to have phones around the President or the Vice President, that they had to hand them in within a certain perimeter.

Bellamy's phone. It wasn't just to make a symbolic bang.

Walker shook his head. *It's not on him – he couldn't have got it in here. Only the VP could get it into the bubble.* He froze. *The VP . . . Bellamy's good friend.*

The Secret Service agent called into his sleeve mike, 'Charlie, have you got Zodiac? Right, copy that.'

Walker looked at the guy.

Four minutes to deadline.

Walker said, 'Zodiac?'

'What did you say?' the agent asked.

'You just said "Zodiac".'

'Crack-head,' Agent Bronson said, looking away.

McCorkell re-entered the room and looked at Walker standing at Secret Service gunpoint.

Walker said, 'Who's Zodiac?'

'Let Walker be,' McCorkell said.

'Due respect, Bill, fuck that,' Agent Bronson replied. 'This guy's getting sorted at a precinct after this; go talk to the NYPD.'

'Walker is one of the greatest operatives this country has ever had.'

'Then we truly *are* fucked,' Agent Bronson replied.

Walker turned and faced Bronson.

The agent looked him square in the eyes, and, sensing something far harder, resisted the urge to force him around to face the other way.

'I need to know right now,' Walker said. 'What is Zodiac?'

The agent looked from Walker to McCorkell. The old man didn't back down.

Agent Bronson shrugged. 'Fine. Add it to your conspiracy. Zodiac is the Vice President's Secret Service call sign.'

Suddenly Walker knew.

Three minutes to deadline.

•

Four FBI agents left their posts, headed to patch into the NYSE's computer system.

That left four seated, and Somerville standing.

Clara moved fast.

She lunged for the holstered Glock at the comms agent's hip—

He reached for it, his hand clamping onto hers.

Somerville turned, took in the scene, rushed forwards—

Clara elbowed the seated agent in the face, pulled his pistol free, brought it up—

CRACK!

Somerville dropped Clara to the ground with a blow behind her ear with the butt of her own service pistol.

The agents in the room watched on, stunned.

'Keep alert, people!' Somerville announced to the room. 'We've got a job to do here!'

•

'The phone!' Walker said urgently.

'What?' McCorkell said.

'The cell phone – it's on the Vice President.'

'Agent Bronson, you have to get the cell phone off the VP and get it out, now!'

'What are you saying? He doesn't carry a phone,' Agent Bronson said. 'His press woman does.'

'But that's the point,' Walker said. 'This isn't an ordinary phone, it's an explosive device.'

'This thing's happening,' McCorkell said, checking his watch, 'in under three minutes.'

'You're both crack-heads,' the agent said. 'Bill, that English air has done something to your—'

'Zodiac isn't a program – it's a target!' Walker grabbed the agent by the lapels of his jacket and pulled him in close, face to face, ignoring the pressure of the Sig that was now being pressed hard under his chin. 'When that bell rings at nine-thirty, an explosive charge will go off. It's the cell phone, on the Vice President. Understand?'

'*You* need to understand that the Vice President's phone is with his press secretary!' the agent said, releasing himself from Walker's grasp and flattening out the front of his suit, the Sig down by his side.

'Bellamy gave him a cell phone to look after,' Walker said. 'You saw the handover; he's your principal, so you *must* have been there until you got the VP inside this building. Think back. Bellamy had it on the inside of his jacket pocket, left side.'

The agent was blank. Then the colour drained from his face.

'Listen to me. If you don't act, you lose a Vice President,' Walker said. 'You have just over two minutes. It's your call. Two minutes and your life goes one of two ways: the guy who lost a Vice President, or the guy who saved one.'

Agent Bronson sped from the room.

Two minutes to deadline.

76

'Today is a great day,' the Vice President announced to the trading room. He stood at the podium, the gavel and electric pad to ring the bell next to his right hand. Beneath him, on the balustrade, the Seal of the Vice President. Either side next to that, the banners and LCD screens carrying INTFOR's logo.

Walker and Agent Bronson ran through the back-of-house area. They could see the trading floor on the internal CCTV screens that they passed. From the room they were in, it was a five-second journey. For both men it was a lifetime.

'To those who say the government can't regulate the market? Sorry, but that doesn't fly.' The Vice President smiled. 'It is the responsibility of the citizens of each country to keep their government in check. The government of the United States is the concern of the people of the United States. Today we are witnessing two great steps forward – one by our government, and one by my great American friend here, Dan Bellamy.'

Walker was a pace behind Agent Bronson. He knew that the floor level of the raised balcony was a couple of metres higher than the trading floor. Walker could see the Vice President behind the ornate stone balustrade, with the murder weapon in his jacket pocket and the assassin standing next to him. It was the perfect alibi; Bellamy might even sustain some minor injuries in the explosion, get some kind of award.

'With a great American company like INTFOR going public,' the Vice President said, 'we will see a progression that is the symbol of this administration. A way forward for this great nation. A new dawn for the security of all of us.'

Agent Bronson spoke into his sleeve mike with every stride. As he and Walker rounded the last corner of the corridor, the two agents at the door sprang to attention.

Walker was a bigger man than Bronson, and by the time they hit the door he was a stride ahead. The agents opened the door to the balcony. Five seconds, and they were there.

The next three seconds were a blur.

Bellamy took a step back.

The Vice President, gavel in hand, said, 'And it gives me great pleasure to ring in the day's—'

Walker crash-tackled the Vice President, the cell phone clattering from his jacket across the balcony floor.

Hands grabbed Walker from behind. The two Secret Service agents pulled him off the VP and a Sig pistol was pressed against the back of his head.

Amid shouting and commotion all around, Agent Bronson and a colleague rushed the Vice President away, turning back and shouting through the doorway to let Walker go, and calling a warning about the bomb.

The cell phone had landed at Bellamy's feet. Bellamy stared at it as the chaos ensued.

09:29:29.

One second to deadline.

•

In that second, Bellamy left the phone and made for the door.

'Stop him!' Walker shouted.

The Secret Service agent moved to apprehend Bellamy.

An NYPD officer appeared at the door, his side-arm drawn.

09:30:00.

•

The bomb detonated.

The sound was unlike any that Walker had heard. A sharp, short report, a tear in the air around him as the shock wave knocked those on the balcony from their feet.

Screens and windows nearby shattered and cracked from the supersonic blast front. Octanitrocubane, or ONC. A detonation velocity of more than ten thousand metres per second.

The work of the bomb-making genius Asad.

Walker got to his feet. The centre floor of the podium was smoking and charred, a fist-sized hole blown in the tiles.

The Secret Service agent was down. Watching the way the guy moved, and seeing the blood seep from his eyes and ears, and hearing his rasping breaths, Walker could tell he had the kind of polytraumatic injuries received by IED survivors in Iraq and Afghanistan. These guys wore the best Kevlar systems money could buy, but just like the soldiers and sailors and airmen on the front line, no amount of armour would protect the fragile human body against the kind of shock waves generated by high explosives.

Walker turned and saw that an NYPD officer had crashed against the doorframe, unconscious, his Glock clattering from his grasp.

Bellamy took the pistol, nudging the cop off the podium, and fled from the scene, through the doorway.

•

Walker knew he had mere seconds. After that Bellamy would melt away. In an hour he'd be surrounded by friends and would check in with the Vice President. It would be his word against that of Walker and, maybe, Agent Bronson. Walker knew that the bomb would never be traced back to Bellamy. Its case would have been made of a ceramic or sugar compound, completely atomised in the blast.

His word against Walker's.

And it wasn't just that Walker would be seen as a disgruntled former CIA agent in from the cold to strike at the very heart of American democracy.

It was the symbolism of the attack.

He knew Zodiac was comprised of twelve targets, each a cut-out cell, triggered by an event.

This was the trigger, the attempted assassination of the Vice President. *Zodiac*.

Walker took the Sig pistol from the fallen agent and went after Bellamy.

•

The corridor behind the podium area was empty.

Two NYPD officers rounded the corner. They saw Walker and raised their Glocks.

'Secret Service!' he yelled.

The officers hesitated. One called, 'ID, now!'

Walker looked to his right, where the door to the restroom clattered closed.

Bellamy?

'Did Dan Bellamy pass you guys?' Walker called to the cops.

'Who?' one asked.

'A guy in a suit – did he just pass you?'

'No—'

'ID now!' the other officer said. 'On the ground! Now! Drop your weapon!'

•

Walker didn't want to shoot a police officer. He certainly didn't want to shoot two. He shot into the ceiling above their heads. Three shots. In the second it took him to raise and fire, the NYPD guys returned with eight shots, each 9-millimetre round wide and low as the officers moved backwards and fired blind, instinctively seeking the cover of the corner they'd just rounded. Walker sent two more rounds down-range, at the corner of the floor and wall, then turned and ran.

•

Walker kicked the bathroom door open, the Sig leading the way.

BANG! BANG!

Two 9-millimetre shots came from behind, embedding in the doorway, splinters hitting him.

Walker dropped as he turned around, returned fire.

BOOM! BOOM!

Silence.

Walker was on the floor, prone, Sig at the ready.

He could hear the cops down the hall, talking into radios, calling in reinforcements, coordinating play, checking on the other 9-millimetre shooter they'd just heard fire at Walker.

Ahead of Walker, in the corridor, was a sheet-rock wall at waist height, with a series of glass windows above. The window three to his left had two gunshot holes.

He looked behind at the toilet stalls. Three cubicles, all their doors closed, and via the floor he could see no feet visible. Three ceramic basins. A wall mirror. A row of stainless-steel urinals. Bellamy could be in a stall, perched on a toilet seat, waiting out the mayhem. *Or he could be in the maze of office space either side of the hallway. Was it Bellamy who had fired those last two shots, or a cop?*

Walker had to find out. He aimed the Sig, which was chambered for the powerful .357 round; fifteen-round-capacity mag; ten rounds left. Through the window he aimed straight ahead and up to the ceiling with a two-handed grip, his right hand on the trigger, left hand over it, pulling slightly in, forming an A-frame to support the fire and combat the muzzle climb.

BOOM! BOOM!

The sprinklers started up – first from the shattered waterhead that he'd just shot out, then one by one, a chain reaction radiating out, in the office and now down the hall. The fire alarms followed, clanging metal bells amplified through the building, then the whoop-whoop of the electronic evacuation siren.

Walker adjusted his grip on the Sig. Eight rounds left.

He crawled across the hallway, below the window level, hidden by the solid partition, his back to the wall. He looked around the corner of the hallway; the two cops were still taking cover. *Good tactics. Hold position, let another force flush from the other side—*

BANG! BANG!

Two 9-millimetre holes punched through the sheet-rock to Walker's left, a foot between them. They were shoulder height; holes the size of silver dollars.

Walker dropped low to the floor to his right.

BANG! BANG! BANG!

Walker fell face down to the carpet as a 9-millimetre round tore through his right forearm.

The Sig hit the floor. He picked it up left-handed and rolled onto his left side, then loosed three rounds back through the sheet-rock, on the same trajectory as those that had just come through.

Walker moved fast. His right arm diagonal across his chest, his hand holding onto his left shoulder, he crouched and ran to the office doorway. He could feel the sticky blood pooling inside his shirt and suit at the elbow, the pain so far all heat and numbness.

At the doorway he saw an open-plan office.

A figure ran across his view.

Bellamy.

•

The office was a big space, housing forty or so workstations in waist-high cubicles, four wide and at least ten long. The sprinklers poured rain over it all. Walker ran into the room and then crouched behind a cubicle wall.

The pain was coming on; throbbing, stabbing in his forearm.

'Give it up, Dan!' Walker yelled to the room.

BANG! BANG!

The Glock 29; a capacity of fifteen 9-millimetre rounds. Bellamy had six left.

The shots had come from the far side of the room, near a doorway that led out to the other side of the corridor, behind the two cops taking cover.

Walker made his way to the middle of the room, his body low, pain beginning to tear at him. 'You're not getting out of here!' he called.

Walker waited. A second. Five. Nothing but the falling water and clanging alarm and electronic wail. He stole a glance over the top of the cubicles. He watched and waited, his vision blurred, a combination of the torrential downpour and the pain of the gunshot wound.

'Give it up, Bellamy!'

Silence.

Walker moved.

Where Bellamy had been there was blood. Not much; a smear against the cubicle wall, and some drops leading around the corner, as if Bellamy were trying to circle around Walker and get back towards the bathroom.

Walker followed the drop pattern to the doorway to the corridor where he'd entered.

The alarms droned. Water fell.

9:35.

Bellamy was gone.

•

Walker was in the corridor, his blood dripping into the water that still rushed from the sprinklers.

He put down the Sig and pulled off his suit jacket. With his foot on the body of the jacket and a sleeve in his tight left fist, he tore off the sleeve. Watching to his left and right, wary, he tied the fabric tightly around his forearm. It was a through-and-through shot, tearing through muscle and possibly grazing bone. He kept the arm close to his chest, his right hand elevated to his left shoulder.

He picked up the Sig. For all his training Walker had never much practised firing a pistol left-handed. The Sig was a good gun, though, the weight and balance and recoil all well designed. If anything, it was a little small in his grip.

A few paces down the corridor he spotted blood in the water; not his own.

Walker switched sides, his back against the other wall, his gun hand leading the way. He stopped at an open doorway. In the reflection of the wet glass opposite he could see that the room held a lot of televisions, most of them playing the same thing: the feed from the trading floor of the New York Stock Exchange.

Looking down, Walker saw that the room held something else: a blood trail, small, already washing away.

Walker inched closer to the doorway and peered around the doorjamb.

A grid of screens lined a wall. This was some sort of control room; perhaps a media-monitoring room. No water fell in here, but everything was covered in a fine white chemical powder. But there was still blood in the water by his feet as it flooded the floor through the doorway.

He heard Bellamy's voice, a low murmur.

Walker stepped inside, the Sig still leading the way. Left-handed, losing blood, he couldn't keep it elevated forever. He lowered the pistol.

Some of the screens showed television channels: the news crews feeding live shots from outside the New York Stock Exchange; cops everywhere; the Secret Service agents largely gone. Walker knew they would stay on scene until they got their man. They would be quarterbacking this; ordering the NYPD's SWAT guys to be sure that there was no way out of the building before they stormed the place. Easily done, Walker could see, since the outside windows and doors had automatically shuttered with heavy-duty steel screens in response to the attack.

Walker moved closer to the screens. Bellamy's voice emanated from behind them, in an adjoining room.

Walker moved around the screens. He saw a final shot of the Vice President being half-carried with Bronson and the other agent into an armoured Suburban and whisked from the scene. Blood was smeared down the Vice President's neck, and the cameras froze on that, zoomed in. A disturbing picture. The ticker was already screaming out the assassination attempt.

Walker edged towards the open doorway to the adjoining room. The wet soles of his shoes mixed with the residue of the dry-chem extinguishers, sticky, claggy, a wet dough that sucked at his feet.

Bellamy's voice grew louder as Walker stood to his right side and looked in, his left arm raised straight, sighting Bellamy's centre mass down the iron sights of the Sig.

'Put the phone down,' Walker said.

Bellamy turned.

Walker kept the Sig levelled at the traitor's heart.

Bellamy said another few words, too low to make out, then put the phone down in the cradle.

Two men. The end of the line for one.

Walker saw blood on the floor at Bellamy's feet. Not a lot; perhaps a leg wound, a shard of shrapnel from a close encounter with one of the .357 rounds. Not enough to be life threatening, but it would slow him down. Then Walker became aware of something else, something in Bellamy's demeanour. Confidence. The kind of confidence that came from knowing that everything is all right. From knowing that he had the upper hand.

Then, movement behind Bellamy.

Another man.

77

'Walker's still in there,' said Bill McCorkell.

He looked around the FBI room – and stopped, seeing that the two agents had Clara cuffed and subdued. 'What happened?'

Somerville looked at Clara, said, 'She'd turned. Working with Bellamy. His back-up plan.'

McCorkell said, 'Clara – a double for Bellamy?'

'Triple, quadruple, I'm losing count,' Somerville said. 'Either way let's just worry about Walker.'

Fiona Somerville listened through headphones to the progress of the Hostage Rescue Team. 'We've got audio from inside,' she said. 'Listen.'

She pulled the earphone jack out of the speakers so that all in the FBI control room could hear.

•

Walker looked from the man back to Bellamy, who now held a Glock pistol aimed at him.

A stand-off: 9-millimetre versus .357. Both men wounded. Each with everything to lose.

'The ultimate insider trading,' Bellamy said. 'This is Barry, my guy. He works here. Works for me. He's made a lot of money doing it for, what, four years now, Barry?'

Walker looked to the man named Barry.

Barry was silent. Barry was sweating. Barry looked like a scared boy.

'Barry?' Bellamy said.

Silence. Sweat. Strain.

'Barry!'

'Yes?' Barry said. 'Yes!' His wide eyes looked from Bellamy to Walker.

'That's a boy,' Bellamy said. He took a pace from the phone and the desk, the Glock still levelled at Walker. The 9×19-millimetre Parabellum was the most popular calibre for American law-enforcement agencies.

It probably contained Hydrashock rounds, 124 grain. Five metres between them. No chance he'd miss.

Walker wouldn't miss either. He watched and waited.

'See, Barry here did a little job for me, didn't you, Barry?' Bellamy said. 'Barry . . .'

'Yes, sir,' Barry replied. He looked ill, as though he only now realised the price that came with doing whatever that job was. 'I did it.'

'See, Barry works in IT here, and he placed these new hard drives like the one he's holding all around the place.'

Walker looked at the black box in Barry's hands. It was small but it looked heavy; a quarter the size of a shoebox; maybe ten times the mass of the cell phone Bellamy had handed the Vice President.

'As of nine-thirty this morning they've all been activated,' Bellamy said. 'And they have a sound activation. Want to know what that is, Walker?'

Walker remained silent.

'Of course you do,' Bellamy said. He looked around at the screens, smiling when he saw the news images flash up: the Vice President being rushed out, Walker being tackled to the ground – and then the explosion. 'I'm not a betting man, Walker. I cover all bases. Sometimes I've got to steal a base. See?'

Walker watched in silence. Barry continued to sweat as he held the black box. Ten times the mass of the cell-phone bomb. At least. ONC explosive. Practically untraceable and undetectable. It would vaporise them all. According to Bellamy the building was full of them. *But how'd that get through security . . .*

'You see, Walker,' Bellamy said, taking a step back, his left hand feeling for the desk next to him, his right steady with the Glock. 'I'm everything you are and more.'

'Why like this?' Walker finally spoke.

'Why?' Bellamy said. 'Why not?'

Walker did not reply; he merely watched as Bellamy's eyes shone. The sales pitch was coming.

'It's our system,' Bellamy said. 'The government had grown too bloated. It's full of waste and needs to be cut down to size. It needs to better serve its purpose. And I'm just another guy in a long line of guys with a solution.'

'A delusion,' Walker countered. 'They'd never hand over the intelligence services to a private company.'

'Your head's in the clouds, Walker,' Bellamy said. 'Maybe you've been dead too long. Private companies *are* the intelligence community. They're the military. Who do you think makes everything? Who develops the software to eavesdrop? Who owns the phone lines that we tap into? Who runs the databases that we mine? Who staffs it all?'

'What, so you want to make INTFOR the new CIA?'

'It worked for the military and the private contractors,' Bellamy said. 'Without the latter? We would have lost a hell of a lot more lives in the mid-east.'

Walker shook his head.

'The government tries to control us,' Bellamy said. 'But we won't just stand and take it. I won't watch my country become everything that is loathsome. So, you ask *why*? It's written in our history, that's why. The second amendment gives us the right to bear arms, but the government wants to take that from us. No. Not today, not tomorrow, not while I'm around. I'm taking up arms to do what has to be done. It's my right – my duty – to do this, for all of us. I'm protecting us.'

Walker wanted to tell Bellamy he was crazy, but he didn't. One thing he had learned a long time ago: never laugh at a man who has a gun pointed at you. And close behind that was: never insult a crazy man who has a gun pointed at you.

'Then why not just wait?' Walker said evenly. 'The Vice President would have pushed your company along. It would have grown, would have proven itself over time.'

Bellamy shook his head. 'He's part of this. Part of big government. They move too slowly. We're losing the war, Walker, don't you see? Losing it here as well as out there.'

'Where?'

'The front line. Our nation is the last superpower on earth and we're a joke. No-one respects us. We're stuck in a holding pattern. Locked in a bloated, obese state of denial. You think China is dragging its feet like we are?'

'So, you're doing this for the country – what, before it's too late?'

Bellamy smiled. 'Something like that.'

Walker looked to the phone on the desk. 'Who were you talking to?'

'My daughter,' Bellamy replied.

Walker knew it was a lie. 'Try again,' he said.

Bellamy smiled. 'A friend.'

•

'Who'd he call?' McCorkell asked, listening in to the conversation playing out between Bellamy and Walker.

'We're working on it,' Somerville said. 'We only picked up the number.'

'And?'

'Bellamy's office. Press-release stuff. Selling himself as a hero, telling the world that he's in there, talking down the perpetrator, Walker.'

'Where's this audio from?'

'Hacked a desktop computer's microphone.'

'You're recording all this, right?'

'Right.'

'Then we've got enough,' McCorkell said. 'Heard enough. Send your boys in.'

'They're already in there,' Somerville replied.

•

'Asad,' Walker stated rather than asked. 'You were talking to Asad.'

Bellamy chuckled. 'No. He has his instructions already. Perhaps if you watch the screens, you'll see. You'll certainly hear it. Feel it, perhaps.'

Walker looked to the screens and saw his own face. It was his graduation photo from the Air Force Academy in Colorado Springs. He looked young, fresh faced, tanned, fit, full of fight.

The ticker underneath said, 'JED WALKER, FORMER AIR FORCE OFFICER, ATTEMPTED TO ASSASSINATE THE VICE PRESIDENT THIS MORNING AT THE NEW YORK STOCK EXCHANGE. WALKER IS CURRENTLY HOLDING AN UNKNOWN NUMBER OF HOSTAGES INSIDE THE NYSE, INCLUDING THE VICE PRESIDENT'S CLOSE FRIEND, DAN BELLAMY, HEAD OF INTFOR...'

'See,' Bellamy said, watching Walker's reaction. 'That's the system I believe in, working as it should. Now, put your gun down. On the floor.'

'That's not going to happen.'

Walker could see Bellamy's finger tighten on the trigger. No doubt he'd get off a round as Walker did. Maybe they'd get off two shots each.

'Put the gun down,' Bellamy said, 'or the consequences will be severe. And I'm not talking about you.'

•

The HRT operators moved in three groups of four. Two teams headed up fire ladders to the roof; the third moved to the front doors, where security disengaged the heavy steel blast door. The news cameras outside broadcast it all, the big tech vans with their antennas and satellite dishes beaming footage live from the scene.

•

'Here comes your big government at work,' Walker said.

Bellamy glanced at the screen, and smiled.

Now the only sound was Barry panting. All three men knew that Barry didn't belong in this world; he belonged in a world of numbers and computer screens and derivatives and put options and IT equipment.

'The gun, Walker, or a lot of lives will be lost.'

Walker looked at the box in Barry's hands, and realised his mistake. It couldn't be ONC; the place had been swept for bombs for weeks, and the sniffer dogs were very, very good. There was no way an explosive device could have been hidden in here before the Vice President's arrival.

'What do the boxes do?' Walker asked, looking to Bellamy.

Again came silence – the silence of having the upper hand. *Bellamy had a contingency plan.*

Walker put his Sig down on the floor and kicked it forwards, halfway between him and Bellamy. Two and a half metres.

•

'What boxes?' McCorkell said to the room. 'What's he talking about?'

No-one knew. They had ears in the room but no eyes.

'Video coming up!' a tech agent said. 'Got a webcam activated . . . hard to be certain, but it looks like Bellamy has a wireless hard drive.'

'A hard drive?' Somerville said.

'Wireless . . .' McCorkell said.

'It's a receiver,' the tech replied. 'For data storage.'

'A receiver . . . and a *transceiver*?' McCorkell added, thinking back to Walker's head-case chip. He looked to Somerville. They each came to the same conclusion at about the same time. 'Jam all signals, all frequencies – now!'

•

'You put the kill order on me in Yemen,' Walker said.

'You were unravelling a project that I'd put my life into,' Bellamy said. His elbow rested against his hip, his arm at a ninety-degree angle and the Glock steady in his hand, as if he could stand like that all day.

Walker felt dizzy. Blood dripped from his gunshot wound to the floor. Much more than Bellamy's. *Gotta make a move . . .*

'You knew that Louis Assif was a double, that he was DGSE,' Walker continued. 'But you needed to know more. You needed more, so you had someone work him. You had me assigned to State to look into him, to get close.'

Bellamy nodded.

'And you were letting him run . . . letting me get close.'

'As long as he kept the bad guys in cash, he was useful to me. And I knew that someone would tail him, so I wanted to be sure that it was someone we knew.'

'Through Heller.'

Bellamy nodded.

'What's in it for him?'

'The future,' Bellamy said. 'He spoke highly of you. Said that it had to be you; that if anyone could crack this, it'd be you. See, you were so good, you had to be used, and you had to die. Pity. I would have recruited you, but Heller wouldn't have it. You were untouchable, he said. Uncorruptible. A rare breed. A dinosaur. Just like your father . . .'

'And Assif, in Yemen?' Walker said, ignoring the personal remark. 'What, he outgrew his role? He'd followed the money . . . and he knew about your plan. About Zodiac. About the chain of attacks that were going to play out.'

'No. He only knew the first step. He helped set that up, to catch a bigger fish that never existed. He knew this would happen, and he knew it would lead to more.'

'More? You failed, Bellamy. The VP's not dead. Zodiac, these twelve attacks – it's all over.'

Bellamy shook his head, and gestured at the television screens.

'The VP didn't have to die,' Bellamy said. 'This is just as good. An assassination attempt at the New York Stock Exchange. That was the trigger. So, it's starting. The ball's rolling. Isn't it, Barry?'

Walker looked at Barry, shaking, hard drive in hand. He looked to Walker, and Walker saw flight in his eyes.

'Why do it this way?' Walker said, looking back at Bellamy.

'Are you looking for an origin story?' Bellamy said. 'Sorry to disappoint you. I arrived fully formed. I'm everything you are and more, because I'm all that you're not.'

'A lunatic?' Walker responded. *Never insult a man who's pointing a gun at you – unless all other options are off the table.*

Bellamy was silent, but only for a moment. He then spoke slowly, deliberately. 'The war on terror – it bred new terrorists.'

'Bullshit,' Walker replied. 'It brought out the opportunists. Like you.'

Bellamy smiled.

'All this time,' Walker said with renewed vigour despite the painful throb pulsing through his arm. 'All this time, and up until a day ago I was ready to leave it all at Heller's feet. But *you're* the puppet master. You're to blame.'

'I'll take that as a compliment.'

'And you're going to kill me now?' Walker said.

'Sure,' Bellamy said.

'Shoot straight,' Walker said. He rehearsed his movements in his mind. *Two and a half metres. Three steps. Inside of a second and a half.* He tensed his thighs, his weight slightly forward, ready to spring. 'Because if you don't put me down by the time I get to you, I'm going to tear you apart.'

'This close, my seven-year-old daughter could shoot you dead,' Bellamy said. 'Watch the screens. I want you to see this.'

Walker kept his weight at the balls of his feet, ready to pounce. He looked at the screens. Every local network and cable news channel, as well as plenty of foreign ones – BBC World News from the United Kingdom, Deutsche Welle from Germany and RT from Russia – tuned into live streams out the front of the New York Stock Exchange.

An audience of millions, beamed live from the TV vans parked out front.

'This wasn't about the Vice President,' Walker said slowly, staring at the screens. Millions of people were watching, waiting for Bellamy's showstopper. Outside the New York Stock Exchange, somewhere – octanitrocubane, or ONC. A detonation velocity of more than ten thousand metres per second. Invented in the US of A and used by a terrorist.

'It was, but that's not all.' Bellamy went quiet.

Walker imagined a bomb going off outside. The world watching via all the media on scene. A spectacular thing; 9/11 all over again. Get the world to tune in, then show them what you can really do. Use ONC, invented in American labs, traceable back to none other than the CIA.

'You're going to detonate ONC for all to see,' Walker said. 'On live television . . .'

'You see,' Bellamy said, smiling, 'in the world of intelligence, it pays to know more than the other guy. You've been out of the game too long. You have no idea the magnitude of what's at stake here.'

Go for the box, Walker willed him. *Reach for it and see what I'll do.*

But the box remained in Barry's hands. Bellamy didn't try to take it. He didn't need to.

Because then, a phone rang. The phone Bellamy had just used.

Bellamy said to Walker, 'That'll be for you.'

Walker looked at the phone.

Ring ring.

Bellamy said, 'Better get it. Tick tock.'

Ring ring. Walker picked it up. He expected it to be Eve. But it wasn't. It was a voice he thought he'd never hear again.

His father's.

78

His father's voice said, 'Jed . . .'

Walker gripped the phone receiver, his knuckles white.

'Son, you can't understand why, or what's going on, but you *have* to trust me here. You've got to let this slide. Get out of there, with Bellamy. You can come to me. Start a new life.'

Jed Walker, a dead man, listened to another dead Walker.

'Son, please, there's a time to explain but it's not now – get out of there while we can still clean this up, and I'll explain everything. You'll understand . . .'

Walker stared right through Bellamy.

'Son, listen . . . we're family. Always. You'll understand soon enough – just let this play out. This is bigger than you could ever know.'

Walker said into the phone, 'You're working with Bellamy?'

'Jed, this is bigger than that. You have to let it play out. You'll see. It's for family – the American family, all of us. You'll see.'

Walker said, 'You once told me that families are always rising and falling in America, right?'

Walker's father was silent.

'You were right,' Walker said into the phone. 'And you're wrong. Yes, this does end now. But then I'm coming for you, and I'll get the answers I need.'

Walker hung up the phone. Bellamy looked surprised.

But then he surprised Walker. He started whistling.

Bellamy whistled the opening bars of 'The Star Spangled Banner'.

Walker knew the words; knew them well. The national anthem of the United States of America. He also knew the United States military code that stated what an enlisted man in or out of uniform was supposed to do on hearing it; the thing was, he already had his right hand over his heart.

Bellamy's whistle sounded the tune to the lyrics: *O say can you see by the dawn's early light . . .*

Bellamy stopped. Smiled.

It was the fifth line of the first stanza that replayed in Walker's head. It wouldn't let him go: *And the rockets' red glare, the bombs bursting in air . . .*

Wherever Bellamy had set the ONC charges, somewhere outside the building, they would go off in spectacular style. A whole new 9/11, after which INTFOR would rise from the ashes and take the lion's share.

As Bellamy watched Walker, his expression changed. He looked to Barry, to the box.

'Give it to me,' he said, panicked, pacing to the trembling man and taking the transceiver. He looked down to check—

Too late.

Walker sprang forwards. As he moved towards Bellamy, the Glock went off with a muzzle flash and the BANG! of a 9-millimetre round.

Walker pushed the weapon aside. Another round went off. Walker pressed onwards, tackling Bellamy, his full weight dropping onto him – 230 pounds of crazed momentum crashing the guy to the floor. Walker landed with his elbows close to his chest, pointing down. He felt Bellamy's ribs dislodge from the sternum and crack under the pressure; heard the air knock out of him. Significant, life-threatening, blunt-force trauma.

Bellamy's eyes bulged with the pressure wave. He brought the Glock up to Walker, but Walker sat up, took the man's right arm in his left grip and held it down to the ground, tight.

Bellamy was red faced with the exertion and the pain, but he drew enough strength to land a punch on Walker's wounded forearm.

Walker reeled back, his left hand still tight around Bellamy's wrist.

Bellamy sucked air: short, sharp gasps that made him wince. He was alive, but not for long. On his back. Looking up. Blinking. His mouth moving.

'Help . . .'

'It's too late for you,' Walker said as he took the Glock and tossed it.

•

Somerville and McCorkell listened as the HRT teams ran through corridors from three different directions, converging on the room. Over the computer terminal's mic, and those on the HRT's tacticalcoms systems, they heard two gunshots, the distinctive claps of a 9-millimetre weapon.

'I'm going in there!' McCorkell yelled.

'I'm right behind you,' Somerville said, grabbing a hand-held radio on her way out.

•

Bellamy's focus drifted. At the most he had a couple of minutes to live.

Walker looked to Barry. The guy was on the floor, motionless, a small gunshot wound to the right side of his chest, low. A lung shot. Not much blood. The Hydrashock round was devastating, the ballistic impact producing pressure waves that propagated at close to the speed of sound. Hydrostatic shock through the body cavity meant near to instant death.

Walker turned his attention to Bellamy, who sucked air like a goldfish out of water.

'Talk,' Walker said to him.

Bellamy reached a hand up and gripped Walker's shirt. His eyes begged for reprieve.

Walker's eyes were cold. 'Talk.'

•

McCorkell crashed into the corridor and raced towards Walker, Somerville a step behind. Then the three squads of Hostage Rescue Team operators converged and provided cover. In five seconds twelve sub-machine guns were pointed at Bellamy by some of America's finest marksmen.

'My . . . daughter,' Bellamy gasped. 'Please . . . can you . . . call her? I need to . . . talk . . . to her.'

'No,' Walker replied. 'Talk to *me*. How do we stop the rest? How do we stop the other attacks?'

'My . . . daughter.'

'I'll make the call,' Somerville said, picking up the hard-line phone. Bellamy recited a number, and Somerville dialled.

Walker considered holding the phone from Bellamy as soon as the kid's voice came on the line, using it as leverage to get him to talk, but Somerville put the phone on speaker.

A young girl answered.

Bellamy gargled a hello.

'Daddy?'

'Darling . . .'

'Talk to her,' Somerville said quietly to Bellamy as she crouched next to Walker. 'Tell her goodbye.'

Bellamy did, then told her he loved her. Walker reached over and ended the call.

'Now, tell me, for her,' Walker said. 'The rest of these attacks. The other eleven. How do I stop them?'

'Twelve,' Bellamy said, starting to pant for breath as his heart and lungs raced for oxygen and blood that just wasn't there anymore. 'There's twelve.'

'This wasn't the first one?'

'This was . . . the trigger.'

Walker looked to Somerville and McCorkell.

'There's twelve,' Bellamy said. 'Each named after . . . after a Zodiac sign, and falls . . . in sequence. This will be reported as what it was, an assassination attempt. It's started.'

'How do we stop them?' said Walker.

'Can't.'

'There's got to be a way.'

Bellamy's eyes were glassy. He stared up at the blank ceiling. He was checking out and he knew it, and he knew he'd lost.

'Once one sees . . . their trigger, they activate. Cut-out cells, see? None knows . . . the others.'

Walker said, 'Someone knows.'

'Not me.'

'Who?'

'No . . .' Bellamy tried to reach up to the back of his head, but his hand never got there. A gurgle emanated and then his body went limp as each muscle gave out.

Walker touched the back of Bellamy's head, felt the tiny bump under the hair. A head-case chip.

EPILOGUE

'We squeezed Senator Anderson,' Bill McCorkell said. 'He talked. Told us everything in a plea bargain to save his life. Said he knew nothing about an attack on US soil let alone against the VP. He'll still do ten years at a fed pen, keeping Heller company.'

Walker remained silent as he sat opposite McCorkell; the two of them alone in a busy New York street. SoHo. Not far from where it all went down less than a week ago. Those events already felt like a lifetime ago.

McCorkell continued, 'Bellamy knew he couldn't get this administration to concede to a bigger role for INTFOR. His only ally in the Cabinet was the Vice President. He hatched a plan whereby the Vice President's death at the hands of terrorists would act as a catalyst to galvanise support in the Cabinet Room. We tossed Bellamy's office and found files for release the next day – he was proposing that the bill to make INTFOR the lead intelligence agency be named after the Vice President, as a tribute.'

'Linking the assassination to a bomb-maker killed while meeting the courier with the bin Laden cell-phone number would have iced the cake,' Walker said. 'The whole country would have been onside to give Bellamy, the great American patriot who was right there at the Vice President's side at the time of his assassination, a blank cheque to look after them.'

McCorkell nodded. 'We're working through that list you got from Hong Kong now. It seems those put options went out to a select few of Bellamy's former clients. If we can unravel that, it might lead to what's next in the Zodiac cells.'

Walker sipped his coffee. 'They find the explosives linked to the wireless hard drive?'

'In the news crews' TV vans,' McCorkell said. 'If we hadn't jammed the frequencies, well, people would have seen a hell of a sight on their screens at home.'

'I can't believe the lengths he was willing to go . . .' Walker said.

'What are you going to do?' McCorkell asked. 'Keep running? Keep living with nothing in your pockets but a fake passport and some cash?'

'I'm not running from anything,' Walker replied. 'I'm chasing it.'

'You've got nothing left to chase. The truth about Yemen is coming out. You'll be reborn. Free.'

'Free? Are you kidding? Besides, there's always something to chase.'

'You know what I mean. Come back, into the fold.'

'I can't work for the Agency again.'

'That's not what I meant. I mean, take your life back. Like this, you can never be the Jed Walker you were. You're a ghost, living in the shadows, always looking over your shoulder.'

'So, I should come home and get a parade?'

'Join my team; you'd be a free man to chase whatever you want.'

'You reckon you're free?'

'I have no reason not to.'

'I have plenty of reasons not to.'

'Like Eve? Is she still a reason?'

'You know nothing about her.'

'True, nothing of import. But I have no doubt that she'd like to know the truth of what happened, about you not being dead.'

'She's over it. She's moved on. She doesn't need a ghost to pop up in her life.'

'People don't get over what she's been through.'

'I can't undo it, either. This isn't some lame TV show where I come back from the grave a year later and say, "Honey, I'm home."'

'It couldn't hurt to try, to give her the option of how to move ahead.'

'Of course it could hurt. It would make her a target. Have you thought of that? It would show anyone watching me that she's a weakness of mine, a way to get to me, to force my hand.'

They both sat for a few long moments.

'You still love her,' said McCorkell eventually, watching Walker.

'Of course. I married her, didn't I?'

'You were separated before you went to Yemen.'

'Thanks to my shitty job.'

'No, it was your attitude towards it. That's changed now.'

'No. I haven't changed. That's the problem. I can't stop, don't you see? I will track down every single cell of this Zodiac program or I'll die trying. Asad is still out there, building bombs.' Walker pushed his empty coffee cup away roughly. 'You think I want to be like this? I can't help it.'

'If you join us, that can change. It won't be one man against the world; it'll be you and me and a group from the UN.'

'Sorry if I don't see that option as an improvement on what I can achieve alone.'

McCorkell chewed at his bottom lip, as if trying to keep himself in check, and then said, 'Okay, well, you know where I am.'

He offered a hand.

Walker shook it.

'Where will you go?' McCorkell asked.

Walker shrugged.

'You know the score,' McCorkell went on. 'You're in the arena, dealing with the worst, and that means that you can't have a normal life. Normal for you is the war that soccer moms see on TV. I get it, okay? When you're in that world, you can't be close to someone, because when you get hurt, they get hurt. One way or another, they get hurt – and you may think you've hurt her all you can but you know, deep down, that isn't true. There's pain and then there's *pain*, and you know you've put her through enough. You need to see her, though, and you will, but you probably won't talk to her, won't let her see you.'

A thousand thoughts ran through Walker's mind, a part of his brain filtering them to some succinct possibilities and musings, which he categorised and prioritised and compartmentalised into a few distinct lists. Less than a minute and he knew what he had to do, today, tomorrow, and for the rest of his life. Marty Bloom would have been proud.

•

Pip Durant sat at the window of an apartment block in Broome Street, New York. He adjusted the scope on his Steyr SSG 69, which fitted with the silencer, was accurate to sub-MOA at a range of up to 600 metres.

He watched the two men sitting outside the cafe. The crosshairs of the Kahle's scope magnified six times, trained on Jed Walker's heart.

He switched to Bill McCorkell. He could kill them both within a second, as long as it took him to re-engage the compact manual bolt mechanism and shift targets.

'Walker, you're not the only dead man still alive,' he said quietly to himself.

•

'Where's Somerville?' Walker asked.

McCorkell smiled. 'She's around.'

'Clara?'

'Deported back to Italy. We let her superiors know she was selling out. Facing espionage and treason charges.'

Walker squinted at the sun's reflection off a passing cab.

McCorkell said, 'You're going to need new ID to get out of the country.'

'Do you think I can't get that? Shit, I'll take you down to Canal Street, get you a bazooka for fifty bucks.'

'It'd probably be a Chinese copy that would blow your head clean off just aiming the thing.'

Walker smiled.

'You'll need more than just ID,' McCorkell said. He placed a parcel on the table, slid it over to Walker. 'For you, from the Vice President's office. It's the least he could do.'

Walker looked inside the envelope: a new passport, made out in his own name, social-security card, money in accounts, cash – the works.

'A clean slate. A thank-you. Nothing more. No commitment. Between you and him.'

'The least he could do,' Walker echoed.

Silence fell again between the two men. Walker looked left and right along the street. Just another hot June day; maybe a summer storm tonight.

'What are *you* going to do now?' Walker asked.

'I've got a new cell to take down,' McCorkell replied, 'and I've got less than a month to do it. I'm going to need to set up a proper team. Of course if I could just draft the MVP . . .'

'Sounds great. Living the dream.'

'Yeah, well, like you I can't find it in myself to walk away.'

'What was on Bellamy's head chip?'

'Not much. But enough to start with. We have a date. A location.'

'You knew about my father being alive?' Walker said. 'His involvement?'

McCorkell looked uncomfortable. 'No. But we do now. The auto wreck, the closed casket – we exhumed the grave yesterday. It certainly wasn't your father's.'

'They planted DNA in the medical exam,' Walker said. 'He planted it . . .'

McCorkell nodded.

'Where is he?'

'We don't know.'

'He's running Zodiac?'

'I'm working to find out.'

'And they think by doing these twelve attacks they're strengthening America?'

McCorkell nodded, said, 'I'm sorry. I'm as shocked as you. But I won't rest until this is sorted.'

Walker looked around again. Something was making him uneasy. *Enough done here today. Time to go. Got to keep moving.* He stood, and pocketed his new ID.

'Where will you end up?' McCorkell asked.

'I'll be around,' Walker said. He took a step away—

'Jed?'

He turned at the sound of the familiar voice.

Eve. She stood next to a patched-up Andrew Hutchinson, his arm in a sling.

Walker said, 'Eve . . .'

A shot rang out.

If you enjoyed *The Spy*, read on for the beginning
of the next book in the Jed Walker series . . .

THE HUNTED

Prologue

The gunshot sounded. Then another.

Walker looked up. Alert, not alarmed.

Nine-millimetre. Double-tap. Fired from an elevated position. A couple of blocks east, atop one of the multi-storey buildings. Fired downwards and at close range to the target, minimising the report.

No-one in the New York street seemed to notice. Just another sharp sound in a big city: a car backfiring or machinery clanging or something big and heavy hitting the deck.

But Walker knew. And the man seated in front of him knew. And the guy standing two yards away beside Walker's ex-wife knew.

'Somerville,' Bill McCorkell said from across the table. He shifted in his seat and added, 'Right on time, I'd say.'

Walker looked up at the rooftop and saw Somerville, five storeys up, a foot on the parapet, holstering her FBI-issued side-arm. He waved. She waved back.

Walker said, 'She wasn't shooting at birds, I take it.'

'Tying up a loose end,' McCorkell replied.

'Durant?'

McCorkell nodded.

Walker looked back up to the elevated position. She'd tracked Durant up there; it was a no-brainer what he'd been up to. Walker pictured the ex-CIA man's body sprawled next to a sniper's rifle. Walker wondered who would have been lined up in the scope first – him or McCorkell. On the street, a team of heavily armed NYPD uniformed officers appeared on foot from around a corner and entered the building. She'd planned it well. A good job all round.

'Thank Somerville for me,' Walker said, his eyes returning to McCorkell.

'You can thank her yourself,' the older man countered. He leaned forward on the table. 'This is the beginning of things, Walker, not the end.'

Walker paused for just a moment. 'This changes nothing.'

McCorkell sat there, silent, waiting.

'I'm not working for you,' Walker said. 'Just tell Somerville she and I are even.'

'You two will never be even.'

Walker didn't answer; instead he turned and walked the four paces to where the FBI man Andrew Hutchinson stood with Walker's former wife, Eve.

Separated. Then widowed. Grieving for more than a year, never knowing what really happened to her estranged husband who'd been listed dead by the CIA and State Department.

Now this.

The two of them, standing there, facing each other on the Manhattan street.

She was smaller than he remembered. A little older. Sadder. Beautiful.

Hutchinson stepped around Walker to join McCorkell at the cafe table. Walker could hear them talking, animatedly, but he blocked it out.

Eve.

Looking into Eve's eyes, he felt that it could have been yesterday he'd last seen her. A bunch of yesterdays ran through his mind. Most of them were firsts. Their first meeting, first kiss, first time they'd slept together, first time they'd fought. The last time they'd fought.

Standing before her, Walker was ready for war. For tears and fists. Anger. But if all that was there, it was coming later.

For now, Eve hugged him. Tight. Silent.

He'd always loved that about her: no matter what happened, she knew what to say, and what not to say. They stood together, embracing, until McCorkell tapped Walker on the shoulder.

'We've just had word,' McCorkell said, moving into Walker's line of sight over the top of Eve's head. 'We know where he is.'

From the tone, the poise, Walker knew what McCorkell meant before he elaborated.

'We've found your father.'

•

'He's in the UK,' Special Agent Hutchinson said to his boss, Bill McCorkell. 'That's David Walker, right there.'

Walker looked over the photographs.

The four of them – Walker, McCorkell, Hutchinson and Special Agent Fiona Somerville – sat in an office of the FBI's New York Field Office. Eve sat at a desk outside the glass-walled office, waiting. The Lower Manhattan office building was a shared federal government space, and staffers milled about, looking busy.

Fair enough, thought Walker. They'd almost lost a VP on their turf just a few days back. The same day that Walker had heard from his father.

'Near Hereford,' Hutchinson said, showing a map on his iPad. 'West Midlands, near the Welsh border.'

'I know the place,' Walker said. He looked at the long-lens shot of the man who had raised him. The man he hardly knew. 'I spoke at the SAS once. My father did too, several times.'

'So he had friends there,' Somerville said.

'Probably. None I recall, no names,' Walker said. He stared blankly, remembering the place. 'Hell, as a teenager I went with him on one of his trips and we fished the Wye together. How'd we get these photos?'

'British intel, about two weeks back,' Hutchinson said. The FBI man used a pencil to itch at his bandaged arm. 'They're investigating someone he was seen with.'

'Why?'

'We're not sure yet,' Hutchinson replied, as he brought up a satellite map on a large screen. 'The call that your father made to you at the New York Stock Exchange? It came from a location not far from the barracks.' He zoomed in on a dot on a tiny road at the centre of a cluster of small buildings. 'It came from a landline phone in this tavern.'

'That call was made three days ago,' Walker said. 'He won't still be in the area. The trail's long dead. He'll be gone. He's good at disappearing.'

'I've just run his image through TrapWire and Scotland Yard's

CCTV program,' Somerville said. 'He's come up four times over the past six months, all within fifty klicks of that tavern.'

Walker studied the images that Hutchinson had brought up on the screen. A couple were grainy and blurred, taken from ATM cameras. Another showed his father in the background of someone's Facebook photo. The last was a grab from a CCTV camera in a shop – in this last one the subject was looking directly up at it, as though he knew he'd been caught out.

'That last one,' Walker said. 'Where's that?'

'A gas station, just on the outskirts of Hereford on that same road headed to our tavern, soon after he called you,' Somerville said, checking the surveillance notes. 'Later that night it was robbed. All on-site stored footage was taken but this had been backed up off-site to the security company.'

'Does all that sound like the actions of a guy *leaving* the area?' McCorkell said to Walker. 'He's still there.'

'Covering his tracks . . .' Walker said, seeing his father's eyes for the first time in a long while. He looked over to Eve, silent, present, but not taking it in, as though the reappearance of yet another dead Walker was one revelation too many. 'You think he's been there for the last six months?'

'At least,' Hutchinson said.

'Seems he's made it something of a home base,' Somerville said. 'He could be running Zodiac from there.'

'We don't know his involvement in that,' McCorkell said.

'Yeah, well he *did* have contacts there,' Walker said. 'He had a hand in the psych training and debriefing of SAS guys, since at least the Falklands.'

'No-one you remember?' Hutchinson asked, cradling his bandaged arm. 'Anyone there particularly close to your father?'

'Nope,' Walker said, thinking back. 'But he had a few friends there, I'm sure. He'd go there every few years. They'd be drinking buddies and the like. Not close.'

'Close enough to work with,' Somerville said. 'Then, and now.'

Walker nodded.

'You got dates for those trips?' Somerville asked. 'I can get British Ministry of Defence personnel records to match, go through them.'

'Maybe,' Walker said, nodding. 'But this is the SAS we're talking about – whether serving or former, they're not going to lay out the red carpet for a group of outsiders to look into their people's whereabouts.'

'Worth a shot,' McCorkell said. 'Let's see where we can get.'

Somerville nodded.

'Why haven't we heard about this sooner?' Walker said. 'Why didn't his presence, plus the fact that MI5 are looking into him too, flag something months ago?'

'We're still waiting on answers to that too,' Hutchinson said. 'Brits are dragging their feet in cooperating – we don't know who they're surveilling, or why.'

'But we're working on it,' McCorkell said, looking to Walker as he spoke.

'I just can't imagine him being in a place like that,' Walker said, 'a place people might recognise him, when he's playing the dead man.'

'He's hiding in plain sight,' Somerville said. 'It worked for you for near-on a year.'

'Yeah, but I was trying to stop a terrorist attack,' Walker said, 'not playing a part in it.'

'You really think he's a part of this, don't you?' McCorkell said, matter-of-fact.

Walker remained silent.

'At any rate,' Somerville said, filling the silence, 'no-one's been looking for David Walker until now.'

'News travels fast, even over the pond,' Walker said. 'They'd have known he was supposed to be dead.'

'So, he's staying off the grid over there,' Hutchinson said. 'Maybe only a local friend or two know of his resurrection.'

Walker shook his head. 'It's not like him. He's too smart, and being over there seems too risky.'

'He's there because of something he needs,' Hutchinson said. 'Protection. Connections. Something.'

'Maybe he's retired there,' McCorkell said, leaning back and sipping a steaming tea. 'For the fishing.'

'Right,' Walker said, deadpan. 'You think he faked his death, had a hand in a terrorist attack on US soil, knew of an internal CIA takeover and an attempt on the Vice-President's life – all from a tavern in rural England?'

McCorkell shrugged.

'You're a pro at this, right?' Walker chided.

McCorkell feigned indifference. Walker looked from him to Hutchinson, then to Somerville. The three of them watched him. Waiting. For an answer. An answer they'd been waiting to hear for three days.

'Look, Walker, this, with your father. It's a lead,' Somerville said. 'The best lead we've got to break into the Zodiac terror network. And we're going to check it out. With or without you.'

'So tell us,' Hutchinson said. 'Are you in?'

Walker looked from the UN intelligence team to the larger office beyond the glass wall. Eve sat there. She was looking at him. Her eyes showed nothing.

Walker nodded. 'I'm in.'

1

'Nine years ago,' Walker said, looking through the car's windscreen at the English town. 'That's when I spoke here, after my first tour of Afghanistan.'

'For the CIA?' Somerville asked.

'No, before that,' Walker said.

'When you were Air Force?' Somerville asked.

Walker nodded.

'I still don't get how the Air Force has boots-on-the-ground frontline guys,' she said. 'Airplanes, airbases, the Pentagon, sure. But humping around in the mountains with SEALs and Delta?'

'Someone has to have the brains in those Special Forces teams,' Walker replied.

McCorkell and Hutchinson rode in the back of the hire car, a Land Rover Discovery. Bill McCorkell was not a field man. Never had been. Just past sixty, he'd spent a lifetime as an intelligence and international-affairs expert, rising to the post of National Security Advisor to presidents from both sides of politics. His current role was driving a specialist UN desk, from which he ran a small team of multinational investigators in the field and reported directly to the Secretary-General. The intelligence outfit was known simply as Room 360, named after its office number in the United Nations building in Vienna, and its members were sequestered from the world's best intelligence and law-enforcement agencies.

Walker watched the familiar streets slip by. On the flight here, plans had been made. He and Somerville would check out the tavern. McCorkell and Hutchinson would visit SAS headquarters, Hereford, to see if any old-timers had had contact with David Walker, the dead man.

Andrew Hutchinson was lead investigator and, like Somerville, was on loan to the UN from the FBI. Just a few days earlier, in the events leading up to the terrorist attack at the New York Stock Exchange, he'd been badly wounded. Walker glanced back at the guy. He had a lot to be thankful to him for – the lawman had saved Eve's life, and because of this his face was a mask of green and purple bruising, and his arm was in a sling.

Walker would not forget that.

And he would not forget Eve, who was now in temporary witness protection courtesy of the FBI. In Maine; that's all Walker knew.

The English town slipped by. The trees were losing the last of their leaves. The sky was one big cloud of grey.

Whatever happened here, there would be tomorrows with Eve. Maybe not like those yesterdays, but at the very least, there would be closure. Answers. Discussions. Decisions made. Progress. For more than a year he'd been thinking about it, about her, never finding the courage to make the first move, allowing her to believe he was dead, always justifying his actions as a form of protecting her while completing his mission.

'This is us,' McCorkell said from the back seat.

Somerville took the exit to the old RAF base, drove up to the guardhouse and stopped. The two men in the back got out.

'Keep in touch,' McCorkell said as he departed, Hutchinson close behind him.

Somerville nodded. Walker remained silent.

She drove back to town, tapping the sat-nav to take them to the tavern on the B-road.

•

The Boar and Thistle was some twenty minutes' drive west of Hereford.

There were four cars in the gravel car park: two rentals and a couple of locals.

Walker stood by their parked car and looked around. Twelve houses in view, all well-kept stone cottages. Dark stone, white-trimmed windows. Gardens set up with precision and allowed to overgrow just so. The road through was two-lane blacktop; cars, trucks and vans passed at an average rate of one every fifteen seconds or so. It was just after midday. The sky was darkening. A typical Midlands affair, the lot of it.

'You coming?' Somerville asked.

'That's what she said,' Walker replied, walking towards the FBI agent who stood waiting by the front door. 'Trading to thirsty travellers since 1514' was stencilled inside the entrance. Somerville had a hand on her hip, her jacket open, revealing where her side-arm would have been back in the US. Her bobbed blonde hair was tucked behind her ear against the wind. She dressed well, for a Fed.

Somerville said, 'What's what she said?'

'Joke.'

'Oh. I didn't know you had a sense of humour.'

'I don't,' Walker said, opening the door.

2

McCorkell looked across the desk at the SAS Squadron Commander, a Brigadier Smith.

'UN?' the Brigadier said, looking at McCorkell's card. 'Are you guys still around?'

'Our pay cheques say so,' Hutchinson replied. He and McCorkell were seated across the 1980s-era laminate desk.

'We need your help on finding this guy,' McCorkell said. They would have preferred to meet with the man at the top, a Major-General in charge of the regiment, but he was away. 'Never mess with the man in the middle', was one of McCorkell's mottos, and it had served him well in cutting through bureaucracy. He suspected that they would not get far here.

'And which guy would that be?' the Brigidier said.

'David Walker,' Hutchinson said, fumbling with his iPad with one hand as he showed the Brigadier the recent picture of David Walker. 'We checked records. You were here when he was.'

'Yes, I remember him. Walker. Yank. Intel expert, anti-terror specialist. Academic and policy man from DC.'

'That's right,' Hutchinson said. 'When did you last see him?'

'And where?' McCorkell said.

'Years ago. Here, on base.'

'What can you remember?' Hutchinson asked.

'Well, let's see. I was a lieutenant then, just over from the paras. He spoke to us during the first Gulf War, the week before we deployed, about what to expect to extract from prisoners – should we take any.'

'Right,' Hutchinson said. 'And you're sure you haven't seen him since?'

'Yes.' The Brigidier passed back the iPad. 'Why the interest?'

'He's dead and buried back home, full honours and mourning,'

McCorkell said. 'But he's been seen around here over the past few months.'

'Oh?' The Brigadier leaned back. 'You're sure?'

'Certain.' Hutchinson tapped on the iPad screen and brought up an image of the Boar and Thistle, which showed the front of the building and a couple of guys in the background, and passed it back.

The photo stirred something in the Brigadier. He stared at his desk, then said, 'Come with me. There's something I'd like to show you.'

•

Walker took in his surroundings within seconds.

The publican was a no-nonsense man who had served in the military. The publican saw Walker too and probably figured the same.

Three groups of people sat eating at tables; two were clearly tourists from the rental cars outside, and the other was locals.

Five people sat on stools at the bar, drinking. Three were inconsequential. Two were of interest. Also ex-military. Walker recognised one from the picture of his father taken here.

Walker ordered a pint of dark ale and turned to his colleague. 'Drink?'

Somerville paused a beat, then said, 'Cabernet.'

'And a glass of red,' Walker said to the publican, who went about the task with a laconic proficiency, placed the drinks on the mahogany bar and said, 'That all?'

'And a question,' Walker said, handing over a twenty and producing the photo of his father. 'Have you seen this guy in here?'

The publican's eyes shifted from Walker's to the pic and lingered a bit, then he said, 'Nope.'

Walker nodded.

The publican went back to his other patrons at the bar. The two ex-military types.

Walker picked up his drink, looked at Somerville and sipped.

'He's lying,' Somerville said, watching the publican keep busy.

'Yeah . . .' Walker said, placing his half-empty pint on the bar. 'That's all right. These boys will help us.'

Somerville looked up at him.

Walker felt a tap on his shoulder. He held Somerville's eye briefly and then turned. The two men from the bar. Each well on the other side of forty, each shorter than Walker but wiry with lean muscle. Former SAS men, or close to it. A lifetime of keeping fit the hard way, their former occupation's hazard writ large in their bones and joints and expressions and scars.

'We heard you're looking for someone,' the tapper said to Walker. He was the guy he recognised from the photo.

'Sure,' Walker said. He slid the photo of his father from the bar and held it next to his face. He was unsure whether the familial traits would be evident to the two guys. The first man stood two yards from him, the second just a yard behind his comrade's right shoulder, the bar to their left. Both wore khakis with flannel shirts and light jackets. Unshaven, hair a little unkempt, just as they would have looked back in their SAS regiment days.

'What's it to you?' he said, looking at Walker.

'I need to find him.'

'Well then, you got a problem, mate,' the tapper said to Walker.

'Oh?' Walker replied.

'That wasn't a question,' he said to Walker, and took half a pace forward. 'I said, you got a problem.'

'How you figure that?' Walker replied. He relaxed his shoulders, let his arms hang loose by his sides, kept his body weight at the front of his feet.

'You're in a tight community here, lad,' the guy behind the tapper said. He looked ten years older than Walker but showed no obvious sign of diminished skill in unarmed combat. 'We look after our friends, including that guy you're after – who, by the way, doesn't want to be disturbed. So, best you leave then.'

'On your way, mate.'

'Yeah,' Walker said, putting his drink down, his head tilted slightly to the left. 'About that . . .'

•

'Some time in the past six months we had a break-in, to our archival armoury,' the Brigadier explained as they walked across a green grass field, dotted with small hillocks. 'Though we didn't know it at the time.'

'Didn't know?' Hutchinson said.

'It gets audited just twice a year, so there's a six-month window.'

Hutchinson asked, 'When was the last audit?'

'Not four weeks ago. That's when this was reported as missing.' They stopped at a metal door where three uniformed soldiers were busily stacking crates inside the earth-covered storage bunker. He handed an inventory to the Brigadier.

McCorkell looked over the list, and Hutchinson read over his shoulder. Twelve Browning Hi Power pistols. Four MP5Ks. Two crates of ammunition totalling a thousand 9-millimetre rounds. And a box of thirty way-out-of-date flash-bang grenades.

'How do flash-bangs go out of date?' McCorkell asked.

'Corrosion,' the quartermaster replied with a shrug. 'It's rubbish, though. They work just fine for at least twenty years; I've seen it myself. The company just wants to sell more to the MoD, and we're not allowed to use the old ones in case one does go wrong.'

'This is enough firepower to start a war,' Hutchinson said.

'It certainly is,' the Brigadier replied. 'And there was a crate of C4 too, we think.'

'You *think*?'

'That stuff goes boom all the time; it's hard to keep track of exactly how much the lads use.'

'Someone broke in here?' Hutchinson said, looking around the armoury. Two corporals and a sergeant looked pissed at the two American suits poking around in their den.

'Not on your life,' the Brigidier replied. 'The archival storage is in another above-ground bunker the other side of the base. Reinforced concrete with a hundred tons of earth all around, dating back to the war. One door is made of three inches of hardened steel from when battleships were a thing. A modern combination lock that's got a whiz-bang security guarantee.'

'Inside job,' Hutchinson said.

The Brigadier nodded. 'It's happened before. Those pictures you showed me? There's another guy in one of them. In the background. He used to work here. Real bastard, or SOB as you might call him.'

'I'll need everything you know about him,' Hutchinson said.

'Right,' the Brigadier said.

McCorkell watched the three other soldiers keep themselves busy as their boss explained the theft, full of silent professional fury at whoever had committed the crime.

Hutchinson said, 'You don't change the locking code?'

'Not as often as we should have,' the Brigadier replied. 'Remedied, by the by.'

'What's the relevance for us?' McCorkell asked. 'There's no way our man had that combination.'

'That's right,' the Brigadier said. 'But if your man is up to no good around these parts, then he's had a hand in this.'

'How'd you figure?' Hutchinson asked.

'Because,' the Brigadier said, 'I know for a fact that the geezer who once stood in my shoes knew that man. And he's the one in that photo of yours.'

ACKNOWLEDGEMENTS

A new series character took a lot of work to create, and to all those who've had a hand in discussing this project, I thank you.

Firstly, thanks to my family and friends for putting up with my absence. Guess you're used to it by now.

Special thanks are due to those who have been invaluable and integral to this project seeing the light of day. I had unwavering support from my three families: Phelan, Wallace and Beasley.

Thanks to my pro readers Tony Wallace, Jesse Beasley and Emily McDonald. Thanks also to Mal, Michelle, Tony and Chaz for your early feedback.

My agents, particularly Pippa Masson, Laura Dunn, Leslie Conliffe and Josh Getzer, for their enthusiasm and belief in my work.

My editorial team at Hachette, Vanessa Radnidge, Kate Stevens and Claire de Medici have been outstanding and understanding in dealing with an author bringing a new baby into the world.

My thanks to my writer friends, especially Lee Child. While writing this book, two good thriller writers died: Vince Flynn and Tom Clancy. I owe those guys a lot.

Nicole Wallace, as always, has been my muse and support. Thanks babe. x